# THE TIME-TRAVELLING ESTATE AGENT

DALE BRADFORD

Copyright © 2024 Dale Bradford

All rights reserved including translation into other languages.

The characters and events portrayed in this book are fictitious. Any similarity to real persons, living or dead, is coincidental and not intended by the author.

No part of this book may be reproduced, or stored in a retrieval system, or transmitted in any form or by any means, electronic, mechanical, photocopying, recording, or otherwise, without express written permission of the author.

All trademarks and copyrights are recognised and are acknowledged to be the property of their respective owners.

*Thanks to Jo, Naomi, Lauren, and Ronnie for their ongoing support, and to Toni and Tabitha for their enthusiastic encouragement. I'll try to make the next one shorter.*

## CHAPTER 1

### SATURDAY 3RD JULY 1976

"What is that, some new kind of television?" an elderly man in double beige asked in a disapproving tone.

Eric quickly slipped his iPhone into his jacket pocket. He had been alone at the bar reviewing the footage for his presentation, and the old man's soft soled sandals had allowed him to stealthily creep up behind him and peer over his shoulder. "I suppose it is," Eric said.

"What's the point of that?" the old man scoffed.

Turning to face his inquisitor, Eric took in Woodland Manor's garish red patterned carpet and dark wood panelled walls laden with unpolished horse brasses. He took a deep breath, inhaling the less than enchanting confection of last night's beer slops and this morning's spray polish, which now had a hint of citrus from the old man's Blue Stratos aftershave. "Oh, it's got a point," he replied.

"But it's microscopic," the old man sneered. "Japanese, I suppose?"

"China actually," Eric said.

"China?" the man guffawed so hard he made himself cough. "That I very much doubt."

The commotion attracted the attention of a young barman with a wispy beard and shoulder-length brown hair. "Good afternoon Mr Reeves," the barman greeted Eric's companion while placing a short-stemmed glass on the bar. "Bristol Cream?"

"Croft Original," Reeves corrected him. "Dry sherry when light, sweet sherry at night."

"I'll try and remember that," the barman said, reaching behind him for the distinctive dark green bottle and bringing it towards the glass.

"Though I could have sworn you had a Bristol Cream last Saturday lunchtime."

"Dry sherry should be served in a glass with a long stem," Reeves chided him. "Otherwise, your hands will heat the drink."

"I do apologise," the barman said, pouring the sherry into a long-stemmed glass.

Reeves handed the barman 30p in small denomination coins and tutted. "This place has gone downhill since—"

"Come on now, don't upset yourself on this beautiful day, Mr Reeves," the barman gently cut him off, aware of how the sentence would end. "It's been over ten years since you passed on the baton. Wasn't it Menander who said, 'time heals all wounds'?"

"Never heard of him," Mr Reeves retorted, holding his glass up to the light. "And he's wrong. It doesn't."

"Looks like another scorcher today," the barman said. "They say it's going to be hotter than the Costa del Sol..."

"Even this glass is grubby," Reeves grumbled. "How often are they cleaned?"

"...And it looks like we're going to have one of the warmest summers on record," the barman continued, while nodding a greeting to Eric.

"Famous last words," Reeves mocked, taking his sherry and choosing a stool further down the bar, close to the big television.

"For the record, my last words are going to be 'I wish I'd spent more time in the office'," Eric said.

The barman lowered his head, allowing his hair to fall forward and frame his face. "That's a slightly unusual thing to say, sir."

"Yes Seb, it is," Eric conceded. "But the next time you hear someone say, 'No dying man wishes they'd spent more time in the office', you can reply 'Actually, Eric Meek did'."

"Are you dying?"

"I hope not, but wouldn't it be satisfying to shut down the next bore who comes out with it?"

Seb frowned in confusion. "Actually, it was you who brought it up," he said. "Are you here for the tennis?"

"Not really," Eric replied.

"We're having Wimbledon on the big television today," Seb continued. "When the women have finished."

The Ladies' Singles Final was between Chris Evert and Evonne Goolagong Cawley, two of the finest players of their generation, but the big television wouldn't be switched on until the men – Bjorn Borg and Ilie Nastase – arrived on court.

"It's the Men's Final later, and we'll be serving complimentary salmon and cucumber sandwiches," Seb explained.

"I'm more interested in a cold lager, Seb," Eric said, eying up his options. "What do you recommend?"

"We've got Harp, Carlsberg, Heineken, and the new Stella Artois," Seb said, extending his arm along the bar taps with a flourish. "But can I ask, why you—"

"I'd better stick to Skol," Eric said, pointing at the tap.

Seb dutifully filled a pint glass, etched with another brand of lager, and placed it in front of Eric, who offered him a ten-pound note. Seb glared at the large denomination note. "I'm afraid we haven't long opened, sir. Do you have anything smaller?"

Eric didn't. "Will it help if I have another?" he asked.

"Another Skol? Already?"

"It is pretty hot out there today," Eric said, gesturing towards the windows as he gulped down the cold yellow liquid. "Have one for yourself and get Mr Cheerful over there another Croft Original."

"Thank you very much, sir," Seb said, pouring another pint from the tap. "I'll have a tomato juice so that will be £1.26 altogether but—"

"You didn't even need the till to add that up," Eric observed. "That's quite a skill."

"It comes with practice," Seb said, slightly blushing. "But I'm afraid I still won't be able to change—"

"Don't worry about the change," Eric said, placing his now empty glass on the bar and immediately starting on the freshly poured one. "It's only money, right?"

"Very droll, sir," Seb said. "I'll see if reception can break a tenner."

"I'm not joking," Eric said. "Keep the change."

"But sir, you've given me a ten-pound note and—"

"Tell you what, throw me a packet of JPS and we'll call it quits," Eric said, pointing to the packs of cigarettes lined up along a glass shelf behind the bar. "Because there's no problem with me smoking in here, is there?"

"None whatsoever," Seb said, handing Eric a pack of John Player Special along with a box of matches. "Let me get you an ashtray. And thank you so much."

Eric unwrapped the cigarettes, savouring the aroma that escaped from the distinctive black and gold box. JPS had been his brand. He'd quit decades ago but recent events had seen him relapse on a few occasions. He lit the thin white tube, inhaled, and blew a plume of smoke into the air. It took on a blue hue from the harsh midday sun pouring in through the dusty windows.

"Can I just ask," Seb said, placing a chunky glass ashtray on the bar in front of Eric, "why you called me Seb?"

"You are Seb, aren't you?" Eric said, taking another gulp of Skol.

Seb whispered: "No one in Cwmbran calls me Seb, only my college friends. Everyone around here knows me as Simon."

Eric studied him. "You're not really a Simon though, are you?"

Seb stared suspiciously at Eric. "Are you trying to pick me up?"

Eric guffawed: "In your dreams!"

"What does that mean?"

"It means I am absolutely not trying to pick you up."

"You wouldn't be the first older man to come on to me," Seb said. "And you'd be surprised how many of them were supposedly happily married."

"You know, I'd completely forgotten how enjoyable it is to be able to smoke indoors," Eric said, ensuring that he blew smoke in the direction of the empty lounge rather than towards Seb.

After delivering the Croft Original to Reeves, Seb returned to Eric and said: "I don't think I've seen you in here before. Are you new to the area?"

"You could say that," Eric replied.

Yes, you could say that. Or you could say the opposite.

Eric had been a kitchen porter at Woodland Manor Hotel and Restaurant for a brief period when he was 16. 'Kitchen porter' was a rather grandiose title for the work he was expected to do, which consisted of scrubbing greasy pans and trays, cleaning the work surfaces and floors, scraping the waste food from diners' plates into the pig bins, and even feeding the on-site pigs that provided the kitchen with pork, bacon, gammon, and sausages.

The job had its upsides though, particularly during the Saturday night Dinner & Dance. Eric and a selection of the more presentable kitchen porters – all of whom went to the same school – would wear little red jackets, with their school uniform shirts and trousers, and bring diners their meals in the ballroom. The youthful waiters were able to supplement their 25p per hour wages with tips from customers. The more the diners drunk, the bigger they tipped, so running drinks errands could be quite lucrative, even though Big Ben Butcher disapproved of the practice. He reasoned that any money leaving punters' pockets should only be going into his tills, and he would literally kick the arse of anyone he caught doing it.

"Well, if I see you again you can count on me serving you first, no matter how crowded the bar is," Seb said conspiratorially.

"You'll definitely see me again," Eric said. "Though maybe not for a while."

Reeves interrupted their conversation by complaining about a cobweb he could see on one of the wall lights, and while Seb left the bar in search of a duster, Eric retrieved his iPhone from his jacket pocket. Its screen asked him to either turn off airplane mode or use Wi-Fi to access data, as the phone was out of service reach. Well, it would be. The first mobile phone mast wasn't due to be erected for another decade. But Eric had no intention of making a call, he just wanted to cue up the relevant footage he'd shot outside the Old Oak.

"How can you watch anything on that?" Reeves sneered, repeating his trick of silently creeping up behind Eric and catching him unawares.

Eric hastily placed the device on the bar, screen side down. "No need to thank me for the sherry."

"Why even bother with a television that small?" Reeves scoffed. "I've got a colour Sony Trinitron at home, and you can see every detail. It cost over two hundred pounds."

Eric took a large gulp of his lager. He briefly considered pointing out that the iPhone's 458 pixels per inch screen resolution was far superior to a 1976 Sony Trinitron television, but he thought better of it.

"Who would buy something like that?" Reeves continued. "What sort of person is so addicted to the telly that they need to carry one around in their pocket?"

With the wall light freshly free of cobwebs, Seb was back behind the bar. "What's that, Mr Reeves?" he asked. "Were you talking to me?"

"I was just wondering how depressing someone's life must be for them to bring a television into a bar," Reeves said to Seb.

Seb looked around the bar. "Who has done that?"

Reeves jabbed a finger in Eric's direction. "Mr Big I Am here."

"This gentleman has just bought you a drink," Seb pointed out. "And the only television in here is ours."

Reeves pointed at Eric's iPhone on the bar. "That's it, there."

Seb stared at the device and frowned. "If the gentleman told you that was a television, I'm sure he was only joking."

"I saw it working," Reeves said. "He obviously wants attention, throwing his money around buying drinks for strangers and showing off his tiny little television."

"I can assure you that attention from you is the last thing I want," Eric said.

"Honestly, it's pitiful," Reeves persisted. "He's so desperate for everyone to see his pocket television."

"I haven't seen it," Seb said.

"He's probably waiting for me to go," Reeves said. "So he can impress you with it. He looks like a pervert to me."

"If I was waiting for you to go I wouldn't have bought you a drink," Eric pointed out. "Which you still haven't thanked me for, incidentally."

Reeves continued: "Can you imagine trying to watch the cricket on it? You wouldn't be able to see the players never mind the ball."

"Actually, it's not just a television," Eric blurted out. He held the iPhone in front of Reeves and pointed to his apps. "It's also a cinema, notepad, address book, organiser, newspaper, dictionary, thesaurus, encyclopaedia, banking portal, weather forecaster, street map of the world, calculator, music player, instant messenger, camera – for still and moving images..."

Reeves was staring incredulously at Eric, as was Seb.

Eric finished with a flourish: "Oh and it's also a phone."

After several seconds of astonished silence, Reeves said dismissively: "A telephone? Utter rubbish! Where do you plug it in, for a start?"

"It doesn't need to be plugged in," Eric said.

"Ring someone then," Reeves challenged Eric, removing a crumpled white handkerchief from his shirt pocket and wiping the perspiration from his balding pink head. "Let's see you use it."

"I can't do that," Eric said, starting to regret his outburst. "It's currently experiencing technical issues as a result of this being 1976."

"I thought as much," Reeves said, shuffling back to his stool. "It's just a children's toy. Telephone indeed. It hasn't even got a dial!"

Eric downed the last of his lager and considered having another. Probably best not to. Getting half-sloshed would only undermine his upcoming presentation.

Reeves was now ranting at Seb from the other end of the bar. "You shouldn't let shysters and con men in here," he yelled. "There are plenty of other pubs in Cwmbran for people like that. I'll speak to Mr Butcher about this."

"I'm sure the gentleman wasn't being serious, Mr Reeves, let me get you another sherry, on the house," Seb tried to placate him, before rolling his eyes at Eric and asking: "Seriously sir, what is that thing?"

"It's an iPhone XS Max," Eric replied.

"But—"

"Remember the guide in 'The Hitchhiker's Guide to the Galaxy'?"

"The what?"

"Sorry, forget I said that," Eric grimaced. "It might not have been published yet."

"Can I see it?"

"Probably best if you don't."

The door to the lounge bar suddenly swung open, and filling its frame was the intimidating figure of Big Ben Butcher. Sweat was running down his enormous bald head and, with no eyebrows to halt its progress, cascading into his eyes.

"It's bastard hot out there," Big Ben announced. "Chuck me a towel, Simon, I'm sweating like a glassblower's ballbag."

Big Ben perched on a bar stool between Eric and Reeves with all the casual arrogance of someone who owned the place – which he did – and mopped his head and face with the bar towel. He pointed to the Stella tap and Seb immediately began pouring him a pint. He knew the drill.

"The weather people say today is going to be the hottest day of the year," Reeves said to Big Ben.

"I can believe it," Big Ben replied, then turning to Seb, he demanded: "Why haven't you got the tennis on? The tarts must have finished by now."

"The Men's Final is due to start at quarter past one," Eric said.

Big Ben turned towards Eric. "And it will probably be over by two," he said, slamming his empty glass on the bar and pointing at the Stella tap for another. "It's going to be a walkover."

"I don't know about a walkover," Eric said.

"Mark my words, it's going to be a straight-sets victory," said Big Ben. "Bang, bang, bang."

"You've got that right," Eric agreed.

Big Ben laughed: "Nastase is going to knock that Swede all over the court."

Eric shook his head. "No, it's going to be a straight-sets victory for Borg," he said.

Big Ben roared with laughter, and looking at Seb and Reeves in turn, asked: "Has this nutter escaped from the Grange?"

"He's been coming out with all sorts of nonsense," Reeves said, obsequiously laughing along with Big Ben.

"They should never have been allowed to build a loony bin so close to a residential area," Big Ben said. "They haven't got enough staff to keep tabs on them all."

"The man's a charlatan," Reeves declared. "He was just bragging to me that he had a telephone in his pocket."

Big Ben continued: "Borg hasn't got a cat in hell's chance. Not a cat in hell's chance."

"You're wrong," Eric said.

Big Ben glared at Eric. Very few people would have the audacity to tell him he was wrong. Especially not in his own bar. "What did you say?"

Eric replied confidently, though without making eye contact: "You're wrong. Borg is going to win in straight sets."

"What are you, an astronomer?" Big Ben sneered.

"In a way."

Big Ben moved his head closer to Eric's. "And I suppose you can predict the score too, can you?"

"Do you want to know the score?"

Big Ben leaned even closer to Eric. "Go on then, smart arse," he said, eyeballing him aggressively.

Resisting preceding his prediction with the term 'spoiler alert', as it would have been wasted on this audience, Eric said: "It finishes 6-4, 6-2, 9-7."

Still remaining seated, Big Ben stretched an enormous arm across the bar and pressed the 'no sale' button on the cash register. He removed Eric's ten-pound note from the drawer and slapped it down in front of him. "Put your money where your mouth is then," said Big Ben. "I'll give you odds of ten-to-one on that being the score."

Eric smiled to himself for a few seconds before slowly removing three ten-pound notes from his wallet. He ostentatiously waved them in the air before placing them down on the bar next to Big Ben's tenner. "Ten-to-one? I'm not really a betting man but I can't turn down those odds. Let's make the bet £30, shall we?"

***

Big Ben retrieved the last of the cash from the safe in the office and furiously stuffed it in a plain white envelope. As he entered the bar area, his entire head, as well as his face, was deep purple in colour. "Can you bastard believe this?" he snapped at a uniformed policeman who was glaring suspiciously at Eric. "He got the score exactly right. What are the chances?"

"Sounds very fishy," the policeman replied, using his fingers to slowly caress his bushy horseshoe moustache. "Very bloody fishy."

Eric smiled at PC Roy 'Spanner' Tanner. He'd seen that look many times before on Spanner's chiselled face.

"He didn't even watch the match," Reeves piped up. "He spent most of it sniffing around the girl on reception. It's disgusting. He's old enough to be her father. I said when he walked in that he was a pervert. I could tell."

"There you go," Big Ben said, handing the envelope crammed with £300 in used notes to Eric. "A bet's a bet. Never let it be said I don't pay my debts."

The lounge bar was almost full now. Most had come to watch the tennis and take advantage of the free sandwiches, but word had also spread during the afternoon that Big Ben was in danger of losing a huge bet, and there were plenty of people eager to witness what would happen next. Some of their faces were familiar to Eric, especially the kitchen staff, but he was a stranger to them.

Eric opened the envelope and started counting the cash onto the bar. "I'd better check it, Mr Butcher," he said. "Just in case you've given me too much."

Several people laughed, until Big Ben silenced them with a glare.

"As you can see," Big Ben said in a loud voice that carried over the heads of the crowd. "I am a man of my word. And now PC Tanner has kindly agreed to escort this gentleman to his vehicle, to ensure that nothing untoward happens to him or his winnings."

The look on Spanner's face strongly suggested that something very untoward would definitely happen to Eric once the two of them had left the building.

"What a generous gesture," Eric said, as he divided the cash into two piles. "But that won't be necessary as I won't be taking the money off the premises."

"You what?" Big Ben said.

Eric handed one of the piles to Seb and said: "Would you mind dividing this up among the staff, including the kitchen porters?"

Seb accepted the cash and some of the younger members of staff descended on him, squealing with excitement.

"And I'd like all you lovely people to join me in celebrating Borg's victory," Eric barked at the gathering while offering the other pile of notes to Reeves.

"Why are you giving me this?" asked Reeves, unsure if he should accept it.

"Mr Reeves here is holding the money," Eric said. "So please ask him to get you whatever you would like to drink for as long as the cash lasts."

A loud cheer erupted in the room, and as Eric made his way through the pile of bodies rushing to the bar he was slapped on the back and even granted a brief chorus of 'For He's A Jolly Good Fellow'.

Big Ben's face suggested it was about to commit murder.

## CHAPTER 2

## TUESDAY 3RD DECEMBER 2019

Woodland Manor's entrance drive was originally connected to the Cwmbran to Caerleon road, but the front section had been sold off in the 1950s, and a dozen detached houses had been constructed up each side of what became Lôn Heddychlon – Welsh for 'peaceful lane'. Ultra-modern in their time, they featured integral garages, large gardens front and rear, and were designed to appeal to executives relocating to the area to oversee the development of the new town. A contemporary property developer would have crammed three, possibly four, times as many houses into the same area, so these properties genuinely were – in estate agent speak – highly sought after, ranking second only to The Meadows in local desirability.

Eric knew all about Lôn Heddychlon. He'd grown up in the last house on the left, just before the pillars that marked the new entrance to Woodland Manor. Uniquely, the double garage of his house had been extended into the ground floor and converted into a shop – leaving the residential part of the property as just a flat above it – and Eric's father had been the proprietor for many years.

Originally his parents ran it as a couple, but his mother absconded with the Associated Welsh Bakeries delivery driver when Eric was ten. She crammed her belongings into a single suitcase and left, with the week's takings from the safe, to start a new life while Eric was at school and his father was at the wholesaler. Eric missed her but he didn't blame her for leaving. His father was an overbearing, mean-spirited curmudgeon. And it's fair to say the loss of his wife did not improve his disposition.

The most surprising thing about the shop was not that it closed in the 1990s, but that it lasted as long as it did with his father as front of house. It sold newspapers, cigarettes, wines and spirits, and a limited selection of groceries but with just two dozen houses as its local customer base, it was the shop's proximity to Woodland Manor – with its constant stream of visitors passing through its gates on a daily basis – that provided most of its business.

Eric parked his Lexus RX 450h outside the house he had come to value. He knew it well. It was directly opposite his old home. After his father closed the shop and downsized to a terraced property in a less exclusive area, the shop was snapped up by a developer and converted back into a house. Now there was no exterior evidence that Meek's Mini Market had ever existed.

Houses in Lôn Heddychlon rarely came on the market. Over half of them were still owned by the same families who had originally purchased them, so there was little historical data for Eric to study to arrive at a valuation for the house, but he knew the location would justify a premium price.

"It's a beautiful house, Mrs Freeman," Eric said dipping, a digestive biscuit into the bone china cup and saucer perched on the largest member of a G Plan Astra nest of tables. It looked like the entire house had been furnished and decorated at the height of the swinging '60s and then forgotten about. "And the period details are very... authentic."

"How well do you know the area?" the old lady asked as she slowly lowered herself onto the faded orange and red check fabric sofa. She precariously balanced her cup, which wasn't accompanied by a saucer, on the sofa's thin wooden armrest.

"Like the back of my hand," Eric replied, pleased to have been given the opportunity to demonstrate his local credentials. "In fact, I used to live directly opposite you."

Mrs Freeman studied Eric's face. "Did you?"

"When it was a shop," Eric explained.

"Oh, we never used to go in there," Mrs Freeman said. "It was very expensive and the man who ran it was rude."

Eric decided not to continue strolling down that particular memory lane and returned to business. "Do you mind telling me what the rows of metal poles in the rear garden are for?"

Mrs Freeman shrugged: "They're supposed to reduce our energy bills, but I don't know if they do."

"Is that why the lawn has so little grass on it?"

"They've ruined all the plants in the garden," Mrs Freeman tutted. "I don't go out there any longer."

"I must admit, it's a feature I've never seen before so I'm not sure how I'll describe it."

"You'd have to ask my husband," she replied. "He put them up many years ago."

"They look to be around six-feet tall and there's quite a lot of them, so they will limit the house's appeal to families," Eric pondered. "Are they easily removable?"

"I just said you'll have to speak to my husband about all that," Mrs Freeman snapped. "Now, have you finished?"

"My tea?"

The half of Eric's biscuit that had been dunked suddenly broke away from the dry part, falling into his tea with a splash.

"Writing up your report," she said, glaring at the droplets of tea on the table. "I've got things to do."

"I've got all the internal measurements of the rooms, but could you just open the door that leads down to the garage for me?"

Mrs Freeman hesitated. "That's my husband's domain," she said. "He keeps it locked."

"What's he got in there, a meth lab?"

The Breaking Bad reference went over her head: "It's his dark room," she said, failing to hide the irritation in her voice.

"Do you know when he will be back?" he asked.

"He usually puts in an appearance just after lunch," she said. "Then he goes off again and spends his evenings down there."

"Would it be alright if I come back this evening, so I can get the internal details of the garage and have a chat with him about the poles in the garden?"

"Can't you just measure the outside of the garage?" Mrs Freeman said. "That's what the others did."

"The others?"

"The other two agents who have been to value the house. They didn't mess around with internal measurements of the garage. And they didn't even mention the poles."

"That's where we're different, Mrs Freeman," Eric said, delighted with the opportunity to blow his own trumpet. "We go the extra mile. Some of these newcomers don't even use a proper camera to take pictures of your property. I've even heard of one who uses his phone."

Mrs Freeman didn't react, so Eric continued: "Attention to detail appears to have gone out of fashion in the modern world but not at Barrington Meek. Do I need to get the exact internal measurements of your garage just for a valuation? Probably not. But did Mozart need to put that high F note in the Queen of the Night aria in The Magic Flute? Did Rembrandt need to paint a little dog barking at the drummer in The Night Watch?"

Mrs Freeman scowled at Eric. "I don't want tradespeople calling in the evening," she said, ignoring his flowery attempts to impress. "I go to bed at eight and I don't want the bother of you traipsing around the house. I can't manage the stairs very well at my age."

"In that case I will be back just after lunch," Eric said. "And I hope to meet your husband then."

***

"Another?" Seb asked, pointing at Eric's glass.

"Better not, I've got a lot on this afternoon," Eric replied.

"Take some time for yourself," Seb said, pouring a second pint of Guinness anyway. "You can't serve from an empty vessel and no one's last words have ever been 'I wish I'd spent more time in the office'."

"I really shouldn't," Seb protested, accepting the glass even before the head had settled. "I doubt my client will appreciate me breathing alcohol all over her. I don't think she likes me as it is."

"Fuck her," Seb said.

Eric laughed. "I don't think that option is on the table," he said. "And I need the business."

"Are times really that hard?" Seb asked.

They were. The housing market slowed dramatically in the winter anyway, but Brexit – the UK's withdrawal from the European Union following a 2016 referendum – was looming, and opinions varied so widely about the impact this would have on the economy that many people were, to quote an overused phrase, battening down the hatches and waiting to see what happens.

"They are, actually," Eric said.

"Sorry to hear that," Seb said, sliding a platter of peanuts, olives, and spicy little biscuits across the bar towards Eric. "Help yourself to nibbles at least," he said.

"Cheers," Eric said, taking a handful of peanuts. "You never used to put these out before you had all these butch builders in here."

The tables in the lounge bar of Woodland Manor Hotel and Restaurant were starting to fill up with construction workers from the nearby Grange University Hospital, most of whom were perusing Seb's lunchtime menu of classic pub grub favourites. The original Grange hospital was established in 1953 as a medical facility for people with learning disabilities, but work began in the summer of 2017 on the construction of a new £350m 'super hospital' on the site. Due to open in 2021, the new facility was separated from the hotel by around two acres of woodland and its 600 workers had provided Seb with record takings over the last two years.

"I should think not," Seb said, stuffing a few of the miniature biscuits into his mouth, splattering his majestic white hipster beard with crumbs as he spoke: "Not at Waitrose prices."

"These are from Waitrose?"

"That's what I tell everyone," Seb said, grabbing another handful. "So they must be."

"You're eating all your profits in that case," Eric said.

Seb patted his plump tummy, which was straining the fabric of his black polo shirt. "The real cost is to my figure," he sighed. "I wanted to be slim for Christmas this year."

Seb was a giant bear of a man, standing over six feet tall and weighing almost 20 stone, and despite being in his early 60s he still dressed sharper than most men half his age.

"Why do you want to be slim for Christmas?" Eric asked.

Seb stared at him, horrified. "For the 'gram of course! Do you know, I actually envy old fossils like you who don't have to care about their appearance. I can't be pictured looking like a fat dowd."

***

"Hello again, Mrs Freeman," Eric said as the front door opened. "Is your husband back yet?"

"He's in the garage," she replied.

"Okay if I pop in and finish up?" Eric said, pointing to his clipboard and swallowing the mint he was sucking to negate his alcohol breath.

Mrs Freeman nodded, invited Eric in and quickly returned to the lounge and BBC2's coverage of the eighth day of the UK Snooker Championship.

Eric walked through the hallway to the half-glazed door that led to the garage and tapped on the glass. "Hello? Mr Freeman? Can you open the door please?" he said.

There was no response.

Eric tapped the frosted glass a little harder and called out again.

There was still no response.

This time he banged with his fist and raised his voice. "Mr Freeman! Can you open the door, please?"

"Do you mind?" Mrs Freeman hissed, as she emerged from the lounge. "Andrew abhors people raising their voice."

"Andrew?"

"My Yorkshire Terrier," she said, pointing to a tiny bundle of hair staring back at Eric from the sofa.

"I am so sorry," Eric said. "I will try from the outside."

All the houses in Lôn Heddychlon had identical layouts, with the integral double-garage taking up part of the ground floor. Five steps led up to the main entrance which contained a spacious hall with wooden doors leading to a lounge, dining room, kitchen, and downstairs cloakroom. The half-glazed door was the internal access point for the garage, and the four bedrooms and family bathroom could be found on the first floor.

Eric put the latch on the front door, so he could get back in without disturbing Mrs Freeman, and rapped on the double-width up-and-over aluminium garage door at the front of the property.

There was no response, but Eric could hear a faint humming sound coming from inside. "Hello?" he called out. "Mr Freeman?"

The handle to open the door was located around a foot above the ground. Eric bent down and tried to turn it.

Locked.

Not a problem, Eric thought, retrieving his keys from his jacket pocket. He had a key that opened most locks of this type. He was a professional, after all. The large bush at the front of the property partly blocked the drive and hid his unauthorised activity from any passers-by or neighbours. He made a mental note to suggest the vendor cuts that back before the staged photos of the house were taken.

The lock put up very little resistance and Eric raised the door. Both side walls were of standard brick construction, but Eric was surprised to be faced with another wall, made from unpainted breeze blocks, built across the entire width of the garage about five feet from the entrance. His heart sank. Even the smallest of cars wouldn't fit in that space. He would have to place lifestyle accessories, such as a bike or canoe, there for the photo. And the lack of a full-size usable garage could knock up to 10% off the asking price he had in mind, depending on what use the vendors had put the freed-up space to. Did she say a dark room?

Built into the breeze block wall was a thick metal door, with a large black and yellow sign which warned 'Live electrical equipment, danger of death' in a bold font. That would obviously have to be removed for the pictures.

Eric banged on this door with his fist. "Mr Freeman? Are you inside? Would you mind opening the door for a few minutes?"

No response.

Eric put his ear to the door but could only hear the humming noise coming from the other side. It was almost a throbbing sound now he was closer to it. He tried knocking again, a little harder, hurting his hand in the process.

Still no response.

Eric was about to try yanking the door open when a slightly distorted voice came from behind him: "Who are you and what do you want?"

Eric turned around in surprise and saw two small CCTV cameras, one in each corner of the entrance to the garage, trained on him. There was also a tiny speaker below one of them.

"That door was locked, and you are trespassing," the voice added. "I have called the police, and they are on their way."

Eric took a business card from his jacket breast pocket and held it up to each camera in turn. "Mr Freeman? I'm from Barrington Meek, the estate agents, here to measure up," he said. "It will only take a few moments."

The voice replied: "Close the garage door immediately and leave the property."

Eric was confused. "Your wife asked me to come here to value the house," he protested.

"You have bypassed the lock on my garage. That's breaking and entering in anyone's language. It could even be argued that it's home invasion."

"I just need to measure up inside," Eric said.

"No you don't," Mr Freeman said. "Like I told the others, the house is not for sale and nor will it be."

"But your wife..."

"My wife gets confused. Now, for the last time, close the door and get off my property."

Eric slammed the garage door. Instead of getting off the property though, he retraced his steps and returned to Mrs Freeman, who was still engrossed in the snooker. "Your husband tells me the house is not going to be put on the market," Eric said testily.

Mrs Freeman looked up. "Did he?"

"He said he told the other estate agents the same thing."

"That probably explains why they didn't get back to me," Mrs Freeman said.

Eric exhaled loudly in frustration. "Do you have a spare set of house keys?" he asked her.

"On the hook in the kitchen," she replied. "Why?"

"I need to have a word with your husband," he replied, darting out of the room and grabbing the bunch. He could identify each key by sight: front door, back door, garage, patio door... which left just one oversized four-sided key. Eric inspected the lock on the door that led to the garage. This was definitely the one. This type of lock was an uncommon choice for an internal door in a residential property, as it would normally be used in commercial premises where the priority was security: the two extra sets of teeth on the shaft made the lock particularly tricky to pick.

The door opened with just a single turn of the key and the hum he could hear from outside became more pronounced. It was similar to the sound a hi-fi makes after playing a record on maximum volume, and it seemed to be all around him.

A single lightbulb hung from the ceiling and illuminated the area. The narrow concrete steps led down to a rectangular space, with the original brick garage walls behind and to either side, and an additional wall – like the one at the front, constructed from breeze blocks and with a heavy door built into it – separated the rear of the garage from the front and led to a central chamber. This door also had the same warning notice as the one at the front of the garage. There were several industrial-looking metal cabinets lining one side wall, a wooden desk and chair on the other, and what appeared to be a coat and a large hat were hanging from hooks on the back wall.

"Mr Freeman?" Eric called from the doorway.

There was no answer.

Eric entered the garage, closing the half-glazed door behind him, and noticed the concrete floor was gently vibrating. As he got closer, he could see the items hanging on the back wall were actually a matte black deep-sea diving helmet and a large, hooded garment. Was it a wet suit of some kind? Eric examined the material. Or was it Latex? Did Mr Freeman host fetish parties in his dark room? The garment was an all-in-one construction, and it seemed designed to enclose every part of the body from the head to the feet, as it had reinforced soles, and the arms culminated in ten sausage-like tubes to accommodate individual fingers. This was definitely a bit kinky, Eric decided.

The hood of the suit had two small slots where the eyes would be and two even smaller ones for the nostrils. A heavy-duty zip went up the front of the garment, from the crotch to the chin, and was hidden beneath a flap. Presumably the wearer got into it, zipped himself up, and then pulled the hood over his head so he was completely encased within it. Although Eric's knowledge of the fetish scene was limited – he had only lasted six pages into Fifty Shades of Grey – he knew that outfits of this nature were usually tight, and he was surprised to discover that the fit of this one appeared to be quite generous. Loose, even. He could probably get into it himself, if he tried.

On the desk was a notebook, which Eric flicked through. Each page had headings for date, time, location, duration, and reference. The entries were a mass of numbers, apart from the locations, which all appeared to be in and around Cwmbran. Were these records of kinky parties Mr Freeman attended?

Where was Freeman? He must be in the centre section of the garage, between the 'danger of death' doors. Those signs were obviously designed to keep people away from his kinky activities – no one would be allowed to have live electrical equipment that powerful in their garage – but the centre section didn't appear to be large enough for, well, whatever went on at those functions.

Like the door at the front, this one had a large metal handle and Eric gave it a yank. It didn't budge. He scrutinised the door. There was no conventional lock, just a magnetic latch at the top. These were usually operated by card readers but there was no obvious sign of one.

Eric opened a few doors on the metal cabinets. They were filled with tools, cables, and brightly coloured electrical components. He picked up a magnetic screwdriver and waved that in front of the door, and the latch itself, to no avail.

Still holding the screwdriver, he examined the back wall, where the suit and helmet were hanging. With his left hand he took the helmet from its hook for a closer look. Suddenly he felt movement in his right hand. The screwdriver appeared to be trying to move away from the helmet. Eric laughed. Aren't magnetic things supposed to be attracted to each other? He tried to bring them together. The helmet remained stationary, but the screwdriver was desperately trying to escape. Eric could feel the muscles in his right arm tensing. The helmet appeared to have anti-magnetic properties. Did such things exist? And was this how the door opened?

Eric went to put the helmet on his head and noticed a faded white sticker inside it with a hand-written message: 'Not to be used without suit'. He studied the garment hanging on the wall. Could this be the key to opening the door? Wearing the helmet and the suit? What could Freeman be doing in that 'dark room' that required such an elaborate entry procedure?

Eric pulled the chair from the desk and slumped down into it. He checked his phone for messages – there were none – and sighed. Should he wait for Freeman to emerge? Or would that be wasting even more of his time? He hadn't sounded particularly amenable when he ordered him off his property. Eric exhaled again. The temperature in the garage was so low he could see his breath. It was almost like smoking again. Maybe he should climb into the suit to stay warm. He laughed at the absurdity of the suggestion. And then decided to do it. Not to keep warm but to confront Freeman in his central chamber. At the very least it would make an interesting story to regale Carol with.

Eric grabbed the suit and examined it. He found he could remain fully clothed, even keeping his shoes on, and still fit inside it. It was more comfortable than it looked apart from the hood, which restricted Eric's ability to see and breathe. He could see even less with the diving helmet on, which had just a thick transparent plastic letterbox slit for the eyes.

He pulled the handle and this time it moved, and the door swung open for him. He stepped inside. He tried to look around, but he could hardly move his head and his eyes stung like he was swimming underwater in an over-chlorinated swimming pool. This pain was accompanied by a horrific high-pitched whine assaulting his ears. He went to turn back but his entire body felt like it was made of stone, and his skin was beginning to tingle unpleasantly. He could just about make out the door that led out to the front section of the garage and he staggered towards it.

As Eric burst through the door, it automatically slammed behind him, leaving him stumbling into the front area of the garage. He collapsed to the floor, removed the helmet, and yanked down the hood. His lungs were gasping for oxygen, and he took a succession of deep, heaving breaths. It took a few moments before he noticed the air he was gulping down was dry and hot. His entire body was starting to perspire uncomfortably inside the suit, so he pulled down the zip and clambered out of it. Once his breathing had settled, he twisted the lever on the garage door that led outside, lifted the large aluminium structure, and was dazzled by a blinding light.

## CHAPTER 3

## SATURDAY 3ᴿᴰ JULY 1976

The sun was high in the sky, its rays warming everything it touched, including Eric, and it took a few seconds for his eyes to acclimatise to the intense brightness. His lungs burned momentarily as the damp winter air he had been breathing was replaced by air scorched by the dry heat of summer.

His stomach turned over when he noticed his Lexus was no longer parked outside the Freemans' house. He hadn't finished paying for that. He couldn't afford to lose it. Not when he hadn't taken the GAP insurance option. Where the Lexus had been was a beige Austin Princess which looked brand new. It even had an authentically '70s brown vinyl roof.

Baubles of sweat formed immediately on his forehead and started trickling down his face. The bush that hid the garage entrance from the road was much smaller than he remembered. He closed his eyes, which were still stinging, and noticed the absence of traffic noise from the Cwmbran to Caerleon road at the bottom of the Lôn Heddychlon hill. And in place of the distant drone that could usually be heard from the nearby A4042 dual carriageway, Eric could hear the chirping of grasshoppers coming from the grounds of Woodland Manor.

His stomach turned over a second time when he opened his eyes and saw that opposite the Freemans' house was Meek's Mini Market. He'd spent his formative years living in the flat above the shop and he couldn't wait to get away from it. Now, his eyes moistened as he took in the special offer posters that were stuck to the inside of the shop windows. They were hand-written in thick black marker on fluorescent green paper.

Eric shook his head and blinked several times, but Meek's Mini Market was still there, and in next door's garden was a bright orange Space Hopper and a red Raleigh Chopper bicycle.

"I must be hallucinating," Eric said aloud, his voice trembling. "There must have been LSD in that garage."

He took several deep breaths. The scent from the brightly coloured flowers in the Freemans' garden reminded him of funerals. Was it normal to be able to smell in hallucinations? And why did everything look so mundane in this '70s theme park? Where were the newspaper taxis and the rocking horse people?

"Maybe there really was a danger of death in that garage," Eric said, "and I'm reliving parts of my life as I die."

If that was the case, he wasn't particularly looking forward to it. If his highlights reel had been a movie genre, it certainly wouldn't have been 'action'.

He pinched his cheek, hard. It hurt. What did that prove? Only that he could still feel pain. He stared at the shop posters: a box of cheese crackers was 11p, a large tube of toothpaste was 16p, a box of ten frozen fish fingers was 25p, and a tin of four hamburgers in gravy was 28p. No wonder his father only ever scraped a meagre living from the business: it was obviously summer so why wasn't he promoting ice-cream, soft drinks, and chilled meats to go with salads and picnics?

His father.

Just saying that word in his head caused his stomach to flip once again. Was he in the shop, leaning on the counter and complaining about the world, like Eric remembered? Eric slowly approached the storefront. The windows did not look as if they had been cleaned in months, the paintwork was chipped, and the fascia was cracked in several places. Such detail. This version of Meek's Mini Market was more downmarket than he remembered the original being.

Next to the shop door was a wire rack which held half a dozen copies of the local newspaper, the Cwmbran Evening Star. Eric looked at the date on the masthead: 3$^{rd}$ July 1976. For the third time in as many minutes, his stomach turned over. Out of every day he had lived, why would his dying subconscious conjure up this one for him to relive?

But wait. He caught sight of his reflection in the glass of the shop door, expecting to see the gauche teenager he once was staring back at him. He was relieved to instead see a slightly distorted version of the overweight 60-year-old man he started the day as. He pushed the shop door and it swung inwards, setting off a clanging bell.

Inside, Meek's Mini Market was just as he remembered it: dark, dingy, and dusty. The left wall was taken up by grubby metal shelving, which held the tinned goods and general provisions, such as bread, biscuits, and home baking items. With no 'best before' dates on the perishable goods, it was astonishing that more people hadn't died of food poisoning in the '70s.

Cleaning, washing, and paper products were presented in a gondola that took up the centre of the store, including five different shades of toilet paper, designed to match the coloured bathroom suites that were popular at this time. Now he thought about it, Eric couldn't recall when he last saw toilet paper that wasn't white.

The right wall showcased newspapers and magazines while the interior of the window area contained two refrigerated cabinets: an upright one for fresh foods including milk, cheese, savoury pastry products, sliced meat, and yoghurts; and a large chest freezer for frozen items such as vegetables, fish fingers, boil in the bag ready meals, and ice-cream.

Stretching the entire length of the back wall was the counter: spreading over half of it was a series of moulded plastic confectionary displays, provided by manufacturers to hold and present their products, and the other half held the cash register and a flat surface for customers to stack their purchases on. His father had never seen the benefit of investing in customer baskets, as most people only tended to buy a handful of items. Behind the counter were wide shelves containing wines, spirits, and beers, and a white plastic display cabinet housing the cigarettes and tobacco products.

It took a few seconds for Eric's eyes to adjust to the gloomy interior, after the dazzling sunlight outside, but the smell hit him straight away: stale smoke. It was not frowned upon for shopkeepers to puff away on a cigarette while they were serving customers back in the '70s, and his father was doing just that behind the counter while talking to a large stocky man who was leaning on it. His father was shorter than Eric remembered, and thinner, with lank greying dark hair flopping in his eyes and a bushy moustache engulfing his top lip. He would have been in his late 40s in 1976, but he looked at least a decade older.

There was a stack of a dozen or so tins of soup on the counter and, while he talked and smoked, his father was scraping off the price tags and replacing them with ones for a higher amount.

The sound of the bell had interrupted the men's conversation. His father stared at him and the giant form of the other man turned around to face him. Eric recognised him instantly: PC Roy 'Spanner' Tanner, who 'looked after' this area.

Spanner looked Eric up and down, appraising him in the way that some policemen did when meeting people, like he was expecting his memory banks to throw up a match from the 'wanted' files. Spanner used his forefinger and thumb to pat down his facial hair, a thick horseshoe moustache that covered not only his top lip but also the sides of his mouth down to the tip of his chin. Peter Wyngarde's Jason King character had a lot to answer for.

Eric marvelled at the branded products on the shelves, many of which he had long forgotten, and wondered how to introduce himself to his father. Hello Dad, I'm your son, even though I'm older than you.

But before Eric could say anything his father pre-empted him: "We're closing at one," he said in that surly tone Eric remembered so well. "So you've only got a few minutes."

Spanner continued to stare at Eric. Although Woodland Manor brought strangers to the area during the week, particularly commercial travellers, it was more unusual for Spanner to encounter new people at weekends. "Bit warm to be wearing a suit," Spanner said to him.

This was true. Eric hadn't really noticed until now but the dramatic change in temperature was draining sweat from his armpits into his thick cotton shirt.

"It's a bit old fashioned, isn't it?" Spanner asked, his fat hand reaching out to pinch Eric's thin lapel. "Just come out of the nick, have you?"

Eric pushed the policeman's hand away. "Do you mind?" he said.

Spanner straightened his back and pushed a sausage-like finger into Eric's sweating face. "That's assault," he snapped. "I could arrest you right now for raising your hand to an officer of the law, in front of a witness."

"I'm sorry," Eric said, holding his hands up in front of him and backing away. The rough tip of Spanner's finger had been pushed so hard into Eric's cheek that it felt like it was still there. "I'm not used to being touched like that."

"Oh, how are you used to being touched?" Spanner took a step towards Eric. "Are you one of those homosexuals?"

"You're the one with Freddie Mercury facial hair," Eric said.

"Are you giving me lip?" Spanner snarled. "You must be a long way from home, cock."

"What do you want?" Eric's father said to him, interrupting Spanner. "I told you, I'm shutting in a few minutes."

Eric backed further away from Spanner and looked at the newspaper racks. He picked up a copy of Melody Maker. The front-page headline read 'Stones, Dead Santana Set', which confused him until he realised the subject of the article was which bands were expected to headline the Knebworth and Wembley festivals. The sentence could have done with an Oxford comma, really.

"I'll take this," Eric said.

Both his father and Spanner eyed him suspiciously. "That's 15p then," his father said, holding out his hand.

Eric patted his pockets for change. There was none. The need to carry coins had greatly diminished in recent years. He reached for his wallet instead. "I've only got a note," he said.

"A note? I've already cashed up the till," his father grumbled.

"I'll have some cigarettes as well," said Eric, pointing to the multi-coloured boxes behind his father. "A pack of John Player Special please."

His father sighed and retrieved one of the distinctive black and gold packs, which had always looked so glamorous to young Eric due to the company's sponsorship of the Lotus Formula One team. "That's 52p altogether," he said.

Eric's wallet contained a five-pound note and two ten-pound notes, and as he was about to pull the lower denomination one out he suddenly realised that it wouldn't be legal tender, and being accused of trying to pass off counterfeit money in front of a belligerent policeman from 1976 who already seemed to have a grudge against him might result in unpleasant consequences, even in an hallucination. He quickly returned his wallet to his pocket.

"Didn't you hear me?" his father said, slamming the cigarettes on the counter. "I said 52p."

"I've changed my mind," Eric said, returning the Melody Maker to the rack and heading for the front door. "You really need to work on your customer service skills."

As he opened the door and set off the bell again, he could just about hear his father mutter "Timewasting twat" to his back.

Eric exhaled deeply and wiped the sweat from his forehead with his jacket sleeve. So much for being an end-of-life highlights reel. That encounter hadn't happened. He had felt genuinely afraid for his safety back there, and with good cause: the Spanner he remembered had a reputation for dishing out his own form of justice to those who crossed him, or indeed to anyone he took a dislike to.

"Oi!"

Eric turned to face the direction of the voice and froze.

"Oi cock, I'm talking to you," Spanner yelled at Eric as he marched towards him.

"Yes officer?" Eric said politely.

"What's your game?"

"I realised I didn't have any money on me," Eric said.

"What middle-aged man buys Melody Maker?" Spanner said. "And has a wallet with no money in it despite wearing a suit on a Saturday?"

Eric shrugged guiltily and could feel his face reddening. Like most of the local youths, he had been wary of Spanner as a teenager, and waves of unease were now washing over him.

"Let me see your wallet," Spanner demanded.

Eric stared in fascination at Spanner's hostile face. He could make out every wrinkle and every strand of hair. If this was an hallucination, it was in ultra-high definition. Eric was amazed his subconscious mind had stored so many details of someone he hadn't thought about in decades.

The growing awareness that this encounter could not be real emboldened Eric who replied: "On what grounds?"

Spanner punched Eric hard in the stomach. "On what grounds? On what grounds? On these fucking grounds, cock."

Eric doubled up in pain and, completely winded, was unable to speak. This suddenly felt very real indeed.

Spanner reached into Eric's jacket and snatched the wallet from him. He pulled the plastic cards out one by one, gave them a cursory glance, and tossed them back at Eric. "What are these, business cards?"

Eric nodded.

"Why are they made of plastic?" Spanner said, before removing the money and pulling a surprised face at the unfamiliar notes. "What have we got here? You said you had no money."

Eric was incapable of answering as he was still gasping for air.

"Are you deaf?" Spanner punched Eric on the side of the head. It was a casual punch, with no real force behind it, almost conversational compared to the first.

"No," Eric protested, reeling backwards and almost falling to the ground.

"What's this shit? Scottish money?"

Eric nodded, grateful for the explanation provided by Spanner.

"What's your business here, cock?" Spanner demanded, folding up Eric's money and cramming it into the breast pocket of his uniform.

"I'm visiting friends," Eric replied, still gasping from the punch.

"Who?"

Eric pointed to the Freemans' house.

"Right well get out of my sight," Spanner said. "I don't want to see you around here again. If I do, you can expect a proper kicking. Do you understand me?"

Eric understood him. He gathered up his wallet and plastic cards, scampered towards the Freeman's house, lifted the garage door, and slammed it shut behind him. Despite the rivers of sweat now engulfing him, he clambered into the discarded suit, clamped on the welding helmet, and threw himself through the internal door.

## CHAPTER 4

### TUESDAY 3RD DECEMBER 2019

"Are you with me so far?" asked the shaven headed man with the thick-framed black glasses sat opposite Eric.

Eric wasn't with him. This was not a good day to discuss business, even though the bloke had made an appointment to come and see him. He was still disoriented from his experience earlier this afternoon in the Freemans' garage. Everything was back to normal when he emerged from it after escaping from Spanner: Mrs Freeman and Andrew were watching the snooker, his Lexus was parked outside, the property opposite was a residential house, not Meek's Mini Market, and he could once again see his breath in the cold winter air.

What kind of a dark room induces hallucinations? And of all the hallucinations he could imagine, why would his subconscious have chosen that one? He rubbed the side of his face, which was still tender from Spanner's punch. This wasn't normal for a hallucination, was it?

"It's like I said, you're living in the past, Mr Meek," the man said, pointing at the wooden literature racks that lined the interior walls.

So it would seem.

"The world has moved on and this place, frankly, hasn't."

"Did you make this appointment just to tell me that or was there something else?" Eric said, looking down at the business card that had been presented to him. "Mr Mason?"

"The days of the traditional high street estate agent are coming to an end," Mason said. "But most of them don't know it yet and I can—"

"Is that your real name?" Eric interrupted. "Jason Mason?"

"Does it matter, as long as people remember it?"

Eric theatrically checked the time on his fitness tracker watch and rose to his feet. "Well, Mr Mason, I've given you five minutes of my time and I'm no nearer to knowing why, so I wish you all good fortune with your venture, whatever it is, but I've had quite a day and I've still got things to do."

"I'm not finished," Mason said. "Please allow me to finish. You'll want to hear what I've got to say."

Eric studied Mason, who appeared to be around half his age. He exuded the easy confidence of someone life had yet to kick in the balls. "Two more minutes then," Eric said, sitting back down.

"I'm offering you the chance to walk away from all this," Mason said, gesturing at the showroom again. "Nobody wants printed information sheets anymore. By the time you've got someone to lay it out and print it I'll have listed it online and already sold the house."

"In that case you must be a very wealthy man," Eric said.

"I'm getting there," Mason said, slowly stroking his chin in a way that showcased his Apple Watch. "This is the Series 4 model."

"I didn't ask," Eric replied. "But thank you for letting me know."

"Look, I'm not here to impress you but to impress upon you that it's not just the future that's online," Mason said. "It's the present, and yet here you are still operating like it's the 20th century."

"Do either of you want a tea or coffee or a sandwich?" asked Carol. "I've done a plate of spicy chicken and avocado today, ideal to warm you up in this bitter weather."

"No thank you Carol," Eric replied. "Mr Mason is not staying."

As Carol walked away from Eric's large mahogany desk that dominated the rear of the showroom, Mason whispered: "Christ, how old is she? Shouldn't she be collecting her pension by now?"

Eric glared at Mason. Yes, she should be, but Carol showed no signs of losing interest in working, even though she had been here almost as long as him.

"I would have thought a wrinkled old bat like that would drive people away," Mason continued in a louder voice now Carol was out of earshot in the staff-only kitchen area.

"I'm always telling him we could do with a bit of totty," chimed in Alwyn, the other member of staff, cupping his hand over his phone. "To be fair to Carol though, she makes awesome sandwiches."

"Does she really?" Mason said in mock appreciation. "That's what every modern estate agent needs: a ready supply of sandwiches."

"The clients love them," Alwyn said. "Everyone will offer you a tea or coffee but when Carol whips out her sarnies... Honestly, they're better than Marks & Spencer's. There was a bloke on the radio this morning saying we buy 20 million pre-packed sandwiches every day, and I'm telling you, she'd make a killing if she set up a catering business. I'd be a customer."

"I bet you're popular with all the single mothers looking for rentals," Mason said, admiring the tribal tattoos on Alwyn's muscular arms.

"Oh aye, the yummy mummies appreciate a bit of Alwyn love," Alwyn crowed, stretching his arms above his head, emphasising his burly chest. "The rentals are the only thing that keeps us going because sales are dead at this time of year anyway, but with Brexit—"

"That's enough, Alwyn," Eric cut him off. "And why are you wearing a short-sleeved polo shirt in the showroom?"

"None of my white shirts fit me," Alwyn said, flexing his biceps. "They can't contain my guns."

"If you can't find shirts that fit you, you should keep your jacket on," Eric said.

"This is like being back in school," Alwyn complained.

"Who are you on the phone to anyway?" Eric said.

"I'm on hold," Alwyn replied. "Trying to get Mrs Wilson's gas reconnected."

"When you've finished, go and buy a bigger shirt," Eric said. "It looks very unprofessional."

"I don't know," Mason said approvingly. "He's one of the few things in here that looks like he's from this century."

"Cheers, butty," Alwyn said to Mason, giving him a thumbs-up.

"Your time is nearly up," Eric said, tapping his watch.

Mason returned his attention to Eric. "As I was saying, Jason Mason is an online estate agent that works for a flat fee rather than commission. That means our charges are considerably less than yours, but we still provide all the same services—"

"I doubt that very much," Eric said, thinking of the hoops he was jumping through to get Mrs Freeman's house listed.

"We will own the online space," Mason continued. "Absolutely own it. Our site is interactive and dynamic while yours looks like it was built in the 1990s by a ten-year-old. And where are you on mobile?"

Eric nodded his head in the direction of his iPhone on his desk. "There I am," he said.

"Boom!" Mason said, clapping his hands together. "That's the perfect metaphor for this business. No one uses an iPhone 4 these days."

"It's a 5 actually," Eric said, slipping it into his jacket pocket and getting to his feet.

"I'm surprised you're not still using a BlackBerry," Mason said. "No wonder you've got no social media presence. You wouldn't even be able to run the apps on that. Did I mention that we've got thousands of Facebook Likes and Twitter followers?"

Eric checked the time again. "Last few seconds, you'd better get to the point."

"My point is you have this prime location in the town centre," Mason said. "It's been an estate agent for over 50 years, so everyone knows it's here, but it's crying out for a makeover—"

"A makeover?"

"You can't say it doesn't need it," Mason said, gesturing at the literature racks. "Those fixtures belong on the Antiques Roadshow. And it also needs a rebrand. As Jason Mason's first bricks and mortar branch it would allow us to better service our existing clientele while also targeting the large local rental sector, which I understand you currently do pretty well with, combining the best of both worlds."

Before Eric could reply, Carol returned from the staff-only door with a tray containing a mug of tea, a packet of biscuits, and a tall glass containing a thick mud-coloured liquid.

Mason looked horrified. "God, she looks even older close up," he said out of the corner of his mouth as Carol placed the glass and biscuits down in front of Alwyn and took the mug to her own desk. "I can't believe you let clients see her."

Alwyn gave a thumbs-up sign to Carol and took a huge gulp from the glass. "Cheers Carol, you make a great protein shake, you do," he said.

Eric glared at Mason. "Carol's a valuable part of this office and she has been for many years."

"Has-been seems an appropriate term," sneered Mason.

"You can address her employment status when you buy me out – that is what you are leading up to, isn't it?"

"Not quite," Mason said, removing his oversized thick-framed glasses and wiping them with his shirt. "I'm proposing that Jason Mason takes over the lease rather than buys you out. We'll be happy to keep you on as a general manager of the branch for an agreed period, as a figurehead, or you can just walk away."

"What are you offering?"

"No money," Mason said. "But something even more valuable – a viable exit route."

Eric frowned at Mason. "I must admit that's not a particularly tempting offer," he said. "I might even use the word 'disappointing' to describe it."

Mason moved closer to Eric. "I would strongly advise you to think it over."

"You can absolutely rely on me not doing that," Eric replied. "I've got your business card and I'll retrieve it from the bin if I change my mind."

"I would strongly advise you to keep hold of it," Mason said, handing Eric a transparent plastic folder containing several documents. "Here's the proposal."

Eric gave Mason a thin smile, accepted the folder, and manoeuvred his way around him, but in doing so his knee bumped into Alwyn's desk. The impact caused the tall glass to wobble and then fall, disgorging its contents over an open book about bodybuilding.

Alwyn leapt to his feet and scooped up the book, causing rivers of the murky liquid to run from its pages to his shirt. "Are you joking me?" he cried.

"Sorry Alwyn," Eric said. Nodding towards the protein shake he added: "But I have told you before, too many of those protein drinks could be bad for you."

"I have to drink them every three hours," Alwyn protested, his hands pressing his wet shirt in a way that accentuated his muscular torso.

"I'll leave you to it," Mason said, heading for the door. He paused at the large rubber plant that greeted visitors. "Why on earth have you got a giant plant in one of your key display areas?"

"That plant has been with us since Mr Meek took over the business," Carol informed him. "It's got great sentimental value."

Mason shook his head as he left.

"I'm guessing he'd strongly advise us to get rid of it," Eric said to Carol.

"He was a bit too full of himself for my liking," Carol said.

Mason's unwanted presence was immediately replaced by a smartly dressed woman who brought the scent of expensive perfume into the showroom. She appeared to be in her 50s but was wearing so much makeup it was difficult to tell.

"Are you having a Mister Wet T-shirt competition in here?" she asked, staring approvingly at Alwyn. "Because I think we've got a winner."

Alwyn returned her gaze and a huge grin spread across his face.

"Can I help you?" Carol asked.

"I think he probably can," she said, pointing to Alwyn. "He looks quite charming."

"I'm so charming I'm like charmageddon," Alwyn said.

"He's just on his way out to get a new shirt," Carol said. "Aren't you, Alwyn?"

Alwyn frowned in disappointment but took the hint.

The woman stared at Alwyn's back as he left the showroom. "God, I love ugly men, don't you?" she said to Carol.

"What is that heavenly perfume you're wearing?" Carol asked, changing the subject.

"Do you like it?" the woman asked unnecessarily, delighted her good taste was recognised. "It's French. Something unpronounceable."

"It's absolutely gorgeous," Carol added.

"Isn't it? The January Sale has started early in House of Fraser so I thought, why not? I'm totally worth it."

Carol smiled in approval.

"The name's Ducreux," the woman said, offering Carol a business card.

"How chic," Carol gushed.

Mrs Ducreux laughed. "The name might be but the bastard who gave it to me wasn't."

"Are you looking to buy or sell?"

"Buy."

"And do you have a property to sell?"

"No, I'm a cash buyer," Mrs Ducreux replied. "So I expect to be treated like royalty in the current market."

"You will be," Carol assured her. "Not because you're a cash buyer but because all our clients are."

"Is this all you've got at the top end?" Mrs Ducreux said, pointing towards the brochures stacked under the 'luxury and executive' section of the racks. "I'm looking for something in The Meadows or Lôn Heddychlon."

"I'm afraid there's nothing available in either location at the moment," Carol said. "We do have a lovely bungalow in Brookvale though."

Mrs Ducreux shook her head dismissively. "Too small," she said, without looking at it.

Carol guided the woman to one of the agency's most expensive properties, but Mrs Ducreux wrinkled her nose. "Darling, I'm opening a gallery in two weeks' time, I can't be seen to be living in a semi."

"There's this one," Carol suggested, handing Mrs Ducreux a brochure. "If you don't mind a project, it's got fantastic potential."

After taking a cursory glance at the details, Mrs Ducreux remarked: "Darling, you might call this 'a timeless blend of rustic charm and warmth', but to me it just looks like a shithole."

"How soon do you want to move?" Eric asked.

"I'm living on the streets at the moment."

Carol looked horrified.

"Don't feel sorry for me, darling," Mrs Ducreux cackled. "I'm only talking figuratively. I've got a chunky settlement and I'm living my best life, without some overbearing old sod constantly holding me back."

"Hence the gallery?" Carol asked.

"Hence the gallery," the woman confirmed. "I've always fancied one and with no man in my life there's no one to tell me why it won't work."

Carol's eyebrows lifted and she pursed her lips. "Where are you opening it?"

"Here, in the centre," Mrs Ducreux said. "In the upstairs bit, the week before Christmas."

"Oh," said Carol. "That's not long."

"It's going to be fabulous," Mrs Ducreux said. "We're debuting with the work of a very talented young photographer friend of mine, charting the changing seasons of the River Usk. You must come to the opening."

"I'd love to," Carol said.

"There will be lots of minor celebs and plenty of bubbles," Mrs Ducreux laughed.

"So when would you like to move?" Eric asked again.

"Is tomorrow out of the question?"

Eric and Carol exchanged glances.

"I'm in a short-term let that expires at the end of the year," Mrs Ducreux continued. "So ideally I'd like to be in by Christmas."

"This Christmas?" Carol gasped.

"Of course," the woman replied. "Is that going to be a problem?"

While Carol was considering her response, Eric stepped in: "I probably shouldn't say this, but I am going to value a property in Lôn Heddychlon this evening," he said. "So we may have something very soon, but getting you moved in less than a month will be a pretty tall order."

"That would be wonderful," Mrs Ducreux said.

"Would you like to leave me your details?" Eric asked. "And I can call you if it becomes available?"

Mrs Ducreux smiled coquettishly at Eric. "Ooh, aren't you Mr Slick?"

"I'm sorry?"

"Way to get a girl's number," she said, batting her false eyelashes in his direction as she handed him a business card.

Eric blushed. "No, I really am going to value a property there right now. In fact, I should have left a few minutes ago."

"I was only pulling your pisser," she said to Eric. "No offence darling, but you're a bit old for me."

"I'm sure I am," said Eric, somewhat relieved.

"Don't forget I'm a cash buyer, so make it a low valuation," Mrs Ducreux said.

"I can't promise that," Eric said. "Houses in Lôn Heddychlon rarely came on the market, and they get snapped up when they do, but you're in a proceedable position so you'll have an advantage over other interested parties."

While Eric gathered his things, Carol brought a plate of sandwiches from the kitchen fridge. "Can I interest you in a spicy chicken and avocado?" she asked, removing the aluminium foil covering. "The kettle's on and I'd love to know more about your gallery."

"They look so good," Mrs Ducreux said approvingly. "Are they from Mark's?"

As he made his way towards the underground car park below the pedestrianised town centre, Eric's phone rang. It was Carol.

"Just wanted to wish you luck," Carol said. "It would be great if you could get the business, particularly now we've got a motivated cash buyer."

"I'll do my best," Eric said. "But she's probably going to be an absolute nightmare to deal with."

"There is one other thing," Carol said in a quieter voice. "I didn't want to say anything in front of Alwyn, but we've had a letter from the bank today."

"Whatever it is, I'm sure it can wait," Eric said. "I probably won't get back in time to deal with it today."

"That's why I'm ringing you," Carol said. "It's important."

"Are they offering us free money?"

"We're over our overdraft limit and we need to get it down before the rent goes out at the end of the month, otherwise it might not get paid."

"Why are you telling me this now?" Eric groaned. "I need to be focused, not distracted by financial hypotheticals."

"Sorry," Carol said. "But think of it as an extra incentive to get the business."

***

It was once again Mrs Freeman who opened the front door to Eric. "You left in a hurry this afternoon," she said.

"Yes, I'm sorry about that," Eric replied. "I got called away on urgent business. Is your husband in?"

He was, and Mrs Freeman led Eric through the hall and pointed at the closed door of the study. Eric knocked and gently opened the door. He had seen the room earlier when measuring the internal dimensions with his laser distance metre. He hadn't noticed at the time, but he could now see that the ceiling-high bookshelf that took up one entire wall was crammed with photo albums rather than books.

"Hobby of yours, is it?" Eric asked, gesturing towards the albums.

Eric instantly recognised Freeman, now he could see his face. The old man was sat with his eyes closed behind a large desk on a plush leather chair, wearing enormous noise cancelling headphones, from which snippets of classical music leaked out into the small room.

Eric lifted one of the headphones from Freeman's head and repeated his question.

Freeman's head snapped back, his eyes wide with shock. "Who are you?"

"I'm your friendly local estate agent," Eric replied. "Going above and beyond the call of duty for the benefit of my clients."

The only other items of furniture in the study were a metal filing cabinet behind Mr Freeman's desk and a rudimentary wooden chair, which looked like it had escaped from the kitchen, parked against the other wall. Eric positioned it so it was opposite Freeman and sat down. The floor behind Freeman's chair was a jumble of cables and several black plastic boxes covered in brightly coloured knobs. There were also two small CCTV monitors and a microphone.

"You must have been in here this afternoon when you spoke to me on the camera," Eric said, gesturing towards the screens. "And presumably you didn't hear me calling you when I was inside the house because you had your headphones on. So where were you when I was measuring up?"

Perched on the edge of his chair, Freeman eyed Eric warily.

"Were you in your 'dark room' in the garage?"

Freeman continued to glower at Eric.

"You don't recognise me, do you?" Eric said.

"Of course I do, you're the estate agent," Freeman said, settling back into his chair. "The one who broke into my garage."

Eric scrutinised Freeman. Although it had been over 40 years since he had been a pupil in his physics class, apart from acquiring a slight tremor in his voice, the old man had barely changed. To Eric, he had looked ancient back then, with his grey beard, bald head, and thick black glasses – all of which were still present.

"Why are you back?" Freeman continued.

"Because I take my job seriously," Eric said. "This is actually my third visit to your house today."

"We're not moving," Freeman replied. "Didn't I make myself clear? It's your own time you're wasting."

"I don't want to get involved in a domestic dispute, but when I originally spoke to your wife she seemed absolutely certain that she wanted to sell the house, and I'd like to clarify why my company would be the best choice for you," Eric said.

"It might well be, but I'm not interested," Freeman said.

Eric stared at him. "Are you aware she is in pain every time she goes up or down the stairs?"

Freeman glared back at Eric. "It's not exactly a picnic for me, either. I'm older than her."

"Why don't you downsize to a bungalow? We've got a lovely one in Brookvale, just a stone's throw away. Everything's on one level and there have been extensive modifications installed for people with limited mobility."

"I told you, I'm not interested," Freeman said, swinging around in his chair to open the third drawer of the filing cabinet.

"This would be an excellent time for you to sell," Eric persisted. "Once the new hospital is built it's going to be like Piccadilly Circus around here. There will be issues with traffic, and parking, and noise…"

Freeman retrieved a bottle of whisky and a glass from the filing cabinet. "You can see yourself out, can't you?" he said without looking up. "You'll obviously know the way, if this is your third visit."

"Mr Freeman, if I list this house tomorrow, I can guarantee you a quick sale. I have a client waiting, a cash buyer. If you were prepared to move to Brookvale – and my firm can handle the whole process for you – you will be able to free up a quite substantial amount of equity. You and your wife might want to go on a world cruise—"

"We went on one once before," Freeman said, pouring a large measure of whisky into the glass and then returning the bottle to the filing cabinet. "I hated every minute of it."

"Perhaps you'd like to see the Seven Wonders of the World," Eric persisted, pointing at the photo albums. "Or maybe you could photograph big game in Africa—"

"Do you know how hot it is in Africa?" Freeman retorted. "I can't abide the sun."

"You remind me so much of my father," Eric sighed. "When was the last time you took your wife on holiday?"

The defiant look on Freeman's face softened a little.

"I don't think you can remember, can you?" Eric continued.

"I don't see the point of holidays," Freeman said. "Why pay to sleep in someone else's bed when it will inevitably be inferior to your own?"

"You don't have to go on holiday, you could do whatever you wanted with the money," Eric said, a slight tone of exasperation creeping into his voice. "You could buy an Aston Martin—"

"What would I do with one of them at my age?" Freeman scoffed. "I can only just manage my Yaris. And the insurance on that goes up every year, even though we barely do any mileage. You'd think it would go down, wouldn't you?"

"Perhaps you'd like to financially help your family—"

"We don't have any family."

"You could buy a mink-lined gimp suit then," Eric finally said.

"A what?"

"Or a diamond-encrusted diving helmet."

Freeman glared at Eric. "I'd like you to leave," he said. "Or do you want me to phone the police?"

"Again? And tell them what?"

Freeman sipped his whisky. "That you are trespassing on private property. Again."

"What did they say the last time?"

Freeman said nothing.

"I was invited here by your wife," Eric said, repositioning himself in his uncomfortable chair. "You remember her? The woman who is a prisoner in her own home, who hasn't been on holiday in years."

"It's not about her," Freeman said.

"That's obvious," Eric said. "Everything around here is clearly all about you."

"What I mean is—"

"You were a shit teacher and you're evidently a shit husband too."

Freeman looked up at Eric, who had risen to his feet. "What did you just say?"

"You taught me physics for three years in the '70s and I learned absolutely nothing in your class," Eric said. "I still haven't got a clue how electricity works."

"Good grief man, that's basic stuff," Freeman said. "When electrons move round a circuit, they carry electrical energy—"

"It's too late now," Eric cut him off. "No need to get up, Mr Freeman, I will see myself out."

"Thank you."

"But before I leave, I will of course explain to your wife why I won't be listing the house, despite her wishes. And I will also arrange for a business associate of mine to visit her in the morning for a no obligation consultation. He's a local solicitor who specialises in divorces for people in later life and he always ensures the wives are very well looked after, which is more than you have done."

Freeman started breathing heavily. "That is an appalling suggestion!"

"He will recommend that she'd be much more comfortable in a luxury retirement home, with all her needs catered for. Do you know there is a self-contained community near Abergavenny which has a beauty salon, gym, cinema, bar, and restaurant? It's practically a village in itself – but without any surly teenagers hanging around and moaning that there's nothing to do."

"I will never agree to that."

"That is your prerogative, of course, but it won't be your decision. Obviously, the house will have to be sold to pay for it – I've checked the deeds and it's in joint names – and I feel duty bound to point out that a 'forced sale' is rarely beneficial to the vendor. And that's before we even discuss your rather unconventional garage conversion."

Freeman scowled at Eric, his lips trembling.

"That's the other thing I'd like to talk about," Eric said. "What have you built in there?"

"It's just a project I've been working on," Freeman said.

"I assume you have written authorisation for what a planning officer would consider to be a structural alteration?" Eric said. "If so, I would very much appreciate catching sight of the application. And am I right in thinking your 'project' is connected to the national grid in some way? If so, there should be certificates of conformity, signed by a qualified electrician."

"That's none of your concern," Freeman spluttered.

"As a concerned citizen, Mr Freeman, I think it is," Eric said. "If it's too much trouble, I can ask a friend of mine in the Planning Inspectorate to email the details to me. I should warn you though, if you haven't applied for planning permission then he will probably want to pay you a visit. And you should be aware that retrospective planning applications are rarely successful."

"Please, sit down," Freeman sighed, a look of resignation on his face. "Let me pour you a drink and explain a few things."

Eric pointedly looked at the time on his fitness watch. Yet another day when he would come nowhere close to attaining his 10,000 steps target. He raised his eyebrows. "To be honest, Mr Freeman, I've wasted enough of my time here today, as you said earlier. You often said that to your class too. 'It's your time you're wasting, not mine'."

"Was I really that bad a teacher?" Freeman asked, retrieving a second glass from his filing cabinet.

"The worst," Eric replied, sitting back down and accepting the glass which Freeman half-filled with whisky. "I wasn't joking when I said I learned nothing in your class. Most of the time you were doing your own thing, and we were just told to copy passages out of textbooks. Or you were stood outside in the corridor, smoking your pipe."

"I needed quiet," Freeman said. "I couldn't think with you all staring up at me."

"How inconsiderate of us," Eric said, sipping the whisky. "I do apologise on behalf of all my classmates."

Just then the whisky registered with Eric's taste buds. "What is this?"

Freeman held the squared bottle in front of him. "Johnnie Walker Blue Label, an exquisite combination of Scotland's rarest and most exceptional whiskies – or at least that's what it says on Amazon."

"Amazon sells this?" Eric gazed adoringly at the caramel-coloured liquid in his glass.

"Indeed," Freeman confirmed, his breathing steadying. "A snip at £149 a bottle."

"My day hasn't been completely wasted then."

"You approve?"

"So much so that I will accept another when you're ready."

"I'm sure you're right, I probably was a poor teacher," Freeman said. "It was only ever a way of supporting myself while I was doing my real work."

Eric jerked a thumb in the direction of the photo albums. "Is that this?"

"No, that's a sort of by-product," Freeman said.

"Is it something to do with all those poles in the garden?" Eric said. "And your three-chambered garage?"

"How do you know the garage has three chambers?"

"Because I went through them today when I was looking for you."

"You went through them?" Freeman stared at Eric. "That's impossible."

Eric showed Freeman the side of his face, which was still red from Spanner's attack. "I can't believe I went all the way back to 1976 and all I got was a lousy punch in the face," he said.

Freeman's face turned white. "You would not be able to withstand the forces…"

"Just as well I wore the suit and helmet then," Eric said. "How does it work? What's in that middle chamber?"

"This is a gross invasion of privacy," Freeman said. "And what's more, you've committed a criminal offence."

"I think you're the one who's done that," Eric replied. "Because whatever equipment you've got installed down there, I strongly suspect it's not something you can buy over the counter at your local DIY store."

Freeman paused for a few seconds. "You really travelled through the chambers?"

"I did," Eric confirmed. "And, when I came out the other end, the house opposite was Meek's Mini Market, just like it was in the 1970s."

"It was the 1970s," Freeman confirmed. "Saturday 3$^{rd}$ July 1976, to be exact, a little before one o'clock in the afternoon."

Eric took a steadying sip of whisky and eventually said: "That was the hottest day of the year."

"It was actually the hottest day of the hottest year of the century," Freeman said.

Eric remembered it well. How could he not? It had started off as the best day of his 16-year-old life. And ended as the worst.

## CHAPTER 5

## SATURDAY 3RD JULY 1976

"I've never seen so many ladybirds," Verity said, gently flicking several from the edge of the tartan blanket while allowing another to crawl on her hand.

"The papers say there's an epidemic," said Eric, waving his hand in front of his face to fend off one of the red and black irritants that had become attracted to him. "Must be something to do with the heat."

Everything was to do with the heat. Cwmbran Boating Lake was noticeably shallower than normal, but it had fared better than the nearby Llandegveth reservoir, which had dropped several feet in the drought, and there were fears of it drying up completely unless there was rain soon.

They lay on the grass between the top of the artificial boating lake and the Afon Lywd river, which meandered past on its way through the valley from the mountains of Blaenavon into the River Usk in Caerleon. Even though it was still early July, the grass beneath their blanket was yellowing and dry, and there were brown cracks appearing in parts of the earth.

"They say it's going to be even hotter today," Verity said, attempting to remove a pork pie from its cellophane wrapper.

Eric smiled, hoping he didn't look as anxious as he felt. What did people talk about on first dates? He could think of absolutely nothing. And was this even a date? They both worked Friday and Saturday evenings in Woodland Manor. She as a barmaid – even though she was just 15 and not legally allowed to be behind the bar – and he as a kitchen porter, a far less glamorous position despite him being a year older.

During a quiet period at work the previous night, she had mentioned to Eric that she fancied spending Saturday afternoon having a picnic at the lake. She went on to ask if he was busy and, if not, whether he would like to join her. Eric readily agreed. Verity was elegant, attractive, with natural blonde hair and a smile that would not have looked out of place in a toothpaste commercial. One of the other kitchen grunts had described her as 'like a prettier Chris Evert' but, more importantly, she was clever, funny, and kind.

"Listen to us," Verity said, still grappling with the wrapper, "talking about the weather like a pair of old codgers."

"It is unusual to have a heatwave in Britain," Eric said. "Most areas of the country have had less than half their typical summer rainfall."

"Alright, Michael Fish," Verity teased, pulling a face she imagined resembled the BBC weather forecaster. "Was that in the papers too?"

It was. Eric helped his father mark up the morning newspapers for a small team of delivery boys, and he couldn't help but absorb information from the front pages as he was writing house numbers and street names on them. He had been about to mention that the last week had seen a significant increase in hospital emergency admissions but thought better of it.

"Here, let me open that for you," Eric said, taking the pie from her.

Verity raised her eyebrows at him.

"There is a knack to it," he hastily explained, and in less than two seconds he presented her with the now naked pork pie.

"Thank you so much for deigning to help a weak and feeble-minded female," Verity said in mock gratitude. "One day, when we know each other better, would you magnanimously agree to educate me in the mysteries of the Pork Pie Unwrapping Ceremony, so that I might one day be able to tackle one alone?"

She examined the hard pastry crust. "Actually, don't bother. I don't imagine there will be many pork pies in my future."

"Are you working tonight?" Eric asked, changing the subject as he rummaged in his carrier bag which contained a selection of items he had liberated from Meek's Mini Market. He brought out a polony, a pack of sliced turkey and ham loaf, and a flat pasty.

"Mmm," Verity said enthusiastically. "What girl wouldn't love a selection of mechanically recovered meat products on a hot summer's day?"

Eric could feel his face reddening, and it wasn't from the burning sun.

"Did you bring any fruit?" Verity asked, wrinkling her nose as she scrutinised each item in turn.

"No, my father doesn't sell fresh fruit," Eric replied. "He did at one time, but it goes off so quickly."

"I'll just stick with the warm pork pie then," she said, nervously taking a small bite.

"I've got crisps though," Eric said triumphantly, tossing several bags in her direction. "And some cheese triangles and two cans of lemonade shandy."

"Ah, the vegetarian options," Verity said. "How thoughtful."

"You'll have to take a bigger bite than that, you'll just get pastry and jelly and none of the filling," Eric advised.

"That's what I was trying to do," she said. "I don't really fancy the pink stuff."

Ignoring the feast Eric had provided, she stared into the distance at some of the teenage boys who had jumped in the lake to cool off and were now getting shouted at by the man who rented out the boats. "Boys are so annoying," she said.

Eric sighed. Did she mean him? Had she expected him to bring a wicker hamper with china plates, silver cutlery, and cucumber sandwiches? Eric, think of something to say quickly, you're losing her...

After a gap of what seemed like several minutes, Verity broke the silence by saying: "Little Len asked me out last night."

Eric could feel his cheeks flushing even more. He tried to look nonchalant, unwrapping the pasty and taking a huge bite. Flakes of crumbly pastry escaped from his mouth as he chewed on the tepid lumpy contents.

"One of the other barmaids said he is always talking about me, and he looks forward to my shifts," Verity continued.

How should Eric respond to this? Len was two years older than Eric. And although he was just five-feet tall with acne and a frizz of unkempt ginger hair, he could drive – he had a car – and his father was Big Ben Butcher, owner of Woodland Manor.

"The thing is," Verity said slowly, "he likes the Bay City Rollers."

"What music do you like?" Eric blurted out. At last, a subject he could talk about.

"Just the usual," she said. "Bowie, 10CC, Roxy Music..."

"Me too!" Eric said.

"But I'm not keen on Queen."

"Neither am I!"

"I love seeing bands live," she said. "Do you ever go to Cardiff for gigs?"

He shook his head slowly.

"You should, you would love it."

"I'm sure I would," he said.

After a few seconds of silence, Verity said. "Anyway, I said no to Little Len, in case you were wondering."

"Oh, right," Eric said, taking another bite of pasty.

"Because I was rather hoping someone else would ask me out," she said, demurely avoiding eye-contact.

Eric stared at her. Did she mean what he thought she meant? How could he know, without committing himself and looking like an idiot if she was referring to someone else? Those were her words. Someone else. She couldn't have meant him. He was right here sat next to her. He wasn't someone else.

Suddenly Verity reached across to him and gently pulled his head closer to hers. "You're not very good at reading signals, are you?" she whispered into his ear.

Eric felt like he was going to burst.

"Now finish that pasty and kiss me."

Eric moved in, his lips touching hers for the first time.

"I said finish that pasty!"

Eric had no idea how long they'd been kissing. The outside world still existed – he heard someone remark how distasteful it was to see people kissing in a public place where children were playing – but he didn't care if he never saw it again.

"That's quite long enough for a first kiss," she said, pulling away and wiping her smiling mouth with the back of her hand. "Shall we go and get an ice-cream?"

Eric nodded. The inside of his mouth could do with cooling down, it felt a little pummelled from her tongue.

As they slowly walked hand in hand from the top of the boating lake towards the bottom end, to the boat hire shed and snacks kiosk, Eric wondered if he had ever had a better day in his entire life. Maybe Christmas Day 1968 when he excitedly unwrapped the Johnny Seven OMA (one man army) multi-firing toy gun he had badgered his mother all year for?

No, on considered reflection, this was even better than then. Mothers with children and men with dogs were milling all around them, old men were sat together on benches wiping their burning red heads with handkerchiefs, groups of barely dressed teenagers lay on the grass verge that surrounded the lake, transistor radios tuned to Radio One. As they passed one gathering, Eric could hear Louis Armstrong's 'What A Wonderful World' playing through a tinny speaker.

Eric looked at Verity, who returned his gaze and smiled happily. You're right Louis, it really is.

"Are you in tonight?" Verity asked.

It was Eric's turn to raise his eyebrows.

"I meant are you working tonight?" Verity confirmed, poking his arm.

Eric nodded.

"Me too," she said. "What time do you finish?"

"Probably not until about midnight, by the time we clear up."

"Same for me," Verity said. "Would you mind walking me home?"

"I'd love to."

"Good," she smiled and gently kissed him on the cheek. After a short pause she added: "My folks are on holiday, and I've got the house to myself."

# CHAPTER 6

## TUESDAY 3rd DECEMBER 2019

"What exactly have you got in your garage?" Eric asked Freeman. "Is it some kind of virtual reality device that's had that date programmed into it?"

"It's rather difficult to explain," Freeman replied.

"You take your time," Eric said, as the warm glow he felt inside spread to his cheeks. "Just keep the Blue Label coming."

Freeman laughed for the first time. "Imagine that, an ex-pupil of mine..."

"Not only that, an ex-neighbour too," Eric said. "I grew up in the house opposite you, when it was Meek's Mini Market."

Freeman's eyes widened behind his glasses. "Really? I don't remember seeing you."

"I spent a lot of time in my bedroom," Eric said.

"Does that mean Mrs Meek was your mother?"

Eric nodded.

"She was a lovely woman. The shop was never the same after she left."

"It never sold bread from Associated Welsh Bakeries again."

A half-smile came to Freeman's lips. "Oh yes, I did hear about that."

They drank another generous measure of the whisky.

"I will only ever drink pure single malts from now on," said Eric appreciatively.

"It's a blend," Freeman informed him. "Most single malts are blends, it just means they are a blend of whiskies from the same distillery."

"I've already learned more today than in three years of your physics class," Eric said. "If this was a movie, we'd get drunk together and catch a man-eating shark or something, but I have to drive and—"

Freeman lifted the now half-empty bottle and raised his thin wispy eyebrows at Eric. "Is that a no?"

"Go on then," Eric said. "Now perhaps you can explain what happened to me this afternoon?"

Freeman stared at Eric. "Can I trust you?"

"Mr Freeman, I'm an estate agent, I would have thought that would go without saying."

Freeman paused.

"Yes, of course you can trust me," Eric added.

"I suppose someone else had to know about my work at some point," Freeman said. "My real work that is, the work I've been doing for over 50 years. But I don't know if you will believe me. Or even if you can believe me."

"Try me."

After a pause of several moments, Freeman eventually pulled an album from the bookcase and handed it to Eric. "Have a look at this," he said.

Eric opened the album. Every page contained full-colour photographs of Cwmbran town centre. Eric could tell they were taken decades ago by the mix of shops that were represented, many of which were long gone. "The Cwmbran of my teenage years," Eric said. "This takes me back. I spent far too many Saturday afternoons flicking through the racks in the record store."

"What do you notice about the photographs?" Freeman prompted.

"The resolution is pin-sharp," Eric said. "They must have been taken with hugely expensive professional equipment. I've never seen any shots of the town as good as this. Where did you get them?"

"I took them last year," Freeman said, handing Eric another album.

Eric noticed this new album had the words 'Cars - General' written on the spine, and it contained page after page of photographs of pastel-coloured Hillman Avengers, Ford Capris, Austin Allegros, Vauxhall Chevettes, Mini Coopers, and unidentifiable Jaguars.

"These are beautiful pictures," Eric said. "Where did you get them?"

"I told you, I took them," Freeman replied, removing a camera from the drawer of his desk and handing it to Eric, "with this."

"It's a Sony digital camera," Eric said.

"Yes, the ILCE7M3KB, with optional lens kit," Freeman confirmed. "I've had it a while now and it knocks all my other cameras into a cocked hat, so much so that I've been revisiting many of my previous albums."

Eric stood up and walked towards the rows of albums. Every album had a title printed on its spine. Some referred to local places, others referred to groups of people, shops, and pubs. Eric grabbed one at random, after noticing its title was 'Birds Eye Ready Meals'.

"This is incredible," Eric said. "I remember these so well. We had a small freezer in the shop full of them. Boil in the bag Cod in Parsley Sauce, Chicken and Mushroom Casserole, Beef Stew and Dumpling, Liver with Onion... These packshots are such high quality. Are you sure you didn't download them from the original artwork?"

"No, I photographed them myself," Freeman said. "Keep going and you'll see the Birds Eye China Dragon range, which was launched in 1975. Do you know there is not a single image of any of those products on the internet?"

Eric slumped into his chair. "This is astonishing," he said. "I loved the Sweet and Sour Pork Balls. Those green boxes really stood out in the freezer."

"So now you know," Freeman said, grabbing the whisky bottle. "Another?"

"Now I know what?" Eric asked, while simultaneously nodding confirmation to the offer – a combination that wasn't as easy to pull off as it would have been several drinks ago.

"What my work is. I am cataloguing every aspect of Cwmbran life in the 1970s."

Eric narrowed his eyes. "That's quite a niche."

"It is," Freeman agreed. "It's going to be a comprehensive visual record of all aspects of the town, captured on a single day."

"You've discovered a resource where you can download this stuff?"

"You're not listening," Freeman tutted. "I am creating that resource. Imagine what this will mean to future historians who up until now have—"

"Hang on," Eric interrupted, looking at his whisky glass. "There are a few things I don't understand here."

"I did say I don't know if you will believe me," Freeman chuckled amiably. "Or even if you could believe me. Because if you still don't understand how electricity works then the mechanics of being able to return to 1976 will be quite a stretch."

After a pause of a few moments Eric pulled a sceptical face and said, very slowly, "Are you telling me that a retired physics teacher – a terrible physics teacher at that – has access to time travel?"

"Not exactly," Freeman said. "Well, yes and no."

"You were right about one thing: I don't believe you. I can't believe you."

"How do you explain these?" Freeman said, pointing to the pile of albums.

"They are just photographs," Eric said. "Phenomenal quality photographs, I'll grant you, but hardly proof that you travelled back to 1976. You or someone else might have taken them at the time."

Freeman snorted. "Do you think cameras capable of taking such high-resolution pictures were commercially available in the 1970s?"

"I don't know," Eric said. "I had a Polaroid that I couldn't afford to buy film for. Isn't time travel just science fiction?"

"You tell me," Freeman said. "Didn't you experience the phenomenon yourself?"

"I experienced something," Eric said. "I thought it was an hallucination at first. Then I thought it had to be one of those virtual reality simulators."

Freeman looked disappointed. "I'm afraid you lack the mental capacity to comprehend what I'm telling you."

"I am going to blame my comprehensive school education for that," Eric said, bristling at the insult. "Because just about any dickhead was allowed to teach in the 1970s."

Freeman looked down at his drink. There was an element of truth in Eric's words. Some of the teachers were even worse than him. "I'm sorry," Freeman said. "That was uncalled for."

"If you can really go back to 1976, why are you not a multi-millionaire? Couldn't you bet on the Grand National, deposit all your winnings in a compound interest account, and then take it all out when you return?"

"Is that really the extent of your imagination?" Freeman said, looking up from his drink at Eric. "A get-rich-quick scheme?"

Eric laughed.

"What's so funny?"

"This!" Eric replied, opening his arms like a fisherman boasting about the size of his biggest catch.

"I promise you I'm not lying."

Eric reached for his iPhone. "In that case, you won't mind if I ring my contact at the Cwmbran Evening Star and give him the story?"

"Just like you don't believe me, even after you've experienced it, he wouldn't believe you. He'd think you were a drunken idiot."

"He already thinks that," Eric said, replacing his phone in his jacket.

Freeman stared at Eric for a few moments and eventually said: "Look, I'm sorry I wasn't a very good teacher, but the reason I cannot sell the house is because the thing that allows me to revisit 1976 is installed in the garage."

"Don't worry, we'll dress it up as a feature," Eric said. "Four-bedroom executive-style detached house for sale. Desirable location, large garden, garage converted to time machine – available via separate negotiation."

"The gubbins is located under the garage, actually," Freeman said. "It cannot be moved, but it's not strictly a time machine."

"It can't be moved?" Eric's face fell. "You can't take it with you?"

"Not without practically demolishing the house," Freeman said. "And it would never work again. So you can see why I won't be moving."

Exhaling heavily, Eric slumped forward in his chair. "I can," he said. He wasn't going to list the property. Mrs Ducreux would not be buying it.

The commission would not be landing in his bank account in time to pay the rent on the showroom.

"I'm sorry to disappoint you," Freeman said. "But I did tell you this from the beginning."

"Just out of interest, how much does a time machine add to your quarterly energy bills?" Eric enquired. "Mine shot up when I bought an extra fridge."

"It's not connected to the national grid," Freeman said.

"How does it work?"

"How familiar are you with the work of Nikola Tesla?"

"The car man?"

Freeman rolled his eyes in exasperation. "Tesla predicted cars could be powered by the AC induction motor he designed, and a development of it is indeed used in the car, which was why the founders named the company after him, but it's a travesty that he's only known for that. Some people believe that Nikola Tesla will one day be spoken of in the same terms as Leonardo da Vinci. Have you heard of the Tesla Coil?"

"Is that a contraceptive?"

Freeman, ignoring Eric's flippancy, continued: "The Tesla Coil was a magnifying transmitter capable of generating high voltage, low current, high frequency, alternating current electricity. Tesla claimed it could create limitless power by harnessing, magnifying, and distributing the electrical energy found within the earth itself."

"Could you try and keep this intelligible, please? My mind is still processing a crushing disappointment and I'm finding it hard to concentrate."

"Think of the Tesla Coil as a radio frequency oscillator that drives an air-core double-tuned resonant transformer."

"Do you honestly consider that last sentence to be intelligible?"

"It was designed in 1891 and if it had been built to the specification Tesla wanted, in the size he requested, and used in the ionosphere, Tesla believed it would have resulted in free energy for everyone on the planet."

"It obviously didn't work then," Eric said. "Because here we are over a century later and energy is not free."

"Do you honestly think it would be?" Freeman asked. "Even if the Tesla Coil worked in the way he predicted, there were too many vested interests for that to be allowed to happen."

"What did happen?"

"Ask the internet, if you've got a free week," Freeman said. "And watch some of the documentaries about his life and work. They're not all made by conspiracy theorists."

Eric's despondent face suggested he was unlikely to do either.

"After World War II, Britain's scientific community was also conducting investigations into the technology," Freeman said. "And this continued right up until the 1970s when the plug was pulled because the country was essentially broke. I was one of the people working on it. When we were all made redundant, some colleagues and I continued developing the device in a private capacity. We wanted to bring to life Tesla's original vision for the device, but we had limited resources and were just working on a prototype. Our goal was to prove the concept would work and then seek funding to make a full-scale version."

"And did you?"

"After several years of getting nowhere, most of my colleagues lost interest and I carried on alone, apart from my assistant. He stayed with me, and we finished it together. Obviously I had to support myself, so I became a teacher, specialising in physics. It gave me a decent salary, lots of free time, and access to some of the materials I needed. And, as you rightly say, any dickhead was allowed to teach back then."

"Is that what all the poles in the garden are for?"

"Did you think they just supported a washing line?"

"Weren't the neighbours curious? If you were experimenting with electricity, wouldn't there have been lots of sparks and flashes?"

"There is," Freeman confirmed. "But all the dramatic stuff takes place underground. The system harnesses the electrical energy within the earth and concentrates it on a square metal frame inside my garage."

"You're mining electricity? How is that possible?"

"Mining electricity isn't possible, I said harnessing. Having said that, our definition of what's 'impossible' changes over time. Television was 'impossible' 100 years ago, your mobile phone was 'impossible' 50 years ago, but I digress. I had hoped it would generate enough energy to power the house, but it turned out to be far more potent than I expected."

"It sounds like a fire risk," Eric said.

"More than that," Freeman said. "It burned a hole in space-time."

Eric raised his eyebrows and looked at his empty glass. "And that means...?"

"It means that a 'door' was ripped open on the day it was powered up," Freeman explained. "And going through that door now takes you back to the day it was created."

"The door being the frame in the central chamber of your garage?"

Freeman nodded.

"Time travel!" Eric gasped.

"No, I told you, the device just opened a door to a specific day."

"But if going through that door takes you back to 1976 then surely that's time travel!" Eric argued. "You've created the greatest invention since... I don't know... sliced bread doesn't really seem adequate."

Freeman shook his head. "All I've done was attempt to follow in Tesla's footsteps, guided by his vision, and I failed. I was trying to generate free electricity – think what that could mean for people all over the world – and what I inadvertently 'created' is something else entirely: an interesting but ultimately pointless diversion."

"You've invented time travel!" Eric persisted. "I experienced it, and that's surely more revolutionary than cheap electricity!"

"Free, not cheap," Freeman corrected him. "And it's not time travel as you understand it."

"It is," Eric said. "Earlier today I met my father – who has been dead for over 20 years. And I know it was him because he was just as miserable as I remember him."

Freeman shook his head with disapproval. "You could have been killed. What were you thinking?"

"If I'm honest, I was thinking I would find you in a kinky sex dungeon," Eric said. "And I only put the suit and helmet on because I thought it unlocked the door."

"You would have been pulled apart if you had walked through the frame without the protection," Freeman said, "which is why the door will only open when the helmet is adjacent to it. But why did you go in there?"

"I was looking for you," Eric said.

"You were prepared to put your life at risk? Because you wanted to list my house?"

Eric sighed. "I just assumed you were in there, and the signs were a bluff."

"A bluff?"

"Like properties with scary dog warning signs. 'Dogs running free, owner accepts no responsibility for trespassers'."

"They're bluffs?"

"I always assumed they were," Eric said. "Maybe I'm wrong."

"Anyway, I had been in there earlier," Freeman said. "But I was in here when I spoke to you through the CCTV. Perhaps I should put cameras up in the back end of the garage as well…"

"Perhaps you should," Eric said, looking past Freeman at the monitors. "How long have you been making these trips?"

"A few years."

"And when did you realise what your device could do?"

"Emily had a previous Yorkshire Terrier, a horrible yappy thing that was always running around the house. One day I left the door to the garage open, and the dog came bounding in and ran straight into the frame."

"What happened to it?"

"I think there might still be microscopic fragments of him stuck to the sides of the frame."

"Oh."

"That's why I made the garage so secure – or I thought I had. I hadn't reckoned on over-zealous estate agents barging their way in. It took me years to develop the right protective gear before I could enter the frame.

Of course, I didn't realise it would send me back to 1976 until I actually walked through it."

"But why would you walk through it, if it had killed your wife's dog?"

"To measure the output. I quickly discovered it was futile passing instruments into the frame because they went the same way as Andrew the first. That was when Rory, my assistant, and I parted company. He thought we'd made a 'death ray' – something else that Tesla theorised was possible – and disagreed over what path to follow next. He wanted to start again, while I wanted to continue exploring what we'd created. After he left, I began developing an outer casing to put the instruments in. After much trial and error, I ended up with the material that the suit is made of. It's crafted from dozens of microscopically thin, yet extraordinarily strong, metallic sheets and it contains all sorts of reflecting technology woven into the fabric and between the layers."

"You developed that as well?"

"I was helped with the formulation by an ex-colleague in a senior position at a university that works with industry," Freeman said.

"And the helmet?"

"That's just an extra thick version of the same material, formed with the help of a diving helmet mould. I don't think it's actually needed, given the protection the suit affords, but it's better to be safe than sorry when we're dealing with the brain. Anyway, when my instruments were encased within the material, they weren't immediately destroyed when they were passed through the frame: instead, they just disappeared. When I looked at the other side of the frame, from the front of the garage, there was no evidence of them."

"That must have been annoying."

"It was, but to quote Madeleine L'Engle, experiment is the mother of knowledge."

"I remember you saying that in class."

"I probably did," Freeman said. "I conducted many more experiments, and the result was always the same, so I decided the only way to find out what was happening was to go through the frame myself. It wasn't easy getting a whole suit made from the anti-magnetic material, but the university's science division funded it, even though it didn't know it at the time. It actually paid for two suits and two helmets to be constructed – my former colleague and I were going to go through together – but sadly he was asked to leave his post when the enormous hole in the university finances was discovered. It was all hushed up of course. These things usually are."

"Then what happened?"

"I went through the frame with instruments strapped to me under the suit. And that's when I discovered that the frame was maintaining a portal back to the day it was first powered up in 1976," Freeman's speech was slowing. "I was elated at first, of course I was. I thought, like you, that the by-product of my experiment was far more significant than my original goal…"

Eric stared at Freeman expectantly.

The old man was silent, though his breathing had become noticeably louder.

"Are you going to add a 'but' to that sentence," Eric asked, after a long pause.

Freeman was still silent, and Eric noticed that behind his glasses his eyes were closed.

"Hello?" Eric said loudly.

Freeman's head slumped forward onto his chest and his deep breathing became a guttural snore.

Eric finished the bottle.

## CHAPTER 7

## WEDNESDAY 4TH DECEMBER 2019

The persistent ringing of Eric's phone eventually prompted him to open his eyes. He was in pain. And confused. Why was he laying, fully dressed, on top of an uncomfortable single bed surrounded by chintz? Then he recognised it as bedroom two of the house he had photographed and taken measurements in the day before. Was that really only yesterday? It felt like a week ago.

The inside of Eric's head was banging like a Ginger Baker drum solo and his face was sore and swollen. He could feel dried saliva crusted around the edges of his mouth as he massaged the side that had been punched. His phone rang again. It was Carol.

"Where are you?" she asked.

How could he answer that? "Why? Is something up?"

"Only that I've been ringing you all morning," she said.

"Carol, I sometimes feel that I work for you," Eric said.

"You wouldn't last five minutes," she replied. "And neither would Alwyn. He went out to get a printer cartridge almost an hour ago. How long does it take to buy a printer cartridge?"

"I don't know," Eric conceded.

"Have you noticed how much time he spends looking at himself? He's got a compact mirror on his desk and earlier this morning I had to tell him not to pluck his eyebrows in the showroom. Anyway, Mrs Ducreux has been on the phone this morning. Did you get the instruction?"

"I'm still working on it," Eric said.

"And the bank wants you to ring them when you get in."

Eric ended the call, laid back on the bed, and let the events of the previous day wash over him. Pitching Mrs Freeman for business, the drink-fuelled discussion with her husband, and – oh yes – travelling back through time to 1976 where he met his long-dead father and was assaulted by an officer of the law. These were all vivid, but he had no memory of going to bed.

He staggered into the bathroom – in need of some updating, he noted – and lowered his face into the peach-coloured wash basin. The whole suite would need to be pulled out by the next owner as it was dragging down the value of the house. Splashing water on his face helped bring him back to life a little, and he ventured downstairs.

"You've surfaced, have you?" said Mrs Freeman from the kitchen. "No offence, but I think it's very unprofessional for an estate agent to drink himself into a stupor in a customer's property."

Eric agreed it was. And after learning that her husband was 'out' he apologised and said he would come back in the afternoon, when Mr Freeman was due to return.

As soon as he climbed up into the cabin of the Lexus, he knew he shouldn't be driving. Not before he'd had some industrial strength painkillers and a full English breakfast, both of which he knew he could find just a short walk away at Woodland Manor. Maybe he would also book a quiet room where he could lie down and die in.

He walked between the two stone pillars that straddled the entrance to the drive. They each had short flagpoles protruding from them, and the flags adorning them left visitors in no doubt of the politics of the proprietor: one carried the blue and gold-starred EU insignia and the other featured the visually striking rainbow Pride design.

When Eric lived in the area, and Woodland Manor was owned by Big Ben Butcher, nothing but the Union Flag and the Welsh dragon would have been allowed to fly on those poles.

Eric passed through the reception area, with its huge portrait behind the desk of a rather plain woman riding a majestic horse, and made his way to the lounge, where Seb was wiping down the bar top in preparation for the lunchtime trade. "Any chance of a breakfast?" Eric asked.

"One: breakfast is only available to residents, and two: we stop serving it at ten and it's now nearly midday," replied Seb. "Does that answer your question?"

"This place has gone downhill lately," Eric sighed. "I'm sure if I was a hunky construction worker I'd be able to order anything I wanted."

"Piss off you twat," Seb said, tapping the code for breakfast into the EPOS system behind the bar. "It's far too early for awkward customers. You're lucky I've had some good news this morning."

"Cheers," Eric said. "Can I have no beans with it, please? I don't consider them part of a full English. Perhaps you can throw on an extra sausage instead. And would it be sacrilege to order a coffee rather than alcohol in here?"

Seb returned to the machine and typed in the appropriate number. "Coffee instead of alcohol? I never expected to hear those words from you," he said. "Having said that, you look like you need it. Big night, was it?"

"Sort of."

Seb looked closer at Eric's face. "Were you in a fight?"

"Not exactly," Eric said. "It was more like a mugging."

"You should do what I do," Seb said, pulling out a small metal bottle that looked like anti-perspirant from his trouser pocket. "Carry a personal defence spray."

Eric looked at the bottle. "Is this legal?"

"Probably," Seb replied. "It doesn't cause death, just a burning sensation, pain, temporary blindness, and shortage of breath."

"Where do you buy things like this?"

"Same place you buy everything these days," Seb replied. "Here, put this one in your pocket in case you get caught again."

"Are these available in Sainsbury's?" Eric asked, accepting the gift.

"You really should get up to speed with how society operates these days," Seb said. "You're one of those dinosaurs who still thinks the internet is 'the future' when it's been the present for over 20 years. You're not even on social media, are you?"

"No, because I'm really not interested in learning what people had for dinner, where they've been on holiday, or how ignorant they are politically," Eric protested, remembering when Carol had introduced him to Alwyn's Facebook page.

"I meant for your business," Seb said. "A lot of our customers find us through Facebook competitions and Twitter promotions and, of course, the building and the grounds are very Instagramable."

"I don't know what you're talking about."

"That's because you're an idiot."

Eric was about to reply when he was distracted by two smartly dressed young men making a dramatic entrance into the bar, giggling in high pitched voices.

"Oh great, a pair of queers," Seb said under his breath.

Neither of the two young men heard Seb's comment and he was the model of politeness while he poured their Dirty Martinis.

"You can't say that," Eric admonished him, as the men retreated to a sofa in the corner of the bar. "Can you?"

"I can," Seb said. "If I'd walked in here like that when Big Ben had the place I would have been beaten up."

"Did you come in here then?" Eric asked. "I wouldn't have thought it was your kind of hangout."

"I used to work here," Seb said.

"I didn't know that," Eric said. "I worked here myself for a while. Only for a couple of months. I was a kitchen porter but on Saturday evenings I would be transformed into a red-jacketed waiter."

"You were one of the ladybirds, were you?" Seb laughed.

Eric winced a little at the word. The black buttons on the front of the jackets had prompted Big Ben to name his young team of workers after the insects. "At least the menu was easy to remember, and I can still recite it now," Eric said. "Steak and chips, chicken and chips, gammon and chips, or scampi and chips. All served in a wicker basket for £2 apart from scampi which was 50p extra. And we had to bring them a sharper knife if they ordered steak because it was supplied by a local shoe manufacturer. We were always told to push the gammon."

"Good advice."

"It wasn't a euphemism."

"Did you know Big Ben Butcher actually was a butcher before he bought this place?" Seb said. "If you worked here you'll remember he kept his own pigs in the woods, and seeing them being fed on all the slops and shit from the kitchen turned me vegetarian."

"Can you not?" Eric said. "I've got bacon and sausages coming."

"Do you remember Little Len?"

Eric nodded. He remembered him only too well. "He would make us porters carry the pig bins up into the woods," Eric said. "And then he'd throw scraps into the pen to try and get them to fight over them. He was a horrible little bastard."

"He was," Seb agreed. "We were all amazed when he upped sticks with one of the waitresses to follow the hippie trail. It was so out of character."

Eric's face clouded over. "She wasn't a waitress, she was part-time bar staff, and she was only 15."

"That would be a scandal these days," Seb observed. "But people did what they liked in the '70s."

Little Len did, Eric remembered, as he always had his father and Elvis to back him up.

Seb continued: "Still, he must have found some form of enlightenment, because he never came back."

"Neither of them did," Eric said.

"I don't remember you though," Seb said.

"My tenure was brief."

"Have you got any pictures?"

Eric shook his head. Ordinary people didn't carry cameras around with them back then.

"God, I'm glad there was no social media in the '70s," Seb said. "The hairstyles I used to try and pull off. When exactly were you here?"

"In 1976, when it was considered acceptable to pay teenagers 25p an hour."

Seb checked his watch and frowned. "I'll go and chase up your breakfast. I don't want you eating it when the builders come in or they'll all want one – and, between you and me, there's a much bigger margin on the lunch menu."

Eric rubbed the swollen side of his face. He hadn't thought about Little Len for years, but yesterday's trip had brought back memories he thought he'd taken to the end of his garden and buried. Deep. Yet here they were again. Hello Eric. Remember us?

Little Len. Destroyer of worlds. Destroyer of Eric's world, at least, with one malicious act, on one fateful day. And that, of all days, was the one Freeman's time machine took him back to. There was probably a term for that. Was it kismet?

After 'the boating lake incident', instead of going back to school in September and taking A-Levels in the sixth form, which would have allowed him to go on to university, Eric dropped out of education to work full-time in his father's shop.

Even now, the question nagged away at him: how could Verity have chosen Little Len over him? She was clever, funny, and kind – and Little Len was horrible. Over the years, when he was melancholic and drunk, he had made a few half-hearted attempts to find out what became of her. But his limited knowledge of Google interrogation techniques meant he never did.

Just as the waitress brought his breakfast and coffee to the bar, Eric suddenly leapt off his stool, causing her to take evasive action and drop his plate onto the unforgiving woodblock floor. It shattered into hundreds of sharp china fragments, scattering his fried egg, sausages, bacon, mushrooms, tomatoes, and beans along the area in front of the bar.

Seb glared at him, mouth open in shock.

"I'm really sorry Seb," Eric said excitedly, rushing out without even glancing back at the full English carnage he had created. "But I specifically requested no beans."

***

Eric pounded on the Freemans' front door. Eventually Mrs Freeman answered, and she was far from pleased to see him.

"What do you want now?"

Eric marched in past her through the open door. "I need to speak to your husband," Eric said. "Where is he?"

"He's in the study," she said.

"Thank you," Eric replied, using his knuckles to rap loudly on the study door, which Eric noticed was locked.

"This is intolerable," Mrs Freeman said, retreating to the lounge and slamming the door behind her.

"I need to speak to you, Mr Freeman," Eric yelled, this time using his fist to thump the wooden door. "If you don't open this door I'm going to break it down, and I'm still drunk enough from last night to do it."

Eventually the door opened. And the expression on Freeman's face suggested he was equally as happy to see Eric as his wife was. "I knew this whole thing was a bad idea," Freeman said, gesturing for Eric to join him inside.

The two men retained their seats from the previous evening, but this time Freeman showed no signs of producing a bottle of expensive whisky from his filing cabinet – which was a relief.

"I need to know more about your time machine," Eric said.

"It's not a time machine."

"What is it, then?"

"Based on last night's conversations, I don't think you will understand," Freeman said dismissively.

"Imagine you had to explain how your device works to a complete idiot," Eric said. "What would you say?"

"Nothing, because a complete idiot wouldn't understand what I was talking about."

"Okay, not a complete idiot, but a not terribly well-educated person. Someone whose lack of knowledge in this area could be blamed on a teacher who didn't give a toss about teaching because he was too busy dicking around with his own project."

A slight twitch appeared above Freeman's right eye. "Dicking around?" he bristled. "In the 1960s I was one of the country's top physicists. If I was a young man now, I would probably be as famous as Stephen Hawking. Well, maybe not Stephen Hawking, but certainly Brian Cox."

"In that case you should be able to tell me – no, teach me, you owe me that – how it works."

Freeman picked up a sheet of lined A4 paper and a pencil from his desk and scrawled an 'x' in the top margin and a 'y' in the bottom margin. "To get from 'x' to 'y' you need to do this," he said, drawing a line between the two points.

Eric nodded. This he could understand.

"But suppose you could do this," Freeman said, folding the paper in half so that the marks were touching. "Suddenly 'x' and 'y' are right next to each other."

Freeman stabbed the 'x' and 'y' marks on the still folded paper with the pencil. "Think of this pencil as the portal, with 'x' and 'y' not being two different geographical points but two chronological points: 1976 and 2019. And just as the universe is constantly expanding, so too is the space – or more accurately the time – between the two points. Last year they were 1976 and 2018, and before that they were 1976 and 2017, and so on, right back to the first day it came into existence."

"Are you saying the time machine will only go back to 1976?"

"It's not a time machine," Freeman emphasised. "You're thinking of the device HG Wells described, with two levers to go either forwards or backwards. This is just a portal between two points. While one of them is constantly advancing in real time, in common with everything around it, the other is fixed at Saturday the 3$^{rd}$ of July 1976. You cannot travel back any further because the portal didn't exist before then."

Eric considered this information. "How many times have you gone back?"

"Hundreds over the last couple of years, that's how I collated my archive of Cwmbran," Freeman said, pointing to the shelves of photo albums.

"Is that really the most imaginative use for the invention you could think of?"

"No, but I soon discovered it was pretty much the only practical thing I could do."

"Why? Is that because you can only go back for a short time?"

"No, theoretically I could stay there for as long as I like, though however long I'm there I will be absent for the same amount of time from 2019. Not that anyone will miss me."

"But if you've gone back hundreds of times, don't you keep bumping into yourself? And aren't you worried about your actions in the past changing things in the present?"

Freeman stared approvingly at Eric. "They are both good questions," he said. "And the answer is the same to both: no. Firstly, the past cannot be changed. Although I have gone back to the past, it has already happened and nothing I can do will change it."

"But suppose I went back and murdered you in 1976?"

"It wouldn't matter."

"How can it not matter? You wouldn't be alive to design the suit that allowed me to go back in time to kill you."

"There are no paradoxes," Freeman said. "You've obviously heard the expression time heals all wounds?"

Eric nodded.

"It's more accurate than you might think, certainly in this case. Each trip is unique and when you return it is wiped from existence, as far as the universe is concerned. Or at least as far as this universe is concerned."

Eric's still-hungover brain was struggling to understand what he was hearing. "Can you say that again, but in different words?"

"Every time we go through the portal from this side we emerge into a fixed point and this action creates a new world," Freeman said. "And when we return that world vanishes, like it never existed – which of course it didn't. That's why you can't bet on the result of a horse race, open a bank account with your winnings, and then withdraw the money when you come back to the present. Whatever you did while in the past will have been overwritten by what actually happened when you return."

"No, those words are no help either," Eric said, narrowing his tired eyes in concentration.

"Or maybe the world we create when we go through the portal carries on existing in an alternative universe or dimension," Freeman said. "There's no way of knowing that. Are you familiar with the concept of the multiverse or the many-worlds interpretation?"

"Are you familiar with the fact that I'm an estate agent? Let's assume I'm not familiar with the multigym, or whatever you just called it."

Freeman sighed in frustration. "As its name suggests, the many-worlds interpretation – or MWI for short – implies that there are many universes, perhaps infinitely many. The MWI views time as a many-branched tree, wherein every possible quantum outcome is realised and exists in its own universe."

"Obviously I didn't understand any of that," Eric said. "But what would happen if you were to go through the portal and not come back?"

"Clearly I haven't done that, but I suppose the world my journey created could remain open indefinitely," Freeman considered. "But every world is unique, even though it starts from the same point in time and space."

"But it was the same version of 1976 that I remember," Eric protested.

"Yes, but if you had got into trouble while you were in 1976 yesterday, I could not have put the other suit on and gone through and rescued you. I would have emerged into the same point in time as you, but in an entirely different world. Think of the portal as a soap solution, and every time we go in it a new bubble is created. That bubble only exists for as long as we are in that world. Once we return here, it pops. As far as we are concerned, at least. Maybe it carries on existing without us."

It was Eric's turn to sigh in frustration.

Freeman tried again. "Imagine loading an image of the Mona Lisa into your computer and drawing a moustache on it in an art package. As soon as you close the program, the new image is wiped out of existence and next time you load up MonaLisa.jpg it will still be in its original state."

"Not if I'd saved it as MonaLisa1.jpg after drawing the moustache," Eric said.

"There is no save function," Freeman said, picking up a battered paperback called Great Welsh Walks from his desk. He flicked through it and stopped on a picture of a grinning man in baggy shorts standing on top of a hill. Pointing to the picture, Freeman said: "Let me put it another way: if I scan this picture into my computer and edit this chap out of it, will he know he's been edited out of it?"

"Of course not."

"That's right, and he'll still be in every other copy of that photograph. So yesterday, whatever you did in 1976 didn't actually happen to anyone but you – you're the man in the photograph."

"Are you saying that if I went back tonight and met PC Tanner again, he wouldn't remember attacking me?"

"Not unless he actually did it in the original 1976 timeline that you both shared."

"Does this mean that nothing I might have done when I went back would have impacted on the present I returned to?"

"That's right," Freeman said. "Each world is entirely self-contained. You can take small objects with you in either direction, such as the camera I used to photograph Cwmbran, as long as it can fit inside the suit with you."

"I need to go back again," Eric said.

"That's absolutely out of the question," Freeman said.

"But if nothing I do will affect the present, what harm is there in me going through again?"

Freeman pointed to the red swelling on the side of Eric's face. "What harm was there in you going through yesterday? You were only there a few minutes and you managed to get beaten up. What if you don't come back?"

"That's my problem," Eric said.

"No, it's mine," Freeman retorted. "I would have lost the suit."

"You've got another."

"Yes, as an emergency backup," Freeman said. "I also hoped, one day, to take Emily through."

Eric sat back in his chair. "She doesn't know about this, does she?"

Freeman shook his head and gestured towards his shelves of photo albums. "She thinks it's just a dark room for my photography."

Eric put his hand into his inside jacket pocket and removed the Barrington Meek cheque book. Although cheques were declining in popularity, Eric still used them to pay creditors because they took considerably longer to clear than bank transfers or debit cards. "How about if I leave this with you, and if I don't come back or I damage the suit I will pay for another one?"

Freeman frowned at the cheque book. "Is Barrington Meek a division of Microsoft? Or Apple? Or Google? Or Amazon? Because it would need to be."

Eric tore a cheque out of the book, dated it and signed it and handed it to Freeman. "If I don't come back, all you have to do is fill in the amount you want and pay it into your bank," Eric said, knowing that his bank would probably return it unpaid regardless of the amount. But Freeman didn't need to know that.

Freeman picked up the cheque and examined it.

Eric said quietly: "To be completely frank with you, and I don't expect you to understand this, but my life hasn't exactly turned out the way I would have liked."

"Whose does?" Freeman replied.

"There was a girl who I don't think I've ever got over," Eric continued, despite the lack of encouragement from Freeman.

"There's always a girl," Freeman said. "In my case, it was Emily."

"Your wife?"

Freeman nodded.

"Now you're really confusing me."

"I go back to visit her," Freeman said, his cheeks reddening. "She was so beautiful when she was younger, and I never noticed because I spent every waking second working on this. I often go back just to follow her around, watching her shopping, visiting the library, or walking around the boating lake. She's always alone, of course, because I completely neglected her. I spoke to her once in Sainsbury's but she recoiled in horror at the sight of me, so I had to run away. It caused quite a commotion. Imagine if they'd called the police and I'd been arrested. Who would I say I was? Of course, as soon as I returned the bubble burst, and it was like it hadn't happened."

Eric stared at Freeman. "Stalking a younger version of your wife – I wouldn't have thought it possible, but I think you may have actually come up with a more bizarre application for the portal than photographing frozen ready meals."

Freeman was embarrassed. "You wouldn't understand."

"I do actually," Eric said, in a more conciliatory tone. "In fact, that's the first thing you've said that I find easy to understand. And that's why I hope you'll understand why I want to go back again."

Freeman's eyes were glistening, and he bowed his head to wipe them with his fingers. "You told me yesterday that I was a terrible teacher and a terrible husband. You were right on both counts."

Eric pointed in the direction of the study door. "That wasn't the word I used," he corrected him. "But she's still here. It's not too late. You can make it up to her now."

"It is too late. There have been too many empty years."

"Take her away to somewhere sunny. You could make it a second honeymoon."

Freeman shook his head. "I still love the woman I married but I'm afraid that sullen drudge watching snooker isn't her: the woman in 1976 is. But I turned the woman from 1976 into what she is today by starving her of companionship and affection."

Eric reached across and held Freeman's trembling hand. "Maybe it's time you told her what you've been doing all these years?"

Freeman shook his head. "She was a music teacher, she had no interest in my work, she had no interest in science, and she's had no interest in me for many years."

"I'm sorry to hear that but let me make one more trip," Eric pleaded. "Let me find out what happened to the girl I was in love with in 1976. I need to know why she left me for someone else."

"You don't need to use the portal to find that out, I can tell you that," Freeman said.

"Can you?"

Freeman nodded.

"Please do," Eric said.

"You were teenagers," Freeman said. "Teenagers are all slaves to their hormones."

"I know."

"And nothing you do or say back there will make any difference to your life today."

"It could make a difference to me, though," Eric argued. "And I think you owe me—"

"I owe you nothing," Freeman said.

Eric stared at him. "Do you remember that time when you set our class a test and you ended up giving everyone ten extra marks because their scores were so poor?"

Freeman exhaled non-committedly. "You were allowed to use your initiative as a teacher back then, before all this national curriculum nonsense."

"The boy next to me scored 11," Eric said. "And you mark-shamed him by telling the rest of the class that his actual mark of one must have been for spelling his name right."

Freeman shook his head. "I have no recollection of that."

"And then you came to me, and read my score out," Eric said. "My mark was ten, and you made a great show of letting the class know it, in a shameless attempt to court popularity."

"I gave you a corrected mark of 20?"

"No, my corrected mark was ten."

"You scored nothing? You didn't even spell your own name right?"

"Of course I did, but you claimed my handwriting was unintelligible and you made me stand up in front of the whole class," Eric said, a tremor entering his voice. "You said that I was one of the dullest boys you had encountered in your entire teaching career."

"I have no recollection of that either," Freeman said. "But I would have only done such a thing for your own good."

"My own good?"

"When I take my wife's dog to the vet for his jabs, the bloody thing yelps in terror and urinates in his carrier because he knows what's coming," Freeman explained. "He's learned to expect pain, but he's too ignorant to know that what I'm doing is for his own benefit."

"For the rest of my school life I was the butt of the class jokes," Eric said. "What's Meek's favourite TV programme? The Undersea World of Jacques Cousteau, because it's got a nought-ical theme. What's the only board game Meek can play? Noughts and crosses... It went on for years, so I think you do owe me something."

"It worked though, didn't it?" Freeman said. "You clearly bucked your ideas up because you ended up as an estate agent. And how many people can say that?"

## CHAPTER 8

### SATURDAY 3rd JULY 1976

Eric and Verity were still over a hundred yards away from the snacks kiosk when they realised the hoard of people surrounding it was in fact a snaking queue, leading up to the single sliding window which faced the patio area. Two red-faced women were valiantly attempting to match consumers with items from their fridges, but they were rapidly running out of options as stocks became depleted.

"Look at those idiots," Eric mocked. "Are they really so desperate for an ice-cream that they will join a queue like that in this heat?"

"I am," Verity replied. "Even if it means I'm going to miss the start of the finals."

"The finals?"

"You are aware it's the finals of Wimbledon today?"

Eric was. It was on the back pages of every newspaper this morning. "Yes, but it's not something I follow."

"I can see you're going to need a bit of work," she said, pulling a solemn face. "I suppose this also means you don't play?"

Eric shrugged. "Where would you play tennis around here?"

"My family are members of Cardiff Lawn Tennis Club, in the grounds of the castle," Verity said. "It's got a great social side as well."

They had reached the end of the queue and Eric turned to Verity in surprise. "You go to Cardiff? Just to play tennis?"

"We go to Cardiff for lots of things, not just tennis," Verity said. "We're also members of Radyr Golf Club and of course there's the theatres and the concerts. What do you and your folks do recreationally?"

A family lined up behind them, and Eric could feel a small child treading on his toes, which were naked and exposed in flip-flops. "Nothing," he said, annoyed with the child's disregard for his defenceless tootsies, and slightly envious –resentful even – of Verity's perfect-sounding life.

"Come on, you must do something?"

"There's just me and my father, and he's always either working in the shop or drinking in front of the telly."

"That's a shame," she said, gently squeezing his thigh. "I bet you'd look good in tennis shorts."

Eric blushed. He knew he didn't look good in any shorts.

"What are your plans for the summer?" Verity asked, her hand still on his leg.

"I'm probably going to work in the shop most days," Eric replied. "But I'll be free on Saturday and Sunday afternoons as we shut half-day then."

"I meant what are your plans for holidays?"

"I don't have any," Eric replied, turning to stare in disapproval at the child who had trodden on his toes again.

"My folks book the same gîte in Dordogne every year. That's where they are now."

"That sounds fun." Eric didn't know what else to say, since he didn't know what a gîte was. Or where Dordogne was.

"It's pretty basic but it's got a small pool," she said casually. "I quite fancy buying an old double decker bus and following the hippie trail to South Asia, but my dad's not keen on the idea. He says I'm only going to be able to do that if I've got a boyfriend to look after me."

"Didn't Cliff Richard go travelling on a bus in Summer Holiday?"

"He did," she squealed. "Do you like Cliff Richard films?"

"Well…"

"It's okay to admit it," she prodded his tummy playfully. "It's cool to like Cliff Richard again since 'Devil Woman'."

"That was a pretty good song," Eric conceded.

"It's outrageous that it only got to number nine," Verity said, frowning.

One of the red-faced women from the kiosk thrust her head out of the sliding window and addressed the crowd: "We've sold out of lollies," she bellowed. "We've only got ice-cream from the machine."

There was a collective groan, and some of the people in front of Eric left the queue.

"That's good news for us ice-creamers," Verity said. "We'll soon be there."

The foot-stomping child behind Eric burst into tears. "I wanted a Funny Face!" he whined.

"He's already got one," Eric whispered to Verity.

"That's so mean!" she rebuked him, with a firm poke in his arm.

"I want to go home!" the child yelled, between deep sobs.

"Don't be dull," the child's mother yelled back at him. "We've only just got here. Keep on moaning and you'll have a smacked arse. Is that what you want? Is it?"

The child pulled a sullen face.

"Are you going back to school in September?" Verity asked Eric. "Or are you heading straight to college?"

"I'm going into the sixth form," Eric replied, "and taking A-Levels."

"That's good," Verity said approvingly. "I couldn't go out with a thickie."

"Does that mean we're going out then?" Eric asked, but Verity didn't hear him as the child behind them suddenly screamed in terror when a ladybird landed on his arm.

"It's okay," Verity stooped to the boy's level and reassured him. "Ladybirds won't hurt you. And look, we're nearly at the front of the queue now."

They were. There were just two people ahead of them. With no children transfixed by the posters of iced lollies and having to make a choice, the queue had thinned out and sped up.

"Do you know what you want to do?" Verity asked, before Eric could repeat his question.

"At A-Level?"

"In general, in life?"

Before Eric could answer he was knocked sprawling to the ground. He looked up in shock at the smirking face of Little Len.

"Thanks for keeping my place in the queue, Meek," Little Len chuckled.

"I saw that," the woman behind the counter said. "You pushed in."

"No, I didn't," Little Len replied, his voice defiant with entitlement. "He works for me and he was keeping my place."

"Is that right, love?" the woman asked Eric, who was slowly getting to his feet.

Reluctantly, Eric nodded in acquiescence. Out of the corner of his eye he could see Elvis – Big Ben's sidekick and Little Len's minder – grinning at his plight.

A former amateur rugby player with an unfashionable quiff – hence the nickname – Elvis usually crammed his large frame into a black suit for his role as doorman during Woodland Manor's weekend Dinner & Dance. Today he was wearing jeans and a black T-shirt with a cartoon image of a sexy woman astride a US chopper motorcycle. The tagline was 'Ass, gas, or grass – no one rides for free'.

"I'll have a 99," Little Len said to the woman.

"We're out of Flakes," the woman replied. "They've melted in the heat."

"A cone then," Little Len said. "Actually, better make it three."

Eric got to his feet, his cheeks burning with embarrassment.

Verity stared at Eric. "Are you alright?" she asked, with genuine concern.

"That's 33p," the woman said, handing Little Len three cones filled with bright white ice-cream that was already starting to drip.

"That's a bit steep," Little Len said, passing one of the cones to Elvis, who had sauntered over to join them. Little Len pointed to Eric. "It's just as well that he's paying."

Eric slid a 50p coin across the counter to the woman, while Little Len took a bite out of one cone and passed the other to Verity.

"What's my girlfriend doing here with another bloke?" Little Len said to Verity.

"I'm not your girlfriend," she replied.

"Yes, you are," Little Len said, grabbing her wrist. "Now why don't me and you go for a walk around the lake while we eat our ice-creams?"

Verity tried to pull Little Len's hand off her wrist. "Get off," she cried.

"Come on Len, let her go," Eric said to him.

Little Len increased his grip on her wrist while his other hand, still holding his cone, formed a fist. He swung it at Eric, connecting with his lip.

Eric was knocked backwards several feet, as much by the cold ice-cream splattering against his face as the force of the punch, but he remained standing, wiping the ice-cream from his mouth with his hand.

Little Len stared at the shattered cone remnants he was still clutching. "You're going to have to buy me another one now," he said to Eric.

Eric was surprised to discover he could taste his own blood. He wiped his mouth again and a streak of red mixed with the white ice-cream on his hand. His lip had been cut after being smashed against his teeth.

Little Len released his grip on Verity and now both his hands were shaped into fists. A crowd was quickly forming around them and one of the women from the kiosk was shouting, but Eric couldn't hear what she was saying.

Little Len made eye contact with Elvis, who nodded in approval.

"This is going to be fun," Little Len said loudly, raising his fists into a boxing pose and approaching Eric.

"Please Len, stop," Verity pleaded, inserting herself between Eric and Little Len. "Don't hurt him, we were only talking."

"I don't want you talking to him anymore, you little scrubber," Little Len said, poking his finger in Verity's face. Then he turned to Eric: "You'd better stay away from my girlfriend, Meek, or next time I'll kick your head in."

Addressing the still grinning Elvis, Little Len pointed to the lake and shouted: "Meek's looking all hot and bothered. Why don't you help him cool down?"

Before Eric knew what was happening, he was scooped up in Elvis's powerful arms and being carried towards the lake. He struggled, but Elvis was far stronger than him.

"Make no mistake, you're going in the lake," Elvis sang to the tune of one of his namesake's old songs, as he tossed Eric into the lake.

The water was warm as Eric hit it, but it was also full of slimy vegetation beneath the surface, and unidentifiable strands of green stuck to him as he recovered and tried to stand up. The water came up to his waist, so he was able to walk back towards the bank with relative ease, if not dignity. Little Len and Elvis were laughing loudly and pointing at Eric, who had become the centre of attention for almost everyone at the lake. The only person not looking at him was Verity.

## CHAPTER 9

### THURSDAY 5TH DECEMBER 2019

Carol had already opened the Barrington Meek showroom by the time Eric arrived just after nine. She always did if he was late. Which he often was, even though his house in The Meadows was just a few minutes' drive away. The traffic had been particularly bad today though, due to the torrential rain.

"Good morning, Mr Meek," Carol said cheerfully. "It's a bit wild out there today, can I get you a tea or coffee?"

"Coffee would be good," Eric said, slinging his wet jacket on the back of his chair.

"That's the worst thing you can do," Carol said, removing it and inserting a large wooden hanger into the arms. "It will lose all its shape and you'll look like a tramp when you call on clients."

"We could do with some of them right now," Eric said, noticing there was an unopened letter from the bank on his desk. "Clients, that is, not tramps. Bloody Brexit."

"Everyone is waiting to see what happens," Carol said. "But Marks & Spencer closing back in May hasn't helped footfall. And it's always quiet at this time of year anyway. People want to stay cwtched up in the warm. Are you going to open that letter from the bank?"

Eric placed it into the drawer of his desk. "Later."

"Can I make a suggestion?"

"Of course."

"If you sold the Lexus and leased something cheaper, like a Fiesta van, there would be tax advantages because it's a commercial vehicle, it would cost a lot less to run, and we could advertise the business on the side panels."

"I'm not selling the Lexus," Eric said. "Clients want reassurance that they're dealing with people who know what they're doing. They want to be associated with success. If I suddenly started driving a Fiesta van—"

"We wouldn't have an overdraft," Carol finished the sentence for him, though not in the way he wanted.

All his life, Eric's father had owned cheap cars that were one step away from the scrapyard. Rusting heaps that often failed to start, regularly broke down, and would have failed their annual MOT without the help of 'a mate in the trade'. Eric was never going to drive a car he couldn't rely on, and nor would he be seen in something as mundane as a Fiesta van. That wouldn't impress potential clients.

He changed the subject. "I've had an idea for a TV programme," he said to Carol.

"What's that?"

"A Victorian consulting detective who buys up old properties at auction and renovates them on a budget," Eric said.

Carol looked confused.

"It would be called Sherlock Holmes Under the Hammer," Eric said with a flourish.

Carol didn't laugh. "Shall I at least find out how much your car is worth?"

"We haven't got to that stage yet," Eric replied.

"Morning," bellowed Alwyn, bursting in through the showroom door.

"Perhaps we'll talk about it another time," Carol said.

Frowning, Eric tapped the face of his watch. "You're late."

"That's because I've brought something in to give this place a bit of life," Alwyn replied, removing a tiny object with a cable wrapped around it from a carrier bag. He unwound the cable and placed the Bluetooth speaker on the edge of his desk.

Eric and Carol exchanged looks.

"Now, I just need to get my Spotify playlist running," Alwyn said, stabbing the screen of his iPhone. A few seconds later the familiar opening chords of Slade's 'Merry Xmas Everybody' clanged out of the tiny speaker.

"No thank you," Eric said. "It's not Christmas and, even if it was, I can't stand that song."

"Don't be so miserable, Ebenezer Scrooge," Alwyn chided him. "I've got Wizzard, Mud, Elton John, Showaddywaddy, Boney M, Greg Lake—"

"No to all," Eric said. "No."

Alwyn looked offended. "That's nice," he said. "I thought a '70s boy like you would appreciate all the time I spent putting this together."

"I hate the way the same old songs get exhumed every year," Eric said.

"How about if we play ABBA?" Carol suggested. "Everyone likes ABBA."

"If we were to play music in the showroom – which we are not about to – it wouldn't be on a tinny little thing like this," said Eric, picking up the speaker and searching for the power-off button. He pressed it and the sound died. "When I was your age, I had two-foot-high speaker cabinets mounted in the corners of my room."

"Here it comes," Alwyn said. "You must be voting for Jeremy Corbyn next week?"

Eric hadn't even thought about the forthcoming general election. "Why would you say that?"

"He's determined to drag the country back to the '70s, isn't he?" Alwyn said, taking a copy of the Daily Mail from his carrier bag. "Nationalising the railways and all that."

"I never had you down as a Daily Mail reader," Eric said to Alwyn. "I thought The Sun would be more your style…"

"They were sold out," Alwyn said, raising a clenched fist in the air and parroting Boris Johnson's campaign slogan. "Let's get Brexit done, innit?"

Eric groaned.

"Honestly, I don't know why I bother, it's like a bloody morgue in here," Alwyn said, booting up his computer. "Everywhere else is getting in the Christmas spirit."

"Maybe you should consider going to work somewhere else?" Eric suggested.

"This place would be right in the shit if I did," Alwyn said, clicking on the Facebook icon. "If it wasn't for my lettings side there wouldn't be anyone coming through the door."

"You're not paid to dick around on social media," Eric said when he saw the familiar blue and white colour scheme fill Alwyn's monitor.

"I have to be on it," Alwyn countered. "It's how most of my tenants communicate with me. Oh, that's cute, Haley's son has caught a mouse."

A look of concern crossed Eric's face. "In one of our properties?"

"No, in the field behind the house. He'll have probably tortured it to death by now though, he's a bit of a headcase."

"Well, on that bombshell," Eric said, removing his jacket from the hanger Carol had hung it on. "I am going to leave you two to it."

"When will you be back?" Alwyn asked Eric.

"Why?"

"You know I'm finishing early today, don't you?" Alwyn said. "I'm picking up my new wheels."

"I'll probably be back by five," Eric said.

"But I'll need the afternoon off," Alwyn protested. "I have to go through all the paperwork with the dealer. I even got to choose my own registration plate."

"You're buying a brand-new car?" Carol looked shocked.

"Aye, and it's fully loaded," Alwyn confirmed. "It goes like stink, and it'll piss all over his Lexus."

"When I was your age, you could tell a lot about someone by their car," Eric said. "You had to be really doing well to have a newish one. Now, thanks to PCP, you see brand-new Audis and BMWs being driven by people in baseball caps."

"What's PCP?" asked Carol.

"Personal Contract Purchase," Alwyn answered.

"It allows people who can't afford to buy expensive cars to drive expensive cars," Eric explained. "It locks them into an agreement that gets renewed every three years and they never actually own the car."

"You can own the car," Alwyn corrected Eric.

"Sorry, they never actually own the car unless they pay a huge sum at the end of the agreement, which they never do. Instead, they just sign up for another one, like they do with mobile phones. The dealers take care of everything for them. It's absolute genius. Someone really should introduce it to the housing market."

***

Despite Eric's breakfast-based accident the previous day, Seb still appeared pleased to see him as he entered the bar. Seb was stood precariously on the fourth rung of a wooden stepladder, pinning a large poster to one of the walls.

"Does this look okay?" Seb asked.

Eric considered the poster's position and nodded. "Looks straight to me."

"It's one of the few things in here that is then," cackled Seb.

"That's offensive," Eric chided him.

Seb pressed drawing pins into each corner of the poster to secure it to the wall. "What do you think?"

"I don't know," Eric said, reading the announcement. "Do you really need to make Saturday nights themed? I thought business was booming with the hospital expansion."

"It is during the week," Seb confirmed. "But the contractors go back to their families on the weekend."

Eric read aloud from the poster: "'Come back to the 70's every Saturday during December'. I hate to tell you this but the apostrophe in '70s is in the wrong place."

"Who cares?" Seb said dismissively. "The 7$^{th}$, 14$^{th}$, 21$^{st}$, and 28$^{th}$ are all Saturdays. Can you imagine how busy the 28$^{th}$ will be? It falls between the days when people will be with their families, so it gives them an opportunity to get out of the house and party, away from their biddies and kiddies."

Eric continued reading: "'Ticket price of £75 per person includes three-course meal plus one bottle of either house white or red'. That seems reasonable value."

"It is," Seb exclaimed. "We're starting with prawn cocktail, finishing with black forest gateaux, and people can choose either scampi, steak, or chicken and chips."

"Why do I have this feeling of déjà vu?"

"I got the idea from our conversation yesterday," Seb said. "We'll be playing '70s music all night and giving prizes to the best dancers and the most authentically dressed guest. Can I interest you in a ticket for this Saturday? Limited numbers available…"

Eric grimaced. "It doesn't really sound like my cup of tea but I'm sure it will be popular at that price."

"It will, though between you and me the bottle of wine is only 375ml," Seb said.

"That's a bit sneaky."

"How is it?" Seb said. "It's still 'a bottle', isn't it?"

Eric didn't argue the point. "Would it be possible to have another late breakfast? And yes, I know I have to pay for the one I knocked on the floor yesterday…"

"I should charge you for the cleaning too, you clumsy oaf," Seb said, walking behind the bar and ordering a full English breakfast on the EPOS system. "No beans, is it?"

"Please."

"You're lucky that fortune is currently shining on me."

"What's happened?"

"Between you and me, I've reached an agreement to sell the woods."

"You're selling the woods? The ones between here and the hospital?"

"I don't own any other bloody woods," Seb replied. "I'm not Prince Charles."

"Who wants to buy your woods?"

"A property developer. He wants to flatten them and build half-a-dozen blocks of flats."

Eric frowned. "That's never going to get planning permission."

"It already has," Seb said. "In principle at least. I've had several meetings with the council and they're all for it. They couldn't do enough for me. Don't forget, all the people who will work at the hospital, particularly if they're not from around here, will need affordable housing."

"But that's going to change the character of the whole area," Eric said.

"What do I care?" Seb countered. "I'm nearly 60—"

"You're at least 62—"

"The point is I've got a fuck-off mortgage on this place that I'll still be paying when I'm 80. But when the deal goes through, I'll be debt-free and able to take more holidays. I might even buy a dog. I've always wanted a dog, but I've never had the time. They need to be walked every single day."

"You're not thinking of retiring, are you?"

"Too right I am. No one on their deathbed wishes they'd spent more time in the office. This is the first time this place has been making a decent profit since the '70s, and if I can get out with a few quid in my back pocket while I'm still young and fit, I'm going to jump at it."

"I'll be sorry to see you go," Eric said. "Seriously."

"I'll still pop in now and again," Seb said. "But I'll employ a general manager to run it day to day. I'll be breaking the cycle."

"The cycle?"

"None of the previous owners had a happy ending. Do you remember the old boy who had it before Big Ben?"

Eric didn't.

"He basically had it stolen from under him," Seb explained.

"By Big Ben? How can you steal a hotel?"

"It's a long story," Seb said. "I'll tell you when I've got more time. Suffice it to say that Big Ben was a horrible bastard."

Eric said: "We all knew that. Like father like son."

"Little Len? Big Ben wasn't his father," Seb said casually.

"What?"

"Come on, that's hardly a surprise," Seb said. "Big Ben was over six feet tall and built like a brick shithouse, and that scrawny little runt barely came up to his armpit."

"I know that, but—"

"His mother used to buy his clothes from the children's section of Kay's catalogue because he was too embarrassed to go shopping," Seb continued. "And when he wore platform shoes, he had to stuff the toes with socks because they didn't make fashionable footwear in his size."

"I didn't know that," Eric said. "I wish I had."

"And of course, Big Ben's stewardship of the place ended unhappily too, as I'm sure you're aware," Seb continued. "After Little Len went off with that young waitress, Mrs Ben buggered off too."

Eric knew. Without her steadying influence behind the scenes, Woodland Manor went downhill and eventually closed in the '80s. "I remember it closing because my father had the shop near the entrance," Eric said. "And when people stopped coming here, they stopped going there too."

"Wow, I'd forgotten all about that shop," Seb said. "It got turned back into a house. That must have been so hard for your dad."

Eric shrugged. "It obviously didn't improve his mood, but he was a miserable sod at the best of times."

Seb gave Eric a stern, disapproving look. "That's no way to talk about your father! Is he still alive?"

Eric shook his head. Although, having said that, if you knew where to look...

"Destroying the woods won't go down well with the locals," Eric said, changing the subject.

"Developing, not destroying," Seb corrected him. "And fuck them. They don't support this place. I can't wait to see their revised Zoopla estimates after the flats have gone up."

***

Eric wondered if he should share his inside knowledge about future developments with the Freemans, as he tucked the carrier bag under his arm and rang their bell. Normally such news would hasten a homeowner's desire to sell their property, but Mr Freeman's house had an added feature that trumped all the hot tubs, saunas, granny annexes, and stables that more desirable properties in the surrounding area boasted.

Not that Barrington Meek had listings with such features – they tended to go to the upmarket estate agents, who had logos formed from cursive fonts. Eric composed the opening paragraph of the sales blurb in his head: unique property in an exclusive, much sought after location with stunning, far-reaching views into the past...

The door was opened by Mr Freeman, who invited Eric in and shepherded him into the study. "I've got some good news for you," Freeman said. "I've had a change of heart. I'm ready to sell the house and we're going with you as the agent."

Eric clutched his carrier bag and stared at him. Was this good news?

"Isn't that what you wanted?" Freeman said, confused by Eric's lack of enthusiasm.

"Yes, but that was before I learned about—"

"Obviously I'm going to decommission it," Freeman said, sitting down and inviting Eric to do the same.

"But you said it couldn't be shut down."

"I said it couldn't be moved," Freeman corrected him. "It can be shut down."

"Won't that close the portal?"

"It will," Freeman confirmed. "And I'll make sure it can't be restarted."

Eric was aghast. "But you've created the greatest invention since—"

"Let's not go through all this again – I told you, it's of no practical use," Freeman said.

"How can you say that?" Eric's voice rose an octave. "Look at all those photo albums!"

Freeman looked down at his desk. "It's not much to show for a lifetime's work though, is it?"

"But there are so many uses you could put it to," Eric continued. "Imagine how much you could charge for trips to the past. Especially if there are no consequences for your actions, it would be like that Yul Brynner film but without the killer robots."

"That's exactly my fear," Freeman said.

"Killer robots?"

"That it could be misused."

"How is that misusing it? That's what you did with it."

"There are still consequences," Freeman said. "If you were caught doing something illegal, you could be imprisoned for it. And if you got into a fight – which you did within five minutes – then you would have to deal with any injury you sustain. And what if you caught a disease? There have been many medical advances since 1976 that you would be deprived of. People still died from smallpox back then."

"Not in Cwmbran they didn't."

"The point is still valid. If you encounter something life-threatening then you will die. And my irreplaceable suit would be lost forever."

"We can make more suits," Eric protested.

"We could," Freeman agreed. "But only if we had access to millions of pounds."

"If you shut it down, no one will ever know it existed," Eric said. "You could be the most famous physicist since…"

"Niels Bohr?" Freeman helped Eric out.

"I don't know him," Eric said. "It is a 'him', is it?"

"It is," Freeman confirmed. "And while I might like history to categorise me with him, Hawking, Newton, and Einstein, I'm going to do as you suggested: sell the house and spend the proceeds on Emily."

"But if you monetised the portal, you'd be rich," Eric said, frustration creeping into his voice. "You could do so much good with all the money you'd make."

"If I was younger, maybe I would," Freeman said. "But I'm more concerned about it falling into the wrong hands."

"Before you do anything, I have to go through the portal one more time," Eric said.

"Look at yourself," Freeman rebuked Eric. "Look at the effect it has had on you. You are like an addict, desperate for another fix. All I've really created is a pointless folly, with no practical application that the world could benefit from."

"What about something like going back to watch your own wedding?"

Freeman countered: "That would only work if they got married on that Saturday in July 1976."

"But what about rich couples taking a week's holiday in the past together?"

"They would need both suits," Freeman said. "And I would never allow the two of them to go through the portal at the same time. And I certainly wouldn't let them go for a week. What could I do if they didn't come back? Even if I had another suit, which I don't, I couldn't go looking for them as they would quite literally be in a world of their own."

"That's the proposition!" Eric said, suddenly animated. "Offer people a second chance of life in a world of their own. They could go back to 1976 with all their knowledge of today and live a completely different life. They could all become billionaires!"

Freeman shook his head. "There are only two suits."

"I'm sure we could fund the production of more suits," Eric said, exasperated. "Once people know what the portal can do."

"I can't wait to hear your sales pitch to the bank," Freeman said.

Eric sat in silence for a few moments. "If the portal was shut down, could it be recreated? Obviously not by me, but by someone else?"

"It could," Freeman replied cautiously. "But even if you built a brand-new one and powered it up today then this would be the only point someone in the future could return to."

Eric stood up. "I'm making one more trip," he told Freeman. "I have to."

"I've already told you," Freeman said. "I'm shutting it down."

"If you do that then I'll be stuck there and you'll have to explain away my disappearance, because I told the office I was coming here," Eric said. "And everyone will know I'm here because my car is parked outside and I'm taking the keys with me, so you won't be able to move it."

"I forbid this," Freeman cried.

"I'm not asking for your permission," Eric replied, leaving the study and opening the door that led to the garage. He still had the spare set of keys for the house, and he left the four-sided key in the lock on his side of the door so Freeman could not follow him. "Now calm down, you'll give yourself a heart attack."

## CHAPTER 10

## SATURDAY 3RD JULY 1976

Eric knew what to expect this time, so he had brought a carrier bag of summer clothes with him. He had removed his suit and shoes in the garage's first chamber and changed into a plain white T-shirt and a loose pair of beige linen trousers. The ensemble was completed by a vintage pair of brown leather sandals.

Wearing less clothing had made it much easier to get the fetish suit on for his sophomore journey into the past but, despite this, within seconds of emerging from the garage he was sweating from the effort of removing the suit. It would be much easier if Freeman had created a sleeping bag of some description that could just be crawled into and zipped up. That was something he would discuss with him when he returned. He would have to buy him a bottle of Blue Label before he broached the subject though, as Freeman had not exactly sent Eric off with his blessing.

Eric walked the short distance from the Freemans' house to Meek's Mini Market. The sun's intense heat burned his exposed arms and the bald spot on the top of his head. Eric made a mental note to bring a bottle of sunscreen next time, and maybe one of those beige fedoras that old men tended to wear.

Eric pushed the shop door and it swung inwards, setting off that familiar clanging bell. There was that dark interior again, and the smell of stale smoke, and the two men were once again chatting at the counter. Spanner turned around, as he had done the previous time, and both he and his father stared at Eric.

"We're closing at one," his father said in a surly tone. "So you've only got a few minutes."

"Okay, thanks for letting me know," Eric replied, trying to sound friendly. "Alright if I take a look around?"

His father nodded assent, and the two men huddled closer together and resumed their conversation. Eric couldn't quite hear what they were saying so he walked around the centre gondola display and edged back closer to the counter. As he did, he noticed the pile of Smarties tubes stacked next to the telephone. He had forgotten about the Smarties.

The chocolate beans were supplied in cardboard tubes which were sealed with a plastic lid. Eric's father loved Smarties and always had a bowl of them behind the counter to nibble on during the day. Whenever he opened a carton of the products to fill his countertop display, out of sight of customers he would pop open the lids and remove about an inches' worth from each tube and pour it into his bowl. When Eric had first caught him doing this, his father had argued that the tubes carried no details about how many individual sweets consumers could expect. This was true. Back then there were no best before dates, nutritional information, or even a list of ingredients, just the manufacturer's name and address: Rowntree Mackintosh, York YO1 1XY in this case.

Out of the corner of his eye, Eric could see his father unwrapping a bar of chocolate and showing Spanner what was inside. Instead of a firm block, with distinct chunks, a sticky mess clung to the foil wrapper like some form of dirty protest.

"They're all like it," his father hissed, selecting a Mars bar and squeezing it.

Eric was surprised to see that the Mars bar, which had pretty much melted from a solid to a liquid in the heatwave, was around the same size as the modern versions. He was convinced they had been larger in the '70s.

"Alright, I'll be here around ten," Spanner mumbled. "Just make sure you're seen with lots of people. What about the boy?"

"He'll be at the Manor as well, he's working in the kitchen."

"Sound as a pound," Spanner said.

"Hot enough for you?" his father said to Eric, as he saw him approaching the counter.

"It's a real scorcher, isn't it?" Eric replied. "I heard somewhere that this has been the hottest day of the year."

"Right, I'd best be off," Spanner said, lumbering out of the shop.

"Have you got any sandwiches?" Eric asked his father as the bell clanged.

"Sandwiches? How do you mean?"

"Sandwiches," Eric said. "Two slices of bread with a savoury filling."

"I know what a bloody sandwich is," his father snapped.

"Do you sell them?"

"Of course not," his father replied contemptuously. "Can't you make your own?"

Eric looked at Meek's Mini Market display of crisps. Display was perhaps too strong a word for it. It consisted of 12 cardboard boxes containing individual packets of crisps, stacked four-high and three-wide. Eric's father had cut a diamond-shaped hole in the box with a sharp knife so customers could help themselves. This was visual merchandising, '70s style. In addition to standard crisps there were boxes of Skips, Quavers, and Smiths Horror Bags.

"Do you have any Chipmunk Oxo?" Eric asked his father.

"Not unless they are there," his father replied, gesturing towards the stack of boxes.

"I was in early this morning, and I saw a young man take a box off sale and carry them upstairs," Eric lied. "Could you just check for me?"

Eric's father eyed Eric suspiciously. "What time was this?"

"Around seven," Eric said.

"I would have been taking the papers out to the delivery boys in the car," Eric's father muttered. "I'm only gone ten minutes or so and my son is supposed to watch the shop, not steal from me."

Eric shrugged, realising he had dropped young Eric in the shit. Well, this version of him.

"What were you doing in here at seven?" his father asked, narrowing his eyes.

"Just getting a pint of milk for breakfast," Eric said. "I'm staying with the Freemans opposite."

"I didn't think they had any relatives."

"No, I'm a friend," Eric said. "Of sorts."

"I didn't think they had any friends either," his father said. "She just watches telly and he spends all his time in the garage."

"Really?"

"You can see into their lounge from here," his father explained. "When she comes home from work, she just sits there on her own all night. I know he's in the garage because you can hear him banging about."

"If you've got any Oxo I'll take the whole box," Eric said, changing the subject.

"You're like my son," Eric's father said. "He eats them one after another. He's become a right podge."

Eric bristled. "He looked fine to me."

"He's practically got tits!" his father said. "And it's no wonder. The lazy sod does no exercise, he just spends all his time in his bedroom listening to that bloody awful music of his and trying to write songs on his guitar."

Eric glared at his father. Why would he slag off his son to a total stranger?

"He's like his mother," his father continued, his tone becoming bitter. "He'll never amount to much."

The words burst out of Eric before he could stop them. "I'm a bloody estate agent," he snapped. "And I live in The Meadows."

His father stared at him. "What are you telling me for? Listen, I don't appreciate being spoken to in that tone."

"I'm so sorry," Eric said, holding his hands up. "It just came out. My father used to say things like that about me, and you just reminded me of him."

Eric's father's eyes narrowed. "Why are you staying at the Freemans if you only live in The Meadows?"

"We had a few drinks and I stayed over rather than risk it in the car," Eric said.

"What do you drive?" his father asked, looking out the shop window.

"A Datsun Sunny," Eric said, remembering his first car. "A friend picked it up earlier."

"I wouldn't have one of those if you paid me," his father sneered. "If you live in The Meadows you should be backing Britain and buying something like the new Rover SDI, not some imported rice burner."

Eric smiled. That was pretty much how his father had reacted when he bought the Sunny in the '80s, apart from suggesting he should have bought a Rover instead. "Can you just see if there are any Oxo crisps upstairs?" Eric said. "Then I'll be out of your hair."

Meek senior frowned contemptuously at Eric. "You'll do what?"

"I'll be on my way," Eric clarified. "It's an expression where I come from."

While his father begrudgingly traipsed up the stairs towards young Eric's bedroom, Eric dashed behind the counter and slid his hand under the cash register. He expertly located the lever that operated the drawer in the event of a power cut and coughed loudly to disguise the sound of it opening. His father had cashed up for the day but the float of £20 was still there. He helped himself to two five-pound notes and four 50p coins. It's your own fault, Dad, I'm just following in your Smartie-stealing footsteps – though I'm also dropping this young Eric in the shit again, as his father would inevitably blame him if money went missing from the till. Sorry young Eric.

By the time Meek had clomped loudly down the stairs, Eric was standing at the front of the shop inspecting the small display of loaves of bread.

"The greedy sod only left me six bags," Eric's father said. "Is that alright?"

"That will be fine," Eric replied.

"He's going to be for it when he gets home, the thieving little git."

He's also going to have a split lip and be covered in vegetation from the boating lake, Eric mused. Sorry for making the worst day of your life even more shit, young Eric.

"Are these today's?" Eric asked, examining the colour of the tape around the neck of the bread wrapper which retailers used so they – but not the public – would know which loaf came in when.

"Fresh in this morning," his father lied. "And being as I'm about to close you can have one at half-price."

"I'll just take the crisps and a bottle of warm Cresta," Eric said, grabbing a bottle of the strawberry-flavoured carbonated drink from the shelf.

"You drink that stuff?"

"It's frothy, man," Eric replied, imitating the polar bear from the television advert, and handing a 50p piece to his father.

Eric's father took it and rung up 42p on the cash register. He tossed the coin in the drawer, seemingly unaware there was less cash in there than a few minutes ago.

"Don't worry about the change," Eric said. "Put it in the charity box."

"Cheers," his father said.

Eric smiled. He knew that charity box was only emptied once a year, and whatever was in it was donated to the Derek Meek benevolent fund. "Got any plans for this afternoon?"

Derek shook his head. "Catching up with paperwork."

"Really? On a lovely day like this?"

"I can't abide the hot weather."

"It's a wonderful day to be alive," Eric persisted.

Derek shook his head again. "You must be joking," he said with disgust. "The '70s are piss-poor compared to the '60s. Everyone's always on bloody strike these days. As soon as The Beatles split up, everything went downhill."

Oh dear, Eric thought, just wait until the '80s when Woodland Manor closes, and you lose all the passing trade. "At least the tennis is on this afternoon."

"Tennis? I wouldn't watch tennis if you paid me."

Eric couldn't help himself. He was goading him, just like he did when he was a teenager. "If it's not rugby, us Welsh aren't interested, are we?"

"I'm English," Derek replied, pointing to a framed photograph of Bobby Moore, triumphantly holding aloft the Jules Rimet Trophy, which was fixed to the wall behind the cash register.

"Oh really? You do surprise me. You sound really Welsh," Eric said, knowing how deeply this would annoy his father.

Eric reflected on his relationship with his father as he walked from Lôn Heddychlon to Cwmbran town centre, eating his six bags of Oxo crisps. They really were just as delicious as he remembered. The fluorescent coloured Cresta was a bit of a disappointment though, but that could have been because it had been many years since he'd had a soft drink that wasn't served chilled.

Eric hadn't felt any affection for his father today, just like he hadn't the first time he came back to 1976. Derek had been a small and petty man all his life and he just got more belligerent as he aged. When he died there was just a handful of mourners at his funeral, none of which looked particularly disappointed to be seeing the last of him.

Remembering this, Eric felt a little guilty. Perhaps he should go back and introduce himself before he made his return journey? He could tell Derek about the business he had built up and show him the miracle that was his iPhone. Look at this Dad, it's got tomorrow's newspapers on it today, and thousands of photographs, and every song The Beatles ever recorded. It would blow his mind.

As Eric approached Cwmbran town centre, he was astonished at how ugly its vast slabs of concrete seemed in the harsh summer sunlight. And how small it was, even though the giant Woolco had opened in 1975. The next 43 years would see ownership of the centre change hands several times, and the development would branch out in every commercially viable direction.

The centre was packed with people milling around, and they were very different to their 2019 descendants. There was a complete absence of tattoos, for instance, and Eric was disappointed to notice that he was probably the most overweight man there. Men in 2019 tended to be either buff or obese but here just about everyone was thin. Their hair was hilarious though, with the balding attempting to deceive with comb-overs, while the hirsute seemed content to let everything grow how it chose, with some cultivating bushy Noddy Holder-style sideburns. How did barbers make a living back here?

Most of the women fitted into two camps, almost as if they were auditioning for a part in Monty Python's Flying Circus. They were either young and attractive or old frumps. Upon closer inspection he realised that describing all the young women as attractive was inaccurate, but their natural appearance – bright blue eyeshadow apart – was more appealing to Eric than the artificially augmented types of 2019.

Shades of orange, brown, and beige were the 'in' colours as far as fashion was concerned, among both men and women, and tank tops, cheesecloth shirts, and flared denim jeans appeared to be equally androgynous. Surprisingly, given the heat, almost no one was wearing shorts.

More strikingly, no one was staring at a smartphone either. Instead, some of the girls carried small transistor radios playing tinny samples from the current hit parade, and some of the men created their own soundtrack by whistling as they walked. Eric hadn't heard anyone whistle in years. The most common accessory, brandished by all ages, was a cigarette. People were smoking as they walked, while they stood in little groups talking, while they sat on benches, and even while they were eating.

Eric bought a box of fresh cream chocolate eclairs from The Cake Shop and carried it into Barrington Property Services. The wooden literature racks were a little lighter in shade, and had less scuff marks, but they were instantly recognisable as the same ones he was using 43 years later. The garish brown and orange paintwork was a little painful on the eye, and there were four desks for sales advisors – each staffed by a young-looking girl – in addition to the grand one at the back of the showroom where Mr Barrington sat.

The biggest difference between his showroom and this one was the complete absence of computers. Each desk, apart from Mr Barrington's, had a mechanical typewriter, reams of papers, and a rotary dial landline phone.

Behind Mr Barrington's desk, six grey metal filing cabinets, containing paper equivalents of Eric's database, spreadsheet, and accounts package, filled the entire width of the wall.

Eric marched straight up to Mr Barrington, who was examining his competitors' full-page adverts in the Cwmbran Evening Star. "I've brought you some chocolate eclairs," Eric said, depositing the white cardboard box on Barrington's desk.

Barrington looked up at Eric in surprise, peering over the top of his gold-framed half-moon spectacles. "Whatever for?"

"Because I know you like them," Eric replied.

Indeed he did. Every Friday afternoon Barrington would treat his staff to a box of eclairs from The Cake Shop. He would usually end up eating most of them himself as, at any one time, at least half the girls were 'watching their figures' – even though none of them needed to.

"How very kind," Barrington said. "I can't quite place your face though. Give me a clue…"

Eric smiled. *In February 1977 you are going to give me my first full-time job, saying: 'The profession has been good to me and, if you work hard, it will be good to you too'. You will be my mentor and teach me every aspect of the business. When you decide to retire in 1990 you will sell me the business at an advantageous price and help me fund the purchase by accepting staggered payments over the following ten years. You are a benevolent father figure to your staff, and you will be to me too, far more so than my real father ever was.*

"I'm sure it will come to you," Eric said.

"Janice, can you get some plates please?" Barrington asked the member of staff whose desk was nearest to him. "This kind gentleman has brought us some cakes."

Janice smiled at Eric. He didn't know her. She must have found alternative employment before he joined the team.

As Janice returned with some paper plates, Barrington said to her: "I don't know if you should have one Janice, you look like you've put on a few pounds."

Eric was shocked, but Janice just giggled.

A man who was probably in his 50s – though it was difficult to tell from the way he was dressed – had been perusing the properties in the racks and looked over when he heard Barrington's remark. He approached Janice, who was facing away from him, put his hands on her bottom and lasciviously massaged each cheek. "You're right, Mr Barrington," he leered. "She should be eating Ryvita, not cakes."

Eric grabbed the man's shoulder and pulled him back from Janice. "What the hell are you doing?" Eric demanded.

The man stared at Eric, outraged. "Mind your own bloody business," he said. "It's not against the law to have a laugh."

"You can't just touch women," Eric said to him. "How would you like it if someone grabbed your arse?"

"Chance would be a fine thing," the man guffawed.

"Would it? Come here then," Eric said, moving towards him. "It's your lucky day."

Horrified, the man recoiled from Eric. "Bugger off, you bloody poof."

"Come on, you sexy man," Eric persisted, adopting a faux French accent as he attempted to grab the man's bottom. "You said 'chance would be a fine thing', well this is your chance."

"Leave me alone you queer," the man squealed, attempting to push Eric away.

"Stop being a dick then," Eric said, backing off.

The man hurried out of the showroom and Eric turned back to Barrington's desk where his old mentor and Janice were staring at him in astonishment.

"How dare you!" Barrington said sternly. "You might have lost me a customer."

It was Eric's turn to be astonished. "Did you see what he was doing?"

"He was only having a bit of fun," Barrington said. "Who are you to poke your nose in? Is this your business? Is your name above the door?"

"It will be," Eric said. "And that wasn't 'fun', that was almost assault!"

"Where are you from, the nineteenth century?" Barrington scoffed, closing the lid on the box of cakes and handing it to Eric. "I'd like you to leave now, if you don't mind, and you can take your eclairs with you."

***

Eric spent an enjoyable hour wandering around Cwmbran town centre, discovering independently run stores that had long since vanished over the decades. Some may have closed due to mismanagement, but others were just victims of changing consumer tastes. Then there were those traders who chose to vacate their premises rather than renew their lease, when it was time for their upward-only rent review. There was always someone else willing to follow in their footsteps and open a shop of their own.

The fake wood cabinets of the televisions in Radio Rentals were hilariously chintzy but the black hi-fi separates in the Sony Centre looked more desirable than anything he'd seen in 2019, where appreciation of sound quality had seemingly fallen out of fashion – a perfect example being Alwyn's awful wireless speaker. The Sony salesman was happy to demonstrate the high-end equipment, using 'Time' from Pink Floyd's Dark Side of the Moon, and Eric was tempted to buy a system there and then until he realised there were two things stopping him: a valid means of paying for it and a method of transporting it home.

Eric ate the now quite warm eclairs on a bench overlooking the Water Gardens, the one civic amenity provided in the town centre. Its focal point was a large metal pizza-shaped sculpture fixed to the wall of a paved and flooded courtyard about the size of a tennis court. In the centre was an artwork formed from a raised bed of Pilkington glass. Onto this, from a spout in the pizza, gushed a torrent of water which cascaded down into the Sunken Garden, where busy shoppers could take a moment to relax among the trees and shrubs. Eric had never really appreciated the facility before – the water last flowed in 2005, and it was fenced off awaiting redevelopment in 2019 – but the gentle sound of the water was so calming he felt his eyelids drooping.

He closed his eyes. Despite Saturday being the peak shopping day – Sunday opening would not arrive until 1994 – he marvelled at how quiet and civilised the shopping centre was. Not because of a lack of people, but because they were not yelling at each other or their children or having conversations with devices clasped to their ears. Some of the older people were very smart, like they had dressed up especially to go shopping, so not only was Eric the most overweight man his age, he also felt the scruffiest.

He thought back to how his younger self would be spending this wonderful day, and immediately his mood changed. Just about everything that he disliked about how his life turned out could be traced back to the boating lake incident on this day. Verity walked away with Little Len. Eric ran home, humiliated. And instead of seeing Verity that evening, when they were both scheduled to be working at Woodland Manor, and walking her home to her parentless house, Eric didn't turn up for his shift. He was too embarrassed to face her and Little Len, so he never went back, and he never saw either of them again.

Derek, his father, would not allow Eric to idle his time away, so that summer was spent working at Meek's Mini Market. And when it was time to return to school in September and enter the sixth form, he couldn't face it, so he continued working at the shop.

Spending so much time together did not endear Eric and his father to each other. They barely spoke during the day and they avoided each other completely when the shop was closed: Eric locking himself away in his room listening to 'that bloody awful music', his father slumping in front of the television and drinking cans of bitter.

Eric had to get away. He joined Barrington's Property Services in February 1977 as a trainee, intending to save enough money to go travelling in the summer, and his father replaced him in the shop with Sue.

Eric didn't want to think about Sue. She had assumed Derek was well off as he owned a business, so she set her sights on capturing his son, which didn't turn out to be difficult as there were no others competing with her for young Eric.

Sue wasn't aware that the business functioned only due to the forbearance of its bank manager, who provided Meek's Mini Market with working capital in the form of an overdraft. It therefore came as quite a shock when she learned that getting her feet under the table did not mean she could help herself to stock off the shelves.

Sue talked constantly of wanting to get engaged, but she soon grew weary of sharing a workplace with her prospective father-in-law and his cantankerous ways. Just like Eric's mother, she abruptly left one day without saying goodbye. In her favour though, at least she had the good grace to not embezzle the contents of the safe.

Not long afterwards, Eric also moved out, buying his first house – a two-bedroom terraced – in Croesyceiliog, in the north of Cwmbran.

Several astute moves later he had ended up with a four-bedroom detached in The Meadows, a highly desirable location just a few minutes' walk from the boating lake. Yes, that boating lake. Being an estate agent, and thus enjoying mutually beneficial relationships with associated legal and financial professionals, greatly assisted his rise up the property ladder and his father helped him make the final leap to The Meadows. Not intentionally, of course, but by dropping dead and having no one else to leave his estate to.

Financially, at least, life had been more than fair with Eric. But there was something missing. Sometimes, when he had a drink, he thought about Verity. Their relationship – if it could be called that – must have been one of the shortest on record. It hadn't even lasted a day, so why had it left such a large hole behind?

Perhaps if he had seen her again, after the boating lake incident, he would have had what people in 2019 called 'closure', rather than a nagging feeling of 'if only'.

Suddenly his stomach turned over. He looked at his watch and did a quick calculation: if he started walking now, he could be at Woodland Manor in time for Verity to start her shift.

# CHAPTER 11

## SATURDAY 3ʳᴰ JULY 1976

Visitors to Woodland Manor had three culinary options: they could eat an expensive meal in the restaurant, they could have moderately-priced traditional pub grub in the lounge bar, or – on Saturdays evenings – they could choose from an extremely basic menu in the ballroom: scampi, chicken, steak, or gammon, all served in a wicker basket with a portion of chips, which were pre-salted to encourage the punters to drink more.

Live entertainment was also thrown in for Woodland Manor's weekly Dinner & Dance. For special occasions, such as Valentine's Day, Big Ben would pay an ageing crooner to belt out ballads from the '50s and '60s, but usually music was provided by a four-piece covers band called The Faith. At least it was until a dramatic shift in musical direction saw them embrace the spirit of punk and become The Filth.

The first Dinner & Dance they played after their rebrand saw them physically removed from the premises by an outraged Big Ben Butcher. In the melee, tempers flared, punches were thrown, and instruments were broken, resulting in threats of legal action. Tragically, all four members of the band lost their lives not long after this incident, when their van caught fire while they were inside. The cause was never discovered.

As Woodland Manor's Dinner & Dance targeted the bargain conscious and those on low incomes, certain corners could be cut. The restaurant was also packed on Saturday evenings, and as there was very little skill required to take orders from a menu of four items, the real waiting staff worked the restaurant while the kitchen porters became their stand-ins in the ballroom. And the usual bar staff was supplemented by anyone prepared to work their feet off for a few quid cash-in-hand.

As Eric walked up Lôn Heddychlon towards Woodland Manor and passed Meek's Mini Market, he glanced at the front window of the flat above it. Young Eric was in there, eyes closed and headphones on, attempting to lose himself and his shame – and probably the unjustness of being accused of stealing from the cash register – in his record collection, while Verity was just a stone's throw away.

Eric's footprints crunched on the gravel drive, which had long since been paved over in 2019, and several vehicles made their way past him to the car park, far too enthusiastically for the conditions, throwing up stones in Eric's direction. The Jaguar and Rover drivers were probably destined for the restaurant, while those in Fords and Vauxhalls would be releasing their inhibitions on the dance floor once they'd been fed and watered.

He walked through the brightly lit entrance and was mildly surprised to notice it had barely changed. The grand reception desk took up the entire back wall of the lobby, and a large oil painting of Big Ben dressed as master of the hunt astride a magnificent white stallion looked down on the desk and all who stood before it, reminding everyone who the boss was. What did it matter if he'd never been on a horse in his life?

A-frame signs helpfully pointed punters in the right direction: restaurant and lounge bar to the right, ballroom to the left. Also to the left was the staircase which led up to the first-floor guest rooms. They were rarely occupied on weekends, unless the ballroom had been booked for a wedding reception, and this was just as well: the booming of the music resonated throughout the upper floors.

"Good evening, sir," the receptionist said to him. Her blonde hair was permed into loose curls and her heavily made-up eyes were partly hidden by an oversized pair of spectacles. She was dressed modestly, despite the humid weather, in a cotton top with half-sleeves and a mid-length paisley patterned red skirt. "Are you here for the Dinner & Dance? The ballroom doesn't open until six but you're welcome to have a drink in the lounge bar while you're waiting."

Eric didn't need to read the receptionist's name badge to know who she was. "Carol?"

"That's right," Carol replied cheerfully. "Do I know you?"

"How long have you worked here?"

"About six years," she laughed. "But it seems much longer!"

"I didn't realise you worked here," Eric said. He also hadn't realised how glamorous she had been when she was younger.

She looked a little puzzled. "Have we met?"

"Is it alright if I pop in the ballroom for a second? I just want a quick word with someone."

The switchboard phone rang before Carol could reply, and Eric took advantage of the distraction to sneak past her.

The dressing of the ballroom for the weekly Dinner & Dance began at five and had to be finished by six, when the punters were allowed in to secure the tables with the best view of the stage and dance floor. The rectangular tables throughout Woodland Manor were the same size but while they sat four in the restaurant and six in the lounge, the ballroom place settings were compressed so that eight could be squeezed in: three each side and one at each end. In addition to laying out the condiments, ash trays, and rudimentary cutlery, the ladybirds were responsible for lighting a slow-burning candle in the centre of each table, adding a touch of class to the proceedings, and ensuring that smokers always had access to a light.

The red-jacketed youths were being supervised by one of the old waiters. Eric recognised him instantly. It was the one he had been warned not to go into the storeroom alone with, as he suffered from 'wandering hands syndrome' and he liked young boys. The waiter paid no attention to Eric, as he was 'removing the creases' from the trousers of one of the kitchen porters by rubbing his hands up and down the material. Eric glanced in the direction of the bar. And there was Verity.

Eric's stomach turned over. She was just as beautiful as he remembered, and as she stacked clean wine and beer glasses under the bar, in preparation for the busy night ahead, the bright spotlights brought out the natural golden tones of her hair. She was wearing more makeup than he expected, but she was probably instructed to in order to make her look older: she could not legally work behind the bar for another three years.

She looked up and saw him. For a second their eyes connected. "We're not open until six," she said.

"I know," Eric said, walking slowly – and nervously – towards her.

"You can get a drink in the lounge bar," she said.

Eric stared at her. He had become a tongue-tied teenager again.

"You can't reserve a table until the doors open," she added. "And there is usually a queue outside."

"I just wanted to see if you are alright," Eric eventually said.

"Alright? What do you mean?"

"After... the um... I mean... How was your day?"

Her face hardened and she ignored the question.

Eric suddenly realised that although he felt 16, he was actually 60, and to her he was just some creepy old bloke trying to chat her up. She probably had to contend with plenty of others like him, especially as the night wore on and the leering men became more intoxicated.

"I really think you should leave," Verity said.

"I'm sorry, I was only making conversation," Eric said. He wanted to ask her what happened after he'd left the boating lake but couldn't think how to phrase such a question.

"Clive," she called to the waiter. "Can you show this gentleman the way to the lounge bar, please?"

"It's okay," Eric shouted over to him. "I know where it is."

The door behind the bar that led to the offices suddenly swung open, and in walked Little Len. He was grinning as he approached Verity. "How's my girlfriend?" he asked her.

"Busy," she replied.

"Come here and give us a snog," Little Len said, putting his arms around her waist and pulling her towards him. Even in his platform shoes she towered above him.

"Please don't," she said, trying to remove his hand which was moving towards her breasts.

"What's the matter?" he said. "You're my girlfriend now, you can't be tight with me."

Eric slammed his hand down on the bar, startling both Verity and Little Len, who hadn't noticed Eric standing there. "That's enough!" he shouted.

Little Len regained his composure and glared contemptuously at Eric. "What are you doing in here? The bar's not open."

"I did tell him that," Verity said, untangling herself from Little Len's arms.

"She's told you, I've told you, so you better piss off right now while you've got the chance because you won't be told a third time," Little Len warned.

Eric stared down at Little Len, his tormentor, the destroyer of worlds. Eric's mouth went dry, his heart was beating faster, his breathing increased, and he could feel his body trembling: all classic symptoms of the flight or fight response. But this time it wasn't going to be flight. He glared at Len, daring him to follow through with his threat.

Little Len disappeared through the door behind the bar into the offices.

"Honestly, you'd better go," Verity said to Eric. "He'll be getting the bouncer or his father, and you don't want to get on the wrong side of either of them."

"Maybe they don't want get on the wrong side of me," Eric retorted, and instantly regretted it. He was useless at saying the right thing in the company of this girl.

"They'd have you for breakfast," Verity said dismissively. "They're not very nice people. You really should go."

"Okay," Eric said. He wanted to say so much more to her.

"Please," she pleaded. "They'll take it out on me for not calling them earlier."

The bar in the lounge had filled up in his absence, and it took a few minutes for Eric to reach the front. He tried to attract the attention of one of the two members of staff who were serving. The one closest to him was tall, thin, strikingly handsome, with perfectly styled long brown hair. Eric recognised him instantly.

"When you're ready, Seb," Eric said to him, waving one of the five-pound notes he had stolen from his father's shop earlier that day.

Seb looked up in alarm. That name was only known to a select few. And this old man was not one of them. "Do I know you?" Seb asked him.

"A large Pernodka, please," Eric said. He needed something strong.

"A what?"

"A large Pernod and a large vodka."

"In the same glass?"

"That's right."

"A double Pernod and a double vodka?"

"Two measures of Pernod, two measures of vodka, and a single cube of ice," Eric confirmed.

The next few hours flew by. Eric did poke his head around the door of the ballroom, but Verity's bar was four-deep, and she was nowhere to be seen. He was forced to leave because The Faith were attacking Free's 'Wishing Well', and the bass was punching his chest. The paying customers loved it though.

As Eric walked back through reception to reclaim his seat in the lounge bar, he noticed there was another figure behind the reception desk with Carol. It was Big Ben. And he was drunk. There was nothing unusual about that, but he was sat in Carol's seat and was trying to persuade her to sit on his lap, like a good girl.

"Come and sit here," he said, pointing to his crotch. He then leered: "I can guarantee you won't fall off."

"Honestly, I'd rather stand, thank you Mr Butcher," she said, pulling her skirt down so it covered her knees. "Shouldn't you go back upstairs now and rejoin the poker game?"

"In a minute."

"They'll be waiting for you," Carol said. "You don't want to keep your friends waiting."

"Come on Carol," Big Ben slurred. "I know you've always had a soft spot for me."

"I don't think Mrs Butcher would be happy to see you behaving like this," Carol said.

Big Ben grinned and shook his head. "Not a problem," he said, leaning forward in the chair so he could reach her. "She's gone to a wedding so I'm all on my own this weekend. You don't want me to be lonely, do you Carol?"

"You're not on your own," Carol said, pointing to Elvis, who was leaning on the reception desk. He was squeezed into a tuxedo and the white collar of his dress shirt was saturated with sweat.

"Been with Elvis all day," Big Ben replied, manoeuvring the wheeled chair so it trapped Carol between him and the desk. Still sitting, he put his hand on her knee and slowly slid it upwards. "I would like some female company now."

"You can tell she likes it," encouraged Elvis, placing his pint of lager on the reception desk and grabbing his crotch.

While his one hand was still on her leg, Big Ben's other hand touched her breast. "What's this, Carol?" he asked. "Not wearing a bra?"

"Please don't," Carol pleaded with him.

Elvis crooned: "Pretty little girl with hair of gold, looks so hot but acts so cold…"

Eric grabbed Elvis's pint and slammed the glass down on the desk with such force that it shattered, showering himself, Carol, Big Ben, and Elvis with shards of glass and cold lager: "What is wrong with you people?" Eric barked at them.

Both men, along with Carol, turned towards Eric, their mouths gaping in disbelief, like a synchronised comedy routine.

Big Ben was first to react, despite his inebriation, rising to his feet. "You're paying for that glass," he shouted at Eric. "And the cleaning of the carpet."

"Let her go," Eric said.

Grabbing Carol roughly by the arm, Big Ben said: "What do these teases expect when they wear short skirts and show off all that flesh?"

"Let her go," Eric said, more forcefully.

Big Ben leered at Carol: "You love the attention, don't you?"

Carol shook her head but seemed too shocked to reply.

Elvis backed Big Ben up. "They take it as a compliment," he said, removing a sliver of glass from his hand. He watched, captivated, as a thin river of blood gushed out. "It's only a bit of fun."

"Let her go," Eric repeated. "You bald bullying twat."

The words had an instant impact. "You must like hospital food," Big Ben snarled, emerging from behind the desk and heading for Eric.

He really was a big bastard. He was probably about 15 years younger than Eric, taller, stronger, and he had just been insulted in front of his staff. Someone was going to have to pay for that.

Elvis gestured in Eric's direction and improvised: "Crazy old man came looking for a fight, he's gonna wish he'd stayed home tonight."

"You really should write some of these couplets down," Eric said to Elvis. "They deserve a wider audience."

Big Ben charged towards Eric, his face contorted with fury. "You really are going to wish you'd stayed home," he snarled.

Heart racing, Eric whipped out the personal defence spray that Seb had given him and aimed it directly into Big Ben's eyes. As he squeezed the trigger Big Ben recoiled in pain, his fists unfurling as his hands tried desperately to protect his face. Eric squeezed again, causing Big Ben to scream. He fell backwards, Elvis gracefully moving aside so his boss could fall awkwardly to the floor among the glass fragments. His anguished cries were masked by The Faith in the ballroom, and the Saturday night hubbub in the lounge, so no one came to investigate the cause of the commotion.

Big Ben could no longer open his eyes, which were rapidly being reduced to swollen red slits streaming with tears. "I'm blind, I'm blind, I'm fucking blind," he cried.

Eric stood over him and taunted: "What do you teases expect, flashing that big bald head to the world? You love the attention, don't you? You're taking it as a compliment, aren't you? It's only a bit of fun!"

The expression on Carol's face was flickering between gratitude towards Eric and concern for Big Ben. "Was that deodorant you sprayed him with?" she said.

Big Ben was now clutching his throat. "I can't breathe, I can't breathe..."

"Call an ambulance," Elvis urged Carol, as he wiped Big Ben's eyes with a handkerchief, which made the pain worse. "He's dying here!"

"He's not dying," Eric said. "It's just chilli oil extract."

Carol asked Eric: "Will it have any lasting effects?"

"I'd love to say that he will now treat women with a bit more respect," Eric said. "But that's probably wishful thinking. It will wear off in a couple of hours and he'll no doubt be back to his usual belligerent self."

"He'll have it in for you," Carol warned him.

"He's not the only one," Elvis said, rising to his feet, his lip curling upwards in a fair impression of his hero. Baring his teeth like an attack dog, his giant hands were forming fists as he advanced on Eric.

"Do you want some as well?" Eric said, holding up the cannister and gently shaking it. "There's plenty to go around."

Elvis gave him a look of pure hatred and dashed off into the bar.

"You'd better get out of here," Carol urged Eric. "He's gone to get reinforcements."

"You're right, I really should," Eric agreed. "It's been a fun night. Five stars. Would recommend."

"And thank you," Carol said, in a quiet voice. "I'll never forget this."

Sadly you will, Eric thought, as he briskly made his way down the gravel drive and reflected on the day's events. He hadn't realised so many men were such obnoxious dicks in the '70s. They were annoying in 2019, of course, with their high-fiving and fist-pumping, and their shouts of 'Get in!', but what he'd encountered today was next level twatishness.

It was getting dark, prompting Eric to check the time. It was nearly 10:30pm but the air temperature was still like the middle of the day. Before jumping back to 2019 he just wanted to have a final word with his father. He wasn't sure what that word would be, but he'd cross that bridge when he came to it. He'd just taken down Big Ben, in front of his sidekick, and he felt he could do anything now. If only he'd had this confidence when he was 16…

As he approached Meek's Mini Market he noticed that young Eric's room still had a light on. He knew only too well that he was up there alone, wallowing in despair from the boating lake incident earlier that day, trying to lose himself in music. Perhaps he should have a word with him?

There was a bell to the right of the shop entrance which rang in the flat upstairs. As Eric got closer to it he realised something was wrong. The glass in the shop door was broken. This was no mindless act of vandalism though, as the shards that would have remained in the frame had been knocked out, leaving a space large enough for someone to walk through.

Eric poked his head into the dark shop and shouted: "Hello?"

There was no response. Young Eric would have his headphones on but what about his father? He rarely went out because he had no real friends. And because he was a miserable bastard.

"Hello?" Eric called again.

The shop door consisted of a single pane of toughened glass inside a six-inch wide wooden frame, and to ensure no one mistakenly walked into it there was a large open/closed sign stuck to the inside of the glass. Eric noticed this lay on the floor just inside the shop entrance, surrounded by broken fragments of glass. He lifted his leg over the bottom frame and stepped carefully into the shop. Even though young Eric had been in the premises when the break-in took place, he had heard nothing at the time. Headphones, loud music, and shame were a powerful combination when it came to shutting out the world.

"What's all this then?"

Eric swung around in alarm, recognising the voice immediately.

"Looks like we've caught you red-handed, cock."

Eric turned towards Spanner, who was casually ducking and walking through the frame. "I was just passing," Eric said. "And when I saw the door was broken, I thought I should alert the shop owner."

"Is that a fact?" Spanner sneered, removing his handheld radio from his belt. The brick-shaped device was large enough to be used as a weapon. "716 requesting backup to Meek's Mini Market in Lôn Heddychlon," he said into it. "Incident in progress. Suspect cornered, possibly armed."

Spanner replaced the radio in his belt and removed his truncheon. "You're not going to give me any trouble, are you?" he said, looming over Eric. "I must inform you though, I'll be more than happy if you do."

Eric's eyes were now accustomed to the lightless interior. The upright chiller containing the cooked meats and dairy products had been vandalised. Thick black paint had been thrown over the fridge itself, as well as its contents. Splashes of the same paint could be seen on the countertop display units that housed individual confectionary items. And behind the counter, there were large gaps in the cigarette display cabinet and on the shelves where the whisky was displayed.

"This is nothing to do with me," Eric said, slowly removing his personal defence spray from his pocket. "I've been up Woodland Manor all evening."

"Any witnesses to that?" Spanner was now just a few feet from him.

"I think Mr Butcher will be able to remember me," Eric said, finger poised on the spray trigger.

"What's that?" Spanner said, noticing the object. "Is that a weapon?"

Eric held the spray in front of him and aimed it at Spanner's face. "It is."

Spanner charged, truncheon aloft.

Eric pulled the trigger.

Nothing happened.

Spanner's truncheon smashed into the side of Eric's head.

Shit.

Everything went dark.

*** 

Eric opened his eyes. His head was throbbing with pain and his face was being slapped, hard and repeatedly.

"It's alright, he's still with us," a young police officer was saying. "Thought you might have done him in."

"It was self-defence," Spanner said. "He attacked me first."

"What with?"

"This," Spanner replied, holding up Eric's personal defence spray.

The other policeman held his arm out and Spanner passed the weapon to him. The officer read aloud the label wording: "Block! Personal Defence Spray. Walk away safe, every time." He laughed and said: "He attacked you with a can of anti-perspirant?"

"It was dark," Spanner said. "It could have been a gun."

"In Cwmbran?" the other officer laughed. "You've been watching too much Kojak."

"I've never seen that brand of anti-perspirant before," Spanner said defensively.

"You've never seen anti-perspirant at all," the officer replied. "Or at least your armpits haven't. The name is obviously a gimmick, like Hai Karate."

Eric's head throbbed. "How do I file a complaint about police brutality?"

"You don't," the officer replied. "Because that would result in an officer being tied up all night in paperwork. I would strongly advise you to keep your mouth shut and bugger off."

"Is that a threat?"

"No sir, it's advice. I understand a certain Mr Butcher, currently residing in the A&E department of the Royal Gwent Hospital, is very keen to be reacquainted with you."

"You can't let him walk," Spanner protested. "He's the prime suspect."

"He was at Woodland Manor, causing quite a scene apparently," Spanner's colleague said. "The receptionist confirmed that he left a few minutes before you attacked him. There's nothing to connect him to this, and where's the stolen goods? Whoever done this got away long before you turned up."

Eric sluggishly slowly rose to his feet and surveyed the scene now the shop lights were on. The confectionary display was ruined, as was the chiller fridge and all its contents. Apart from the whisky and cigarettes, nothing else appeared to be missing.

Eric's father was on the phone behind the counter, talking quietly into the mouthpiece. "They've practically cleaned me out of spirits," he was saying. "And all the cigarettes are gone, and they've even vandalised my fridges."

Eric tried to interrupt him, but the police officer stopped him. "He'll be on the blower for some time," he said. "He's speaking to his insurance company. He's obviously very upset."

Eric remembered the loss adjuster turning up early on Sunday morning, and how his father had roped him into helping clear up the mess. Eric had been amazed at how cheerful his father had been throughout the whole process, despite the disruption and the hassle of having a brand-new chiller installed.

The police officer guided Eric towards the door. "I'd like you to come to the station tomorrow to make a statement. Not a complaint, just a statement. Can you be there for two?"

Eric nodded. He wouldn't, obviously. His head was pounding from Spanner's truncheon. His mouth was dry from the alcohol. He was more tired than he could ever remember. He wanted to go home.

It was after two as he left the shop. He had forgotten how dark the nights were in the '70s. There was just a single streetlight at this end of Lôn Heddychlon and as he approached Spanner's Mark II Ford Escort, which was parked behind the other officer's car, its light was reflected by something glistening on the front passenger seat. Eric peered through the window. On the seat was a cardboard box crammed with bottles of the same brand of whisky that had been stolen from Meek's Mini Market. There was also another box in the passenger footwell, piled with individual packets of cigarettes.

## CHAPTER 12

### SATURDAY 7th DECEMBER 2019

Eric woke up cold, in pain, confused, and in a completely silent house. Why was he in an awkward position on the Freemans' sofa, fully clothed? And where were the Freemans? His watch informed him that it was just after eleven. On Saturday. What had happened to Friday? Had he spent so long in 1976 that he missed an entire day?

A glance at the missed calls on his iPhone suggested that might well have been the case. Closer inspection revealed they were all from Carol. He swung his legs down from the sofa and sat up. There was a large swelling on the side of his head. He swore as he touched it.

He walked into the kitchen and poured himself a glass of water. After he had gulped it down, he went from room to room, in search of the Freemans. Some people might have felt awkward doing this, as if they were intruding, but Eric had been an estate agent for over 40 years. It came natural to him.

He sat on one of the uncomfortable wooden kitchen chairs. There was an empty space outside the house where the Freemans' Toyota Yaris was usually parked. Perhaps they had gone shopping. Why hadn't they woken him though? Or covered him with a blanket? Or put him in one of their spare bedrooms?

He entered the garage and changed from his summer clothes into his 2019 suit, which had been left crumpled in a heap on the floor. Back in the house, he searched in vain for painkillers. If only there was a shop nearby...

As he left the house he stared at the property opposite, the scene of last night's burglary. Or insurance fraud, as he now knew it to be. He already had a very low opinion of Spanner, but it was even lower today. And should he really be surprised his father was involved? He had always been dishonest in small ways, such as occasionally ringing suppliers after a delivery and claiming an item was missing, plus there was his longstanding misappropriation of Smarties to take into consideration. 'It's just a bit of bunce,' he would say to young Eric. 'It helps to cover the shoplifting'. A brand-new top-of-the-range chiller cabinet was more than just a bit of bunce though. Eric recalled his father saying gleefully at the time that the cost had been in four figures.

Eric smiled to himself as he entered the reception area of Woodland Manor. Although the décor had been updated several times during the intervening years, the enormous wooden reception desk was still where it had been in 1976, and it still had an oil painting of someone on a horse behind it. He must remember to ask Seb about the identity of the female subject.

He glanced in the direction of the ballroom – or the function room, as it was called today – and thought back to the exchange he had witnessed between Verity and Little Len. They did not look like a couple about to run off and start a new life together, on the hippie trail or anywhere else. He passed the spot where Big Ben lay screaming and took a seat at the bar in the lounge. After a few moments, the receptionist poked her head around the door and informed him the bar did not open until midday.

"Is Seb around?" Eric enquired.

She nodded and vanished.

Eric cycled through the text messages on his phone. All six were from Carol and alternated between 'Where are you?' and 'Ring me!' so he called the office.

"Where have you been?" asked Carol. "We've been worried about you."

"We? Alwyn has been worried about me?"

"No, he hasn't, and that's one of the reasons I need to speak to you." She lowered her voice. "Yesterday he spent his lunch hour with Jason Mason. I think they're planning something."

"Okay, I will be with you in about an hour," Eric said. "We'll talk about it then."

Seb appeared behind the bar, a look of concern on his face. "Jesus Christ, what happened to you this time?" he asked, examining Eric's dishevelled appearance and the swelling on his face which had spread from the side of his head.

Eric placed the can of Block on the bar. "This worked fine once," he said. "But when I went to use it again, nothing happened."

"They're only single-use items," Seb explained. "You can get multi-use cans, but they're a bit large to fit in your pocket."

"Could you let me have a couple more?"

"What's going on?" Seb asked, bending down and retrieving two cans from beneath the bar. He handed them to Eric. "Why are you getting into so many fights?"

Eric sighed. "You wouldn't believe me if I told you."

"You're not wandering the streets of Cwmbran at night looking for rough trade, are you?"

"Is there much around here?"

"I wouldn't know."

"In that case, can we talk about something else, such as breakfast?"

***

Carol was alone when Eric arrived at Barrington Meek. She hadn't heard him come in and was bent over the ancient wooden racks with a duster and a can of polish.

"Do you think it's time we had a refit, Carol?" Eric said.

Carol jumped up, startled. "You scared the life out of me."

"And while we're at it we'll get a bell for the door," Eric said. He studied Carol. Although she was 43 years older, she was still identifiable as the woman from the previous night. Her hair was shorter and straight, but it was still blonde – though he conceded that might not be its natural colour – and behind her more subtle spectacles her eyes were almost identical. She'd stayed slim too. He'd never noticed before, but she was attractive. And there was no need to add 'for her age' either.

"He's gone out with Jason Mason again," Carol said, indicating Alwyn's empty desk. She went to her desk and collected several notes she's scribbled. "I've sorted that… he can wait…" she said as she cycled through them. "But can you ring Mrs Freeman on this number?"

Eric accepted the paper with a mobile number scrawled on it.

"Does this mean we've got the house?" Carol asked. "Have you told Mrs Ducreux yet?"

"It's complicated," Eric said.

"How?"

"I'll tell you later."

Carol backed away from Eric. "Shall I nip out and get you a toothbrush and some toothpaste from Boots?"

"Do I need them?"

Carol nodded. "And you could do with a shave too."

Eric called the number. It rang several times.

"Hello?" Mrs Freeman answered.

"Hello Mrs Freeman," Eric said cheerfully. "It's Eric Meek here, returning your call."

"Who?"

"Eric, from Barrington Meek. The estate agents."

"Oh."

"Is everything alright?"

"My husband wanted to speak to you."

"Can you put him on?"

"Not really, he's resting," she said. "He's had a heart attack."

***

The crawling December weekend traffic between Cwmbran and Newport, and the search for somewhere to park, resulted in Eric arriving at the Royal Gwent Hospital's cardiology unit late in the afternoon.

"The doctor said it's unstable angina," Mrs Freeman said as Eric showed her to a table in the hospital's cafeteria.

"Is that good?" Eric asked nervously, as he set two coffees down on the table.

"It's the less serious type of heart attack," Mrs Freeman replied. "They're giving him blood-thinning medication for now."

"Do you know how long he'll be in?"

"It depends on the results of the tests," she said, sipping the hot coffee. "At least he's stable."

"That's good."

"But I can't cope with all this at my age, I really can't. You know I sleep downstairs?"

Eric nodded. He'd suspected one of them did when he encountered a single bed in the secondary reception room when he was measuring the house. "The stairs leading up to the first floor are quite steep in properties of that period."

"He's not going to be able to manage them either now," she said. "I don't know what we are going to do."

Suddenly Eric had an epiphany. "I can help," Eric said. "The last conversation I had with your husband, he told me he was prepared to put the house up for sale. And I have on my books the perfect property for you, a bungalow in Brookvale."

She looked disdainfully at Eric. "Is that why you're here, touting for business?"

"No, of course not," Eric said. "I came to see how your husband is. I don't know if you're aware, but I was a pupil of his."

Mrs Freeman's face softened. "I wasn't aware," she said. "But I did wonder what the two of you were talking about for so long the other night."

"I apologise if broaching the subject at such a time is inappropriate, Mrs Freeman, but a bungalow will make life so much easier, for both of you."

"I don't know," she said. "I'd have to see it."

Eric removed his phone from his jacket pocket and opened the web browser. He typed in Barrington Meek's URL and clicked on the property in Brookvale. He handed her his phone after setting up the slideshow option.

"That's lovely," Mrs Freeman said approvingly as she flicked through the pictures. "That would be much better. The garden is wonderful. I've really missed having a garden."

"It's closer to the shops and the doctor's surgery, and the boating lake is just a few hundred yards away," Eric said, before realising that Mrs Freeman would be unlikely to be doing much walking.

"Could we afford it though?" she asked.

"Easily," Eric assured her. "If you sold your property, you could not only afford to buy this one, which is ready to move into with no onward chain, you would also be able to bank a quite significant sum."

Mrs Freeman's mouth fell open, before widening into a smile. "Really?"

Eric returned her smile. "And we could make this happen very quickly indeed if you wanted to go ahead."

"But I'd need to find a buyer for our house."

"I've already got one for you," Eric replied.

"You've got one? How? The house isn't on the market."

"I'd like to buy it myself."

"You?"

"As I told you, I grew up opposite your house," Eric said. "It would be a homecoming for me."

"Is it ethical for you to buy it?"

"Estate agents are allowed to buy houses too," Eric said. "And I'd be extra incentivised to ensure the process went as smoothly as possible."

Mrs Freeman frowned. "There's so much involved in moving house."

"I will take care of everything," Eric said, taking a mouthful of coffee. "Just say the word."

"I do know the area," Mrs Freeman considered. "I've got a dear friend who lives in Brookvale. We don't see each other as much as we'd like because she has trouble walking."

"This would be ideal for you both," Eric said. "And there's a thriving social scene in the area. The lady who moved out of the house—"

Mrs Freeman interrupted him. "Why is she selling it?"

"She's moved in with her daughter in Tenby," Eric said. This was mostly true, as that's where her ashes were currently located. "She always wanted to live by the sea."

"Tenby is nice."

"She was part of a book group, a choir, and the local WI branch," Eric said. This was entirely true: her son had told Eric all this when he put the house up for sale. "You certainly wouldn't be bored there."

"I will have to talk it over with Frank."

Eric reached across the table and put his hand on hers. "You would be doing this for him just as much as you," he said. "As you say, I don't think your husband will be climbing stairs for a while."

Mrs Freeman looked uncertain.

"That is one of the downsides of the Lôn Heddychlon properties," Eric said. "They all have steps leading up to the front door. And because they are on a hill it is not easy – or cost-efficient – to have a ramp installed."

Mrs Freeman looked downcast. "We had a quote for a stairlift once," she said. "It was thousands."

"Like I said, you would be doing this for you," Eric said, maintaining eye contact and ever-so-gently squeezing her hand to emphasise his sincerity. "But you would also be doing it for him."

"It would be such an upheaval though," she said. "Packing everything up, informing people of the change of address…"

"You won't have to worry about any of that," he replied. "My office will manage every aspect of the move."

After a few moments of silent contemplation, Mrs Freeman said to Eric "In that case, and because you and Frank know each other, I am prepared to put myself in your hands."

"Thank you, Mrs Freeman," Eric said. "I won't let you down. Now if you'll excuse me for a few minutes, I just have to make a couple of phone calls to get the ball rolling."

Eric walked outside the hospital to where the smokers congregated and rung Carol. He told her to take the Brookvale property off the market and to contact the deep cleaning specialists Barrington Meek used once a tenant had moved out of a rented property. "Tell them I've got an urgent job," he said. "I want it done this weekend and I don't mind paying extra."

"Brookvale has already been cleaned," Carol said.

"It's not for that house," Eric replied.

"Where then?"

"The Meadows," Eric replied. "And call Mrs Ducreux and tell her she can have first refusal as she's a cash buyer, but only if she acts quick."

"But we don't have any properties in The Meadows," Carol protested.

"We do now," Eric replied. "My house."

Eric returned to the cafeteria and Mrs Freeman. "The wheels are in motion," he said. "All you have to do is sign a few forms."

"How long will it all take?"

"I'm going to be pulling out all the stops and calling in favours," Eric said. "I'll try to get everything completed before the end of the month."

"Will it take as long as that?"

Eric laughed. "That's what I'm aiming for," he said. "Normally a straightforward move would take at least six weeks, longer if there is a chain involved, and longer still at this time of year."

"Where will I stay?"

"We'll put you up in a luxury suite in Woodland Manor while it's going through," Eric said. "There's television and Wi-Fi provided, and room service can bring you breakfast, lunch, and dinner. I will also arrange for a taxi to take you between the hotel and the hospital as often as you like."

"I don't know what to say," Mrs Freeman said, dabbing her eyes with a tissue. "That's really very kind of you."

Before Eric could respond, his phone rang. It was Carol.

"They can't do it until Tuesday," Carol said.

"That's no good," Eric said. "I'll have to do it myself."

"If it's really urgent," Carol said, "I don't mind helping you do it tomorrow."

"That's a generous offer, Carol," Eric said. "But it's a big job."

"I've got nothing better to do," Carol said. "Besides, I've spoken to Mrs Ducreux. She wants to see it at ten on Monday morning, so it's a case of needs must when the devil drives."

"Okay, I will take you up on that," Eric said. "Is there anywhere that will hire us a van for the weekend this late in the day?"

"I'll sort that," Carol said. "I'll bring it with me in the morning."

After Eric ended the call, Mrs Freeman said: "She sounds like someone you can depend on."

"She is," Eric replied. "She really is."

A few seconds later, a nurse approached their table and gently tapped Mrs Freeman on the shoulder. "He's awake, and asking for you," she said.

Eric accompanied Mrs Freeman into the lift, and she held on to his arm as they slowly made their way down the corridor to Mr Freeman's ward. His bed was with five others, all of which held men who looked to be around the same age as him. His eyes widened when he saw Eric was with his wife.

"Hello Mr Freeman," Eric said. "I'm pleased to see you're looking well."

Mrs Freeman took over, fussing over her husband's appearance, making him take a drink of water, peeling a satsuma and separating the segments for him. Eventually, she said to him: "I've got good news."

"I could do with some of that," he wheezed.

"We're moving," she said, clapping her hands. "Mr Meek is sorting everything out for us."

"Is he?" Freeman glared at Eric.

Turning to Eric, she said: "Show him the pictures of the new bungalow."

Eric did.

Freeman watched the slideshow in silence.

"Won't it be wonderful not to have stairs?" she asked him.

"I think I'd better have a chat with Mr Meek," Freeman said. "Why don't you go and get yourself a cup of tea or something?"

As she left the ward Eric turned to Freeman, shrugged, and said: "She wants to move. You want to move. What's the problem?"

"You know what the problem is," Freeman said, with as much indignation as he could muster in his weakened state.

"You won't have to worry about anything," Eric said. "My office will take care of it all."

"You think you've got me over a barrel, don't you?"

"I'm helping you," Eric said.

"You're exploiting me!"

"Remember what you said about taking your wife's dog to the vet for his jabs, and how he's too ignorant to know that what you're doing is for his benefit?" Eric said. "You're the dog and I'm the vet."

Freeman winced.

Eric continued: "Without that thing dominating your life you'll at least get to spend your remaining time together. Have you thought what would have happened to the portal if that heart attack had killed you?"

"No," Freeman conceded.

"Emily would have been left to deal with it," Eric said. "I would imagine it could cause quite a disturbance if someone who didn't know what they were doing began dicking about with it."

Freeman winced again.

"Look, if your house goes on the open market a surveyor is going to come across the portal and ask a lot of awkward questions. If you sign the house over to me, I will ensure it doesn't fall into the wrong hands, and we can also discuss decommissioning it safely at some point."

"How do I know you're not ripping us off?"

"That's your biggest concern? Your wife has already had two valuations from other agents," Eric said. "Without seeing them, I'll pay you whichever valuation is the highest. And you've seen the asking price of the bungalow, which is very fair."

"You're railroading me," Freeman said.

"How? This is what you said you wanted. You'll come out of this with a lump sum to spend on making your wife happy. Because despite what you said, she still really cares about you even though you've been a terrible husband."

Freeman sighed. "You have got me over a barrel."

"Don't be the dog again," Eric chided him. "If you look at the bigger picture, you'll see that I am taking care of you and Emily."

"Looks like someone took care of you," Freeman said, pointing at Eric's swollen face.

"Spanner," Eric sighed. "Again."

"You should try staying out of his way."

"I tried," Eric said, then recounted what happened at Meek's Mini Market.

Freeman chortled, causing his frail torso to painfully shake. Clutching his sides, he warned Eric: "It's not in your interest to make me laugh. I might drop dead before I sign the papers."

Eric explained to Freeman why the date the portal was connected to was so significant to him, recounting his humiliation in the boating lake incident, and how betrayed he felt when Verity switched allegiance to Little Len. "She just went off with him, hand in hand," Eric said, his voice barely more than a whisper. "She didn't even look back."

"Of course she went off with him," Freeman said. "Are you really as dull as you present?"

"What do you mean?"

"Even now, after all these years, can't you see?" Freeman wheezed. "She did it to protect you."

The blood drained from Eric's face. His throat grew tight, and goosebumps formed on his arms. "To protect me?"

Freeman nodded. "That's obviously why you're still bothered by this incident. You know, deep down, that it should have been you protecting her."

## CHAPTER 13

### SUNDAY 8th DECEMBER 2019

"Oh, they don't do the two-for-£10 offer on Sundays," Carol said after spending several minutes staring at the menu in silence. "That's a shame, because I was going to have the fish and chips."

"Have whatever you want," Eric said. "Two portions of fish and chips is not going to break the bank."

"It's almost a tenner each," Carol was outraged.

"We're worth it, Carol," Eric said. "And we can claim the VAT back if we say we're entertaining clients."

"No, we can't," Carol said. "Because HMRC guidelines state that entertaining clients is hospitality—"

"I was joking, Carol," Eric said. "I'm obviously more than happy to buy you lunch myself, out of my own pocket."

Carol's face shaped to say 'But you can't afford it' but instead she smiled gratefully. "Thank you, it's a long time since I've been out for Sunday lunch."

The branch of the casual restaurant dining chain wouldn't have been Eric's first choice for Sunday lunch, but it was just a few minutes' drive away from his house, and it was surprisingly affordable – despite what Carol thought – when compared to Woodland Manor.

Whatever the cost, he would have willingly paid it: Carol had turned up just after nine with a van and helped him declutter his house. The van contained boxes of gadgets and home gym equipment which, if left in place, would have dragged down both the appeal and the value of the property. Eric didn't use any of it anyway. Then she fired up her steamer and gave the kitchen and bathroom a deep clean while Eric removed anything else that might detract from 'the show house look' that buyers expected these days. Carol had even suggested popping out to B&Q for some white emulsion, but Eric pointed out that houses smelling of paint were often treated with suspicion by potential buyers. Instead, she used her phone to order flowers for 9:00am delivery the following morning and positioned an empty wine carafe on the hall table and another in the kitchen. Eric was ordered to place the flowers in them as soon as they arrived, after cutting the stems at an angle and adding water.

After they ordered their food, they sat in awkward silence for a few moments. They were surrounded by the sounds of families and friends enjoying each other's company, laughing at private jokes, chastising the odd misbehaving child, and predicting the outcome of the following week's general election.

"I usually go to Woodland Manor for Sunday lunch," Eric eventually said. "Would you like to go there sometime? My treat, obviously."

"No thanks," she replied.

"No? It's where all the local glitterati go to stuff their faces."

"Do I look like glitterati?" she asked, pouting her lips.

"Didn't you work there at one time?" Eric asked.

Carol looked suspiciously at Eric. "How did you know that?"

"Er, I'm not sure," he said.

Carol took her phone from her bag and started flicking the screen with her finger.

"What's your husband up to today," Eric said, slightly irritated by her rudeness.

"Fishing," Carol replied, without looking up. "He goes fishing every weekend, even at Christmas."

"Your freezer must be full of trout then?"

"He never catches anything," she replied, still engrossed in her phone. "I don't think catching fish is the point of fishing."

Their meals came and they ate in silence. The fish and chips was much better than Eric expected for the price, and to his surprise he also enjoyed the mushy peas.

"I would expect to pay more than double for that at Woodland Manor," Eric said as he placed his cutlery on his empty plate. "But that's probably why I've got no money."

Carol was absorbed in her phone again and didn't look up or respond.

"That was very enjoyable," Eric said. "And thanks again for all your help today."

"You should see this," Carol said, handing her phone to Eric. "Jason Mason is slagging us off on Twitter."

"You're on Twitter?"

"According to this, he's opening a branch in Cwmbran in 2020," Carol said. "Because, according to him, the existing agencies in the town centre are either stuck in the last century or they're corporate branches staffed by disinterested wage slaves. He doesn't lack confidence, does he?"

"He got all that in one tweet?" Eric said. "Isn't there a character limit?"

"It was doubled last year," Carol replied. "You really should be on Twitter. Hand me your phone and I'll download it for you."

Eric did as he was told.

After a few seconds Carol said: "How long have you had this? The memory's full and it takes ages to open apps. Get it upgraded and then I'll install Twitter for you."

"I don't want to pay for a new phone just so I can hear what Jason Mason is saying."

"You'll be a lot better informed," Carol said. "20 years ago, you had to buy a newspaper or listen to the radio to find out what was happening. These days the news comes to you. Also, the cameras on the latest models are better quality than that old digital you use, and you'd be able to transfer pictures straight to the office while you're still on site."

Eric pouted: "Guess I'm getting a new phone then. Not sure when I'll get chance to do it though."

"You're spending a lot of time out of the office lately," Carol said. "Is everything okay?"

"I've got a lot on," Eric said. "Ideally I need to sell my house tomorrow to that woman so that I can buy the house in Lôn Heddychlon that I went to value earlier this week."

Carol looked shocked. "You're buying it yourself? Is that sort of thing above board?"

"It's fine," Eric assured her. "I'm paying the figure that another estate agent has valued it at."

Carol looked unhappy and exhaled loudly.

"Is that a problem, Carol?" Eric asked.

"It's probably not my place to say."

"But?"

"Some people might say you should be concentrating on your business rather than worrying about moving house."

"That's exactly what I am doing," Eric replied. "I'll be using some of the equity from the sale of my house to make a director's loan to the business, which will get the bank off our back and tide us over until Brexit is sorted and the market gets going again."

Carol's eyes widened and she raised her eyebrows. "Oh."

"And I'll extend my personal mortgage for another few years to cover the stamp duty and legal fees. So don't worry, the business is being taken care of and it should be around for a good few years."

"In that case, we really need to do some marketing," Carol said. "Whatever you think of Jason Mason, he's right about the way business is changing. We need more of an online presence. It won't necessarily cost a lot of money, but it will be a lot of work."

Eric pulled an unhappy face. "A lot of work? I don't like the sound of that. I heard someone in the pub say that estate agents were lazy. I was so shocked I nearly fell off my mobility scooter."

She looked puzzled.

"It's a joke, Carol," Eric explained. "I don't really have a mobility scooter."

"People don't have mobility scooters because they're lazy," she chastised him.

"I know, it was in poor taste, and I apologise," Eric said.

"And we need a tagline. Something like 'Barrington Meek, where the service is unique'."

"I like that, Carol," Eric said considering her suggestion. "Do you want another drink?"

"I won't be able to drive the van back if I do."

"Don't worry about the van, I'll take it with me."

"But how am I going to get home?"

"I can drop you off or you can take a taxi back and put it on expenses."

"A taxi? On a Sunday? No wonder you've got no money," she said.

Eric repeated the phrase when he brought the two glasses of merlot back to the table. "Barrington Meek, where the service is unique."

"It's not though, is it?" said Carol. "And it doesn't scan terribly well either. If only your name was Jerome."

Eric took a large glug of wine. Go on, his expression said.

"Find your dream home, at Barrington Jerome."

Eric grinned, exposing his red wine-coloured teeth. "That's almost worth changing my name for," he said.

"But the name is our heritage," Carol said. "It's the strongest thing we've got going for us. A young woman from a marketing agency gave a talk to our WI group and—"

"You're in the Women's Institute?"

"What's wrong with that?"

"Nothing," Eric shrugged. "I just didn't know."

"It was really interesting," Carol continued. "The business was here before you took over, wasn't it? When did it become Barrington Meek?"

"July 1990," Eric replied. "But Barrington Property Services originally opened in the early '60s."

"If we just focus on 1990, that's a great hook for a marketing campaign in the New Year," Carol said, repeating a phrase she had heard at the WI. "30 years of Barrington Meek. 30 years of service to the local community. The filing cabinets are full of papers from the early days so I'm sure we could come up with a press release about how house prices have changed since 1990. And we could list the top ten things people bought for their new homes back then."

"How will we find that out?"

"My sister-in-law works at the Office for National Statistics, which keeps records of things like this. I'll give her a call. We could also ask the Cwmbran Evening Star to do a profile piece on us."

"I'll give Zack a ring," Eric said.

"Do it now, while you think of it," she urged him.

"On a Sunday?"

"Sunday is just another day," Carol said. "And regional newspapers are crying out for 'good news' stories amongst all the Brexit doom and gloom."

Eric left the table and went outside to make the call.

"You were right," Eric said when he returned. "It's all arranged for tomorrow afternoon: a puff piece profile and interview, photo of the staff, and a picture from the early days. And no charge because I said we'd be doing a campaign with full page ads in the New Year."

"Wear your smartest suit tomorrow," Carol said. "I'll send Alwyn a text to make sure he does as well. I'm sure he'd love to be photographed in the Star."

Eric stared at Carol admiringly. "You're the real star around here, Carol."

"Stop it," she said, her cheeks blushing. She was clearly unfamiliar with praise. And not just from Eric.

"It's true," Eric said. "And I'd like you to take a more active role in the business. Would you be up for doing that?"

Carol nodded, cautiously.

"You can start tomorrow by showing that woman around my house," Eric said. "I'm sure you'll do a much better job of it than me."

Carol protested: "Oh that's not true."

"It is," Eric said. "It's a well-known fact that vendors are the worst people to present their own properties because they get all defensive at the slightest bit of criticism. You do it, Carol, I have absolute faith in you."

"Thank you," she said, her red wine lips breaking into a rare smile.

"I won't be in the office so much over the next couple of weeks so I'd like you to take charge when I'm not there. Give that marketing woman a call if you like and invite her to pitch a campaign for us."

"Is there the budget for that?"

"You can spend up to five grand," Eric said. "She should be able to do something with that."

"She will," Carol beamed. "Especially on socials."

They sat in silence for a few moments, lost in their own thoughts. A bell rang behind the bar, indicating last orders. The family groups were standing around and helping each other with their heavy winter coats before they ventured outside into the December cold.

"Right, we'd better make a move," Eric said.

"What's the rush?" Carol protested. "We've finished at your house."

"There's something I want to do at the property I'm buying in Lôn Heddychlon," he said, looking at his watch. "And time is ticking away, so if you don't mind could you call yourself a cab?"

"Do you need a hand at the other house?"

"No, you've already done far more for me than I deserve," Eric said.

Carol emptied her glass. "Why do you want to move there anyway? Isn't it a step down from The Meadows?"

Eric replied: "It is, certainly in financial terms, but I suppose you could say I want to go back to my roots."

Carol sighed as she picked up her phone to summon a taxi. "I never managed to bloody escape mine," she grumbled.

## CHAPTER 14

## SATURDAY 3ʳᴰ JULY 1976

The hot sun burned Eric's face as he emerged from the garage. He was wearing the black shorts he used to play squash in, an old faded grey T-shirt with a Mötley Crüe logo, and a pair of Nike running shoes which he'd bought after Carol had signed him up for a local charity fun run several years ago, which he did not participate in. He was going to run now though, from Lôn Heddychlon down to the boating lake, carrying the few possessions he'd brought with him in an old wash bag he'd strapped around his wrist.

As he jogged in the scorching heat, his motivation to keep going came from Freeman's last words to him – you should have protected her – and although each stride inflicted pain on his out of condition body, he kept pounding the harsh unforgiving pavements, sweat streaming down his face, neck, and chest.

The boating lake was separated from its own car park by a large open field and the Afon Lwyd river, and it was accessed via a pedestrian bridge. As Eric reached the bridge, he stopped to give his body a few moments to recover. He bent down and gulped in the hot dry air. Other people using the bridge were staring at him. Everyone was staring at him. Men of his age did not dress like this in 1976. His grey T-shirt was almost completely dark with sweat, and it clung to his podgy stomach, making him look even more comically plump than normal.

Still panting, Eric walked across the bridge and into the children's area, which consisted of a smaller boating lake and a selection of playground rides. It was packed with families and all he could hear was the shrill sounds of small children enjoying themselves.

Suddenly one child's voice cut through the rest: "I said I want to go home!"

Eric frantically looked around.

The child's mother replied irritably: "And I told you we've only just got here!"

"It's too hot, mam!"

"Stop moaning," his mother shouted. "I bought you an ice-cream, didn't I?"

Eric rushed towards the kiosk which dispensed the snacks and refreshments. There was now no queue at all, and just a few children with disappointed faces were listening to the red-faced woman in the serving window deliver the heartbreaking news: "I'm sorry but we've got no ice-cream left now, only teas and coffees."

Eric's stomach turned over. He didn't remember this. He walked from the kiosk to the lake itself, where he could see a familiar looking youth trudging out of the water towards the bank.

"Bollocks!" Eric cried loudly, to the obvious disgust of the people within earshot.

"Oi butty, watch your language," one old man reprimanded him. "A man of your age should know better."

Eric held his hands up in a feeble gesture of apology, but no one noticed as most people were all pointing and laughing at young Eric, who was walking as fast as his wet clothes would allow him towards the bridge. Eric could feel his eyes welling up in empathy with young Eric. Was empathy the right word? Could you empathise with yourself?

Eric positioned himself so he blocked young Eric's way. "Go after her," he said.

Young Eric looked up in alarm at the oddly dressed butterball looming over him, dripping in sweat.

"You've got to fight for her," Eric encouraged.

"That's easy for you to say," young Eric replied, tears welling in his eyes.

Eric grabbed young Eric by the shoulders. "Len is a weedy little shrimp," he said. "You could beat the crap out of him if you wanted to."

Young Eric stared at his older self. "Were you watching?"

"I, er, saw it out the corner of my eye," Eric said.

"He's Big Ben Butcher's son," young Eric said. "No one can touch him."

"Or what?" Eric said. "Do you honestly think that whatever happens after you punch that little twat in the face could be any worse than how you feel now?"

"He's got a bodyguard," young Eric protested. "Do you think he'll just stand there?"

"I'll take care of him," Eric said.

Young Eric snorted with disbelief as he evaluated the sweating old man's ability to follow through on his promise. "You?"

"Look, if you don't go after her now and fight for her, you'll regret it for the rest of your life," Eric said. But young Eric swerved around him and ran off. The opportunity had passed, and old Eric watched young Eric retreat to the shelter of his bedroom.

Eric bought himself a Styrofoam cup of tea with some of the cash he'd stolen from his father's till and joined two other men sat on a wooden bench overlooking the lake while his body recovered. The men appeared to be much older than Eric, and they both held wooden walking sticks in their hands. They were thin, frail, and having a mumbled conversation about how overweight and sweaty Eric was, and how ridiculous he was dressed.

"Hot enough for you?" one of them eventually turned and asked Eric.

"I don't mind this heat at all," Eric replied. "It tends to thin out the herd by killing off the old and infirm."

***

The trek from the boating lake back up to Lôn Heddychlon was considerably harder than the journey down. It was mostly uphill for a start, and Eric's feet and legs were aching from his earlier efforts, plus the sun's heat became even fiercer as the afternoon wore on. If only he'd arrived at the boating lake a few minutes earlier.

Instead of entering Freeman's garage Eric kept on walking, into the grounds of Woodland Manor. He needed to rest his aching limbs and rehydrate with a cold pint of lager or two before returning to 2019.

As he approached the entrance to the building, he noticed a green MGB GT coupe parked at an inconsiderate angle right in front of the 'Strictly no parking, please use car park to the rear' sign. The final letter on the insect-splattered – there's something you don't see any more – registration plate was K, which suggested the MGB was a 1971 model. Eric stopped to admire the vehicle. The driver's window had been left open, allowing him to appreciate the black leather seats and wooden steering wheel.

"I wouldn't go too close, if I was you," cautioned Carol, who had emerged from behind the reception desk to put out an A-frame sandwich board promoting tonight's Dinner & Dance. She had no petticoat beneath her red paisley patterned skirt and the blazing sun made the thin material almost transparent.

Eric tried not to stare at the silhouette of her legs. "Why is that?"

"It's the owner's," Carol explained. "And he's very possessive."

"It's a fine car," Eric said. "I've always fancied one."

Carol smiled weakly at him but said nothing.

Eric could see what she was thinking. "I know," he said. "I should really get a move on if I'm going to have one as I probably don't have long left."

Carol didn't disagree, returning behind the reception desk to answer the phone. "Woodland Manor Hotel and Restaurant, how can I help you?" she said in the same sing-song voice Eric was used to hearing at Barrington Meek.

The tennis was in full swing on the big television when Eric slumped onto a bar stool. He unzipped his wash bag to retrieve some more of the local currency, liberated from his father's shop during his last visit, and placed a 50p piece on the bar.

"Can I help you sir?" Seb asked him.

"He shouldn't be allowed in here dressed like that," complained Mr Reeves, his tone dripping with contempt.

"To be fair, Mr Reeves, it is the hottest day of the year," Seb said on Eric's behalf.

Reeves held up his small ornate glass. "Is that why the Croft tastes watered down?"

"Thank you," Eric said to Seb. "I'll have a pint of lager please."

"Any particular one?" Seb asked.

"It doesn't really matter, they all taste about the same," Eric replied wearily.

"Stella?" Seb prompted. "It's new and it's become our most popular lager."

"Actually, I'll have a Harp," Eric said, pointing to the yellow and blue livery of the branded tap. "I haven't had one of them for years."

As Eric sat back and savoured his lager, Big Ben appeared behind the bar. His looming presence blocked Eric's view of the television but Big Ben didn't seem to care. He slapped his wallet and car keys down on the bar and began pouring himself a Stella. He glared at the television screen in disgust. "Come on Nastase," he urged. "You should be knocking that big girl's blouse all over the court."

Eric was the only person in the bar not watching the match. He was trying to think of a way to shave a few minutes off the time it took him to get from Lôn Heddychlon to the boating lake. He ran there today, and arrived a few minutes too late, so if he could get there quicker than he could run, he might be able to prevent 'the incident' taking place.

While Eric was thinking about this, Elvis sauntered into the bar. He stared disdainfully at Eric and his unusual attire and sat at the table by the window which looked out over the entrance. Elvis signalled to Seb to bring a drink to him, and Big Ben picked up his pint and joined him, leaving his wallet and keys on the bar.

Mr Reeves was engrossed in the tennis, and while Seb was taking a pint of Stella to Elvis, Eric calmly stood up, walked to the end of the bar and scooped up Big Ben's wallet and keys with his right hand in one smooth motion.

"Are you off?" Seb called after him, as he returned to the bar from Big Ben's table.

"See you later," Eric replied, picking up the pace as he made his way from the lounge through reception and out into the burning sun. He slid into the MGB's driving seat, the hot leather inflicting more pain on his legs, and turned the key in the ignition. The 1798cc engine was still warm and it roared into life, the deep throb from the exhaust echoing off the wall it was parked by. It had been quite a while since Eric had driven a car with a manual gearbox and it made a horrible metallic crunching sound as he tried to engage first.

"Come on," Eric chided himself. "There's only four bloody gears."

Out of the corner of his eye Eric could see that Carol was staring at him, her mouth gaping open in horror. Was she going to let Big Ben know his car was being stolen? She didn't need to, because here he was, rushing towards him, followed by Elvis.

Eric forced the gearbox into first and dumped the clutch, causing the car to leap forward in an awkward jerky manner. The engine was screaming as Eric wrenched the gearstick into second and headed down the drive.

Big Ben had caught up with him and was attempting to wrench the driver's door open. Eric stamped on the accelerator pedal. It didn't make a huge amount of difference. Even though it was only five years old, the engine in the Mark III MGB GT could only summon 95bhp, so it struggled to reach 60mph in less than 15 seconds – almost twice as long as his Lexus.

Big Ben was furiously banging his fist on the car roof, threatening to do all sorts of horrible things to Eric unless he stopped – even though he would definitely have done them if Eric had stopped – but then he tripped over one of the stone flowerpots dotted along the drive which were designed to prevent vehicles driving on the lawns. Suddenly Big Ben was no longer trying to drag Eric out of the car, he was screaming with fury as he came to an abrupt stop on the gravel.

Eric roared out of Woodland Manor's entrance and down the length of Lôn Heddychlon. He stopped where it met Caerleon Road and retrieved his iPhone from his wash bag. He started the phone's stopwatch function and headed for the boating lake car park. Pulling in, he could see that all the allotted spaces were full, so he mounted the curb and brought the MGB to a halt on the grass fields that surrounded the car park, before sprinting across the bridge to the kiosk.

Out of breath, he arrived at the now closed kiosk and checked his time: just over six minutes from Lôn Heddychlon, including the final section which he had run under his own steam. Assuming he was going to steal the car again – and he could, anytime he liked, if he kept the keys – he would have to get from Freeman's garage up to Woodland Manor in under three minutes if he was to prevent 'the incident' taking place.

Eric turned around and walked back over the pedestrian bridge towards the boating lake car park. He could see, even from this distance, that the green MGB was no longer where he parked it. Presumably someone had hot-wired it and stolen it, as Eric hadn't locked it. He hoped the police caught whoever stole it before Big Ben did.

As Eric stepped off the bridge onto the grass, he stopped. Two cool teenagers were smirking at his Mötley Crüe T-shirt as they walked past him. They would soon change their attitude when 'Too Fast For Love' was released in the '80s. That wasn't what was at the forefront of Eric's mind though: he was looking at where he parked the car compared to where he stood now. It was a distance of around 100 metres. Next time, if he was going to park on the grass – and he'd have to, as the car park would be full – he could give himself an extra minute or two by parking on the section of grass closest to the pedestrian bridge.

## CHAPTER 15

### MONDAY 9th DECEMBER 2019

As Eric entered the Barrington Meek showroom, Carol rolled her eyes and gently nodded her head in the direction of Alwyn, who was not alone at his desk. Alwyn and his shaven-headed guest had their backs towards the door and were talking so loudly they hadn't heard Eric come in.

"This one time, I was due to show a client a property, but I got there early as I needed a dump," Alwyn was saying. "There's me, sat in the downstairs bog, squeezing out this enormous log, when the woman rings me. She's outside. The bog's right by the front door so after I finish wiping my arse, I just put the seat down. I didn't want to flush it, even though it stunk, because then she'd know I was on the bog when I was talking to her. Anyway, I open the door to her and she rushes straight into the bog herself, because she was pregnant and needed a pee."

Both men erupted into raucous laughter.

"What are you doing here?" Eric said to Jason Mason.

They turned to face Eric. Mason was the first to speak, after ostentatiously looking at his watch: "Bloody hell, what time do you call this? You've already missed half the day."

"Get out," Eric said, pointing towards the door.

"We were only having a chinwag," Alwyn protested.

"Yes, I heard," Eric snapped. "Do you think that's an appropriate subject for the showroom? You didn't even hear me come in – what if I'd been a client?"

"No danger of that," Mason said with a smirk. "Nobody's been in all morning."

Eric grabbed Mason's shoulder. "I told you to leave," he said.

Mason glared at the hand on his shoulder. "You had better remove that before I remove it for you," he warned Eric.

Eric kept it there. He'd faced up to Big Ben. Jason Mason was a nobody. "You've got no business being in here," Eric said, maintaining eye contact with Mason.

"Maybe not now," Mason replied, pulling away from Eric's grip and heading towards the door. "But who knows what's around the corner?"

"If he comes in again Carol," Eric said, "call the police because he will be trespassing."

"Trespassing?" Mason snorted as he opened the showroom door. "In a public place?"

"Even if you have implied permission to enter somewhere," Eric said, "if you have been asked to leave, and you don't, then you will be committing the offence of trespass – if you want to be an estate agent, Mr Mason, I suggest you learn a little about property law."

"Shall I make you a coffee?" Carol asked Eric nervously.

Eric studied Carol's face. She really had not changed a great deal since 1976. She was still recognisable as the same woman. And she was still playing a subservient role.

"No thanks, Carol," Eric said. "From today you are forbidden to make anyone in this office a coffee. And if you are dealing with a client who requests one then you will delegate the task to Alwyn."

It was Carol's turn to stare at Eric.

"But she can still make my protein shakes, can't she?" Alwyn said, with a worried look on his face.

"No beverages of any kind," Eric replied forcefully. "This isn't the '70s and Carol is not your personal assistant, so I don't want to see her running any errands for you either."

Alwyn pulled a sour face and inserted his iPhone earbuds.

Eric waited until he could hear Alwyn's tinny Christmas music leaking out before turning to Carol and asking quietly: "How did the viewing go?"

Carol smiled. "Pretty good. She slagged off your décor – and I couldn't disagree with her – but she likes the house, and she likes where it is."

"Is she going to put in an offer?"

"She already has," Carol replied. "It's £25,000 short of the price I quoted though."

Eric sighed with disappointment. "I don't really want to go that low."

Carol shrugged. "You'll still get £500,000 for it."

"How?"

"Because I told her the vendor was looking for £525,000," Carol said.

"But I told you to put it at £500,000 for a quick sale."

"I thought it was worth more," Carol replied.

Eric smiled with relief. "You really should be running this business, Carol. Give her a call and tell her she can have it."

"Okay, but I'll wait until this afternoon, I don't want to appear too keen," she said, making a note on her pad. "And talking of this afternoon, don't forget that Zack from the Star is coming in at three to do the profile piece for our 30th anniversary next year."

"I hadn't forgotten," Eric said. "I did set it up, remember?"

"I'm sorry if that came across as nagging," Carol said. "I just wanted to remind you."

"And thank you for doing so," Eric said, removing a folder from his filing cabinet and handing it to Carol. "Going back to the sale of my house, although I would normally agree that we don't want to appear too keen, can you chase Mrs Ducreux and express the sale? And can you give the legal people the heads-up so we can exchange contracts on that and these other two properties as soon as possible?"

Carol looked through the documents. "The Freemans are buying the bungalow in Brookvale, you're buying the Freemans' house in Lôn Heddychlon, and Mrs Ducreux is buying yours. This is very nice business for December," she said approvingly.

"It will keep the wolves from the door," Eric said pointedly. "But can you do it in reverse order? My house first, then the Freemans', then Brookvale? It's a self-contained chain so there shouldn't be any complications. It would be great to complete this week."

"This week?"

Eric nodded. "There's no reason why it can't be done, if everyone knows it's a personal favour for me and the circumstances are exceptional, because no one is busy in December. I've already rung the financial advisor but he's with a client, so I've set an alarm to remind me to ring him later today."

Carol shuffled the papers. "Have you got a signed mandate from the Freemans?"

Eric hadn't. And Carol couldn't proceed without one. "I'll get one signed now," he said. "Can you print me out a Sole Selling Rights contract?"

Carol opened a folder on her desktop computer. "What commission fee?"

"Just 1%, there's not going to be much work involved."

She looked at the document Eric had given her. "And you've confirmed this is the right address?"

"Yes Carol," he said. "I'm not Alwyn."

"Just checking," she said, typing in the details. "As you know, his mistake on the house in Fairwater turned out to be quite expensive."

"That's why he's only allowed to do the rentals."

While Carol was filling out the mandate, Eric rang the Royal Gwent Hospital to check that Mr Freeman was still in the same ward. He was, but afternoon visiting times didn't start until three. Eric looked at his watch – that wasn't for another two hours, and if he went then it would mean cancelling Zack from the Cwmbran Evening Star.

"Is Mr Freeman's wife with him?" Eric asked the ward sister.

"She is," the woman said.

"I need to see them both urgently," Eric said.

"Is it an emergency?"

"It is," Eric said. "I'm an estate agent."

***

Finding a parking space in the hospital grounds proved to be less painful than his previous visit – one of the bonuses of visiting outside the stipulated hours – and Eric stopped at the on-site shop to buy a newspaper and a selection of confectionary.

"Hello Mrs Freeman," Eric said as he entered the ward. "How's the patient today?"

"He's a bit dopey," she replied.

Eric resisted the urge to say, 'no change there, then' and instead handed her a carrier bag containing The Guardian and the assorted bars of chocolate. "A little something to keep you going," he said.

Mrs Freeman eagerly tore open the wrapper of the first bar of chocolate, though she looked a little disappointed with Eric's choice of reading materials. "Were they all out of the Daily Mail?"

"I can pop back down and check," Eric said.

"If you wouldn't mind," she replied. "And see if they've got any Maltesers."

Slightly out of breath, Eric returned with the goods. "I've just got two forms for you both to sign," he said.

"Forms?"

"For the move," Eric prompted. "And hopefully you can be in your new bungalow before Christmas."

"I don't know if I could face moving right now," Mrs Freeman said, looking disapprovingly at the Daily Mail's 'PM blasts labour Brexit betrayal' front page headline.

"Brexit's not going to happen for some time," Eric said. "And when it does no one knows what impact it will have on property prices. You might not be able to sell your house at all if the country goes into recession."

Mrs Freeman looked up from her Daily Mail. "Do you think so?"

"Certainly not at the price we agreed. And the bungalow in Brookvale is attracting a lot of interest. Between you and me, I've got a cash buyer from Bristol coming to see it tomorrow."

***

It was after three by the time Eric returned to Barrington Meek's showroom, and he was disappointed to see Jason Mason sat with Alwyn again. Zack from the Cwmbran Evening Star was perusing the premium houses for sale with Carol. "Sorry to have kept you," Eric said to Zack. "I was with a client."

"No problem," Zack replied, shaking Eric's hand. "Business is good, is it?"

"We're still here," Eric replied, handing the signed Freeman documents to Carol and gesturing her to get on with processing them. "And you can't ask for much more than that these days."

Zack sat in the customer chair at Eric's desk and placed his digital voice recorder in the centre. "Ready to go when you are," he said.

Zack's questions were as anodyne as Eric expected – it was a puff piece after all – and Eric was able to reel off stock answers about the high levels of service an independent business like his could provide, how proud he was of Barrington Meek's heritage, and what a privilege it had been helping generations of Cwmbran people move into the homes of their dreams.

The whole interview was wrapped up in less than 20 minutes, and Zack then asked Eric to pose with his staff at their desks and he would photograph them on his phone.

"Use my camera," Eric said, retrieving it from his desk drawer. "It will give a much better result."

"I don't know how to use it," Zack said. "It's dead easy with my phone."

"I'll take the picture," offered Jason Mason. "I've got one just like this – well, mine's the top of the range model—"

"What's he doing here?" Eric hissed at Carol. "Didn't I make myself clear, earlier?"

"I did warn Alwyn that you wouldn't be happy," Carol replied.

Eric reluctantly handed his camera to Jason Mason, who spent several minutes barking orders at Eric, Carol, and Alwyn as he moved them around the showroom.

"He's like a bloody film director," Alwyn said.

"No, just a professional," Jason replied, handing the camera back to Eric. "It's all about depth of field and lighting."

"I see you managed to get all of my double chin in every frame," Eric said as he reviewed the shots on the camera's LED screen.

"Yeah, it wasn't easy though," Jason snickered.

"Good one!" Alwyn guffawed, then turning to Zack he said: "While you're here you can do a story on me. I'm going whitewater rafting in the New Year for charity and I'm after sponsorship."

Zack explained that unfortunately it was the Cwmbran Evening Star's editorial policy not to cover such things, but he wished him every success with his fundraising efforts.

"Isn't it funny how nobody asks to be sponsored to do something useful?" Eric said to Zack. "Like picking up litter or fetching shopping for old ladies. It tends to be something they've always wanted to do, like climbing mountains, cycling around France, or jumping out of a plane."

"I'll sponsor you, Alwyn," Jason said. "If you wear a Jason Mason branded T-shirt."

"Good stuff!" Alwyn replied, punching the palm of his hand with his fist in celebration. "Love it."

"Get out," Eric said to Jason. "I have told you twice that you are not welcome here. You have no business here. You are banned from these premises."

As Jason slowly ambled out, he said to Alwyn: "Don't worry about not being in the Star. No one reads local papers anymore, their circulation has fallen off a cliff. I can get you far more coverage with a single social media post."

After Mason had gone, Carol gave Eric a resigned look that said, 'Sadly he's probably right'.

"Alwyn, I'm giving you a formal verbal warning," Eric said. "If I catch you talking to one of our competitors in the showroom again it will be grounds for dismissal."

"Alright, Hitler," Alwyn protested.

"Do you understand?" Eric said.

"But he's going to sponsor me," Alwyn cried.

Carol attempted to break the tension. "Does anyone want a cup of tea?"

"I would love a protein shake, Carol," Alwyn replied.

Eric held his hand up. "Management does not wait on junior staff. If you want a protein shake you make it yourself."

"Management?" Alwyn queried.

Eric nodded. "Carol is now the branch manager."

Carol looked just as surprised as Alwyn to hear this.

"You report to her and follow her instructions to the letter when I'm not here," Eric said. "And if you don't, you won't only be looking for sponsorship, you'll be looking for another job."

* * *

As he pulled up in Woodland Manor's car park, Eric briefly considered timing the drive down to the pedestrian bridge of the boating lake. Although his Lexus had a kerb weight of over two tonnes due to its cavernous size, modern safety features, hybrid technology, and 4x4 powertrain – more than twice that of Big Ben's MGB – it was also capable of accelerating twice as fast, so their times would not be too dissimilar, even allowing for 2019's road layout being slightly different to 1976's.

Eric ordered a burger from the pub grub menu and nursed a pint of Guinness while he awaited its arrival. Looking around the lounge bar, he marvelled at how little it had changed over the decades. Although the décor was more subtle, the dark wood tables and chairs appeared to be the same ones that Big Ben used. He smiled to himself as he recounted his last encounter with Big Ben and moved to the table he was last sat at with Elvis, by the window that looked out over the entrance.

Although it was now completely dark outside, illuminated bollards – rather than stone flowerpots – allowed Eric to trace the path of the drive down to the gates, and exterior floodlights lit up the area surrounding the entrance. Eric noticed an expensive looking black Jaguar XJ-L crawling out of the car park, and he spotted Seb following behind it on foot, arm raised in a farewell wave to the occupants.

Seb noticed Eric looking out at him and a few moments later he joined him at his table.

"It's bloody cold out there," Seb said.

"They looked important," Eric said.

"They are," Seb said. "Their company will be clearing the woods. But what are you doing here so early? And why are you dressed so smart? I almost didn't recognise you."

"I had to have my picture taken today," Eric said sheepishly.

"What for?"

"Nothing important, just an advertorial piece for the Star – 30 years of Barrington Meek."

"That's an excellent idea," Seb said. "The town centre is getting so homogenised with chain stores that you independents need to remind people that you've got a history in the community. Heritage is hugely important. I'd love to be able to put up some old pictures of this place in the foyer and some of the rooms."

"What's stopping you?"

"There aren't any," Seb sighed. "Or at least there aren't any that I know of."

"Have you tried the library?"

Seb had, unsuccessfully. And even internet searches failed to produce any results.

"I might be able to help you," Eric said. "Tell the kitchen to hold my burger for 20 minutes."

***

When Eric returned, he had a photo album under his arm with the words 'Woodland Manor' printed on the spine. He handed it to Seb, who was still sat at the table.

"These are all from 1976," Eric said, as Seb flicked through the pages. "You might want to have a look at them."

"These are fantastic," Seb enthused. "Where did you get them? The pictures are so clear it's like stepping back in time."

Seb stopped on one page, his hand covered his mouth and tears began to form in his eyes.

"What is it?" Eric asked.

"It's me," Seb sobbed. "There's a picture of me in here, pouring a pint. Look at me, I'm so fucking hot and I didn't even know it. I thought I was fat."

Eric leaned in to see the image. Seb's face was thin, with more sharply defined features, and his immaculately styled long hair cascading around it. Just like it had been when he last saw him in 1976.

"And there's old Mr Reeves, who always spent Saturday afternoons in here," Seb said, pointing to an old man sat at the bar on his regular stool. "Can I have a copy of this?"

"It's not actually my photograph but I'm sure the owner would be happy for you to scan it, or any of the others in the album," Eric replied.

"That's wonderful," Seb said, wiping his eyes. "I'm going to put it as my profile pic as well."

"Could you do something for me?" Eric asked.

"Of course."

"Can I have another couple of cannisters of Block?"

## CHAPTER 16

## SATURDAY 3RD JULY 1976

The MGB's engine was still ticking, indicating it had only recently been parked, when Eric yanked the driver's door open. Big Ben was so confident no one would be stupid enough to steal his car that he never bothered locking it. Not that it would have mattered if he had: Eric still had a key from the last time he stole it. To ensure the operation went as smoothly as it needed to, Eric had removed all the other keys Big Ben kept on the ring, leaving just the one for the MGB's ignition. The engine fired up instantly and Eric slammed it into gear and tore off down the drive.

The MGB roared through Woodland Manor's entrance pillars, down Lôn Heddychlon, pausing briefly at the mercifully clear T-junction where it met Caerleon Road, and headed for the Croesyceiliog bypass which led down to the boating lake. In 2019 it was accessed via a roundabout but in 1976 traffic from Caerleon Road had to queue at a junction and wait for an appropriate opportunity. The driver of the Hillman Imp in front of Eric was clearly in no hurry, as the only car preventing him joining the bypass was still hundreds of yards away. Eric was in a hurry. He swung the MGB onto the opposite side of the road and overtook the Imp, flooring the accelerator pedal to build up speed.

There was a queue of cars waiting to enter the boating lake car park, but Eric mounted the curb and slalomed along the field towards the pedestrian bridge, scattering a group of kids playing football and causing a man with a dog to shake his fist at him. The newly introduced wobble in the MGB's steering suggested the short cut had buckled one or both front wheels, but Eric didn't care. The car had done its job. He abandoned it close to the bridge and sprinted towards the kiosk, ignoring the members of the public shouting that he couldn't park there.

He'd made it. Young Eric and Verity were still in the queue for ice-cream. He slowly approached them. Young Eric looked gauche and awkward next to her, the girl with the sun in her hair.

The young child yelling 'I want to go home!' and his mother's response of 'Don't be dull, we've only just got here' reminded Eric of his mission. He turned away from the couple and scanned the milling crowd.

Just setting foot on the bridge were Little Len and Elvis. They were staring at the MGB, no doubt expecting Big Ben to be at the lake. Patting his jacket pockets to ensure they contained his weapons, Eric marched towards them.

Blocking Little Len's path, he said: "The boating lake is closed to you today."

Little Len glared at Eric in disbelief. No one had ever blocked his way before.

"So just turn around and find some other place to be a twat," Eric said. "And no one will get hurt."

People walking in either direction on the bridge were tutting as they were forced to walk around the group.

"There's only one person who's going to get hurt," Little Len laughed, looking towards Elvis for encouragement.

Elvis was warily staring at Eric who, in response, theatrically patted the bulge in his jacket pocket like he'd seen people do in films when they were packing heat.

Little Len went to walk around Eric but, using his left hand, Eric pushed him back. Even though he was 60, overweight, and unfit, Eric was still physically stronger than Little Len, whose thin pale arms protruding from his T-shirt carried no muscle definition. Why would they? Athletes apart, few people worked out in the '70s. Eric was also almost a foot taller than Little Len. And he had a very determined look on his face.

Little Len looked to Elvis again, expecting him to intervene, but Elvis held back. "Do you know who I am?" Little Len asked Eric.

"Have you forgotten?" Eric replied, with mock concern.

"Listen, you old bastard," Little Len growled. "If you don't get out of my way—"

Eric slapped him hard across the face, causing Little Len to stumble backwards into a group of girls who had stood to watch the drama unfold. They screamed in shock. Little Len's cheek glowed bright red.

"We don't use industrial language like that in a public place," Eric scolded him.

"Kick his head in," Little Len commanded Elvis. "What are you waiting for?"

"Maybe we should go," Elvis said, helping Little Len to his feet by pulling his thin little arms.

"Go?" Little Len was outraged.

"It could be a trap," Elvis said quietly. "It looks like he wants me to react."

"I bloody want you to react," Little Len spat.

"Good decision," Eric said to Elvis, giving him a thumbs-up gesture.

"I'm going to get my dad," wailed Little Len, running towards the MGB.

Elvis glared at Eric, memorising every aspect of him for future reference.

"You'd better go after him," Eric said to him. "The heat tires the little ones out so quickly, don't you find?"

Elvis eventually retreated over the bridge in search of Little Len. He wouldn't be hard to find. His cries for his father were getting increasingly frantic.

As Eric walked back towards the lake, he saw young Eric and Verity sat by the water's edge, eating their ice-creams and laughing. He smiled at them. They had their whole lives ahead of them. Regardless of how long they stayed together, he'd given them the chance that Little Len had taken from him, and tears unexpectedly began to form in his eyes.

But the elation he'd felt at confronting his tormentor and rewriting history proved to be short-lived. He was now engulfed by a crushing, exhausting feeling of grief for the life he'd lost through his own cowardice. The sea of happy, smiling faces surrounding him lowered his spirits even further.

*\*\*\**

By the time he had walked back up to Lôn Heddychlon, Eric was drenched in sweat. He was still wearing the suit he'd chosen for the Cwmbran Evening Star photograph, and while it was perfectly appropriate for a cold December afternoon, he was more than a little overdressed for the hottest day of the century. But he had needed something with easily accessible pockets for his weapons, in case the confrontation with Little Len and Elvis had turned violent.

Eric really wanted a cold lager before he returned to 2019, so he removed Big Ben's wallet from his inside jacket pocket, stashed the notes into his trouser pocket, and flung the wallet into the bushes at the entrance to Woodland Manor.

"Are you here on business?" young Carol asked from behind the reception desk.

Eric smiled at her. "What gave it away?" he replied.

"It's just that the suit—" Carol gestured towards Eric's sweat-stained jacket.

"I know," Eric said. "I was here on business, but now that's sorted I decided to stop in for a cold lager before I go."

Carol pointed to the orange and brown sofa opposite the reception desk. "Why don't you sit here and I'll bring you one out?"

"Why would you do that?"

"It's a bit cooler in the foyer, with the doors open," she replied. "It's very stuffy in the bar with all the smoke and you look like you could do with a sit-down near a breeze."

"That's very kind," Eric said, slumping into the sofa.

"Which lager would you like?" Carol asked, as she stood up.

"Anything will be fine," Eric replied, and closed his eyes. They really did all taste the same.

Carol returned a minute later with the promised pint of lager on a round metal tray. The condensation on the outside of the glass gave it the appearance of a staged image from an advert. Carol placed a branded beermat on the large square armrest of the sofa and carefully handed the glass to Eric. "Are you interested in the tennis?" she said.

"Not really, I know who wins," Eric replied without thinking.

Before she could return to her post or reply, Big Ben stormed into the foyer through the open front door. "What have I told you about leaving the desk unattended?" he snarled at Carol.

"She was very kindly getting me a drink," Eric said.

Big Ben turned to Eric. "I don't pay her to get you or anyone else a drink," he growled. "Are you trying to get her sacked?"

"Look, I'm sorry," Eric said. "There's no harm done."

Big Ben eyed Eric warily. "Are you a resident?"

"No, but—"

Big Ben snatched the pint from the sofa arm, spilling some onto the floor. "Piss off then," he said. "And don't ever show your ugly sweaty face in here again."

Turning to Carol, Big Ben pointed to the lager he'd spilled and snapped at her: "Clean that up."

As Big Ben marched into the lounge bar, Carol said to Eric: "I'm so sorry, he's in a bad mood because his car was stolen earlier this afternoon."

"What a shame," Eric said. "I hope the thief hasn't damaged it."

"You really had better go," she urged him. "Mr Butcher does have a temper."

"I haven't finished my drink yet," Eric said defiantly, following the route Big Ben took into the bar.

"Pint of Harp when you're ready, Seb," Eric said to the young barman as he sat on the empty stool next to Reeves.

Seb looked up startled. No one called him that here. "Do I know you?"

Before Eric could reply, Big Ben stormed up to him. "Are you deaf or just stupid?" he spat in Eric's face. "I said you were banned."

"I know you did, but I unbanned myself," Eric said.

Big Ben grabbed Eric's jacket lapels. "If I have to physically throw you out—"

Eric removed the cannister of Block from his left jacket pocket and sprayed Big Ben in the eyes. He screamed and fell backwards, arms flailing, knocking drinks off the bar.

Seb's mouth dropped open in shock. His wasn't the only one. The other drinkers gawped at the pathetic figure of Big Ben Butcher, writhing on the floor, clawing at his eyes, and wailing like a child.

"I'll have that Harp another time," Eric said to Seb. "I'm not sure I like the ambience in here today."

Carol was stood in the doorway, hands to her head in a fair impression of the subject in Edvard Munch's The Scream. "What's happened to Mr Butcher?" she asked Eric.

"Nothing he didn't deserve," Eric said. "And he certainly doesn't deserve you."

Carol blushed. "Should I call an ambulance?"

"I honestly wouldn't bother," Eric said. "He'll be back to his usual obnoxious self before you know it. Why do you work for someone like that?"

Carol shrugged. "Jobs don't grow on trees around here."

Eric stared at her. "I know this might seem a strange thing to say, but do you trust me?"

Carol stared back at him. "I've only just met you."

Eric held his hand out. "Come with me if you want to live… a different life."

Carol looked confused. "What?"

"Come on Carol," Eric urged. "Don't waste your life working for someone like him. You are capable of so much more."

"You don't know what I'm capable of," she said.

"I honestly do."

"And how do you know my name?" she asked suspiciously.

Eric pointed to her name badge.

"Oh of course," she laughed.

The commotion in the bar was getting louder, and among the crowd gathered around Big Ben were Little Len and Elvis. It was probably best if they didn't spot him. "Are you coming?" he asked Carol as he headed towards the exit. "Because I really should get a move on."

"Where are we going?"

"Somewhere a bit more welcoming," Eric replied. "I'd still like a drink."

"Have you got a car?" Carol asked.

Eric shook his head. He did have, earlier.

"Hang on, I'll see if Sandra will lend me her Mini."

She dashed inside and after a few moments she returned brandishing a set of keys that fitted an ancient looking pale blue Mini. "She's always borrowing my makeup," Carol explained.

*** 

As they emerged through Woodland Manor's entrance, Carol asked again: "Where are we going?"

"What about the Old Oak out the lanes?" Eric suggested.

"Are you from around here?" Carol asked.

Eric nodded. "Do you want me to drive?"

"No thanks," Carol said. "I'm more than capable of finding my way there."

With both front windows wound down, the drive through the lanes towards the rural pub was exhilarating, though the buffeting wind made conversation impossible. They pulled into the small car park and Eric was delighted to see just a handful of other vehicles dotted around.

They took their drinks outside and carefully sat opposite each other on one of the notoriously unstable picnic-style wooden tables.

"Fancy wanting to be stuck inside a dark old pub on a day like this," Carol said, gesturing towards the pub's open door, through which they could see drinkers sat on stools at the bar.

"Indeed," Eric agreed, taking a large gulp of his drink.

"Well?" Carol said. "What's this all about then? Do you want to tell me why you've dragged me out here and almost certainly cost me my job?"

"You can do so much better," Eric said.

"Like what?" she said, removing her glasses to wipe the lens.

Eric gazed at Carol's youthful face. He'd never noticed how captivating her eyes were, as they were always hidden behind frames, and her complexion was so smooth. Why hadn't he spotted how attractive she was when she first started working for him in the early '90s?

"That's nothing then, is it?" she said.

"I'm sorry, I was distracted," Eric said. "I was looking at your face."

"I know, I've got a spot coming," Carol said, ferreting in her handbag for a compact mirror. "It sticks out like a sore thumb. Who gets spots at 26?"

"Sandwiches," Eric suddenly said.

"What?"

"That's what you should do."

Carol stared at Eric.

"I'm serious," he said, removing his jacket and laying it on the bench seat alongside him. "If you go into any corner shop around here for something to eat all they'll have is things like pies and pasties. If you supply them with pre-made sandwiches they'll fly out of the chillers."

Carol laughed. "Sandwiches?"

"Yes," Eric continued. "They'll cost you pennies to make and both you and the shopkeeper will make a huge margin."

"No one buys sandwiches," Carol laughed again.

"Only because no one sells them," Eric replied. "If you make them, they will come."

"Who will?"

"Customers!" he said. "Honestly, you make excellent sandwiches—"

"How do you know?" she interrupted.

"I can just tell," Eric said. "Start with simple combinations, like cheese and onion and ham and tomato, and then go on to introduce more exotic varieties like salmon and cucumber, prawn mayonnaise, and, er, spicy chicken and avocado."

"What's avocado?"

"It's a fruit, I think," Eric stuttered. "It doesn't matter. Sandwiches are going to be big business. I heard somewhere that people in the UK will be buying 20 million pre-packed sandwiches every day by 2019."

"How would anyone possibly know that?"

"Well..."

Carol shook her head. "I think you've had too much sun today. And where would I get the money to start a business?"

Slightly frustrated, Eric downed his pint. "I'm popping to the gents," he said, rising from the table.

There was no internal gents' toilet in the Old Oak in 1976, and Eric walked around the outside of the building to the small extension. It was just as rustic as he remembered it. He stood at the aluminium trough and pondered on the events of the past few hours. It was certainly a day to remember, even though he'd be the only one doing the remembering once he returned to 2019.

Eric's thoughts were suddenly interrupted by his iPhone alarm going off. It was the default tone, which resembled the emergency siren on a World War II submarine, and the sound really carried in the tranquil country air. Shit. He'd left it in his jacket pocket. He finished his business as quickly as he could and rushed out to the table where Carol was sitting. She was holding his iPhone.

"What's this?" she cried.

"It's an alarm clock," he said. That was true. He had set it to remind himself to call his financial advisor to discuss the property chain. He pressed the home button and turned the alarm off.

One of the drinkers from inside came outside. "Everything alright?"

"Yes, it's just my alarm clock," Eric said, snatching the iPhone from Carol and shoving it in his trouser pocket.

"Alarm clock? It sounded like a bloody bomb was going off," the drinker said. "What do you need an alarm clock for on a Saturday afternoon?"

Eric laughed. "It's Monday where I come from."

The man stared at Eric. "What are you on about?"

"I'm so sorry to have disturbed you," Eric said, taking a five-pound note from his trouser pocket and offering it to the drinker. "Please buy a few drinks for you and your friends."

Flabbergasted, the drinker agreed to do just that.

"Are you bonkers?" Carol said to Eric. "That's enough for about 20 pints."

"It's only money, right?" Eric shrugged. And it wasn't even his, it was Big Ben's.

"Let me see that alarm clock of yours," Carol said.

"Why?"

"Because it doesn't look like any alarm clock I've ever seen before," she said.

"I can't."

"If you don't, I'll go in there and tell them it's a bomb," she warned.

"Please don't do that."

"Let me see it then."

"Okay but if I do, you've got to promise not to freak out," Eric said.

She assured him she wouldn't.

Eric removed the phone from his pocket and pressed the home button. The jet-black screen displayed the time in crisp, white numerals.

"That's amazing," Carol said. "How come the numbers are so smooth, and how come they're white?"

While Eric was holding the phone, Carol pressed the home button and the screen now had 20 little graphics, one of which was an analogue clock with a digitised second hand slowly moving around its face.

"What's happened now?" Carol squealed.

"It's basically a computer," Eric said, deciding it was less hassle to tell her the truth than to make something up. "And all these little pictures are programs that run on it."

"What programs?"

Eric took the phone back and gave her a quick guided tour of his most-used apps: "This one's a calculator, this one's for appointments, this one's an address book, this one's a dictionary and thesaurus, this one's a notebook, this one's a map with satellite navigation, this one's my bank account, this one's a news channel…"

Carol reached across and prodded the phone icon and the screen changed to a numeric keypad.

"Don't tell me it's a phone as well."

"It is."

"How gullible do you think I am?" she cried. "Where does it plug in?"

"Please, lower your voice," Eric urged. "It doesn't need to be plugged in."

"Let me see you make a phone call then," she challenged him.

"It won't work," Eric said. "There's no service in this... area."

"How convenient!"

Eric inputted the number for the Barrington Meek showroom and the message 'You must disable Airplane Mode to make a call' appeared. "See?" he said.

She looked sceptical.

Eric prodded the camera icon and the screen immediately changed to a view of the table they were sat at. "This works though," he said, framing Carol's face in the screen and pressing the white button.

The iPhone clicked like a real camera and a small thumbnail of Carol's face appeared in the lower left corner of the screen. Eric enlarged it and showed it to Carol.

"Fuck off!" she shrieked.

Eric smirked. He had never heard her use that word before. He returned to the camera screen and slid the menu to video, and the white button changed colour and became red. "What's your favourite song, Carol?"

She couldn't think.

"Okay, what's number one in the charts?"

She thought for a few seconds. "It's the Real Thing, with 'You To Me Are Everything'."

"How does it go? Can you sing it for me?"

"I can't sing!" she protested.

"Just hum it then," Eric encouraged, framing her in the screen again.

Although clearly embarrassed, she hummed the first line of the chorus.

"That's fine," Eric said, and played it back to her.

Carol was speechless.

Eric played it again. He then switched the camera into selfie mode, holding the phone at arm's length and leaned his head into hers so they could both see themselves on the screen. "Where are we, Carol?" he asked.

"The Old Oak," she replied, pointing towards the building behind them.

"And are you having fun?"

"I'm having a day I'll never forget," she laughed.

Eric cleared the screen and pressed the music icon. "It's also got stored on it every song ever recorded by The Beatles, The Kinks, Kate Bush…"

"Who?"

Eric went into his song library and played 'Wuthering Heights'.

Intrigued at first, a look of horror came over her face as the piano intro gave way to the vocal. "What the hell is that?" she recoiled from the device.

Eric laughed. Carol probably wasn't ready for Kate Bush yet, not on top of everything else she'd just seen. Quite a few people weren't ready for her in 1978, after all. He put the phone back in his jacket pocket. "Sorry, I got carried away there," he said. "It must be the salesman in me."

"How does it work?" Carol asked.

"I honestly don't know," Eric said. "I don't even know how electricity works. I'm pretty sure microprocessors are involved but don't ask me to explain what they do."

"How have you got it?" she asked in awe.

Eric stared at her. In for a penny, in for a pound. "Everyone has them where I come from," he said.

"And where's that, Futureland?"

"Yes, in a way," he said slowly. "I'm from 2019, Carol."

"Fuck off!" she said again. "You're pulling my leg."

"I'm honestly not."

A look of genuine fear flashed across Carol's face. She stood up.

"Please, Carol, sit down," Eric said. "You promised me you wouldn't freak out."

"I said I wouldn't freak out if you showed me your alarm clock," Carol replied. "This is a bit bloody different."

"I'm sorry," Eric said. "I obviously wouldn't have said anything by choice—"

"You're not from the future," Carol said, shaking her head.

"I am, and in a way that alarm was to remind me that it's time to return."

"You're going back?"

"I have to."

"Are you going to take me with you?"

"Would you like me to?"

"Yes!"

"I'm really sorry but I can't do that."

The joy instantly left Carol's face. "Why?"

"Because you need to wear a special suit, and I've only got one."

"Could I fit in it as well?"

"Unfortunately not."

"Maybe you should stay here then?"

Eric considered that scenario. It could work, if he prepared for it, though living in 1976 would mean having to forgo so many of the things that made Eric's life bearable. Imagine having to physically go to a library and search through dusty old books if you needed to look something up. And how would he survive if the supermarket didn't bring his shopping to him? "I'm really sorry, I do have to go," he said.

"But you'll come back for me?"

"I could," Eric conceded. "But if I did, you won't be here. It would be a different you, who I'd have to get to know all over again."

"That's fine," she said. "Let's do that."

"But even if I say I'll do it, you will never know if I do," Eric said.

"How bloody convenient," she said, folding her arms and sighing.

After a pause, Eric said: "Carol, can you drive me back to Woodland Manor, please?"

"Is that where your spaceship is?" she said. "What if I don't want to? Has your thing got a laser gun you can threaten me with?"

"If you don't want to then I'll have to offer one of those drunkards in there a few quid to take me, but they're all so pissed that we'll probably crash in the lanes and burn to death in the wreckage."

Huffing heavily, Carol got up from the table and headed towards the Mini. "If I do this, you've got to tell me something about the future," she said.

Eric thought for a moment. "We eat a lot of sandwiches."

## CHAPTER 17

### MONDAY 9th DECEMBER 2019

As Eric unzipped himself from the suit, he reflected on his trip. He'd achieved his mission objective: he'd stopped Little Len humiliating his younger self and stealing Verity. Or at least he had stopped him doing it at the boating lake on that day. Maybe he would go on and do it somewhere else instead, on a different day. Maybe he'd even made things worse for young Eric. With no way of returning to that world, he'd never know. Just as he wouldn't know if young Carol chose the life of a sandwich entrepreneur.

Maybe his actions had also made young Carol's life worse too. Big Ben would not have been happy with her abandoning reception to spend the afternoon with the man who attacked him. She had been delightful company, and she was genuinely upset when they said goodbye – but the afternoon they shared now only existed for him. It all seemed rather pointless. Maybe Freeman had the right idea after all: go back, take pictures, come home again.

Interrupting Eric's melancholy mood, the screen of his fitness watch exploded with fireworks. For the first time since he'd been wearing the device, he'd reached his steps target for the day. That was something to celebrate at least. As the digital fireworks ended, the time returned to the display: just after ten. There was still time for a drink. He'd decide later whether it was to unwind, drown his sorrows, or celebrate his athletic achievement.

"Christ, what's happened to you?" Seb looked up from his phone as Eric entered the almost empty lounge bar. "Have you been on a tanning bed or something?"

Eric felt his face. It was tingling from prolonged exposure to 1976 sun at the boating lake and the Old Oak. "Just give me a large Pernodka," Eric said as he slumped into a bar stool.

Seb slid the large glass across the bar to Eric. "One large Pernod and vodka, with a single cube of ice, as you like it."

A small smile expressed Eric's thanks. He looked around the bar at his fellow customers. A young couple were arguing about something in hushed voices, an elderly couple sat in silence, and a table of four contractors were discussing football. Eric was the only one here alone.

"Something up?" Seb said. "You were full of beans this afternoon."

"A lot can happen in six hours," Eric said, the alcohol burning his lips.

"Have you been drinking?"

"I've had a couple."

"I can tell."

"Will you join me?"

"Is it a special occasion?"

Eric considered the question. "Not really," he replied.

"I only drink on special occasions," Seb said. "So no, thanks."

Eric looked into his glass. "Have you ever thought everything is just a pointless waste of time?"

"Cheer up, Eeyore!" Seb said, punching Eric's arm surprisingly hard. "You've got a top of the range car—"

"It's six years old."

"You run your own business—"

"We turnover less now than we did five years ago."

"You're still doing better than most people," Seb said, and pointing to the television in the bar that was showing the news with the sound turned down, he added: "You could be him, for instance."

Eric glanced in the direction of the flat screen television, which was ridiculously thin compared to its 1976 counterpart, and offered more than twice the screen area. Footage of Labour Party leader Jeremy Corbyn being jostled by press photographers and cameramen was accompanied by a scrolling headline which explained that with just two days to go until the general election, Labour's Shadow Health Secretary Jonathan Ashworth had been forced to apologise and claim – not wholly convincingly – that he had been 'just joshing' when secretly recorded comments he'd made about the party's chances had been leaked.

Ashworth had said he couldn't see the party winning the election, their prospects were 'dire' and 'abysmal', and that voters 'couldn't stand' Mr Corbyn.

Eric had weightier worries than politics. "Have you ever chickened out of doing the right thing because you were a coward?" he asked Seb.

"Who hasn't?" Seb replied.

"You'd want to put it right if you could, wouldn't you?"

Seb continued watching the television. "Ashworth's being slaughtered for this, but the sad thing is he's probably right."

"But what if putting things right didn't actually put things right? Would you do the right thing even if you knew it wouldn't fix the wrong thing?"

"What are you going on about?" Seb said, backing away from Eric. "If you'll excuse me, I'd rather not be a guest at your pity party."

A few minutes later Eric held his empty glass up in front of him, and Seb put down his phone and brought him another. Neither man spoke. Nor did they when Eric requested a third. When Eric asked for a fourth, Seb shook his head.

"Why not?" Eric said.

"Because the bar's closed, everyone else is going home, and you've clearly had enough," Seb said forcefully. "And you'd better not be driving because I will call the police if I see you get in that car."

"Let me have a room here then," Eric said, taking his wallet from his jacket.

"Okay," Seb replied. "But what's going on with you?"

"My life hasn't turned out the way I wanted it to," Eric said.

"Nobody's does," Seb replied, turning his attention back to his phone.

"Says the owner of Cwmbran's most prestigious hotel and fine dining restaurant…"

"If you saw the size of my mortgage payments you'd shit your pants," Seb replied.

"But you're selling the woods, so you won't have a mortgage at all for much longer."

"Keep your bloody voice down," Seb hissed.

"Is it a secret?" Eric could feel the lounge starting to spin. "I think I drunk those last Pernodkas too fast."

"What's brought this on? Is it Maudlin Monday or something?"

"I should have protected my girlfriend, but I didn't."

"You've got a girlfriend?" Seb looked up from his phone. "What happened? Did someone attack her? Did they attack you as well? Is that why you wanted those cans of Block?"

"Not now, a long time ago, when I was 16."

"Why do you look back so much?" Seb asked. "That's not the direction you're going in."

"That's a good one," Eric said. "Do you subscribe to Motivational Poster Monthly by any chance?"

"Say that again without slurring," Seb challenged him.

"You can be so glib at times," Eric moaned.

"And you can be such a drama queen," Seb replied, pouring himself a tomato juice and adding a generous splash of Worcestershire sauce. "I'm sure she's forgiven you now."

Eric stared at Seb. "Do you think so?"

"You were a teenager. All teenagers are twats. Christ, if people knew about some of the things I got up to…"

"But this is different, she ended up with the boy I should have protected her from," Eric said, noticing the slurring himself. "And she did this to protect me, apparently. How do you think that makes me feel?"

Seb wrinkled his nose and added another splash of Worcestershire sauce to his drink. "Like dancing?"

"And the two of them just vanished. Never heard of again."

"Perhaps they ran off to Gretna Green and got married. Do people still do that?"

"She was too young to get married, and he was totally unsuitable for her."

"That was in the opinion of your hormone-addled and far from impartial teenage brain," Seb argued. "Perhaps she grew to like him."

"He was horrible."

"Perhaps she was as well," Seb said, savouring the now spicier kick of his tomato juice.

Eric's eyebrows lifted. "She absolutely was not."

"If it bothers you that much, why don't you find her and apologise?"

"I wouldn't know how."

Seb held up his phone and said a little impatiently: "You've got the real-life 'Hitchhiker's Guide to the Galaxy' in your pocket. You carry the greatest resource humanity has ever known literally – and yes, that's literally, not figuratively – around with your car keys. You can reach over half the population of the world with it. I'm sure if you asked around, you'd find someone somewhere who knows something."

"I don't know anyone," Eric sighed.

"Who was this girlfriend anyway? She must have been quite something if you're still brooding over her."

"Verity," Eric said. "She worked here the same time as me."

Seb shook his head. "Doesn't ring a bell."

"She worked behind the bar in the ballroom on Saturday nights," Eric explained. "Even though she was only 15. She was beautiful but she was also clever, and funny, and…"

Seb poured himself another tomato juice. "I can't picture her – all the young barmaids looked the same to me, and none of them lasted long. Understandable really, they weren't the best working conditions for young girls."

"She's the one who went off with Little Len," Eric said quietly.

"Oh her!" Seb said. "To be honest, I still can't picture her, but I remember them running off together. It caused quite a stir at the time. When we were talking about Little Len the other day, you never mentioned he was your love rival."

Eric shook his head. "It wasn't love."

"It might have been," Seb said, "if they never came back. Mind you, perhaps he was too afraid to face Big Ben after stealing his MGB. He loved that car. He was apoplectic when he found out Little Len had taken it."

"He stole his father's car? In front of him?"

"Big Ben wasn't here. He was upstairs, hosting a high stakes poker game. Did you ever have to work one?"

"I don't know anything about them."

"He would hold one a couple of times a year in the bridal suite," Seb explained. "Imagine half a dozen or so lairy middle-aged mates of his all crammed into the one room, smoking, drinking, and acting like they were the tits."

"They did that in the bridal suite?"

"They took the bed out first, obviously, to make way for the table, and they kept playing until there was a winner, and it was usually Big Ben. One or two suspected Elvis helped him cheat but no one dared say anything. The games went on for hours and they were a nightmare for the staff."

"I can imagine."

"The table had to have a dealer – which was one of us – and there was someone else on drinks duty. It was a constant cycle of writing down orders, going to the bar to collect the drinks, and then bringing them up on a tray. It was bad enough for us guys, having to listen to all their bullshit, but it was far worse for the girls."

"Please spare me the details," Eric said. "It sounds horrendous. And illegal. Did anyone report them to the police?"

Seb shrugged: "I think half the players were police…"

Eric cautiously stood up. "It's probably best I called it a night if the bar is closed."

"It is. How come you're so hammered tonight?"

"I had a few pints sat out in the sun," Eric said, recalling his afternoon at the Old Oak with Carol.

"What are you on about?" Seb said. "It's been pissing down all day."

The Pernodkas had really caught up with Eric now, and he was slurring his words as he unsteadily made his way towards the reception desk: "You'd think they would have come back at some point though, wouldn't you?"

"Who?"

"Little Len and Verity."

Seb retrieved a room key from behind the desk and said impatiently: "Perhaps they did. Who knows? It was all a long time ago and no one cares now."

"You'd think that, wouldn't you?" Eric said.

Seb handed Eric the key. "Room number two, it's the closest one to the top of the stairs," he said, before turning his attention back to his phone.

Eric removed his own phone from his pocket and pressed the home button. Nothing happened. "Battery's dead," he said. "I don't suppose you have a spare charger lead I could borrow?"

Seb looked disdainfully at Eric's iPhone 5. "Probably not for that antique," he said.

"It uses the same lead as the newer phones," Eric said defensively.

"In that case you can borrow this one," Seb said, yanking one from a socket behind the desk and handing it to him. "Do you want an alarm call in the morning?"

Eric held up his phone. "No thanks," he said. "I've got one on here."

## CHAPTER 18

### TUESDAY 10th DECEMBER 2019

It wasn't his phone that woke Eric, it was the thumping on the door. He opened his eyes and blinked as he took in the unfamiliar surroundings. There was a small desk and chair, which had his jacket slung across it, a built-in wardrobe, and a bedside cabinet with a plastic tray. This had once held tea bags, instant coffee sachets, pods of UHT milk, and individually wrapped biscuits. But they were now scattered across the floor, along with Eric's clothes.

The thumping came again. "Housekeeping!" an unfamiliar female voice said.

"Ten minutes," Eric shouted back, aggravating the headache he just realised he had.

"No ten minutes," the voice countered. "You check out."

Eric's fitness watch informed him it was almost noon. Why hadn't his alarm gone off? Why hadn't anyone woken him? He looked around for his phone. He got to his feet, stumbled into the en suite and ran the tap to irrigate the inside of his mouth. Then he realised his phone was in the sink. He quickly snatched it up and tried to dry it with the fluffy white towel hanging from the chrome rail. He pressed the home button, but nothing happened.

Eric opened his room door and addressed the lady waiting patiently outside, her trolly piled with stacks of new consumables: "I am so sorry, I overslept. I will be out of your way as soon as I can."

He scrambled into his creased clothes, threw his jacket over his shoulders to make himself marginally more presentable, and as he left the room he pulled a five-pound note from his wallet and offered it to the lady.

"What is this?" she asked, inspecting the large blue and white piece of paper which featured a young Queen Elizabeth II and had last been legal tender several decades ago.

His face burning, both with embarrassment and yesterday's sun, Eric ferreted around in his wallet for a contemporary replacement. "I'm so sorry," he said, accepting the 1976 note back. "But I haven't got another one. No one carries cash anymore, do they?"

Seb was behind the reception desk when Eric arrived downstairs. "Good morning, sir, did you sleep well?" he asked obsequiously. "Apologies for our staff inconsiderately disturbing your slumbers, but we do have another guest booked into that room tonight."

"I'm so sorry," Eric said. "Being in the sun for so long must have tired me out."

"There was no sun yesterday, you cretin. Might excessive consumption of Pernodka have contributed to your coma-like state?"

"It wouldn't have helped," Eric conceded, reaching inside his jacket for his wallet. "How much do I owe you for the room?"

"The room – and the drinks you didn't pay for – are on the house," Seb said.

"Oh come on," Eric began to protest.

"No, it's fine," Seb replied, retrieving the Woodland Manor photo album from below the desk and handing it to Eric. "I've taken a few scans from the images in here so let's call it quits, shall we?"

***

Carol was alone in the showroom when Eric eventually arrived at work. He'd dashed home first, to shower and change, but even with shampooed hair and fresh clothes he still felt a little unclean. He must have looked it too, as Carol frowned in distaste as he approached her desk.

"Heavy night?" Carol said.

"Not especially," he replied.

"Do you think I was born yesterday? I can still smell the alcohol on you."

Eric changed the subject. "Where's Alwyn?"

"Out to lunch," Carol replied. "With his friend Jason Mason. They've become very chummy."

Eric shrugged, casually tossed the folders he was carrying onto his desk and slumped into his chair. It was hard to reconcile this Carol with the one he was with yesterday. Was it only yesterday? It felt like weeks ago. And for her it would have been a lifetime. The other her, that is. The bubbly Carol of 1976.

"What's that?" Carol asked, pointing to the Woodland Manor photo album.

"Some old photos," Eric said. "They were taken by Mr Freeman, and I was showing them to the bloke who owns Woodland Manor."

"Can I see?"

"Sure," he said, handing her the album. "You will probably recognise some of the people as they were taken in July 1976, when you were on reception."

All colour drained from Carol's face. "How do you know that?"

"You must have told me," Eric replied.

A slight tremble had entered Carol's voice. "I don't think I did."

"You must have done," Eric said. "How else would I have known?"

Seemingly satisfied with his explanation, Carol skimmed through the pages of the album. She didn't pause for more than a couple of seconds on any of them.

"Bring back any memories?" Eric asked.

"Not really," Carol replied, slamming the back cover closed. "I wasn't there long."

Well, you lasted longer than me, Eric thought. Should he mention that he worked there as well, and at the same time as her? She clearly did not remember him, which was understandable, as he hadn't remembered her, but maybe she remembered Verity?

"Do you recall a girl called Verity who worked behind the bar on weekends around the time these photos were taken?" Eric asked, as casually as he could.

Before she could answer, the showroom door burst open and in crashed Alwyn and Jason Mason. They were laughing and talking loudly in the style of men celebrating a win on the horses. They appeared surprised to see Eric.

Mason was the first to react. "What's this? In the office again, Eric? Anyone would think you worked here," he sniggered.

"Ring the police, Carol," Eric said.

Mason snorted with laughter. "The police!"

Alwyn put an arm on Eric's shoulder. "Overreacting, much?"

"I never overreact," Eric replied. "And in unrelated news, your employment is terminated."

"What?" Alwyn removed his arm and glared at Eric.

"Seriously Carol, ring the police," Eric said.

Carol picked up her phone dubiously. "What shall I say?"

"Tell them we've got a trespasser causing trouble in the showroom."

"Wouldn't I be better off ringing the town centre security team?" she asked. "They could have someone here within minutes."

"If private security attend, then Mr Mason won't end up with a criminal record," Eric replied. "Tell the officer it's a Code One."

"Criminal record?" Mason laughed again.

"Is this straight up?" Alwyn said, a slight hint of anxiety in his voice. "I'm not really sacked, am I?"

"You absolutely are," Eric confirmed. "I refer you to our conversation of yesterday afternoon when I warned you that bringing a competitor into the premises would be grounds for dismissal. You will receive a formal letter of termination within the next few days."

Alwyn went to grab his laptop, but Eric blocked his way. "The laptop stays," Eric said. "It is company property."

"But it's got all my personal files on it," Alwyn protested.

"Don't worry, I'll wipe them before we pass it on to your successor," Eric said.

Alwyn's face reddened with anger. He was, as rugby players say, a big unit. He could easily throw Eric across the showroom without breaking sweat. "Let me copy my files," he demanded. "Or I'll—"

Eric continued to block his way. "Or you'll what? Assault me? You could do that, but only if you plan to retire early, because you'll never find paid employment again."

"I just want my files," Alwyn said, struggling to contain his fury. "I need my files."

"Let him copy his files," Mason urged Eric.

Eric removed a Barrington Meek-branded USB flash drive from his desk drawer and jumped into the chair at Alwyn's desk. He moved the laptop's mouse to disengage the screensaver, popped the flash drive into an empty USB slot, and clicked on the file explorer icon. He double-clicked it and the laptop's folders filled the screen. "Which are your files, Alwyn?" Eric asked.

"You don't know which ones are mine," Alwyn said.

"That's why I'm asking you," Eric replied patiently. "Tell me which ones are yours and I will copy them to this drive now and you can take them away with you. I'll even let you keep the USB drive, as a gesture of goodwill."

Alwyn's breathing became noticeably louder, but he said nothing.

"You can't mean this one, can you?" Eric said in a loud voice, pointing to the folder named 'Rentals'. "Because that holds all the details of the properties we manage, including the contact details of the landlord and the tenant. You can't mean that one, can you? That can't possibly be yours, can it?"

Alwyn protested: "I'd need to go through the whole thing."

"Don't worry, I'll do that," Eric said. "And if I find anything that's not work-related I will either email it to you or post it to you on a USB drive along with your P45 and the letter confirming your dismissal."

"I've only just changed my car," Alwyn wailed. "How am I going to make the payments?"

Eric shrugged. "I imagine you have a cooling off period, but I hope you didn't put down too much of a deposit."

Mason grabbed Alwyn's arm. "Come on," he said. "We're going to the Citizen's Advice Bureau."

"That's a good idea, they might be able to help you with the car finance," Eric called after them. "But if it's about your job then you'll be wasting your time and theirs."

"You'll be sorry," Alwyn said to Eric.

As Mason led him away, Alwyn kicked the showroom rubber plant. Its seven-foot stalk, which brushed the suspended ceiling tiles, flew out of its blue ceramic pot, scattering soil across the carpet.

"He never liked this plant," Eric said, carefully returning it to its home. "I hope he hasn't cracked the pot."

Carol stared at Eric in disbelief. "What's happened to you?" she said.

"What do you mean?" Eric replied, returning to Alwyn's laptop once the plant was restored to its rightful place by the door.

"You've just sacked Alwyn," Carol said. "You know, the bloke who manages all the rentals, which bring in most of our income. I mean, I know he's a twat and everything but was that a wise move?"

Eric swivelled in Alwyn's chair to face her. "He doesn't do anything you can't do," he said. "Which is hardly surprising because you taught him how to do it. Give the temp agency a call and get someone in to cover. You can show them the ropes. We'll be fine. And can you change the passwords on every machine and our log-in details for the site?"

After she finished her call and created new passwords, Carol said, "Do you fancy a coffee?"

"Didn't I forbid you from making other people beverages?"

Carol laughed. "You did, but you're not really other people, are you?"

"I'll make you one, Carol," Eric said. "And we can have a staff meeting."

Carol smiled in gratitude but showed no enthusiasm for the muddy brown liquid Eric presented her with.

"You did say no sugar, didn't you?" Eric said.

"I didn't say no milk though," she replied. "Or no coffee."

"Shall I have another try?"

"It's fine," Carol said. "It's the thought that counts."

They sipped their coffees in silence for a few moments, before Eric asked: "What did you want to be when you were younger?"

"When I was a little girl? I don't know, probably a princess, married to a handsome prince, and living in a palace with lots of children."

"What about when you were a bit older and had more realistic expectations? What did you want to do when you left school?"

"I never really thought about it," she said. "I just found a job."

"Did you consider further education?"

"Back in the '60s, most girls like me didn't go to college or universities," Carol almost snorted. "Not around here, anyway. They just got jobs to tide them over until they got married and had kids. Tragic really, isn't it?"

"It is," Eric agreed, "if it wasn't what you wanted."

"We didn't really have a choice."

"Did you ever fancy running your own business?"

Carol frowned.

"Why are you pulling that face? You are more than capable of running a business. Let's be honest, you run this one."

"I didn't have the confidence when I was young – nor the money."

She had seemed pretty confident to Eric. "What if money hadn't been a problem?"

"I don't know," she said. "I didn't have any ambition or sense of direction either. I wasn't driven, not like you with your successful business and your posh house."

Eric sheepishly looked down into his coffee. He'd only ever been driven by a desire to escape from living and working with his father. He would never have been able to take over this business without the kindness, generosity, and financial help of its previous owner – who turned out to be a bit of a dick, admittedly – and he had his father's estate to thank for contributing towards the house.

"What about now?"

"Now?" she cried. "I've left it a bit bloody late now, don't you think?"

"What if I was to make you a partner in Barrington Meek?"

Carol carefully placed her still full cup down on her desk. "Are you joking?"

"Why would I be joking? I just said that you already run the place."

Carol welled up. "That would be amazing."

"What would you like us to do different?"

She stood up. "This calls for another coffee," she said. "And a proper one this time, no offence."

As she went off into the kitchen area, Eric's thoughts turned to how he could help the younger Carol. Or at least 'a' younger Carol. He'd already given one the idea for a sandwich business, but it hadn't been particularly well received. The concept sounded too ridiculous. But maybe a business based on something familiar would be taken more seriously. Particularly if he was also able to offer direction, a certain amount of mentoring, and seed capital.

"It's like you were saying the other day, about if buying a house could be as easy as buying a car," Carol said, placing a coffee in front of Eric. "That's the one I want, this is my part exchange, just tell me how much extra I need to pay every month."

"The new builds already do something like that," Eric said.

"And look how popular it is with customers," Carol said. "I'm sure the part exchange option is why the new estates fill up so quickly. It can't be down to the quality of construction or the size of the gardens."

"It's a nice idea but it's too ambitious for an independent," Eric said. "Unless we had access to an unlimited line of credit. And if we did, we could probably get a better return by investing it in other areas."

"But we could offer the next best thing," she said. "A bespoke service."

"We can't build houses—"

"We don't need to," Carol stopped him. "The houses are already there. We just need to tap into people's wish lists."

"Their wish lists?"

"Buyers could come to us with a comprehensive list of requirements, such as number of bedrooms, size of garden, location, price range etc and we actively go out and source that house – even if it's not for sale."

"Approach people who haven't got their properties on the market?"

"Exactly," Carol said. "Unless the buyer is after something unique, I'm sure we could find several matches for most people. If we approach the targets, offering them a small premium over market value, they'd probably sell up, especially if we—"

"Do the same for them!" Eric finished her sentence. "Find them their ideal home."

Carol beamed. "And we could manage every aspect of the move for them – like we are doing now for the Freemans, and like car dealers do for the Alwyns of the world."

"I love it, Carol," Eric said. "I want you to write this up as a proposal, explaining every aspect of each step so that a complete beginner could understand what's involved. Also, if someone was starting an estate agent for the first time, outline everything they would need to do – and write it in terms someone unfamiliar to the industry would grasp."

"Like a franchise?"

"Exactly like a franchise," Eric confirmed.

"You'd be in a better position to do that than me," she protested.

"I'll give it a read through when it's done," Eric replied. "And fill in any blanks. I've got a few other things I need to do first though."

"Are you asking me to do all this while I'm also running the branch and training up Alwyn's replacement?"

Eric grabbed her hand and gently squeezed it. "Isn't it amazing what you can do with a sense of direction?"

## CHAPTER 19

### WEDNESDAY 11th DECEMBER 2019

Tom, the sales assistant in the phone shop, had been extremely helpful with the iPhone upgrade, patiently transferring all of Eric's files from his 5 to his new XS Max despite there being a queue of other customers. The screen was huge compared to his previous model, which Eric's ageing eyes appreciated, and the camera quality was far better than he expected – he could dispense with his digital camera when taking shots for the agency now. And by choosing the top of the range 256 GB model, Eric would even be able to make video tours of his properties.

Tom was also quite helpful in suggesting ways Eric could use his phone to trace an old friend. Using his own handset, Tom started by typing a name into Facebook's search bar. "There are over two billion people on Facebook," Tom said. "If they are on here, you will be able to get in touch with them by sending them a friend request."

"What if they are not on Facebook?" Eric said.

Tom gave Eric a pitying look, suggesting that anyone not on Facebook wouldn't be worth looking up.

"And the person I am looking for is quite old," Eric added. "I haven't seen them for over 40 years."

"You could try uploading an image to Google and doing a reverse image search," Tom suggested. "And if that doesn't work, and the only picture you have of him is old, you could try ageing it in an app first and then trying."

With the transaction complete, and the tuts and sighs from other customers getting louder, Eric decided he should take up no more of Tom's time and he left the shop – but not before asking for a business card with his contact details on. Even though the town centre was busy – it was December, after all – footfall appeared to be down on previous years, despite being boosted by activists of all political persuasions handing out party literature for the following day's general election.

The first call Eric received on his new phone came from the removal company Carol had arranged for the Freemans' house. A team of four were outside the premises in a 7.5 tonne box van and were unloading cardboard boxes for packing the couple's belongings into, room by room.

After Eric let them in – and warned them that the garage and its contents were to be left intact and the access doors to remain locked – he confirmed with Carol that there was someone at the house in Brookvale available to receive all the boxes. There was. Of course there was – Carol had arranged it. Everything was under control. And it really was. The equity from the sale of his house would keep the business going and, with Carol running it, Barrington Meek would surely go on to thrive in the future. And he was going full circle, living in a house a literal stone's throw away from where his journey started in Lôn Heddychlon. And not just any old house, a house with a time machine in the garage.

He burst out laughing at the thought, causing two of the removal men to give him quizzical looks. "Sorry," he said. "I was just thinking about something ridiculous."

It was so ridiculous he wasn't sure what he was going to do with it. He had decided that when Carol had completed her 'Beginner's Guide to Running an Estate Agency' document, he would take it back to 1976 and give it to the younger version of her, with enough capital for her to get started, but he had no other plans beyond that. He could afford to take his time and think of a creative use for the device. Surely he could come up with something more imaginative than Freeman's photography excursions?

Or could he? He typed '1976 photographs Cwmbran' into Google and flicked through the results on his new phone. The bigger screen allowed him to see that the quality of the top results was poor, certainly compared to the shots that Freeman had taken, and the majority of them were black and white rather than vivid full colour. Perhaps he could publish the images in photo books, or have them made into jigsaws?

But why restrict himself to still images when he could go back with a video camera – or even just his phone – and make period movies, not just of Cwmbran but also Newport, Cardiff, and Swansea, and the south Wales coastal resorts such as Barry, Porthcawl, and Tenby? And why stay in Wales? Why not go to London? Or Berlin? Or New York? Or Tokyo?

Eric decided to leave the removal men to it and go for a spot of lunch at Woodland Manor while he weighed up the possibilities of his new business idea. As he was walking up the drive, he typed variations on the words 'retro', 'vintage' and 'publishing' into Google in search of an unclaimed URL.

Should he just call his new business RVP? It had a certain ring to it, and although typing the phrase into Google brought up millions of results, most of them seemed to be about former footballer Robin van Persie. Perhaps he could have a side business of sourcing vintage items for people too. They would have to be small, to fit inside the suit, but there was a big market for genuine vintage jewellery and clothes: the woman who owned the Preloved Designer Wear store two doors away from Barrington Meek drove a much better car than him and was always advertising for more stock in the Cwmbran Evening Star.

There were plenty of tables in the lounge bar – it was still early for the hospital construction workers – and Seb was sat at one with just a coffee and his phone for company.

Eric pulled up a chair: "Mind if I join you?"

"Be my guest," Seb said, without looking up from his phone.

Eric pulled his XS Max out of his jacket pocket and placed it on the table. "I've got the same model as you now," he said.

"Very nice," Seb said, still not looking up. He was typing a long message to someone.

Eric picked up the lunch menu and after reading both sides asked: "Is there any chance I could have a breakfast?"

Seb shook his head. "The staff are told there can be no off-menu ordering," he said. "Normally I can override the system and put one through to the kitchen, but they won't thank me for doing that today. We've got a lot of lunch reservations as it's office party season."

"Fair enough," Eric said, returning to the double-sided menu. "I guess it will be traditional sausage and mash for me then. Can I get you a drink while I order?"

Seb shook his head. He was fine. He had a lot on.

Eric returned to the table with a wooden spoon with his table number engraved into it and a pint of Guinness. "Tell me something," he said to Seb. "How do I put Facebook on my phone?"

Seb finally looked up. "You're joining Facebook?"

Eric shrugged. "I know, I never thought I would."

"Just go into the App Store and download it," Seb said.

Eric looked at his phone. "Is that a simple process?"

Seb snatched the new phone from him. "Give it to me," he said, and his fingers flew around the screen. A few seconds later he asked: "What's your Apple ID?"

"I haven't got a clue."

"You need that to download apps," Seb said. "You'll have to go on your account page, put in your email address, and click on 'I've forgotten my password' if you don't know it."

"Right, I'll get Carol onto that when I go back to the office," Eric said, taking a long drink. "And how do I go about getting an image reverse?"

"Do you mean a reverse image search?"

"That sounds more likely."

"You need to upload an image to Google and it will find others that are similar," Seb said, appraising Eric. "What's brought on this sudden need to engage with the online world?"

"It was what you said yesterday," Eric replied. "About how I could use my phone to find someone."

"You're hoping to find your young barmaid? The one who ran off with Little Len?"

Eric nodded.

"Why?"

"I don't know, to apologise I suppose."

"Finding her on Facebook will be difficult. The chances of her still having the same name 43 years later are pretty slim, and even if you do know her current name there could be hundreds of other people with the same one. And as for a Google reverse image search, you need a decent quality image first. Have you got one?"

Eric hadn't.

"Dear God, move on, Eric," Seb urged.

"I have!" Eric protested.

"You clearly haven't," Seb said. "You wouldn't be buying a new phone and talking about all this if you just wanted to apologise to her."

"The new phone is a business expense."

"And even if you find her, what are you expecting? That she's remained chaste all these years on the off chance that you, her handsome prince from half a century ago, would decide to finally come looking for her now she's reached pensionable age?"

"It's not quite half a century," Eric pointed out. "Its 43 years."

Seb continued: "You've never moved out of Cwmbran, so if she had any feelings for you or if she ever wanted to find you, she wouldn't exactly have had far to look, would she?"

Eric had no answer to this, so he waited in silence until his food was brought to his table. As he dipped his premium quality sausages into his red onion and shallots gravy, and savoured his herb butter mash, Seb's phone burst into life.

"Hello?" Seb said.

"We've hit a problem," Eric heard the caller say.

"I have every confidence that you'll sort it out," Seb said forcefully. "Because you are aware we're working to a very tight deadline, aren't you?"

"The men are going to have to down tools," the caller said.

Seb leapt up from the table and marched across the bar. He swore a few times at his handset and conducted the rest of the conversation outside the building, where Eric could not hear.

*** 

Eric was pleasantly surprised to see Alwyn's successor in place and on the phone when he called into the office. And the fact that he was a rather tubby chap in his 30s, with a pleasant face and unfashionable hair, was a bonus. Eric was done with hunks, even if they were popular with the customers.

The new guy already knew the job, Carol explained, as he had spent almost a decade at a rival estate agent in Cardiff. Ryan had been made redundant when the chain went into administration in the summer and was delighted to be given a chance to 'get back in the game', especially so close to Christmas. And as he had provided holiday cover for the chain's now-closed Cwmbran branch in previous years, he knew a little about the local market.

"Did Carol explain that business is pretty quiet right now?" Eric asked Ryan.

"She did, but that's to be expected with Christmas around the corner," he replied. "Plus, there's all the uncertainty surrounding the election and Brexit. The market always picks up in January though, thanks to the holy trinity of Ds: death, debt, and divorce."

Eric smiled. "What went wrong at your previous employer?"

Ryan looked uncomfortable. "I don't really think I should be telling tales out of school," he replied.

"Off the record," Eric encouraged him. "Just between us. How can a firm with a dozen branches go bust?"

"That was part of the problem," Ryan said, after a moment of hesitation. "The business had grown so rapidly that it didn't have the infrastructure to support a chain. And the branches were competing with each other, even though we represented different areas, rather than with our rivals."

"Why would you compete with each other?"

"We had targets to meet, and the worst performing branch would get slaughtered by the boss each month, so we would try and nobble each other. One bloke's speciality was the pish bowl."

"The what?"

"He would pee in a bowl and put it in his freezer overnight," Ryan explained. "The next day he would separate the frozen pee from the bowl and post it through the letterbox of a house that was on the books of another branch."

"Why?" Eric asked, open mouthed.

"The pee would defrost and soak into the mat or the floorboards. It worked best with empty houses, but he also did it with occupied ones late at night."

"Why?" Carol repeated.

"So there was less chance of the house selling," Ryan explained. "If the first thing you smell when you walk through the door of a property is urine, well, it's probably not going to be the house of your dreams, is it?"

"Carol, I think we've both learned something new today," Eric said. "Though we probably won't be in a rush to emulate it. Now can you just help me with something techie?"

Carol had no trouble installing Facebook on Eric's new XS Max as she had set up his original Apple ID on his 5, and while she talked Ryan through the rental properties on Barrington Meek's portfolio, Eric tried to find Verity by typing her name into Facebook's search bar. Although it gave him several results, every one of them was far too young to be 'his' Verity.

"Are you looking for friends to add?" Carol asked.

Eric quickly closed the app. "No, it was recommended that I use it to find someone."

"This sounds interesting – who are you trying to find?" Carol asked.

"Oh, just someone I used to know a long time ago," Eric said bashfully. "I lost contact with them and..."

"And?"

"And, well... look, this is getting embarrassing," Eric said, feeling his face flush. "How would you try to find someone from your past?"

"Is it a him or her?"

"Does it matter?"

"If it's a her then I would get in touch with mutual friends, contact her brothers and sisters, any other family, and if I got nowhere, I would then look for her on Facebook and Google."

"And if it's a him?"

"I cannot imagine wanting to contact any 'him' I lost touch with – I would have lost touch with them for a reason."

Eric typed Verity's name into Google. Unfortunately, she shared a surname with someone famous, so every result on the first few pages was about her namesake. He narrowed the search criteria by adding 'Cwmbran' to her name, then changed her surname to Butcher, in case she had married Little Len, but 20 minutes later he was no closer to finding her.

He thought about Carol's suggestions: there had never been any mutual friends, she was an only child, and her parents had moved abroad permanently at some point in the '90s. He typed 'how many people vanish in the UK each year' and got depressing, and bewilderingly different, results ranging from 180,000 to 275,000. He learned from one report that although the vast majority turn up again, at any one time there were an estimated 1,000 unidentified bodies lying in the country's mortuaries and hospitals.

"You look deep in thought," Carol said. "Do you fancy a coffee?"

Eric nodded, relieved at the opportunity to stop reading the distressing report. He looked up the phrase 'reverse image search' and was delighted to discover he could understand the instructions. There was just one problem – he did not have an image of Verity to upload to Google. But maybe there was one in the Woodland Manor photo album? He smiled as he realised that even if there wasn't, he could just go back and take one.

"Carol, where would be a good place to buy vintage summer clothes?"

"What era?"

"For the summer of 1976."

"Why would you want to do that?"

Because this time when I go back, I want to blend in with my surroundings as I might be there for some time. "Woodland Manor is having a '70s night and I thought I might make an effort."

"Is this for New Year's Eve?"

Eric nodded. "Kind of," he replied.

"It must be lovely to go out on New Year's Eve," she sighed.

"Doesn't Mr Carol take you out drinking and dancing? I can just see you singing along to an ABBA tribute band."

"I would love that," she said. "But my husband hates ABBA."

"How can anyone hate ABBA?"

"And do you know what he does on New Year's Eve?"

"It sounds like he doesn't go to ABBA-themed parties."

"He goes fishing on the canal."

Eric failed to stifle a laugh. "I'm sorry," he guffawed. "I wasn't expecting that."

"I know, it's hilarious," she said.

Eric could see Carol's eyes glistening, even behind her thick glasses. She obviously did not find it hilarious, and he felt guilty for laughing. "So, the vintage clothes?"

"Probably best trying the charity shops," Carol replied.

"Not Preloved Designer Wear?"

"Where do you think she gets most of her stock?" Carol said.

"Do you want to come and help me choose something?" Eric asked her. "I'll treat you to lunch."

"You're going to leave Ryan in charge, on his first day?"

"He seems very capable," Eric replied. "And we won't be gone long because I have to run a few errands this afternoon."

\*\*\*

While they ate their toasted sandwiches in The Steam Room coffee shop, carrier bags of flared trousers and garishly patterned shirts at their feet, Carol said: "You know you said you would make me a partner?"

Eric nodded.

"Did you mean it?"

"Of course," Eric replied. "Let's get Christmas out of the way and we'll get it sorted in the New Year."

She took a sip of her coffee, clearly delighted.

"Why would you have thought that I didn't mean it?"

She sighed. "I've been let down a few times before."

"But not by me," Eric said.

"No, not by you."

"And didn't I treat you to a new dress? Well, a new-to-you dress?"

"You did," she said, smiling down at the bright yellow material sticking out of the bag by her feet. "I had one just like it in the '70s – the same size too. Hey, this might even be my old one. Wouldn't that be a coincidence?"

"How can you have gone all these years without putting on weight?" Eric asked, tapping his tummy.

"Just keeping busy I suppose," she replied. "You might like to try it."

"The thing that amazes me is how expensive these old clothes are," Eric said, ignoring her jibe. "Even in the charity shops. And Preloved Designer Wear must be raking in a fortune."

"Newport and Cwmbran were full of clothes shops in the '70s," Carol said. "I wish I could just walk into David Evans, Chelsea Girl, C&A, Laura Ashley, New Look, and Tammy Girl now."

"Changing the subject a little, do you remember there being poker games at Woodland Manor in the '70s?"

Carol's face clouded over. Slowly and reluctantly, she nodded.

"And did—"

Carol put her hand on his mouth. "Please, don't ruin the day by bringing all that up."

After a few moments of silence, Eric said: "Mr Freeman is coming out of hospital this afternoon and I've arranged to meet them at Brookvale."

"I'm staggered at how quickly this transaction was completed," Carol said. "Even though there was a chain of three."

"What are you implying? That I've done something underhanded?"

"Quite the opposite," she replied. "By calling in favours we've completed in a week what would normally take months."

"That's partly because no one needed a mortgage," Eric said. "And as you say, we called in favours with the conveyancing solicitors, and I might have hinted that this deal was being filmed by the BBC for a property TV show and it had to go through quickly to meet their deadlines, and—"

"You're missing the point," Carol corrected him. "I'm not complaining, I'm saying that more people might be able to move house in a week if everyone involved is incentivised to do it. Now wouldn't that be something worth promoting?"

Eric smiled in approval. "That's a lovely thought. A week would probably be overpromising but maybe we could find a way of streamlining all the processes so we can complete in under 30 days?"

"Prepare to be amazed, and move into the house of your dreams in 30 days – there's our slogan," Carol said.

"Barrington Meek, your moving managers," Eric offered.

"That's good too," Carol said, holding up her hand in a high-five gesture.

"You're getting as bad as Alwyn," Eric said, reluctantly tapping her hand with his.

"You can shut up," she replied. "You're the one who's been on Facebook all morning."

***

When the narrow road leading up into Brookvale was designed, the planners did not expect there to be cars parked both sides for much of the time. Each of the bungalows in the cul-de-sac had a drive and a garage but the advent of multi-vehicle homes, and the 21$^{st}$ century tendency of acquiring so much stuff that garages were invariably used for storage, meant it was a tight squeeze for the removal van to get there without damaging someone's paintwork. Eric had therefore arrived ahead of time and warned the neighbours that a large van was arriving, and most had kindly moved their vehicles well out of the way of the Freemans' new home.

The previous occupier was elderly too, so there was a useful handrail running from the drive entrance all the way up the gently sloping path to the front door. There were no steps or stairs inside or out and as the taxi driver helped Mr Freeman out, Eric rushed down to meet him.

"What do you think?" Eric said, gesturing towards the property.

"It's a bit smaller than I was expecting," Freeman replied.

"And that's what you want at this stage of your life," Eric said. "It's been recently decorated so you don't have to do a thing."

Mrs Freeman had finished paying the driver and now joined them. "Tell those boys to be careful with my things," she said, pointing at the four men who had formed a line and were passing the boxes containing the Freemans' possessions to each other.

The heavy furniture was already inside, and each box was labelled with the room the contents came from. The men had agreed to unpack, under Mrs Freeman's supervision, and take away all the packaging when the job was finished. This had cost Eric an extra £400 but as he watched her walk through the front door, complaining that the men in the house hadn't wiped their feet, he knew they would be earning their money today. Eric turned to Mr Freeman and offered him his arm.

"I've got a stick, thanks," Freeman said, defiantly waving his cane at Eric. "I might be old but I'm not completely enfeebled."

Eric pointed to a wooden bench at the front of the property that had a round iron table with a gift-wrapped package on it. "Would you like to have a sit down before we go in? I've got you a little moving-in present."

Freeman slowly made his way up the path alongside the drive, with Eric walking patiently behind him in case he lost his grip. He lowered himself on to the bench, sat for a few minutes, breathing deeply, and eventually picked up the package and began to tear the wrapping from it, exposing an oblong blue box.

"All you need is a top hat and you'll be just like him," Eric said, pointing to the box's caricature of a dapper Edwardian gentleman, complete with cane, in mid-strut.

"Johnnie Walker Blue Label," Freeman said with satisfaction.

Eric gently tugged a black ribbon which allowed the two halves of the box to separate, revealing a 70cl bottle and two crystal tumblers. He put them on the side table and used his fingernail to break the seal on the bottle. "Here's to your new home," he said.

"A cube of ice would be nice," Freeman replied, as Eric poured a small measure into each glass.

"It would," Eric agreed. "But you'll have to do without it, unless you want to ask your wife to bring some out to you?"

"I shouldn't be having this," Freeman said, sipping the whisky.

Eric joined him. Looking at his glass appreciatively, he said: "Velvety smooth and vibrant, with layers of dried fruits and citrus smoke evolving into honey, sweet spice, and a vanilla finish."

"How long did it take you to memorise the Amazon description?" Freeman asked.

"A lot longer than you'd think," Eric replied. "And I hope you appreciate the effort I went to."

They sipped their drinks in silence for a few minutes, while the removal men continued lugging in boxes to the soundtrack of Mrs Freeman urging them to 'Be gentle!' and eventually Eric said: "Can I talk to you about the portal?"

"I was wondering how long it would take you," Freeman said. "Now the drugs have worn off and I'm compos mentis again, I've had a chance to think about your behaviour."

"My behaviour?"

"You steamrollered Emily into selling the house to you," Freeman said, a touch of anger in his tone. "Just so you would have access to the portal. But how are you going to maintain it?"

"It needs maintaining?"

"It does," Freeman said. "Without which, in a best-case scenario, it will stop working."

"That's a best-case scenario?"

"If it malfunctions, even in a minor way, and you are in 1976 at the time, you would be stuck there."

"That would be unfortunate," Eric said.

"And if it malfunctions while you are in the central chamber, your body will be ripped apart."

"Are we still talking about a best-case scenario?" Eric said.

"Very much so," Freeman said.

"Jesus, what's a worst-case scenario?" Eric asked, taking another sip of the whisky while avoiding eye contact with the removal men, who were now throwing resentful glances in his direction.

"If it malfunctions in a big way, it could potentially tear apart the very fabric of space and time."

"I'm not sure what that means," Eric said. "But it sounds a bit dramatic."

"It could, in laymen's terms, mean the end of the world."

Eric took another sip. "There's a cheerful thought."

Freeman stared at Eric. "You should know that I am not at all happy about how you've engineered this situation."

"I can see that, but I did what was best for you and your wife," Eric said defensively. "You're being the dog again."

"Poppycock," Freeman said. "You did what you did for your own selfish reasons."

"Look, all I want to do is what you've done, just take photographs," Eric said.

"Do you think you can buy my acquiescence with this?" Freeman cried, banging his glass on the table.

The sound brought Mrs Freeman out to investigate. Noticing the small glass tumblers and the bottle, she cried: "Is that whisky? Have you given him whisky? Are you trying to finish him off?"

"It was a moving-in gift," Eric said sheepishly.

She glared at them both, snatched the glasses and the bottle and took them into the house, complaining to the movers about the stupidity of men.

Eric stood in the doorway and watched her pour the contents of the bottle down the kitchen sink. "There goes £150 down the drain," he said. "And I mean that literally. Still, the glasses are nice, aren't they? She might want to grow spider plants in them or something."

"You're in trouble, you are," one of the removal men said as he passed the couple. "She's turning the air blue in there."

Eric returned to the subject of photography, and his idea of starting a new business based on capturing still images and movies of other places in south Wales and beyond in 1976.

"Sounds like a good idea," Freeman said. "You can have all my albums to start you off."

"That would be fantastic," Eric said. "Thank you."

"It'll cost you though," Freeman warned.

"How much?"

Freeman pointed to the empty Blue Label gift box. "One of them. Every week."

"Absolutely out of the question," Eric replied. "It's in my interests to keep you alive as long as possible so my counteroffer is one a month."

"Accepted," Freeman said, offering Eric his hand to shake.

"I am really bad at negotiating," Eric sighed. "The way you readily agreed suggests this was what you wanted in the first place."

***

Walking up Woodland Manor's drive, Eric saw that part of the woods was lit up by huge floodlights. What a shame it would be to destroy these ancient trees and replace them with housing. If it was anyone other than Seb proposing such ecological vandalism Eric thought he might try and stop it going ahead, particularly as he was now a resident of the area once again.

There was a member of staff he didn't recognise on reception, so Eric wandered into the lounge to look for Seb. There were two girls behind the bar, neither of which he knew, so he went back out to the reception desk. "Can you tell me where Seb is?" Eric asked.

The young man on reception eyed Eric suspiciously and shook his head. "Seb is busy," he said.

"I'm sure he is, but so am I," Eric said. "Can you contact him?"

Whatever the young man said in reply was drowned out by the sound of a large black van roaring up the drive and heading for the woods, followed by a police car with a flashing blue light.

## CHAPTER 20

### SATURDAY 3ᴿᴰ JULY 1976

After Eric securely locked the garage door behind him, he headed for Meek's Mini Market. His eyes were immediately drawn to the fluorescent green posters on the windows again. Could they really be an effective advertising medium? Eric's suspended wire window display had cost him hundreds of pounds but maybe he should throw a tenner at some fluorescent paper posters and a thick black marker pen for Barrington Meek's 30th anniversary in the New Year? It would certainly stand out in a modern retail setting.

Eric pushed the shop door, which swung inwards and set off the familiar clanging bell. Once again, his eyes had to adjust to the dark interior after coming in from the hottest day of the century at the point when the sun was at its peak, and the familiar stench of cigarette smoke crept up his nostrils.

The two men, stood either side of the shop counter, eyed him suspiciously and his father said in a surly tone: "We're closing at one, so you've only got a few minutes."

Eric approached the counter and, pointing to the window with his thumb, said: "Have you considered revising your promotions to take into account the seasonal desires of your customers?"

PC Roy 'Spanner' Tanner's mouth dropped open in astonishment. He looked Eric up and down, his nostrils flaring at the flared denim jeans with frayed hems and Ben Sherman red and white gingham shirt.

Derek Meek was also staring at Eric: "Whatever you're selling, I'm not buying," he said.

"I believe that," Eric said. "But I'm not selling anything. I would just like to suggest you use your posters to promote things people actually want. I've got nothing against cheese crackers, toothpaste, fish fingers, and tinned beefburgers – but why not showcase cold drinks, chilled meats, and ice-cream at this time of year?"

Both Spanner and his father involuntarily glanced at the overworked fridge at the front of the shop, which was destined to be vandalised by burglars later that night.

"It is pretty hot outside today," Eric explained.

"I told you, I'm about to close," Derek Meek said.

Spanner used his forefinger and thumb to brush his thick horseshoe moustache, jutting out his chin. Gesturing at Eric's shirt and trousers he sneered: "You're a bit long in the tooth to be wearing that, cock."

Eric's father nodded in agreement.

"Don't you think so, Meek?" Spanner said to his father. "He looks like a refugee from the bloody Dick Emery Show."

Eric had forgotten that Spanner called his father by his surname. And in his own shop too, in front of customers, in a deliberately disrespectful display of alpha male dominance. Eric turned to Spanner and said: "Why don't you fuck off?"

Spanner's fingers stopped, mid-stroke of his moustache. His stunned expression suggested no one had ever spoken to him like that before. Looking down at Eric, he theatrically cupped his hand to his ear: "I beg your pardon?"

"Deaf as well as crooked?" Eric taunted him.

"Do you know what happens to people who spend a night in our cells?" Spanner said, his face flushed beetroot red.

"You take turns having your wicked way with them?"

Spanner leapt towards Eric, who dodged right and avoided the policeman's outstretched arms. Spanner's momentum carried him into the small shop's central gondola, sending bottles of bleach, washing up liquid, and twin packs of pastel coloured toilet roll tumbling across the floor.

"Roy, please, take it outside," Derek Meek urged.

"Yeah, come on Roy, let's take this outside," Eric said, jogging towards the door.

Eric emerged into the blinding sunlight and, turning back towards the door, pulled a small cannister from his trouser pocket. As Spanner burst through the door, Eric fired the spray directly into the policeman's eyes. He staggered backwards, swearing and screaming, and fell over an A-board advertising the Cwmbran Evening Star.

Eric's father opened the door, expecting to see Spanner pummelling Eric, and was shocked to see the policeman rolling on the ground clutching his face and roaring with pain and fury. "Are you alright, Roy?" he enquired.

Spanner roared: "Do I look alright? Ring 999 now! Officer down!"

Derek had the keys to the shop in his hand and Eric snatched them from him. He locked the shop and pulled his bewildered father's arm towards the family car, a putrid-green Hillman Avenger Estate.

"Get in and drive," Eric commanded, throwing the keys back to his father.

"What have you done to him?" his father asked, nervously.

"Something you should have done a long time ago," Eric snapped. "Stood up to him."

The car burbled into life and Eric's father asked in a trembling voice: "Where are we going?"

Eric thought for a moment and replied: "The Old Oak."

"The pub?"

"Do you know the way?"

Eric's father nodded. Of course he knew the way. Back when they were a family, they would sometimes drive out there in the summer. Eric was left in the car with a small bottle of clear lemonade and a packet of Chipmunk Oxo crisps while his mum and dad had a few drinks inside: Brains SA for him and Cinzano Bianco for her.

As the car laboured along the dual carriageway towards the lanes that led to the pub, Derek nervously asked: "What is this about? Are you robbing me?"

Eric wound the passenger window down to let some cool air into the vehicle, which took more effort than he remembered, and stared at his father's frightened face. He had never seen him like this before, ever. "No, I'm not robbing you," Eric said. "If I wanted your car I would have left you behind. And let me just add, if I did want to steal a car, this would be the last one I'd pick."

Eric gestured at the cheap black plastic dashboard, which housed just a radio, air vents – which were blowing out warm air that smelled of curry – and an oblong opening containing white markings for fuel level, water temperature, and speed. Thin orange needles were supposed to tell the driver the status of all three, but they were wildly inaccurate. The numbers on the speedometer went up to 100 but even though the engine was performing at its maximum capability in top – fourth – gear, the marker showed 80 and Eric estimated they were not even moving at 70 miles per hour.

Eric had to yell to be heard over the howling of the engine "Why would you buy this shed?"

"It's an estate," Derek shouted back. "It's handy for collecting stock from the cash and carry."

"But it's shit," Eric said. He was going to explain why but then he realised he was in danger of turning back into his teenage self in the company of his father and the despised family car, which was the poverty-spec DL model with the bottom of the range 1250cc engine.

Most of his friends' dads had stylish Fords – Capris, Escorts, and Cortinas – and Eric was so embarrassed by the Avenger that, if he needed to go somewhere further than walking distance, he would try to cadge a lift with one of them rather than be seen arriving in 'the piss-green delivery machine', as one of his friends had christened it.

They turned off the dual carriageway and entered the lanes which led to the pub. The engine was allowed to gather its breath here, as the road was narrow and could only accommodate two cars in opposing directions if they both slowed to a crawl to pass each other.

Derek wound down the window on his side of the car. He was sweating. "Why are you staring at me?" he asked nervously. "You're not a psycho, are you?"

"Would I be taking you to a pub if I were?" Eric replied.

"Are you a homosexual?" his father asked, even more nervously.

Eric failed to suppress an involuntary laugh. "You might find this difficult to believe but I'm here to help you."

"Help me? With what?"

"Everything," Eric said, brambles from the hedgerows flicking at him through his open window as Derek yanked the car left to avoid a Triumph Dolomite coming in the opposite direction. "Now will you please just look at the road and concentrate? You nearly had us in the hedge then."

"He was miles over my side," Derek complained, turning his head to look back at the offending vehicle that was speeding away behind them.

As they entered the smoke-filled pub, the locals who were sat at the bar all turned to stare at them. No one spoke, not even the burly barman in the white Bri-Nylon shirt who was filling up a traditional 'dimple' pint glass with a foaming liquid from one of the taps. They had all been extremely friendly when Eric was last here, even moving out of the way to allow him to get to the bar – but that was on a previous trip, when he had the alluring young Carol with him.

"Two pints of Harp, when you're ready," Eric said to the surly faced barman.

The locals gawped at Eric. That was nowhere near the level of deference required in this pub. You don't interrupt the landlord when he's pouring a pint. You wait patiently and silently until he deigns to look at you. Those are the rules.

"It is Harp you drink, isn't it?" Eric said to his father, who nodded.

Eric put a five-pound note on the bar and added: "Have one for yourself and put the change in the charity box."

Derek stared at Eric, open-mouthed.

"Thank you very much indeed, sir," the no longer surly-faced landlord said, breaking into a beaming smile. "Do you want to enjoy the sun outside and I'll bring them out to you?"

They did. They sat in silence for several minutes until the grinning landlord brought the drinks out on a round metal tray. "Here you go, gents," he said obsequiously, placing the glasses in front of Eric and his father. "Just give me a shout if there is anything else I can do for you."

Eric took a large gulp of his lager and put the glass gently back on the wooden table. It certainly wouldn't be his choice of drink in 2019 but his options were limited here. And, in this weather, it went down very well indeed. His father took an identical gulp and placed his glass back on the table in the same way. Was he mirroring Eric or was Eric mirroring him through learned behaviour?

"How can you help me?" Derek asked, after taking a deep second guzzle of the yellow liquid. He pulled a crumpled box of Embassy cigarettes from his pocket and put one in his mouth while he fumbled for a box of matches in his other pocket.

Eric stared at the distinctive white box with the red central stripe, which resembled the shirts of Ajax of Amsterdam, his favourite overseas football team at the time. He hadn't seen a pack of Embassy cigarettes for decades.

"Do you want one?" Meek senior asked, which was unexpected. His father had repeatedly warned Eric about the dangers of cigarettes, despite being a lifelong smoker himself. Maybe he was concerned for Eric's health. More likely he was concerned for his stock. Eric had previous after all, most notably with bags of Chipmunk Oxo crisps.

Eric took one and moved his head closer to his father's to receive a light from the same match. His father looked old. Even though, here and now, he was two decades younger than Eric.

After savouring the smoke and lager mix, Eric eventually said: "Don't let Spanner break into the shop tonight."

Derek looked around him in panic. He tried to speak but could only splutter. "Wh... wh... wh..."

"I know what you've got planned," Eric said, blowing a plume of smoke up into the clear blue sky. "You go to the Dinner & Dance at Woodland Manor while he breaks in and pours paint on the fridges and empties the shelves of whisky."

"No," Derek said, his voice trembling. "That's not right."

"Yes, it is," Eric said. "There's no point lying to me, I know what happens."

"How?"

"You wouldn't believe me," Eric said. "You couldn't believe me, but you know I'm telling the truth, don't you?"

Derek took a deep drag on his cigarette. His hands were trembling.

"Look, I'm not going to stitch you up – I said I was here to help you, remember? But first you've got to confirm I'm right."

"Partly," Derek conceded. "I am going to Woodland Manor tonight but to play in a poker game."

"And Spanner?"

Derek took another large gulp of lager and lit a second cigarette, even though the first was still burning in the ashtray.

Eric answered his own question: "He's going to break in and make a mess, and you're going to claim on your insurance policy for a new fridge. Correct?"

Derek closed his eyes and gave a slight nod of his head. "It can't cope in the heat," he said. "The food is going off and I don't have the money for a new one. What was that about whisky, though?"

"He's going to fill his car with all your stock, and he's also going to steal your cigarettes."

"We never agreed to that," Derek said, shaking his head. "He wouldn't do that."

"Not only will he do that but, if you go along with this tonight, you will be beholden to him for the rest of your life," Eric warned. "Every Saturday lunchtime, just as you're about to close, he will come in and take a couple of bottles of whisky 'for the lads at the station'."

Derek gasped in horror.

"And you're going to let him," Eric continued. "Because he'll always have that hold over you. And if you don't like it, if you complain that you can't afford it, he'll threaten to inform the insurance company that you defrauded them."

"How could you possibly know that?"

"Because I've seen him do it. Honestly, Dad, it's not worth it for a new fridge."

Derek had an even more horrified look on his face. "What did you just call me?"

Eric took a huge gulp of Harp. "Dad."

"Are you deranged?"

"No," Eric said. "I'm your son."

"You're pulling my leg," Derek said. "You're older than me!"

"I am," Eric conceded. "This is me, Eric, from 2019."

Derek shook his head. "That's impossible."

Eric took his iPhone out of his shirt pocket. He touched the screen and held it up in front of him so the facial recognition software would unlock it.

"What's that?" Derek asked.

"Something else that's impossible," Eric replied.

The iPhone screen picked up where it had left off, displaying the BBC News app. Most of the stories were about the next day's general election.

"What are they?" Derek persisted.

"I can't really show you them because there's no service," Eric said. "But what's your favourite Beatles song?"

Derek thought for a few seconds. "I don't know, something from Revolver I expect."

Eric tapped the music icon in the bottom right of the screen, then tapped on 'albums' and scrolled down to the thumbnail graphic of the distinctive black and white artwork. "You're in for a treat, this is the 2009 remaster," Eric said as he tapped the image and showed the screen to his father. The individual tracks were listed with a number next to them. "Pick a number," Eric said. "Go on, just touch one of them."

Derek's finger settled on 'Love You To', and the familiar sound of the sitar introduction flooded out of the phone, surprisingly clearly, causing Derek to leap back in shock.

"Is this like a radio or something?"

"Every Beatles song ever recorded is on here," Eric explained as he hastily turned the sound down and handed his father the phone. "Including some you've never even heard."

Derek turned the device over in his hand. "Where are they kept?"

"The songs? They are digitally stored on silicon chips. But this is much more than just a music player."

Derek stared at the iPhone in wonder. "And these little pictures?"

Eric took his father through them with all the patience that Tom had taken with him, explaining their functions, and demonstrating the ones that did not rely on a cellular connection. His father was most taken with the Solitaire app, uncharacteristically smiling at the card animations.

"Can you buy these?"

"Not for a while," Eric said, realising his father would never live to see them.

"If I had one of these, I'd be on it every minute of every day," Derek said.

"That can be an issue," Eric replied. "But would you like this one?"

Derek eyed him suspiciously. "To keep?"

"You could keep it," Eric said. "But if you showed it to the right people, it could make you rich."

They were interrupted by the landlord bringing out two fresh pints of Harp. "Here you go gents, I could see from inside that you were running low so thought you might like a top up."

They thanked him and took large glugs from the fresh glasses.

"Let me get this straight," Derek said, lighting another Embassy. "You're my son and you've come from the future – is that right?"

Eric nodded.

"There's a turn up for the books," Derek said, inhaling deeply. "When do England next win the World Cup?"

"They don't," Eric replied.

"They must do!" Derek protested. "Does something happen to Keegan?"

"Wales become good, if that's any consolation."

The expression on Derek's face strongly indicated it was not. "What happens to me?"

"I've already told you," Eric said. "If you go along with this fraud, the rest of your life will be a misery. But if you take this phone—"

"It's a phone?"

"It's also a camera," Eric said, and moved closer to his father and took a selfie of them both. Then he took a video of his father talking and played that back to him.

"That's not bad quality," Derek conceded. "Does it allow you to go back through time as well?"

"No, you need something a bit more powerful for that," Eric said, disappointed with his father's lack of wonder at the technological miracle he had just been shown, not to mention his lack of curiosity about his grown-up son visiting from the future. He hadn't asked him a thing about his life.

"They serve a decent pint of lager here, fair play," Derek observed, eyeing his emptying glass.

"Dad, I'm giving you the chance to walk away from Cwmbran, which I know you hate, and do what you want for the rest of your life," Eric said, trying to keep a growing sense of irritation out of his voice. "If you took this phone to America and showed it to Steve Jobs or Bill Gates—"

"Who?"

"They're in their early 20s now but they become two of the most influential men in the world. They create global technology empires that—"

"Got their phone numbers, have you?"

"No—"

"Their addresses?"

"No—"

"How am I supposed to find them? Wander from town to town like David bloody Carradine?"

Despite his father's negativity, Eric smiled at his reference to the television series Kung Fu, which was one of the few programmes they watched together. "I don't know," Eric sighed. "I didn't exactly think this through in advance."

"I can't just up sticks and go to America on the off chance that—"

"Alright, you don't need to go to America," Eric interrupted. "Have you heard of Clive Sinclair? He's based in Cambridge, I think."

"You think?"

"I'm pretty sure he is. Or maybe Richard Branson at Virgin."

"Who?"

"You know, the record label that published Tubular Bells, or Alan Sugar of Amstrad – he will be easy to find."

"And what would I say to them? 'Oh hello, my son asked me to bring this to you'. The first thing they'd ask me is how it works. How does it work?"

"It's basically a computer," Eric said.

"But how does it work?"

"I don't know."

"You don't know much, considering you're from the future," Derek said, in that disappointed tone of voice he took so often with young Eric. "Then they'd ask where I got it from. 'Oh, sorry, I forgot to mention my son is from the future!' They'd throw me out. Or they'd take it off me and I'd never hear from them again."

Eric considered how best to respond to this tsunami of negativity. Slapping him across the face would be seen by some as appropriate.

After staring at the device for a few more moments, Derek slid the iPhone across the table to Eric. "Nah, it's not for me," he said.

"But you've seen what it can do!" Eric said through gritted teeth. "You heard The Beatles."

"It didn't sound as good as the record though, did it? It was all treble and no bass."

Eric opened the Kindle app and showed his father some of the dozens of books he had downloaded.

"I don't have time to read books and, even if I did, I wouldn't be able to get on with that," Derek responded. "It would strain my eyes reading on that tiny screen."

"What about the solitaire game?"

"That was good," Derek said. "But I can play that anytime I want with just a pack of cards."

Frustrated, Eric slumped back in the uncomfortable chair.

"I think I should be getting back now," Derek said, looking at his watch.

"You and me both," Eric replied.

They drove back to Lôn Heddychlon in silence. As Eric clambered out of the Avenger, Derek said: "It's too late for me to be doing new things at my age."

"Dad, I'm 20 years older than you," Eric said.

"And you could probably do with losing a few pounds," Derek replied, closing the car door and locking it with the key. "Listen, about tonight…"

"Just do what you fucking want," Eric said.

Derek raised his eyebrows. "Well, that's charming, I must say."

Eric watched his father walk away. Not once did he look back at his grown-up son from the future as he disappeared inside the shop. It was just as well Eric hadn't been expecting an emotional parting, with hugs and tears and I-love-yous. He really should consider making a sharp exit from the area after the incident with Spanner – if he caught up with him, Eric was in no doubt he would be on the end of a brutal beating – but, drenched in sweat and feeling uncomfortably sticky, he decided to have one more cold drink before leaving. Then, when he returned to 2019, he would have a nightcap in the bar, find out from Seb what all the excitement was about, and spend his first night in his new house – assuming Mrs Freeman had finally let the removal men go so they could unload and unpack Eric's possessions.

As he walked into the reception area of Woodland Manor Eric said to Carol: "Only marry for love, Carol, never settle."

Carol looked up at him. "Settle? What does that mean?"

"Never put up with second best," Eric elaborated. "And if anyone says they love fishing but hate ABBA, run a mile in the opposite direction."

Carol laughed. "I love ABBA."

"I know," Eric said. "And I bet I can guess your favourite song."

Intrigued, Carol said: "I don't bet, but if you can tell me my favourite ABBA song, I'll be very impressed."

"'Knowing Me, Knowing You,'" Eric sang the title with a flourish. "Aha!"

Carol shook her head. "I don't know that one," she said.

Of course she didn't, it hadn't been released yet.

"You will," Eric said, slightly embarrassed. "But if anyone tells you they don't like ABBA, think very carefully before you marry them. You don't want to end up spending New Year's Eve alone while your husband goes fishing."

Carol laughed, covering her mouth with her hand. "Fat chance of that happening! Mind you, there's fat chance of me finding anyone decent around here," she said.

"I do believe you're right," Eric agreed, wiping his sweating forehead with the sleeve of his gingham shirt. "So why stick around? You're 26, you've got your whole life ahead of you, so why not go travelling and see the world? If you don't, you might regret it when you're older."

Carol's face turned serious. "Do I know you?"

Eric looked upwards and sighed. "It's complicated."

"How is it?"

"You do know me, but you don't remember me."

She looked offended. "I think I'd remember you if I knew you."

The shrill ringing of the telephone interrupted their conversation and Carol spent the next few minutes explaining how to find the hotel to a guest who was lost en route. After she had finished the call, she said to Eric: "I don't think I like what you're implying."

Eric pulled his iPhone from his pocket and scrolled through his pictures until he found the one he'd taken of Carol outside the Old Oak last time he was here. He held the screen up in front of her.

"When did you take that?" she squealed, and pointing to the phone she added: "And what's that thing?"

After prodding the screen a few times with his finger, he once again held it up for Carol to see. It was a moving image of her, obviously taken at the same time as the picture because she was wearing the same clothes. The clothes she was wearing now.

"What's your favourite song, Carol?" said an off-screen voice.

The real Carol looked down at her blouse. "This is the first time I've worn this," she gasped. "How is this possible?"

The off-screen voice asked: "Okay, what's number one in the charts?"

Carol was mesmerised by the footage, and she had an anxious expression on her face at its conclusion. "That didn't happen," she said. "I don't remember any of that."

Eric played her the next video, which was taken in selfie mode and featured him with her, though his attire was different.

"Where are we, Carol?" the on-screen Eric asked.

"The Old Oak," she replied, pointing towards the building behind them.

"And are you having fun?"

"I'm having a day I'll never forget," she laughed.

The video ended and Eric returned the phone to his pocket. "But you did," he said.

Carol covered her mouth with her hands, which were now trembling. "Seriously, what's going on?"

"You look like you need a drink," Eric said.

"I do," she said, her voice also now trembling. "That's like something David Nixon would have."

Eric entered the bar and approached Seb, who was chatting to Mr Reeves. "Can you get someone to cover the front desk?" Eric said to Seb. "Carol's not feeling well and I'm taking her home."

"Who was that?" Seb said to Mr Reeves as Eric disappeared back into reception.

"Never seen him before but he looked a shady character to me," Reeves replied. "A man of his age in jeans. It's repugnant."

Eric held out his hand and led Carol outside to where Big Ben's MGB was parked. He opened the passenger door for her.

"Have you got Mr Butcher's permission?" she said, with obvious concern.

Eric held up his small bunch of keys. "I've got his keys, haven't I?"

The experience of driving on the hottest day of the hottest year of the century was far more enjoyable in Big Ben's MGB than his father's Avenger. And it felt a lot faster due to it being lower to the ground. Instead of turning right out of Lôn Heddychlon towards the Old Oak – which he knew closed at three each afternoon – he turned left and made for Caerleon.

The narrow streets of the small town were packed with people, many of them young, drunk, and loud. Although Caerleon was the site of a Roman fortress, most of its visitors were attracted by its abundance of drinking establishments rather than its architectural significance. Over a dozen pubs were crammed into its narrow streets, kept in business by students from the local university and drinkers from the surrounding area embarking on ambitious 'pint in every pub' excursions.

Eric wasn't interested in mingling with the rowdy youths though. He steered the MGB into the car park of the Abbey, a former convent that had been converted into a hotel and restaurant. Despite the crowds and the heat outside, it was both quiet and cool within the old building's thick stone walls. A smartly dressed waiter showed the couple to a table for two in the dining room and artfully lit an elegant red candle.

"I just need a drink," Carol said, immediately discarding the leather-bound menu she had been handed. "And an explanation."

Several other diners turned their attention to the couple and Eric was able to hear snippets of their mumbled conversations. Apparently, they both looked common, and a plummy voiced woman observed that Carol was young enough to be Eric's daughter, 'but probably isn't'.

Eric told Carol the truth. That he was from 2019. She didn't believe him but equally she found it hard to not believe him, given the evidence he had presented her with on his iPhone. The conversation followed pretty much the same format as last time, when they were sat outside the Old Oak, with Carol asking questions about the iPhone that Eric couldn't answer.

"It really is like magic," Carol said.

The waiter returned to the table and Eric ordered steak and chips, with home-made pate and toast to start. To his surprise, given her earlier statement, Carol said she would have the same. And when he enquired what drinks they would like she scanned the wine list and requested a merlot.

"Is that a bottle?" the waiter asked.

Eric and Carol looked at each other and agreed that yes, it was.

"I don't think I'm going to be able to drive if I have more than one glass," Eric said, after the waiter had gone. "I had a couple of pints earlier."

Carol kept asking questions about the iPhone over the starter, and Eric held it below table level, so the other diners couldn't see, as he talked her through some of its other functions.

"I should just make a video of me talking you through it all," Eric eventually said. "In case I come back again."

This led on to the subject of why she couldn't remember him from last time, and Eric tried to explain that each world he returned to was unique.

Carol looked crestfallen. "Are you saying that if you came back again, I wouldn't remember you?"

Eric nodded. "You clearly didn't."

"What's the point then?" she said, a little too loudly, once again provoking discussions about their relationship among the other diners. "What did you come back for this time?"

Eric explained about his fractured relationship with his father, and how he had tried to prevent him making a mistake that would have repercussions for many years ahead. And how he didn't think he had succeeded.

"Are you planning to come back for a third time?"

"I've been back a few times actually," Eric said. "One time I stopped Big Ben from mauling you on the reception desk."

Carol shuddered. "He's vile," she said. "He's always touching the staff. When did he try to maul me?"

Eric considered his answer. "Later tonight," he said.

"But you'll be there to stop him?"

"I'm afraid I won't," Eric said. "Not this time."

"How gallant," Carol sniffed.

Eric pleaded with her not to go back to Woodland Manor and tried to encourage her to start her own business. Once again, he explained how sandwiches would become a big thing in the near future: "Honestly, 20m prepacked sandwiches are sold every day," he said. "Over 300,000 people are employed making them."

A pained expression creased Carol's face. "That's ridiculous," she said. "But even if it was true, I can't run my own business."

"Why not?"

"No one is going to take me seriously," she protested. "I'm a woman."

"What if I gave you this?" Eric said, holding his iPhone.

"I wouldn't know what to do with it," Carol said. "And the first man I show it to will just take it off me and tell me to bugger off."

This comment caused a few tuts from the other diners and a look of rebuke from the waiter, who ambled over to their table and enquired if everything was alright.

"Sorry," Eric said. Holding up the now empty bottle of merlot, he gestured for another. He really would not be able to drive after this.

"I fully accept your point about the men of today," Eric conceded. "To live with such toxic masculinity must be unbearable."

"I've never heard it called that before," Carol said. "But you don't have to explain it."

"I thought men would be more courteous in 1976."

"Oh, they'll open a car door for you on a night out," Carol said. "But they'll also black your eye if you as much as look at another bloke."

After the main course had been consumed, the waiter asked if he should bring the sweet trolly out. Eric laughed. He hadn't heard that expression for decades.

"No need," Eric said. "I'll have a Black Forest gateau, to complete the '70s dining experience. And bring us another bottle of wine please."

Carol giggled coquettishly. "How are you getting home?"

Eric pondered the question. "I'm not," he said. "I'm going to stay here tonight."

Carol giggled again. "I wonder if the bridal suite is free?"

"If it is, I might treat myself," Eric replied.

Carol moved her head closer to Eric's and said: "And I might join you."

It was the turn of Eric's mouth to drop open in shock.

"What?" Carol said, reaching out for Eric's hand. "Aren't you attracted to me?"

"It's not that," Eric stuttered. "It's just that—"

"What then? Are you worried about the age difference?"

"It's pretty hard to ignore it," Eric replied.

"Don't worry about it," she said. "I'm not. You're not too old for sex, are you?"

"I don't know," Eric spluttered. "I just assumed that door had closed a long time ago. We've both had a drink and I'm not going to take advantage of you."

"Go on, take advantage of me," she urged, moving her hand from his to under the table. "I've never met anyone like you. You talk to me like I'm an equal."

"You are an equal," Eric said, his voice rising in pitch as her hand rested on his leg. "In fact, it's been recognised that women are superior to men in many ways."

Carol removed her glasses, leaned across the table, and brought her head closer to his. Her eyes glistened in the candlelight and her cheeks were flushed from the wine. She kissed him lightly on the cheek, attracting the attention of other diners. And even the waiter gawped when she kissed him on the lips.

## CHAPTER 21

## SUNDAY 4th JULY 1976

Eric slowly opened his eyes. Lying just inches away from him was Carol's face. And her bare shoulders. And her bare breasts. The rest of her was shielded from his slightly blurred gaze by a white cotton sheet, which was twisted around her torso and legs.

Eric was still wearing his Ben Sherman shirt and flared jeans, which were uncomfortably tight in places he'd prefer them not to be, and he eased himself off the bed, delicately pulling the crumpled sheet up to cover the still sleeping Carol.

Most 60-year-old men who spend the night with an attractive blonde less than half their age would wake up the following morning feeling a little bit pleased with themselves. Smug, even. Eric just felt ashamed. Yes, Carol had been a little forward, but whose fault was that? Who'd turned her head with his 'magic' gadget? And who plied her with wine?

He retrieved his socks and shoes, quietly freshened up in the en suite, and left the room. Not because he didn't like it – the Abbey's Deluxe rooms were exceptionally well appointed – but to spare them both the embarrassment of facing each other sober, in the harsh morning light, with only one of them fully dressed.

After waiting in the corridor outside the room for several minutes, Eric rapped on the heavy wooden door.

There was no response from inside.

"Carol?"

There was still no response, so he called again, in a louder voice, and knocked the door harder.

With his ear to the door, he could just about hear Carol shuffling about inside, followed by the sound of running water.

Once the tap had stopped, he said: "Carol, I have to go."

"Go?"

"Will you be alright?"

"Wait!"

It was more than ten minutes before the door opened and Carol emerged. "You were just going to swan off?"

"I did let you know I was going," Eric said. "I didn't just go."

"What a perfect gentleman," she sniffed. "Who said chivalry was dead?"

At reception, Eric was mortified to discover he had insufficient cash to pay for the room and had to appeal to Carol to make up the shortfall. Her expression suggested this did not endear him to her.

After checking out, they sat on a wooden bench in the rear garden of the hotel, with the sound of nearby church bells rendering conversation difficult.

When they had finished, and the congregation was safely inside its place of worship, Carol opened her purse. "This leaves me with virtually nothing for the week," she complained.

"I'm sorry," Eric said. "But the meal and the wine practically cleaned me out."

"I only got paid on Friday," Carol said. "How am I going to manage?"

"Perhaps you could ask for an advance?"

"Do you know my boss?"

"I've encountered him a couple of times."

"You don't ask him for favours," Carol said. "Because he always wants something in return. Besides, I doubt I've even got a job, after taking off with you yesterday."

"I did say you were feeling poorly."

"He'll have already replaced me."

"You can't be sacked for being ill."

"That might be the case where you come from," Carol said. "But you have no idea what it's like working in Woodland Manor."

He did. But this wasn't the right time to tell her.

"But what am I saying?" Carol ranted. "That won't be a problem, will it? After all, I'm an equal and I've got my whole life ahead of me. You said so yourself. I'll just go travelling and see the world!"

"I did say that but —"

"But what?" Carol counted the coins left in her purse. "I've got almost 40p. Will that get me on a flight to New York?"

Eric tried not to smile. And failed.

"Do you think that's funny?"

"I'm afraid I do," Eric admitted.

Carol visibly mellowed. "I suppose it is," she said. "And we had a pretty good night, didn't we?"

"We did," Eric agreed. "It was one of the most enjoyable nights of my life."

"You're overegging the pudding now," Carol admonished him.

"What does that mean?"

"It means you can save all that old flannel for the next one," she said. "You've had what you wanted."

"What I wanted?"

Looking around, to ensure no one heard her, she said in a whisper: "I woke up naked."

"Carol, nothing happened," Eric assured her. "I woke up fully clothed."

She scoffed: "Do you think I was born yesterday?"

Eric stretched and attempted to insert a finger between the waistband of his jeans and his stomach. "These jeans are so tight that if I take them off I will never get them back on again," he explained.

"Bloody hell," Carol laughed. "You really are not like other men."

"Do you mind if we go now?" Eric asked.

"Suits me," Carol said. "I'm desperate for my own bed. Which way is the car?"

"We can't use the car," Eric said.

"Why not?"

"I'm still over the limit to drive. And so are you."

"We'll take it slowly."

"I stole it," Eric admitted. "The police are going to be looking out for it, and getting stopped and hauled into the station would be extremely detrimental to my health."

"Jesus Christ!" Carol cried in frustration. "I take back what I said about you not being like other men."

They walked in silence to the nearest bus stop. And perhaps I should take back what I said about me never letting you down, Eric said to himself.

"We've just missed one," Carol said, reading the tiny writing on the poster. "And there won't be another one for more than an hour."

"Can we get a taxi?" Eric pleaded.

"Who's going to pay for that?" Carol snapped. "You?"

The walk was over two miles, in the burning sun, and there was very little conversation, especially after they passed through Ponthir and embarked on the hill up to Llanfrechfa and Lôn Heddychlon. Drenched in sweat, Eric had to stop several times to catch his breath. After the third time, Carol didn't bother to wait for him.

Eventually the slope levelled out and he caught up with her as they were getting close to home. His home, anyway. He hadn't even asked Carol where she lived.

"This is where I have to leave you," Eric said, pointing to the entrance to Lôn Heddychlon.

Carol suddenly grabbed his hand. "Take me with you," she pleaded.

"I can't," Eric said. "Even if I wanted to—"

"What do you mean, 'even if you wanted to'? Does that mean you don't want to?"

"I'm sorry Carol," Eric said. "It's physically impossible."

"Okay, bye then," she said, releasing her grip on his hand and flouncing off towards Cwmbran. "See you round. Or not."

## CHAPTER 22

### FRIDAY 13th DECEMBER 2019

As he'd spent a day, a night, and part of the following day in 1976, Eric had missed the corresponding amount in 2019, so when he returned through the portal it was early Thursday evening. Exhausted from the hike in the sun, hungover from the merlot, and jetlagged by the time shift, he took two sleeping pills and collapsed into bed.

His first task, when eventually rising on the Friday, was to hunt for his kettle. He craved a cup of tea. The removal men had seemingly unpacked everything except the kettle, or perhaps it was sent into storage with his other gadgets, so he made an instant coffee in the ancient microwave that the Freemans had left. It was awful. But the memory of Carol's crestfallen face as she walked away was infinitely worse. Even though he hadn't taken advantage of her sexually, in every other respect he'd behaved like a typical 1976 man: acting the Big I Am with his talk of the future and then dumping her. He'd even taken all her money.

He was brought back to 2019 by his phone pinging to inform him he had a message. He had left it charging overnight in the kitchen and as he unplugged it, he saw there were several others, along with a catalogue of missed calls from the office. He opened the most recent message, which was from Carol. 'Where r u?' it read. As did the previous three. She had probably cut and pasted them. He couldn't face speaking to Carol yet, not after everything he'd put a younger version of her through, so he simply texted back that he would be in later. He needed a breakfast from Seb before he could even think about driving.

Two hours later, as he walked up Woodland Manor's drive, freshly showered and back in contemporary clothes, Eric noticed there were several police vehicles in the car park, and three groups of serious-faced people huddled together. There were more serious-looking people at the entrance to the woods, which was cordoned off with blue and white tape, along with two unmarked white vans and a Portakabin.

"What's going on?" Eric asked the receptionist, who was tapping the keys of a computer keyboard and looking down at his monitor.

"Nothing's 'going on'," he replied disdainfully, without even looking up. "It's business as usual."

"I respectfully disagree," Eric said. "There is indeed something going on out there and it's far from usual."

"Whatever," huffed the receptionist. "I'm just minding my own business."

"Has no one informed you of a receptionist's responsibilities?" Eric said irritably. "Key aspects include greeting visitors and making them feel welcome."

The young man stopped typing and looked Eric in the eye. "What can I do for you, sir?" he said, emphasising the word 'sir' in an unpleasant manner.

"Is Seb about?"

The receptionist jerked a thumb in the direction of the lounge bar, threw Eric a 'Satisfied now?' look, and went back to his computer.

The lounge was empty apart from two members of staff, gossiping in hushed but excited tones behind the bar, and Seb, who was sat at his usual table having what sounded like a fraught phone conversation. Eric thought it best to stay away from him until he'd finished his call. He asked the bar staff if it was too late to order a breakfast. It was, and even worse, it was too early to order a bar snack, so Eric settled for a coffee. He was still drinking it when Seb came across to join him.

"That's me fucked," Seb said. "Right up the arse. And not in a good way."

Eric was unsure how to react to this statement. "A problem?"

"You could call it that," Seb said, gesturing towards the scene outside the window. "The sale of the woods has fallen through because of all this shit."

"What shit?" Eric asked.

Seb stared at him. "Are you taking the piss?"

Eric assured him he wasn't.

"Were you in a coma yesterday?" Seb said. "It was all over the news."

"What was?"

"The surveyors were taking soil samples and they found human remains," Seb explained. "And now forensics are crawling all over the site and the developers have pulled out."

Eric's stomach turned over. "Human remains?"

"I know," Seb said. "Have you ever heard anything so ridiculous? I thought they were just using it as an excuse to beat me down on price, but the delicate little flowers apparently don't like publicity."

"Ah."

"The development was all over the Welsh news yesterday," Seb ranted. "You can't buy exposure like that, and they were complaining about it!"

"Do the police know who it is?"

"I doubt it," Seb said. "It might take months to identify them."

"It could be Verity," Eric said, gulping down his coffee. Did coffee steady the nerves? Or make them worse?

"Your teenage crush?" Seb scoffed. "It's not going to be her."

"Think about it," Eric said. "She disappeared."

"Yes, with Little Len," Seb said. "In his father's car."

"What if he killed her?"

"Why would he do that? She'd already chosen him over you – no offence."

Eric was offended but he wasn't convinced. He dashed outside to talk to the police. He was not allowed anywhere near any of the investigators nor the scene itself, but eventually a junior officer was tasked with taking down the details Eric was so eager to provide.

"What did they say?" Seb asked when Eric returned to the bar.

"They palmed me off with a community support officer who said they would look into it," Eric replied. "But I got the impression he was just humouring me. I don't even know if he was taking notes or just pretending to."

"They probably get a lot of nutters appearing out of the woodwork when things like this happen," Seb replied. Gesturing at the television, which was showing the lunchtime news headlines, he added: "Speaking of which, can you believe Boris is our prime minister?"

Eric looked confused. "He has been all year."

"But now he's been voted in with a huge mandate," Seb replied. "We're going to be stuck with him for five bloody years."

"Oh right, the general election," Eric finally understood. "He won then?"

"Seriously, have you been in a coma?"

***

As he approached the Barrington Meek showroom, Eric was shocked to see the glass in the two windows had been replaced with an enormous expanse of cheap MDF. The glass panels in the aluminium door had also been replaced with the material. This was not a look that would have met with town centre management approval.

Eric tried the door and was relieved to discover that it opened but what awaited him inside made the exterior of the showroom look positively upmarket. The wooden literature displays, which had been a fixture of the business since Mr Barrington owned it, had been attacked with what appeared to be an axe, and were split in several places. There were holes smashed in the plastic headers, and many of the front lips that held the property brochures in place had been snapped off completely. The giant map of the local area, which dominated the wall behind Eric's desk, had been defaced with black spray paint spelling out the word 'wanker'.

Carol and Ryan were sweeping the thousands of glass shards that littered the floor into cardboard boxes. They stopped as Eric walked in. Carol's red eyes and smudged makeup indicated she had been crying.

"I am so sorry," Carol said.

"Why?" Eric said, taking in the devastation, which had echoes of the burglary at Meek's Mini Market. "You didn't do this, did you?"

Despite her obvious distress, Carol giggled at his comment. "No, of course not," she replied. "But I've got a good idea who did. He took all the computers too."

Eric inspected the now smashed ceramic pot of his rubber plant. Its seven-foot stalk lay prostrate among the glass, its leaves crushed by uncaring feet. "This plant was a present from Mr Barrington, the previous owner," he said. "It's been with me since I took over the business."

Carol shook her head. "And the bastard deliberately tried to kill it."

"Looks like he succeeded," Eric said, examining the plant's limp stalk. "When did this happen?"

"Sometime in the night," Carol said. "The police have been and taken a statement – they were obviously kept busy last night, with the election and everything – and I've asked the town centre security to check if there are any CCTV images that we can use. I've also spoken to the insurance company, and the glazier is on his way up from Cardiff."

Eric turned his executive leather chair the right way up and slumped down in it. A slash in the seat resulted in most of the air escaping from the cushion, along with particles of ancient yellow foam, as he sat. "To be fair, the old place was due a makeover," Eric noted. "Did he at least spare the kettle?"

"Do you want a coffee?" she asked, incredulously.

"If it's not too much trouble," Eric replied, looking down at his phone.

"I can't believe how calmly you're taking this," Carol said, making her way to the kitchen area. "He's taken the computers with all the client information."

"But you changed the passwords after Alwyn left," said Eric. "And everything's backed up to the cloud."

"They've wrecked our lovely fixtures," Carol said, waving in the direction of the racks.

"But, on the other hand, we can finally get one of those fancy multimedia display units that we saw at the trade show last year now," Eric countered. "And some nice new laptops that don't take all morning to warm up."

"What's come over you?" Carol asked him. "When did you get so zen?"

"Well, it's obviously an inconvenience—"

"An inconvenience?"

"Yes, but we're insured," said Eric. "And it won't interfere with the three-way move."

"Are you letting the papers know?" Ryan asked.

Eric grimaced. "I don't know, I'm not sure I want to be in the news for this reason."

"Could be worse," Ryan said. "At least no one's died."

"What an odd thing to say," Carol said, sorting through the kitchen crockery. "Do you know, the vindictive sod even smashed your 'Best Boss' mug, Mr Meek?"

"Didn't you see the news yesterday?" Ryan asked her.

"I don't watch the news," Carol replied. "If it's not bloody Brexit it's bloody Boris."

"Didn't you hear about Woodland Manor?"

"What about it?" she had to raise her voice, as the volume of the boiling kettle increased.

"They found a body in the woods."

Carol emerged from the kitchen, her face pale.

Eric joined the conversation. "And I think I know who it is," he said.

"A body?" Carol whispered.

"I think it could be Verity," Eric said.

"Verity?"

"She worked at Woodland Manor the same time as me."

Carol's eyes widened. "You worked there?"

"Only for a couple of months back in 1976."

"I don't remember you," Carol said.

"You wouldn't," Eric replied. "I was one of the kitchen grunts, chained to the sinks, though I had a few stints as a ladybird as well."

"That place…"

"Do you remember Verity?" Eric asked her. "I was quite close to her, until Little Len rained on my parade."

The door of the showroom opened, and a serious-looking man in an expensive suit walked in. "Oh my," he muttered. "This is a fine old mess."

"I'm sorry sir but we're closed today," Ryan told him.

"That's probably a wise decision," the man replied, taking in the full extent of the devastation. "I'm the loss adjuster. Is Carol about?"

She was. She patiently answered his questions and dug out receipts for the computers. Not long after he left, the glazier arrived and suggested Eric, Carol, and Ryan might want to vacate the premises for the day, as he would be working well into the evening and there was going to be a lot of noise and mess.

"I'll give you a ring when I'm close to finishing," the glazier said to Eric.

"Don't ring me, ring Carol," Eric said. "I've got things to do."

"So have I," Carol replied. "And you seem to forget that this is your business, not mine."

"Are you serious?" Eric asked her.

"My name's not above the door, is it?" Carol said. "Yet it's me who gets called out in the middle of the night to attend to the break-in. You didn't even answer your phone…"

"I'm sorry, I took a sleeping tablet…"

"And now you expect me to be on call again tonight, putting my own life on hold."

"Look, I'm sorry if I've been taking you for granted lately," Eric said gently, attempting to put his arm around her.

Carol aggressively pushed Eric's arm away. "Only lately, is it?" she cried, storming out of the showroom.

"Jesus, what an old boot," the glazier muttered. "Imagine being married to that."

## CHAPTER 23

### SATURDAY 14th DECEMBER 2019

When she hadn't turned up for work by ten, Eric decided to ring Carol. There was no answer. This was most unlike her. She had never previously been absent without letting Eric know in advance. Not that there was much actual work to do, apart from dealing with the three-way move, at least until the insurance company had finished its investigation, but he still expected her to show up. Ryan had done. Eric had sent him home after the two of them had tidied up and carried the wrecked displays out to the rear of the premises.

Eric agreed to keep paying Ryan's agency, even though Barrington Meek would not be trading for a while, as he didn't want Ryan finding an alternative position. He could be the ideal replacement for Alwyn, and Carol seemed to like him.

Her outburst the previous day had been totally out of character and Eric wondered what had caused it. Could it have been the stress of dealing with the break-in? Was it something he'd said? Or not said? Maybe there was something happening in her personal life? He knew very little about her life outside work. She did not discuss it and, he realised guiltily, he'd never been interested enough to ask. All he could recall was that she was married to a man who went fishing on New Year's Eve.

She lived in what estate agents would describe as 'an up and coming' part of Cwmbran in the sort of terraced house that would be marketed as 'ideal for a first-time buyer'. As Eric parked the Lexus outside, it attracted the attention of a group of adolescents in hoodies who were hanging around and vaping with attitude.

She was still in a dressing gown, a faded blue robe, when she answered the door. Eric had never seen her without makeup before and nor had he seen her looking so despondent. Even behind her glasses, he could see the whites of her eyes were pink, suggesting she had been crying.

"Carol, I've been so worried about you," Eric said. "Have I done something to upset you? Apart from taking you for granted, I mean."

She invited him in. Eric had never visited Carol's home before, but he knew the layout of these properties off by heart as they were all basically the same: two bedrooms, two reception rooms, compact kitchen, and upstairs bathroom. Former local authority houses, many were now in private hands and had lost their previously uniform exteriors: porches, and even loft extensions had been bolted on over the years as families' finances caught up with their need for more space. Carol's exterior remained standard though, and many period features remained inside too, he noted with approval. Such properties were easier to value and were quick to sell if competitively priced.

"Do you want some tea?" Carol asked, as they entered the living room.

"Thanks," Eric replied, taking in the faded orange and brown wallpaper, which looked like it had been up since the '70s. There was no sofa, just two large armchairs. Evidently Carol and her husband were neither cuddlers nor throwers of dinner parties, as the small square dining table also had just two hard wooden chairs. Eric perched on one, awkwardly.

"Sorry about the mess," Carol gestured at the collection of dishes, cups, and pans surrounding the kitchen sink as she filled the kettle.

"It's me who should be apologising," Eric said. "I obviously took you for granted once too often yesterday, and I'm really sorry."

"I've been taken for granted all my life—"

"And that's going to change," Eric interrupted her. "In the New Year, I promise you I will make you a partner in the business."

Carol smiled for the first time as she brought two mugs of tea to the table and sat down alongside Eric. "I was about to say, I've been taken for granted all my life so one more instance wasn't going to make any difference."

"What's wrong then?"

Carol stared into Eric's eyes. She seemed about to say something but then changed her mind and took a sip of scalding hot tea instead.

"Carol, whatever it is, you can tell me," Eric said. "How many years have we been together?"

She looked confused by his choice of words.

"You know what I mean," Eric corrected himself. "How many years have we worked together? And how often have we fallen out?"

She looked down into her tea. "It was when Ryan said a body had been found at Woodland Manor," she said slowly. "I thought I was going to be sick, it brought so many bad memories flooding back."

"I believe it could be Verity," Eric said. "The girl I used to—"

"It's not Verity," Carol said.

Eric stared at her. He felt a cold sensation wash over him. "You knew Verity?"

Carol nodded.

Eric's whole body began to tremble slightly. "Why didn't you say?"

Carol shrugged.

"How do you know it's not Verity?" Eric asked, the mug in his hand also now trembling.

"Verity lives in Bath."

"What?" Eric felt his stomach flip. "How do you know?"

"We send each other Christmas cards," Carol replied.

"You've got her address?" Eric said, trying to remain calm.

She nodded.

"I need it," Eric said. "Get it for me."

"I don't know if she'd want me to do that," Carol replied.

Eric raised his voice. "You must give it to me," he demanded. "I need that address."

Carol stared at Eric's flushed face in horror. He had never spoken to her like that before. She obediently reached for the address book under her landline phone, copied the details down onto a spare page and ripped it out.

"Why didn't you tell me this before?" Eric said, snatching the paper from her.

Tears filled Carol's eyes, but Eric was not there to see them.

***

Eric could have picked a worse day to drive to Bath but only if he had really, really tried. The second Saturday before Christmas is a key day in the city's tourism calendar, with festive events and markets filling the Georgian streets of its centre, and significantly swelling its population. The queues for the car parks were tailing back onto the roads, further slowing Eric's progress.

No doubt the locals could have shown him an easier route to Verity's address, but his car's sat-nav seemed intent on giving him a guided tour of the city's honey-coloured architecture. He had spent nearly as long stuck in Bath's city centre traffic as it had taken him to make the journey from Cwmbran.

Hordes of shoppers in Santa hats, weighed down with bags of Christmas purchases, further slowed the flow of crawling cars by crossing in front of them, rendering the 20mph speed limit signs aspirational at best.

At least the prolonged journey had given him plenty of time to consider his opening line. He'd considered everything from the standoffishly cool 'Hey, remember me?' to the Brief Encounter-inspired 'I say, haven't we met somewhere before?' but whatever he said would have to be appropriate to her situation. In his heart he envisaged her still single, still slim, still with long blonde hair, and still with the same vivacious enthusiasm for life she displayed back in the '70s. Perhaps she would be wearing a short tennis skirt, having played at her club in the afternoon?

Eric conceded that would be unlikely, as even he knew tennis was rarely played in December, but that's what he was willing her to look like. He was also preparing himself for her to be haggard, worn down by life, or morbidly obese. Or she could be happily married to Little Len, surrounded by adoring grandchildren.

Not for the first time during the journey, he asked himself what he hoped to achieve with this trip. Even if she was as he imagined her, he didn't expect her to just fall into his arms and quip 'Hey, what took you so long?'. But he had been holding a candle for her for so many years that he couldn't stop his stupid mind painting pictures of something like that happening. And if he didn't want that as an outcome, why else was he here? Just to apologise and to find out how life had treated her, he answered himself. To insert a page break into that chapter of his life so it would stop bleeding through into the rest of his book.

Eventually the sat-nav implored him to turn right into a residential street, and informed him, with an air of finality: "You have arrived at your destination."

With another vehicle immediately behind him, Eric was unable to pull over as there was nowhere to park. All the houses had driveways, and white lines in the gutter indicated both the areas which were to be kept clear and where parking was permitted. Eric continued up the hill, noticing that the houses increased in desirability the further up he went, then spotted a suitable sized gap. He darted into it without indicating, giving his front nearside alloy a bash and earning a toot of disapproval from the vehicle following him.

He was grateful for the opportunity to stretch his legs on the walk down the hill, after being confined to the Lexus cabin for so long, and it gave him the opportunity to compose himself and think again about what he was going to say to Verity. Assuming she was in, of course. Eric had not even considered the possibility that she might be out.

Now he was almost here he could feel his stomach turning over in anticipation. The last time he felt this nervous he was addressing the membership at his trade association's AGM. What a shitshow that was. He was given a graveyard slot, resulting in a steady stream of people leaving throughout his speech because they wanted to get to the bar. The bastards didn't even laugh at his jokes.

He took in the houses on both sides of the street. They were mainly traditional mid-century modern semis, but outstanding examples of the type. Constructed from the same honey-coloured stone as Bath's iconic Royal Crescent and the Circus, they were complemented by handsome arched doorways and Georgian windows. What a beautiful street to live on, Eric thought: the peace of the suburbs but just a short walk from the city centre. How much would one of these go for? Probably in the region of a million. And while he was mentally spending the commission he would earn from such a sale, he really did arrive at his destination.

It was one of several that had been constructed later than the grand properties in the rest of the street. Although detached, they lacked the charm and elegance of the semis, being basic boxes of the sort that young children drew: two windows upstairs, two windows down, and with a sloping roof and a central door. Eric wondered how much these properties would sell for, compared to their more upmarket neighbours. One was for sale, and Eric snapped a picture of the estate agent's unfamiliar board so he could satisfy his professional curiosity later.

A short wall separated the front garden from the pavement and Eric rested his shoe on it and pretended to tie his laces, though he was actually calculating the square footage of the property by estimating its exterior dimensions. It was dark, and there were no lights on inside the house, so Eric sat on the wall and read the BBC News app on his phone.

After he had read every story, including the sports ones, he stood up to stretch his legs. Maybe he should just go home. Old Eric would have. Old Eric would have bolted for home as soon as he failed to find a parking space. But old Eric would never have even made the trip. And this was new Eric.

He walked up to the front door and rung the bell. A tuneless sound could be heard within but nothing else. He rang again and rapped on the wooden front door. The knocking echoed in the hall, suggesting no carpet and very little furniture.

After a few minutes he pulled a business card from his jacket pocket and scribbled his mobile number on it with the message 'Please call me, Verity'. He was just about to post it through the brass-effect letterbox when he heard footsteps on the path behind him. He turned around and there was Verity.

Her face and figure were fuller, her hair was shorter and a different shade of blonde, but it was unmistakably her. She was wearing jeans and a quilted coat with a faux fur trimmed hood and was carrying two shopping bags.

"Can I help you?" she said warily.

"Hello," Eric said. And then he clammed up. His throat tightened and he couldn't say anything even if he'd known what words he was going to say.

"Hello," she repeated back to him, but with no enthusiasm. "Why are you on my property?"

"Are you Verity?" Eric asked.

"Who?" she snapped. "You must have the wrong house."

"Verity, I'd know you anywhere," Eric said, adopting the standard let's-hug-it-out pose, with arms outstretched ahead of him. "It's me, Eric."

She was glaring at Eric with contempt. "Who?"

"Eric. Eric Meek. We worked together at Woodland Manor in Cwmbran in 1976."

"You're wrong," she said.

"I'm not," he replied gently. "I've never forgotten you."

She continued staring at him. "I don't know you from Adam," she said. "Who are you, again?"

"Eric," replied. "We had a picnic down the boating lake when we were teenagers."

"Who do you work for?"

"I'm an estate agent," Eric said.

"And what do you want?"

"I just wanted to know what happened to you," Eric said. "Carol gave me your address."

"Who?"

"Carol. She was the receptionist."

At last, there was a flicker of recognition on Verity's face. "Why would she do that?"

"She works for me. Well, with me. You are Verity, aren't you?"

"I used to be," she finally said. "I changed my name a long time ago."

"And you honestly don't remember me?"

She shook her head. "I honestly don't."

"My father had the shop in Lôn Heddychlon," Eric said. "I brought pies and pasties to the picnic, and you were disappointed I didn't have any fruit."

She rubbed her chin and narrowed her eyes. "What did you say your name was?"

"Eric. Eric Meek."

"I vaguely remember having a picnic," she said. "But I don't remember who it was with."

Eric found this very hard to believe. Every minute detail of the day, good and bad, was ingrained into his memory. "You don't remember who you had the picnic with?"

"A lot has happened since then," Verity said, picking up her shopping bags. "Now, if you don't mind, I've got frozen food to put away."

"You were spending the day with me, but you went off with Little Len," Eric said in a whisper-like voice.

Verity's face hardened at the sound of his name. "I'd like you to leave now," she said.

"But Verity—"

"Leave me alone," she shrieked, as she scrambled to unlock her front door. "And don't ever come here again."

The door slammed, and Verity was gone. Again.

## CHAPTER 24

### SUNDAY 15th DECEMBER 2019

Eric woke up on the sofa in the lounge of his new house. He hadn't slept well. Although his black leather three-seater was less than a year old, it had proved to be even less comfortable than the Freemans' ancient fabric one.

The events of the last few days finally caught up with him when he returned from Bath the previous night, and he'd fallen asleep in his clothes in front of the television. All these years Verity had been living less than an hour away from him. He had been pathetically pining for her, like a grief-stricken dog whose owner has passed away, and she didn't even remember him. Whatever her story was, Eric accepted he was unlikely to learn it now.

The television's eco mode had kicked in at some point, and when Eric fired it back up, he was less than impressed with what the BBC considered Sunday afternoon entertainment: Bargain Hunt, Songs of Praise, followed by an animated film about animals joining a circus. Reason enough to treat himself to Sunday lunch at Woodland Manor, which he now lived just a few minutes' walk from.

The restaurant was fully booked so Eric sat alone on a tiny table for two in the lounge. All his fellow diners had companions to share their tables with, be they friends, partners, children, or parents, and Eric felt awkwardly self-conscious sat with just his phone and table-identifying spoon for company. The service was slow and there was no sign of Seb.

Only a week had passed since he and Carol had enjoyed Sunday lunch together, but it felt like months. So much had happened since then. He'd thoroughly enjoyed her company, and even though the venue they'd visited was a little downmarket compared to his current location, he wished he was back there with her. That would be the her of last Sunday, not the her of yesterday, which he'd been unforgivably rude to. If only the portal would allow him to replay any day.

His lunch finally arrived. The carrots and parsnips were decent, but the beef was tough, the roast potatoes were stodgy, the Yorkshire pudding was burnt, the peas were as hard as marbles, and the gravy was watery. That will be £27.50, please. Does sir wish to add a gratuity? No, sir bloody doesn't.

Walking back home, Eric glanced across at the house formerly known as Meek's Mini Market. He felt a little guilty at abandoning his father to his fate, and considered what he might do differently, should he decide to try again. Let the police know in advance that one of their own will be committing a crime? That could work, but only if his report is taken seriously. Stand guard outside the shop himself, and prevent Spanner doing the breaking and entering? A nice idea in principle, but Spanner would be a formidable opponent. Ring 999 as soon as Spanner approaches the shop, so he can be caught in the act? That had much more appeal, but there was no phone box in the vicinity. He could call it in from the Freeman's house though, he would just have to come up with a plausible reason why they should invite him in on a Saturday night and allow him to stakeout the property opposite.

Eric's what-if forecasting was interrupted by the ringing of his phone. It was Mrs Ducreux. Oh God, what did she want? He knew she was going to be trouble. He'd told Carol this right from the start. He considered not picking up but that might exacerbate whatever issue she had, and he'd have to face her sometime.

"Hello," Eric said cautiously.

"Eric, I've got a problem," she wailed.

"Not with the house, I hope?"

"No, the house is fabulous," she said. "It's with the gallery."

"That's a relief," Eric said.

"How so?"

"I'm sorry, I meant to say…" Shit.

"I know what you meant," she said. "And I know this is nothing to do with you but, as you know, I'm new to the area and I've got no one else to turn to."

"How can I help?" he asked, attempting to sound enthusiastic.

"The gallery's grand opening is next week," she said. "And that prick of a photographer has thrown a hissy fit because he doesn't like the location. He thinks a gallery in a town centre is too low rent for his work, so he's pulled the exhibition."

"Oh dear," Eric sympathised. "I'm sorry to hear that."

"Not half as sorry as I am, darling," she said. "I know it's a long shot, but I don't suppose you can think of any local photographers keen to exhibit their work at short notice, can you?"

Eric did not need to think for long. "I might very well do," he said.

"You'd be an absolute lifesaver if you did," she said. "But no rubbish, obviously. And nothing that induces seen-it-all-before syndrome."

"Would you be interested in an installation showcasing the Cwmbran of 1976?" Eric asked. "They're beautiful photographs and they've never been shown in public before. And I think they would have far more local appeal than scenes from the River Usk."

"Oh darling," Mrs Ducreux cried. "I could kiss you, I really could. Who is it?"

"It's not someone you'd know."

"I'd have to see samples of their work first," she cautioned.

"Are you in this afternoon?"

She was.

"I'll be down in about an hour," Eric said.

***

Before he got out of the Lexus, Mrs Freeman was standing at the door to greet him. She was smiling, and beckoning Eric in.

"What a lovely surprise," she said to Eric. "Will you stay for tea?"

"That's very kind," Eric said, entering the small hallway of the property. "How are you settling in?"

"I'm only sorry we didn't do this years ago," she said. "Have you come to see Frank? I hope you haven't brought him whisky again."

"Not this time," Eric said, as he was ushered into the lounge. Mr Freeman was sat in one of two winged armchairs, which were positioned either side of a green baize card table. A game of Scrabble was in progress.

"Mr Meek," Mr Freeman said, attempting to rise. "To what do we owe the pleasure?"

"Please don't get up," Eric said to the old man. "I'm only here for a quick chat."

"I'll put the kettle on," Mrs Freeman said, tottering into the kitchen.

Eric sat in her chair and studied the board, the letters in her rack, and the scores. "I hope you two are not playing for money," he said to Freeman. "Because I think she's got you over a barrel."

Freeman smiled at Eric's choice of words. "What can I do for you?"

"Actually, it's a case of what I can do for you," Eric replied.

"Oh?"

Eric explained how Mrs Ducreux had been let down and was looking for a photographer to showcase. "It would be wonderful for your archive to be seen by the local community," Eric said. "And selling prints could be quite lucrative."

Freeman considered the proposal for almost a minute. Finally, he said: "I think it's a marvellous idea, but I wouldn't want to be personally involved. Can I be anonymous?"

Eric shrugged. "Probably," he said. "Artists do use nom de plumes."

"I'd prefer that," Freeman said, stroking his chin. "I don't want to be in the local paper or have people know my business."

"Would you like to meet the gallery owner?"

"Not really," Freeman said. "Can you deal with it all?"

Eric hesitated. "I could…"

"Excellent," Freeman said. "The albums are in the garage."

"What is it with you and garages? Have you never considered just putting a car in one?"

Freeman burst out laughing.

Mrs Freeman returned from the kitchen with a tray containing three mugs of tea. "Sorry for the delay," she said. "I forgot to plug the kettle in. Now, what mischief were you two cooking up this time?"

Eric spent another twenty minutes in the Freemans' company and while Emily washed up, Frank saw him to the door and handed him the garage key.

"Take what you want," he said. "Come and go as you please."

"Thank you," Eric said, unlocking the door. "What shall we do about the money?"

"What money?"

"If you are anonymous, who will Mrs Ducreux pay for any sales?"

"She can pay you," Freeman said.

"She could," Eric said. "And I could then pay you, but there will be tax implications."

"You don't need to pay me," Freeman said. "You can decide what to do with any proceeds. Give them to a good cause or keep them yourself."

"Excuse me?"

"I don't need any more money, you've given me back my life," Freeman said, his eyes glistening. "This move has been the best thing that's ever happened to me. It's like Emily and I are rediscovering each other. You were right."

"About what?"

"About me being the dog."

***

It was strange pulling up outside his old house. It was even stranger going inside and seeing someone else's furniture where his had once been. And the formerly muted beige walls now sung with vibrant, colourful artwork. A psychedelic clown canvas on one wall competed for attention with a screaming nun on another, while three A4-sized abstracts dominated the mantelpiece.

"Obviously I'm not settled in yet," Mrs Ducreux said, noticing Eric's bewildered expression as he placed a large cardboard box on the onyx coffee table and lowered himself onto one of her two purple chaise lounges. "I've still got lots of stuff to retrieve from storage when I get chance."

Eric nodded. There was already far more furniture in the house than he ever had. "It looks great," he said, as convincingly as he could. "Very... homely."

"Don't ever play poker," she laughed. "You'll lose your shirt."

Eric opened the flaps of the cardboard box and brought out six of Freeman's albums. "These are just a sample of his work," he said. "He's probably accumulated enough for you to mount a new exhibition every month for the next five years."

She thumbed through the albums, squealing in delight every now and again. "What period does his work cover?" she asked. "These appear to be all '70s."

"Yeah, '70s is his speciality," Eric confirmed.

"Which years?"

"Just the one."

"One? He took all these pictures in one year?"

Eric confirmed that was the case.

"What about his other work? You said these albums were just a sample."

"They're the same," Eric said. "Every picture was taken in 1976. On July 3$^{rd}$ 1976, to be exact."

Mrs Ducreux stared incredulously at Eric. "How is that possible? There's hundreds of them."

"Thousands," Eric corrected her.

"Are you pulling my pisser, darling?"

Eric assured her he wasn't.

She exhaled deeply. "Well, they do say a narrow focus brings big results," she said, returning to the albums. Gesturing in the direction of a fluorescent orange vintage cocktail bar in the corner of the lounge, she added: "Be a sweetheart, darling. Go and mix us a couple of snifters. It's getting dark outside, so it's allowed."

Several hours, and several snifters later, Mrs Ducreux had selected the images she wanted for her premiere. She had decided against the albums devoted to school sports day at Cwmbran stadium ("Bit pervy for today's sensibilities, darling. All those alabaster pubescent thighs in tight short shorts"), and the boating lake ("How many different views of a shallow pool of water does a visitor need to see?") and settled on shops of the town centre.

As well as being appropriate for her new gallery's location, the exterior shots of long-gone retailers provoked nostalgic I-remember-them feelings, but the real stars were the interiors. Mrs Ducreux loved the record racks in Boots, the electric guitars in Soundwave, the washing powders in Fine Fare, and – her absolute favourite – the pick 'n' mix counter in Woolworths. The cascading displays of colour and confectionary completely captivated her. "I want this on my wall," she said of one. "No, I want it blown up and I want it as my wall."

"That would look striking in the gallery," Eric agreed.

"I'm not talking about the gallery," she said. "I meant here."

After they discussed terms – the split from any sales was to be 50/50 – Eric explained that the artist did not want to be publicly identified.

"That's a shame," she said. "But I can live with that. It might even give the installation more appeal. We'll have to give him a name though. What do you think of Argus?"

Eric looked sceptical.

"You remember your Greek mythology," she said. "Argus was the giant with 100 eyes who never fell asleep."

"Why not South Wales Argus?" Eric suggested.

"That does have a certain ring to it," she said.

"I'm teasing you," Eric said. "The South Wales Argus is the name of a local evening paper."

"You absolute arse," she roared, assaulting Eric with a lime green cushion. "You can mix me another drink for that."

"I'd better not," Eric said. "I'm driving."

"I'll get it myself then," she stormed off in a mock huff.

While she was searching for her swizzle stick, Eric packed the rejected albums back into the cardboard box. He then retrieved the boating lake one and casually flipped through it. He hadn't really seen the pictures earlier because Mrs Ducreux whizzed through it. Now, as he looked at each picture in turn, one stood out from the rest. While most were similar scenes of people standing and sitting around the lake, one shot captured a burly man with a '50s quiff who appeared to be throwing a teenager into the water.

Mrs Ducreux returned with her drink. "Are you sure I can't tempt you, darling?"

"Like I said, I've got the car outside," Eric replied, rising from the chaise lounge.

"I wasn't talking about a drink," she said, pursing her lips. "Have you got anyone to rush home for?"

Eric was stunned into silence.

"I've got a waterbed upstairs," she said.

"I've heard they're, er, quite practical," he stammered. "And you can, er, set them to a specific temperature, so the water is cool in the summer and warm in the winter."

Mrs Ducreux stood very close to Eric, one hand holding her glass and the other gently stroking his face. "Have you ever had sex on one?" she purred. "The motion of the ocean can cause quite a commotion."

"I can't say I have."

"You have had sex, though?" she teased, tapping his nose with her index finger.

"I just assumed that door was closed to me now," Eric said.

"Well, you know what they say," she whispered in his ear. "When a door is firmly closed, it might just need a good bang to get it open again."

## CHAPTER 25

### MONDAY 16th DECEMBER 2019

When Eric opened the door of the newly re-glazed showroom, he was surprised to see Carol already sat at her desk, typing on an old laptop she'd brought from home.

"Good morning," he said. "It's getting quite wintery out there."

She grunted something unintelligible in return but did not look up at him.

Eric was about to try again but, for the first time in his life, he didn't know what to say to her, so escaped to his own desk. He'd brought an old laptop of his own in and, once he'd set it up, checked his email. There were several messages from the insurance company he was expected to reply to, but he had little enthusiasm for anything right now.

After nearly an hour of silence, he glanced across at Carol, who was still engrossed in her laptop. This was the longest they had ever gone without speaking and the atmosphere felt awkward and uncomfortable. He would have to say something. They couldn't go on like this.

"I've got an idea for a TV programme," he finally said.

Carol ignored him.

"Kevin McCloud follows the progress of someone building a house near Silverstone racetrack."

Carol still ignored him.

"It would be called Grand Prix Designs," he said with a flourish.

Carol still ignored him.

"I'm popping out for some lunch," Eric sighed, desperate to escape the suffocating tension of the showroom. "Can I get you anything, Carol?"

She finally looked up at him. "No thanks," she replied in a quiet voice.

"What's upsetting you, Carol?" Eric asked. "I can't help you if I don't know what the problem is."

In a tone harsher than Eric could ever remember her using before, she snapped: "Help me? Why do you think I need your help? Do you think every woman needs a man to solve her problems?"

"No, of course not."

"Do you think all of us pathetic women need rescuing from our sad lives by a dashing knight in shining armour? Is that what it takes for a man to feel good about himself?" She paused for a few seconds, then added: "If we do need rescuing, it's from men – not by them."

***

Pulling into the car park of the Old Oak, Eric noticed how little it had changed over the last 43 years. True, it now had indoor toilets and a garden for families, with play equipment for children, but the exterior of the main building was indistinguishable from when he'd brought young Carol and his father here. Even the wooden picnic tables on the outside terrace were identical.

There had been long queues outside all the eateries Eric usually patronised in the town centre, so he'd decided, on a whim, to go out for lunch. He hadn't intended to come here – he thought he would go to Woodland Manor – but here he was. Perhaps, subconsciously, he was trying to feel closer to young Carol and his father.

The bar area was decorated with tinsel and mistletoe, and the usual '70s Christmas 'classics' were playing over the sound system, but both failed to raise any seasonal good cheer in Eric, who ordered a lasagne and retreated to a table as far away from the other customers as possible. The pub had always had a row of stools perched at the bar, and several customers – clearly locals – were sat discussing current events with the landlord.

The bar line-up changed several times while he ate his meal, with originals going and new arrivals taking their place. After finishing his microwaved lasagne, he made his way past them to get to the exit and heard one of the customers say: "I see they've identified that body they found in the woods."

Well, whoever it was, it certainly wasn't Verity.

"Oh yeah?" the landlord enquired, while he was pulling the man a pint.

"Len Butcher," the man said, accepting the fresh frothing pint and delighting in being first with the information.

"Who?" one of the younger men said.

"Little Len?" one of the older ones cheered. "Good enough for the prick."

"Hey, come on now," the landlord reproached him. "You can't use language like that in here."

"But he was a prick," the older man protested indignantly. "A massive prick. Just like his old man was a prick."

"Even so, show some respect," the landlord admonished. Gesturing towards Eric, he added: "This gentleman has come out here for a nice bit of lunch, he hasn't come here to hear you curse."

As Eric headed for the door, the landlord thanked him for his custom, and wished him a good afternoon and a very merry Christmas, but Eric did not respond. He was deep in thought. So that's where Little Len ended up.

As Eric opened the door to leave the pub, the landlord called after him, loud enough for Eric to hear: "Ignorant prick."

***

Seb was sat at his usual table and deep in conversation with his phone when Eric entered the lounge. He was clearly unhappy with whoever he was speaking to. His face was flushed red and tiny droplets of spittle had been trapped in his bushy white beard. Eric thought it prudent to steer clear of him. Seb had not been himself lately. But then, who had? Not Eric. And certainly not Carol.

Sipping his Guinness at the bar, Eric could hear brief snippets of Seb's conversation. It appeared he was trying to locate someone, but his task was proving problematic because he didn't know the person's name. When he finally finished his call, Seb joined Eric at the bar.

"Have you lost someone?" Eric enquired.

Seb gave him a thin resigned smile. "Kind of."

"Is there anything I can do to help?" Eric said.

"Not really," Seb replied.

"Is it true that the body in the woods is Little Len?"

Seb growled at Eric: "Stop saying 'the body in the woods', will you?"

"What?"

"I am so pissed off with hearing that expression," he said. "It's everywhere – the local radio, the Cwmbran Evening Star, the internet… I never thought I'd hate a phrase as much as 'Let's get Brexit done' but this is doing my head in. They've even started calling it Butcher's Wood."

"Sorry," Eric said.

"It's bad for business," Seb said. "It's not been confirmed by DNA yet, but dental records indicate that 'the body in the woods' is indeed that of Len Butcher."

"I wonder what happened to him?" Eric mused.

"Who cares?" Seb snapped, gesturing to the barmaid to bring him a drink. "He was a nasty little bastard, you said so yourself."

"He was," Eric agreed. "And I did. So much for Elvis protecting him."

"Elvis!" Seb scoffed. "He was a pussy."

This was probably true. Eric thought back to when he slapped Little Len at the boating lake, and Elvis did nothing.

"I wonder if he died the same night he disappeared," Eric said. "The night when everyone assumed he took off with Verity."

"Can we change the subject?" Seb said.

"I came here for Sunday lunch," Eric told him. "I didn't see you."

"I don't work Sundays," Seb said. "No one goes to their grave wishing they'd spent more time in the office."

"It was so busy," Eric said. "I would have thought you'd want to be here."

"I don't need to be here for Sunday lunch," Seb said. "It's lowest common denominator cooking. Pile it high and sell it cheap."

Eric narrowed his eyes and frowned. "I'm not sure I'd call it cheap."

"Can you just stop with all this prattling?" Seb said testily.

"Is something wrong?"

"You could say that," Seb huffed. "The sale of the woods has collapsed, and I'll never get anything like what they're worth now. Not after all this. I'll never be able to retire."

Eric guessed Seb was right. The discovery of a body rarely had a positive impact on property prices, so land was probably the same. He mentally composed the copy for the front cover of the prospective brochure: a select development of spacious apartments with exceptional views, perfectly suited for modern living. Butcher's Wood is located close to the beautiful Monmouthshire and Brecon Canal in the countryside east of the bustling town of Cwmbran. With the stunning landscapes of the Brecon Beacons on your doorstep and just a few miles drive to the historic city of Newport, Butcher's Wood also boasts all local amenities within walking distance and unparalleled transport links...

Eric's creative composition was interrupted by a text message. Removing his phone from his jacket pocket, he saw it was from Carol. Does this mean she was speaking to him now?

"Eric, I've left on your desk a list of jobs that you and Ryan need to do in the next couple of days," Carol's text read. "Some are urgent and only you can do them, so I've underlined these. The ones that aren't underlined can be left to Ryan, who is very capable and will be an ideal replacement for me. Thank you for everything you've done for me over the years, I wish you the very best of luck with the business in the future."

Eric read the text again. What did this mean? Was she resigning? It certainly sounded like it. That would be a kick in the teeth. But it could also be read as a cryptic suicide note. He texted back 'Carol, please ring me' and when he'd heard nothing for a few minutes, he rang her. It went straight to voicemail. He rang the office and Ryan explained she'd emptied her desk and left the keys with him. She hadn't told him where or why she was leaving.

Eric left without finishing, or paying for, his drink and drove the Lexus harder than he'd ever done before. Pulling up at Carol's house, he was perturbed to see a police car parked outside. He banged on the door several times, almost punching it. A uniformed police officer opened the door and Eric barged past him.

"Where is she?" Eric cried. "What's happened?"

Carol's husband was sat in one of the two armchairs, sobbing. Eric had always pictured him as a domineering ogre, neglecting his wife in favour of his own selfish pursuits, but this short, bald man in a grubby grey cardigan did not match that description.

The police officer had closed the front door and followed Eric in. "Can I ask who you are, sir?" he said in a voice dripping with displeasure at the way he'd been shoved aside.

"This is Mr Meek," Carol's husband said. "He's Carol's boss."

Eric was surprised her husband recognised him. They had never met. Eric didn't even know Carol's husband's name. As he considered this, he realised that he really should know it. He offered his hand to the man. "Pleased to meet you," Eric said.

"Likewise," the man said, standing up to shake Eric's hand. "I'm Terry."

"What's happened to Carol?" Eric asked Terry. "I had a text from her about half an hour ago. Is she alright?"

"She's fine," the police officer said. "I'm glad you're here Mr Meek because I was going to be contacting you next."

"Where's Carol?"

"I told you sir, she's fine," the policeman repeated. "I'm officer Ripley and I'd like to suggest that you sit down and calm yourself while I make us all a nice cup of tea and we'll go through everything."

"But—" Eric started to say.

"Do sit down sir," officer Ripley repeated, rather more forcefully. "Please."

While Ripley disappeared into the adjacent kitchen, Eric slumped into the other chair. The two men sat in silence. Gripping the arms of the chair, he eventually said to Terry: "This is very comfortable."

"Yes, we love them," Terry replied. "They were only £600 for the pair. They recline too."

"Just what you need," Eric said.

"We used to have a sofa, but the cats wrecked it," Terry said. "They were always snagging the back of it with their claws."

Bloody cats. One is okay, especially if it can be photographed curled up on a rug in front of a roaring fire, but more than one can be a problem. There will be lots of loose hair, and the smell of litter trays. Three or more cats and that house is never going to sell for the asking price, not until it gets a deep clean while the moggies get shipped off to a cattery.

"Strange that we've never met before," Terry said to Eric.

"Yes," Eric agreed. "It is."

"Does she talk about me?"

Eric considered his response. Sometimes, but not in a positive way.

"I didn't think she would," Terry said. "I've never been good enough for her."

"She's never said that," Eric tried to reassure him. This really was a comfortable chair, especially for that price. "Where did you say you got these chairs?"

"I'm saying it," Terry said. "I can tell by the way she looks at me. She blames me for how her life has turned out."

"I'm sure that's not true," Eric said.

Terry started to weep. "It is true, I've never been nothing but a disappointment to her," he sobbed. "She deserves so much better. She deserves someone like you. She was always talking about you. Mr Meek this, Mr Meek that…"

"Where is she?"

"She's in prison," Terry replied.

"In prison?"

"She's confessed to murdering that bloke in the woods," Terry said.

Ripley emerged from the kitchen, balancing three steaming mugs on a round yellow plastic tray. "That's not strictly true," Ripley corrected Terry. "But she is likely to be charged with perverting the course of justice. I'm afraid I couldn't find any biscuits…"

## CHAPTER 26

## SATURDAY 3ʳᴅ JULY 1976

Eric emerged from the Freemans' garage into the familiar scorching sunshine. He was overdressed for the weather, in dark jeans and a black sweater, but there was a good reason for that. As there was for the pair of high-powered binoculars that dangled from his neck by a strap. As he gently closed the garage door, he stared across at Meek's Mini Market, where his father and Spanner were plotting tonight's break-in. Eric had bigger fish to fry on this occasion. Sorry Dad, but you're going to find out the hard way what a mistake you're making. Now you'll be indebted to Spanner for the rest of your life.

Sweat began to trickle down Eric's face. He couldn't just stand out here in this weather. Besides, Spanner would be leaving the shop very soon and his copper's instinct for a wrong 'un had resulted in the pair of them clashing on two earlier occasions.

Suddenly the unmistakable clanging bell of the shop door broke the silence. Spanner was on his way. Eric approached the Freemans' front door and pretended to ring the bell. He was horrified when the door opened just as his finger was poised.

"Can I help you?" asked Emily Freeman. A much younger Emily Freeman than Eric had seen before. She wore a long-sleeved white linen dress with tassels around the deep cut neckline and hem. The woman from Preloved Designer Wear had one just like it on a mannequin in her shop. Boho chic, she'd called it. Emily's hair was long, dark, and flowing, with strands of grey just starting to appear.

Eric quickly calculated that she would be in her mid-40s but she bore virtually no resemblance to the woman he knew in 2019.

"Hello?" she said. "Are you okay?"

"Yes, thank you," he eventually stuttered. "You must be Mrs Freeman?"

She nodded.

"I'm here to see your husband," Eric said. "Is he available?"

Taking in his unconventional attire, which was totally unsuited to the current weather, she asked cautiously: "Is he expecting you?"

Eric shook his head. "He's not, but I've got some information about his... er..."

"His project?" she suggested, opening the door wide enough for him to enter. "You'd better come in then." While holding the door, she bent down to pick up a leaflet that had been posted through the letterbox.

Eric followed her in, noting the unfamiliar chandelier that hung in the hall: in 2019 there was just a single lightbulb. "What a lovely ceiling rose," Eric commented. "Is that an original feature?"

"No, we had those put in throughout the house when we moved here, along with the cornices. They're a little ostentatious, I know, but it was so plain and boring inside."

"That's mid-century modern for you," Eric replied.

"Pardon?" she stared at him.

"Isn't that what they call houses built after the second world war?" Eric spluttered. "With clean, simple lines and a lack of decorative embellishments?"

"I've never heard that expression before," she said. "Are you a property expert?"

Eric laughed. "I suppose I am," he said.

"My husband is in his den," she said, pointing to the door that led to the garage. "Can I get you something to drink?"

"That would be wonderful," Eric said, surreptitiously wiping the sweat from his forehead with his jumper sleeve.

"Would you like me to mix you a Harvey Wallbanger or a Piña Colada?"

Eric laughed again. He had no idea such cosmopolitan drinks were served in Cwmbran in 1976. "I wish I could," he said. "But I'm here on business."

"Business? On a Saturday? How intriguing. Something non-alcoholic then?"

"Anything cold would be nice."

She yanked open the door of the kitchen fridge. Inside it was virtually empty, apart from some wrapped meat, salad vegetables, yoghurts, milk, and around half a dozen pink cans. "Do you drink Tab?" she asked. "It's like Coca-Cola but for diabetics… and people who are trying to lose weight."

"That'll be great, thank you," Eric replied, wondering if she was alluding to his less than trim body. He'd tried Tab occasionally, when Meek's Mini Market run out of Cresta, Coke, and Lilt, but he wasn't a fan. He was partial to its successor, Diet-Coke, though.

"Ice?"

"Thank you."

She returned a few seconds later with a large glass tumbler, filled with the fizzing brown liquid and four cubes of ice. "I keep it in the fridge, but it still needs ice in this weather," she said.

"I've heard that's a problem for shops," Eric said. "Keeping goods cold."

"I'm sure it is," she said. "Alright if I leave you to it?"

"Leave me to it?"

"Leave you with my husband," she said. "I'm making the most of this weather and getting a tan in the garden."

"I hope you've got plenty of sun cream," Eric called out to her as she walked outside.

"Can't bear the stuff," she called back, before laying down on a flowery patterned sun lounger positioned between the two rows of poles.

Without decades of exposure to the elements discolouring them, Eric could see the poles were made of bright copper which glistened in the sun.

"Nice poles," Eric said.

"Aren't they hideous?" she replied. "But apparently they are going to reduce our energy bills."

Eric considered warning her of the dangers of not using sun cream, how her skin would age prematurely and develop wrinkles, but she was probably in more danger from whatever force the poles were generating. Or conducting. Or diffusing. Eric didn't know what role they played. Then again, thinking of her and young Carol, and how vivacious they were in this time compared to their 2019 counterparts, maybe women were harmed more by staying married to men who neglected them rather than exposure to the sun or time-travelling portals.

The door leading to the garage was locked but Eric used his own key to open it.

"What do you want?" yelled a hostile voice from inside. "I've told you never to come in here when I'm working. It's dangerous."

Eric ignored the warning and closed the door behind him. Still holding his glass of Tab, he took his first swallow of it. He didn't like it. It tasted a bit like medicine, but at least it was cold and refreshing. The layout of the garage was pretty much unchanged, and Freeman was hunched over his workbench with his back to Eric, examining a thin sheet of metallic material under a microscope.

"I told you I was working," Freeman said, aggressively.

"I just thought you might like a drink," Eric said, placing the glass of Tab on the workbench.

Freeman spun around: "Who the hell are you?" he said to Eric. "And how did you get in here?"

Despite being younger than Eric at this time, the 1976 Freeman looked remarkably similar to the 2019 model. He was slightly taller, his face less lined and his features more defined, but his bald head could still only call on a few wispy strands of hair for protection. And he stank of body odour, suggesting he hadn't bathed or showered for several days. The dried sweat stains on his off-white nylon shirt added credence to this theory.

"I would say that you wouldn't believe me," Eric said. "Or even that you couldn't believe me, but I know that you of all people can."

Freeman stared at Eric. "What the hell are you talking about?"

"I'm saying – actually my presence here is proof – that while you fail in your quest to generate free electricity—"

"How do you know about that?" Freeman gasped.

"You do, in fact, create something else entirely."

Freeman stared at Eric expectantly: "Yes? What?"

Eric considered how to phrase his answer. "A hole."

"A hole?"

"In the universe."

"Do you mean a wormhole?"

"Possibly," Eric said.

Freeman fired a series of questions at Eric, none of which he could answer.

Eric eventually held up his hands in a gesture of surrender. "Look, I'm an estate agent, not a rocket scientist," he said. "In layman's terms, your project has opened up a doorway between today and the future."

Freeman collapsed onto a plastic chair that looked like it had been liberated from a school science lab. He grabbed the glass of Tab and downed it. After he wiped his mouth, he ventured: "Are you from—"

"The future? Yes. Well, one possible future."

"I never imagined for one second that this could happen," Freeman said. "But now I think about it..."

Freeman started babbling excitedly, to himself rather than Eric, using terms unfamiliar to 99.9% of estate agents, before concluding: "I've invented time travel! This is a truly momentous day!"

"You don't think so," Eric said. "The future you, that is."

"What do you mean?"

"It's a long story," Eric said.

"I've got time," Freeman replied.

"No, you haven't," Eric said. "You have already spent so many years on this, and it will be many more years before you figure out how to use it without cooking yourself. By the time you have, you will be a sad and bitter old man who realises he has wasted his life."

"I have not wasted my life!" Freeman snapped.

"I'm paraphrasing but those are your words, not mine," Eric said. "Because this thing is useless."

"It's the greatest invention of this century," Freeman cried.

"I thought so at first, too," Eric said. "But while someone from the future can go back in time, they can only come here to this garage and only to this day. Today. Consider that for a second. All you'll ever be able to do is return here, at this time. So why not just enjoy the day now? Spend some time with Emily in the garden, explain why she should use sun cream, have a few cocktails. She knows how to mix a Harvey Wallbanger and a Piña Colada! Or go out to a country pub for lunch—"

"I can't stop now," Freeman countered. "Not now you've told me that the device is operational."

"Yes, it works, but it's got no practical application," Eric said. "You can't change a thing. Everything resets when you return. You've no more impacted on the past than if you watched a documentary about it."

Freeman looked dubious. "That can't be."

"From what little I know, each time you travel through the portal you either create a new world, which you can never return to or interact with again—"

"The many-worlds theory is true?" Freeman asked enthusiastically.

"Maybe. Or the universe observes your actions and cleans up after you, like a dog owner scooping up a turd his pet has left on the pavement."

Freeman bombarded Eric with more questions, few of which were coherent or understandable. Eric eventually put his hand over Freeman's mouth, like Freeman had once done to him in a physics lesson. "Listen, I can't give you answers, I'm an estate agent," Eric said. "And I had an awful physics teacher in school. But I can give you the best piece of advice you'll ever receive."

"And what is that?"

"Stop," Eric said. "It's not worth it."

"How can you say that?"

"You've got a wonderful wife upstairs," Eric said. "Spend your time with her instead."

"Be like everybody else?"

"Yes, be like everybody else," Eric said. "Have an ordinary life. Go places, do things, buy an Aston Martin. Because the you that I know will go to his grave regretting all the years he squandered on this project."

Freeman stared at him. "But if I do that, how will you get here?"

"I told you," Eric said. "Every trip creates a new world, or any changes I make get erased when I return. So even if you do stop now, the you that I know won't have done."

"So why are you telling me this?"

"You know, I've only just realised something," Eric said. "Every time I come back to 1976—"

"You've been here before?"

"I have, and every time I've tried to help people I have failed miserably."

"What people?"

"You don't know them, but you know Emily," Eric said, firmly clasping Freeman's shoulder. "Go and spend your time with her rather than rotting in this self-constructed dungeon."

Freeman looked around his garage, considering Eric's words. "I've already devoted so many years of my life on this."

"You have, but no one in the cemetery wishes they'd spent more time in the office – ugh, I hate myself for saying that."

"You expect me to just walk away from it?"

"And have a shower," Eric added. "You pong a bit."

After a few minutes silence, Freeman brightened up: "But if you help me with it, with your knowledge of how it works, I'll be able to complete the project much quicker, and spend time with Emily as well."

Eric stood up. "Like I said, I've failed every time I've tried to help anyone. I will see myself out, Mr Freeman. I know the way."

***

Eric had spent the rest of the afternoon at the boating lake, savouring once again the sun, sounds, sights, and smells of his teenage years. Actually, this is far superior to watching a documentary, he conceded. With advances in VR technology, this might ultimately be what a visit to the cinema will be like in the future.

An exceptionally large C&A branded carrier bag was floating on the surface of the lake near the bank and Eric reached down to rescue the discarded item. Someone must have been shopping for new clothes – in Newport, where the nearest branch was – and changed into them when they arrived at the lake. It was probably a lacey top or a skimpy summer dress, judging by what most of the women here were wearing.

Eric had rescued the bag partly out of civic duty but mostly out of necessity: he hadn't dared leave the portal suit in the front chamber of the garage in case Freeman discovered it, so he'd been carrying it around all day, rolled up into as tight a bundle as possible. Holding the voluminous bag in one hand, he stuffed the suit into it with the other. He had hidden the helmet in one of Woodland Manor's many rhododendron bushes, which had been allowed to grow unencumbered either side of the entrance, and he planned to store the suit and the helmet in the front section of Freeman's garage before he undertook his night's task. It had seemed so easy when he was planning this trip back in 2019, but now he was here he began to feel apprehensive.

Several hours later, when daylight became dusk, Eric made his way up to Woodland Manor. The waiting around had been frustrating, but far worse was the knowledge that Carol would be enduring the unwelcome attentions of Big Ben, while Elvis watched, and Eric wouldn't be there to intervene.

After stashing the helmet and suit in the garage, Eric furtively made his way along the grass verges that bordered Woodland Manor's drive. They were almost as hard as the gravel, through lack of water, but they made less noise. And he did not want to attract any attention as he was here purely to observe.

The entrance doors to the reception area were wedged open with shrubs in pots and the giant rhododendron bush that Eric was hiding in gave him an unobstructed view of the whole desk and several feet either side of it. A subdued Carol was sat at the desk, attempting to tidy her hair and reapply her smudged lipstick with a tiny compact mirror that was leaning against an empty pint glass – probably the one that Eric had broken on his previous visit. She looked up as Little Len came into view, and Eric could see her mascara had run.

"My dad says you've got to get someone from behind the bar," he said to Carol.

"There's no one spare," Carol said quietly. "Everyone is flat out as it's nearly last orders."

The stillness of the night, and Eric's proximity to the reception desk, allowed him to hear every word of the conversation with absolute clarity, despite the muffled boom-boom of the music in the ballroom.

"Don't argue with me, do as you're told and go and get someone," Little Len ordered, much louder than he needed to. "Go on, I'll watch the desk."

After Carol left, Little Len checked himself out in her compact mirror. He was evidently pleased with what he saw because he was making kissing faces into it, pursing his lips and narrowing his eyes.

Carol returned with Verity, who rolled her eyes when she saw Little Len.

"What do you want?" Verity asked him.

"You've got to go up to the poker game," he said. "They've had their break so now they need more drinks."

"Where's Sandra?"

"She's quit," said Little Len. "The little scrubber just stormed out."

"I'm not going up there," Verity replied.

"You've got to!"

"I am not going into that room with those pigs," she replied.

"Don't make her go up there," Carol said to Little Len. "I'll find someone else to see to the drinks."

Little Len grabbed Verity's arm. "In that case, you can help me feed the real pigs," he said, leading her out of reception and around the side of the building towards the kitchen.

"They stink," Verity protested.

"You should have gone to the poker then, shouldn't you?"

"Why are you feeding them now anyway?"

"To show stupid little girls what happens when they don't do as they're told," Little Len replied.

"You really are a tosser," Verity said to him.

With no other female bar staff available, Carol had despatched one of the red-jacketed ladybirds up to the bridal suite to take the poker players' drinks order. He had complained, as he was about to end his shift, but she promised she would amend his times in the recordkeeping book so he would have an extra two hours' pay. Satisfied, he slunk off up the stairs, though with little enthusiasm.

Eric didn't recognise him so perhaps this was his first shift. Perhaps he was Eric's replacement. Woodland Manor had a rapid turnover of staff. Everyone underage was paid cash in hand and there were no official records kept of all the youths who came and went. Some only lasted a night. Some – like the one Big Ben forced to down a shot of Tabasco Sauce – less than an hour.

Eric's musing on 1976 employment initiations was disturbed by the sound of someone running on the gravel. Suddenly Verity appeared and ran into reception, slamming into the desk.

"I've stabbed him," she cried.

Horrified, Carol came from behind the desk and grabbed Verity. "You've stabbed Little Len?"

Verity wailed: "He made me sit on the pigs' fence and threatened to throw me in with them if I didn't kiss him. I tried to get down, but he wouldn't let me."

"Where did you stab him?" Carol asked, holding both of Verity's arms and looking into her eyes.

"In the neck," Verity said. "And then he fell in with the pigs."

Carol examined the white bow of Verity's blouse. It had red splashes on it. She brought the sobbing Verity behind the desk and sat her in the receptionist's chair. "I'll get you a drink," she said to her. "Sit there and I'll fetch Simon."

Within seconds, Carol had reappeared with what looked like a brandy glass and Seb. Carol gave the glass to Verity, who gratefully sipped its contents.

"You've stabbed Little Len?" Seb said to Verity. "And he's in with the pigs?"

Verity nodded.

"Okay, stay there," Seb said.

"I'd better call the police," Carol said.

"No," Seb said. "I'll go and see him. Wait until I come back, and we know what we're dealing with."

As Seb strode off, Carol put her arm around Verity and tried to comfort her. "What did you stab him with?"

Verity held up the small chrome tool, attached to a lanyard, which combined a bottle opener and a corkscrew. All bar staff wore the devices around their necks so they could open bottles and serve customers faster.

"I doubt you'll have done much damage with this," Carol said. "You've probably hurt his pride though."

Verity tried to laugh but couldn't quite do it. "I hate him," she said. "He thinks if he says I'm his girlfriend that I'll just go along with it. I only took the job because one of my friends from school was too afraid to work here on her own and begged me to apply too."

"It's not a healthy place for young girls," Carol said.

"I know," Verity said. "She quit last week, because Little Len kept coming on to her, so then he moved on to me."

"I'm sure he's learned a lesson tonight," Carol said. "He might think twice about doing that to other girls in the future."

They sat in silence for several minutes and then Seb reappeared.

"How is he?" Carol asked.

"He's dead," Seb replied, stony faced.

Both women burst into tears.

"I'm going to have to ring the police now," Carol wailed, picking up the telephone receiver.

Seb snatched it off her. "Do you want – what's her name?"

"Verity," said Verity.

"Do you want Verity to go to prison for the rest of her life?"

Carol shook her head. "Of course not."

"Neither do I," Seb said. "And she doesn't have to. Leave this to me. First get her out of that blouse and into a fresh one."

While Carol helped Verity out of her blouse behind the desk, Seb made a call. "Hello Sue, it's Seb here from Woodland Manor, can I have a priority taxi straight away please?"

"What's going to happen to me?" wailed Verity.

"Did anyone see you go into the woods with Little Len?" Seb asked Verity.

"Some of the kitchen porters might have," Verity replied. "We went inside to get the pig bin and carried it out with each of us holding a handle."

Addressing Carol, Seb said: "Listen closely. I'm going to send you both to a friend of mine who will look after you tonight. If anyone asks, Carol, you just fancied a trip to Bath for the hell of it."

Carol looked bemused. "Bath?"

Grabbing Verity, Seb said to her: "You and Little Len are boyfriend and girlfriend and you decided to run off together for a few days."

"How would they do that?" Carol said.

"They stole Big Ben's car," Seb replied.

"It's right there," Carol said, pointing to it.

"It won't be for much longer," Seb snapped. "Now, no more questions."

"This is wrong," Carol said. "We should just call the police."

"It'll be fine," Seb said, writing an address on a piece of paper. "As long as you do what I'm telling you. When the taxi comes, you go with her to Bath. A friend of mine has a hotel that will let you in. You don't work Sundays so you can spend tomorrow shopping and come back in the evening like nothing has happened. Verity will have to stay away a little longer."

"And what are we going to use for money?" Carol asked.

Seb emptied both his trouser pockets out on to the reception desk. There were dozens of crumpled up five-pound notes, along with a few one-pound notes. "There's probably a hundred quid there," he said. "That will last you for a while."

Carol and Verity stared at the money. "Where did you get all that?" Carol said.

"I like to gamble," Seb replied with a grin. "And I usually win."

"How long do I have to stay away?" Verity asked.

"I don't know," Seb replied. "Probably just a few days. I know where you'll be, so I'll send for you when everything is sorted."

"What about her parents?" Carol asked.

"They're away on holiday," Verity replied.

"That's good," Seb said. "Do you have a number for them?"

Verity nodded.

"Give them a ring when you get there and just tell them you're staying with a friend for a few days."

"They'll kill me," Verity wailed. "I'm only 15."

"No, your parents won't kill you, prison will kill you," Seb said, grabbing her chin. "What do you think would happen to a pretty little thing like you? They'd be fighting over who'd have you first. Believe me, getting a bollocking from your parents is nothing in comparison."

"This is wrong," Carol repeated, but she scooped the money up and shoved it into her handbag. "What about Big Ben?"

"I'll sort everything," Seb replied. "The poker game will go on for hours yet, he will be pissed as a fart and pass out into a coma. He always does. Now, off you go, I can see your taxi pulling up."

Eric watched Verity and Carol get into the taxi. Carol gave the driver a slip of paper with the address on. He turned the light on in the car, looked at it, reached for his glasses and looked at it again.

"Bath!" he blurted out. "I'm not driving to Bath at this time of night!"

Seb was also watching the drama unfold and came rushing out. "What's the hold up?" he said in an abrupt tone. "These ladies are special guests of the hotel. If your firm doesn't want to be our preferred taxi choice, then I'll let Big Ben know. The fact that you'll never get another penny of our business will be the least of your concerns."

"No problem, sir," the driver backtracked. "It's just that my wife is expecting me at midnight."

"You'd better put your foot down then," Seb said.

The taxi roared off and Seb returned to the hotel. Eric could see him making calls from reception, but he couldn't hear what was being said as the first tipsy patrons had begun making their way out of the ballroom.

Eric crept out of the bush and tried to mingle in with them.

A man who saw him emerge shouted: "Hey, some perv has just been having a wank in the bushes!"

Rather than correct him, Eric thought it wiser to leave. Quickly.

## CHAPTER 27

### TUESDAY 17th DECEMBER 2019

"Do me a favour, have a drink with me," Eric said, slouching into the seat opposite Seb. Woodland Manor's owner was sat at his usual table, the one with the window affording a view of the front gardens, even though it was too dark outside to see anything other than the lights guiding visitors to the car park.

"Hard day?" Seb said, gathering up the papers he had scattered around the table into a folder.

"Very much so," Eric sighed. "Will you have a drink with me?"

"Not tonight," Seb said. "I only drink on special occasions."

"In vino veritus," Eric muttered.

"Come again?"

"In wine, truth."

"I know what it means," Seb said. "I'm wondering about the context. Just because I don't drink doesn't mean I've got something to hide."

Eric shrugged and pulled a I-didn't-say-that face.

"Some of us have got lives," Seb said. "We choose not to piss our money up the wall, bore the arse off people by talking a lot of shit, and then have to write off the following day so we can recover."

Eric winced at the rather pointed insult then took his phone out of his jacket pocket, touched the screen a few times and said: "Verum absque vino veritus etiam."

"What?"

"But even without wine there is truth."

"Where are you getting this from?"

Eric held up his phone. "Google Translate," he said. "I wish I'd found it earlier."

"Okay, I'll have a drink with you," Seb sighed, rising to his feet. "But you're paying, and we're having something respectable."

Seb returned with a bottle of Beaujolais, two large-bowled lead crystal wine glasses, and a combined corkscrew and bottle opener.

"Is this the good stuff?" Eric asked, examining the label.

"It's decent, but without being ruinously expensive," Seb replied as he expertly extracted the cork with the tool. "To put it into perspective, the glasses cost more than the wine."

Eric savoured both the wine and its vessel. "Fruity," he eventually concluded. "Where does this appear on the wine list? Near the top?"

"Mid-range," Seb replied. "It will set you back £40 a bottle, but it's only money, right?"

They sat in silence for a few minutes and then Eric picked up the bar tool. "The staff used to carry these around their necks," Eric noted. "They wore them like a necklace."

"I know," Seb replied. "It would be a tribunal case if someone fell on one these days."

Eric nodded. "It wouldn't kill you though, would it?"

Seb took it from Eric and scrutinised it himself. "It might do, if you were really unlucky."

"You'd have to be really, really unlucky, I would have thought," Eric said.

Seb ignored the comment. "What's brought this on then?" he said. "Why are you going to waste your Tuesday night – and my Tuesday night, more importantly – and £80…"

"£80?"

"We're having more than one bottle, aren't we?"

Eric nodded in acceptance. "It is a very drinkable wine."

"Why do you want a drink tonight? Is it the desire to once again slump into a maudlin state while moaning about your love life?"

"I don't really have one of those," Eric said. "Or at least I didn't…"

"Tell me about it," Seb empathised. "I think the last person to run their hands through my hair was a nit nurse."

Eric didn't laugh at Seb's joke, which he'd heard several times before. "At least I'll be able to walk home tonight."

"How so?"

"I've bought one of the houses at the bottom of your drive."

"Really? You kept that quiet," Seb said. "Does this mean I'll be seeing even more of you?"

"Who knows? Did you hear the showroom was attacked?"

"I did," Seb said, pouring another glass. "A disgruntled ex-employee, wasn't it?"

Eric nodded. "And now Carol is in custody."

"Was she involved as well?"

"No."

"Carol is your receptionist, yeah?"

"No, she's my business partner, but she used to be a receptionist. In this very establishment."

"Did she? Small world, eh? I didn't know you even had a business partner, I thought you were the owner."

"I am, but I was going to make her a partner in the New Year."

"Sounds like you dodged a bullet there then."

"How do you mean?"

"If she's been arrested," Seb said. "You don't want a crim as your business partner. What did she do?"

"Nothing."

"She must have done something."

"She failed to report a crime when she was younger," Eric said, staring at Seb. "And it eventually became too much for her, so she handed herself in."

"They do say confession is good for the soul," Seb said, taking another sip from his rapidly emptying glass. "Time for that second bottle."

"Do you speak from experience?"

Seb waved to attract the attention of the bar staff and pointed at the bottle in the centre of his table. "What?"

"About confessing being good for the soul?"

Seb laughed. "My conscience is as clear as this glass," he said, holding it up to the light.

"You did say you were going to tell me how Big Ben got to own this place," Eric said, gesturing at his surroundings. "When you had time."

"From what I've been told, through rather nefarious means," Seb replied, yanking the cork out of the newly arrived bottle. "You know he used to have a butcher's shop?"

"You said. Big Ben Butcher the butcher."

Seb nodded. "It sounds like a prime case of nominative determinism, but it's more likely he just enjoyed cutting up animals. Anyway, he expanded into supplying local restaurants, including this place, and he used to bring his wife to the restaurant once a week. He obviously took a shine to it because he dropped his prices so low that other local butchers couldn't compete."

"Why would he do that?"

"So that he could become the sole supplier," Seb explained. "And that was when he increased his prices. When the old boy who owned the place got back in touch with other butchers, he was told they didn't want the business. Perhaps they were miffed because he'd dropped them, or maybe they'd been warned off by Big Ben – he could be an intimidating bastard."

"He could."

"Anyway, meat prices kept going up and the old boy fell behind with his bills. Big Ben added interest to the debt, then he started supplying inferior quality meat, which meant that less people came to eat here, and the bloke got into financial difficulties."

"Poor chap," Eric sympathised.

"Don't feel too sorry for him," Seb said. "Mr Reeves was a bit of a grumpy bugger himself. He was also stupid enough to allow Big Ben to bail him out – even though he had caused the debt – and become his business partner. He then started invoicing the business more and more for his meat while he was also drawing a salary, bleeding the place dry, and eventually he owned it all."

Eric shook his head. "What a bastard."

"He was," Seb agreed. "But he had powerful friends, and this became the place to be in Cwmbran in the '70s. Even old Mr Reeves used to come in most Saturday lunchtimes, despite everything that had happened."

"How did you come to own it?" Eric asked. "Did you do to Big Ben what he'd done to Mr Reeves?"

Seb laughed. "Not exactly. I worked my way up to be bar manager. Not because I was better than the other staff – although I was – but because I didn't mind being treated like shit. Most people couldn't cope with it."

"Why would you?"

Seb shrugged. "It paid well."

"Bar work paid well?"

"Very well," Seb confirmed. "But although it was a good business, Big Ben lost interest in it after his wife buggered off. There was also that incident with the band. Everything went downhill while he drank himself to death. Pity really, as that was too good an end for him."

"Is that when you bought it?"

"No. When it closed, I opened my own hairdressing salon in the town…"

Eric appraised Seb. "I don't really see you as a hairdresser."

"It was my childhood ambition," Seb retorted. "I used to practice my styling techniques on my mum. I worked here part-time while I was in college. But, when I qualified, the salary for stylists was so poor that I stayed here full-time. By the time it closed, I'd saved enough to start my own salon."

"Bar work obviously did pay well," Eric said, raising a glass to Seb. "Here's to you. I admire a self-made man."

"I ran that for a few years, opened another two branches, and when this place came up for sale I put in a cheeky bid which was accepted."

"Why would you want to do that, if you had a successful chain of hairdressers?"

Seb topped up his glass. "That's a good question," he said, staring at Eric. "I suppose it was a combination of wanting to go back to my roots while also dancing on the grave of Big Ben Butcher. The building and grounds were run down and needed a lot of work, so I sold the hairdressing business and invested everything into this. I needed a huge mortgage as well – which I've still got. The sale of the woods was going to pay that off."

"But business is booming," Eric said, pointing in the direction of the hospital.

"It is now," Eric said. "But it's been a hand-to-mouth existence until recently."

"Even without the woods, you would be an instant millionaire if you sold up now."

"Have you been listening?" Seb said. "I've still got a huge mortgage and anyone wanting to buy this as a business would base their valuation on the last few years' accounts."

"That's good," Eric said. "They'll show significant growth."

Seb lowered his voice. "They'll show that we've made losses since we opened and are only just breaking even now."

"Really?"

"No, not really," Seb hissed. "But that's what the accounts will show."

Eric took a glug of the deep red Beaujolais. "I'm confused."

"I keep two sets of books," Seb explained. "One for the tax man and one for me. The less income we declare, the less tax we pay."

Eric fell silent, digesting what he'd heard.

"Don't look so shocked, lots of businesses that handle cash do it," Seb said. "Why wouldn't you?"

"Because if HMRC find out—"

"They're not going to find out," Seb said. "Besides, that loophole is pretty much closed now, thanks to the EPoS system and people paying on plastic."

"Even so, what happened to 'you don't want a crim as a business partner'? You might well end up as a guest of Her Majesty yourself if they ever do find out."

"I'm sure I'd survive," Seb said. "But how do you think your receptionist will cope with life behind bars?"

"I don't know," Eric said. "They won't let me see her. I went to the station and made a statement and even though I gave them fresh information they didn't seem bothered."

"Fresh information?"

"About the crime Carol confessed to. She was just a witness to it. But because I couldn't provide any evidence to back up what I was saying, I got the impression they were just humouring me. I was just given a business card and told to get back in touch if I had any further evidence that could help with their enquiries."

"Best to let justice run its course," Seb said, topping up their glasses.

"You're probably right," Eric agreed.

"I usually am."

The wine was giving both men's faces a rosy glow, and they sat in silence for a few moments. Eventually Eric said: "Is Sebastian your real name?"

Seb smiled. "Everyone calls me it, so it must be."

"I used to think I'd have been more successful if I'd had a more enigmatic name," Eric said. "I was the only Eric in my school. I tried glamorising it when I was a teenager by saying I was named after Eric Clapton, but then someone pointed out that he was only a kid when I was born, so I had to put up with taunts like 'Why would your father name you after a schoolboy? Was he a nonce?'."

Seb laughed, surprisingly loudly, attracting glances from some of the other customers. "I think people like you should stick to the truth," he said.

"People like me?"

"You're not one of life's natural liars," Seb explained. "You've got to believe the lie yourself before you can get others to believe it. I adopted the name Sebastian when I first started going out. Back then you didn't use your real name, for obvious reasons, and I thought calling myself after a gay icon – Saint Sebastian – would be self-explanatory. It wasn't, as it turned out, but I was so convinced my name was Sebastian that I became him."

An issue with the bar's EPoS system took Seb away for a few minutes, and Eric used his phone to research Saint Sebastian. Often portrayed in art as a near-naked youth, writhing while being shot with arrows. 'The homoeroticism is obvious,' said one site. It wasn't to Eric.

When Seb returned, Eric asked: "What would you do if you could go back in time?"

Seb thought for just a few seconds and replied: "Have more sex."

"Not be young again," Eric said. "Go back to an earlier time but as you are now. What would you do then?"

"Have more sex," Seb said, in a much louder voice.

Eric took a deep glug of his wine. It was going down too well, and he was starting to feel more than a little lightheaded. "You're not taking this seriously," he said.

"It's not a serious question," Seb protested. "What do you expect me to say? Kill Hitler? Campaign against plastic in the oceans? All I would do – all anyone would do – is what we are already doing. Are you happy Boris Johnson is prime minister?"

Eric pulled a sour face.

"Neither am I, but what are we doing about it? Are we joining political parties opposed to him? Are we out on the streets protesting? No, we're sat here talking bollocks and getting pissed. That's what us little people do, we look the other way – whether it's through ignorance, fear, or indifference – instead of standing up for what's right. We're not heroes."

"Maybe we can be," Eric said.

## CHAPTER 28

## SATURDAY 3ʀᴅ JULY 1976

They finally emerged from the rear door of the kitchen. She was wearing her bar uniform of black skirt, white blouse, and a black bow, and he was in baggy green high-waisted trousers and a denim shirt. They were almost the same height because her footwear was flat while he wore two-tone platform shoes, which were mostly hidden by the excess hem of his trousers.

They carried between them a large aluminium bin, marked 'pigs only' in faded red paint. There was a handle each side and Little Len gripped his with one hand while Verity needed both of hers to keep the bin from scraping along the ground. Her bar tool, which was still around her neck, swung as she struggled with her load.

"You're really weak, aren't you?" Little Len taunted her. "Even for a girl."

Eric, his phone capturing the action as it unfolded, was hidden behind a tree perfectly positioned between the kitchen and the pig pen, which Big Ben had built around a hundred yards away in a clearing in the woods. Even at this distance, the smell was putrid. The pigs were fed on scraps from the kitchen, which were scraped into two bins by the kitchen porters after the waiting staff had cleared diners' tables. It took several days to fill a bin to the top during the week, but both bins could reach their maximum capacity on Saturday nights.

"I shouldn't be doing this," Verity complained.

"You wouldn't be if you'd done what you were told to," Little Len replied, dipping his free hand into the oozing mush, and grabbing a mouldy slice of bread which he theatrically waved in her face. "Hungry, my sweet?"

"You're disgusting," she said.

With dusk setting in, Eric was able to creep from his initial hiding place to a tree closer to the pig pen, and then to one positioned just yards from it. The oaks were estimated to be several hundred years old, so Eric was easily concealed by their trunks. His only worry was whether the available light would be enough for his iPhone to record everything that happened in sufficient detail.

Verity had to stop several times, as the weight of the bin was hurting her hands, but Little Len was unmoved by her struggle, tutting and sighing dramatically, and moaning that he didn't have all night.

They finally reached the pen and put the bin down. The pigs knew what was coming and rushed excitedly to greet them. The pen had been constructed from four-foot wooden poles that had been driven into the ground and were connected by horizontal bars. Inside the pen were two long troughs, one for water and one for food. The water level was almost at the top but the food one was empty. Two round-mouthed shovels, used to scoop the slops into the trough, were leaning against the outside of the fence.

Little Len ignored the pigs' grunts and squeals and perched on the fence. "Come up here and join me," he said to Verity.

"No thanks," she replied.

"You're going to need to get your strength back because we've got to shovel this lot over the fence into the trough," he said, holding out his arms. "Come on, I'll pull you up."

She ignored him.

"Come on, you were happy to walk with me around the boating lake today," he said.

"Only so you would leave Eric alone," she said.

A lump formed in the back of Eric's throat. She was protecting him.

Little Len's tone became more assertive. "Haven't you learned yet that bad things happen to silly little girls who don't do as they're told?"

Reluctantly Verity allowed him to help her up onto the top rung of the fence. She held her nose with one hand and wafted the air with the other. "The smell..." she groaned. "Let's get this over with."

Little Len casually fished a packet of cigarettes out of his shirt pocket. "Smoke?" he said, offering the open pack to her.

With one hand still holding her nose, she waved the other in a gesture of refusal. "They're all looking at us," she said. "Why are you teasing them?"

"You'd know all about teasing," Little Len said, lasciviously eyeing her legs.

Eric swallowed hard. He wanted to intervene. He really did. But it had taken him almost nine hours of waiting to reach this point. He had caught a bus to Newport earlier in the day and browsed the record shops to distract him from brooding over his mission. He knew he had to see this through, without getting physically involved, regardless of how painful and emotionally draining it would prove to be. When he got hungry, he went for a Wimpy Brunch, which consisted of two beefburgers without buns and a portion of chips, followed by a Knickerbocker Glory made with deliciously soft ice-cream.

Little Len's gaze moved up to Verity's torso. "You haven't got much tit, but I bet your nips are soft and puffy, aren't they?"

Verity tried to slide along the fence to get further away from Little Len, but his arm was around her shoulder, gripping her tightly.

"And I bet you're nice and tight downstairs," Little Len leered.

"You'll never find out," she said, almost spitting the words out at him.

"No? Maybe you'd like me to throw you in with the pigs?" Little Len said, pushing Verity backwards towards the animals, which were still jostling each other, grunting with expectation. "They'll rip your clothes off much quicker than I could. And for the same reason too, to get at the meat."

"Let me go," Verity cried, struggling to release herself from his grip.

"My mother once had a yappy dog that my father couldn't stand," Little Len said, pushing her further towards the pigs. "He threw it in there at feeding time. It didn't yap for long."

Verity grabbed her bar tool and swung it at him, digging it into his neck.

Eric was expecting a torrent of blood to shoot out, but it seemed her action had barely broken the skin. Her attack had caught Little Len completely off guard, but he still had an arm around her and with the other he was feeling his neck, assessing the damage.

"That hurt, you little bitch," he yelled. He pulled his hand from his neck. It was red with blood, which was now slowly seeping from the wound.

Verity tried to release herself and in doing so she shoved Little Len away. Unable to maintain his precarious balance on the edge of the fence, he fell backwards into the pen, almost in slow motion. The only thing preventing him fully falling in was one of his platform shoes, which was wedged beneath a bar in the fence. Suddenly the shoe, which was two sizes too big for him, slipped off and Little Len tumbled completely into the pen.

Verity stood transfixed as the pigs crowded around him. Shouting abuse at her, he punched several of the animals and tried to stand up. He managed this, but with one leg significantly longer than the other, and the pigs thronging around him, he found it impossible to escape. The leg with the shoe still on began kicking at the pigs, who squealed in pain and backed away in terror. With his path towards the fence now clear, Little Len ran towards it – but the foot still wearing a shoe buckled, and he tumbled back to the ground.

"I've broken my ankle," he cried.

Gripped by the tableau, Verity giggled at his predicament.

"Why are you laughing?" he screeched, as the pigs charged towards him once again. "This is not funny. Go and get help."

As Verity left, Eric expected the hungry pigs to attack Little Len, but they just pressed their snouts into him, looking for food. A shower of violent swearing came from Little Len as he shoved them away, punching and kicking out at the ones he could reach. The rumpus allowed Eric to move to a tree with a closer and clearer view of the situation. Little Len's face was now clearly identifiable. Eric shifted his position so he would be concealed from view when help arrived and continued pointing the iPhone at the pen.

Eric heard Seb approaching before he saw him, his giant steps crushing the dry twigs underneath his steel toe-capped boots. By now

Little Len had managed to drag himself to the side of the pen, and he sat with his back against the fence.

"Elvis?" Little Len called out, turning his head towards his rescuer.

"Elvis has left the building," Seb replied as he approached the pen and stared down at Little Len. "Actually, that's not true. He's playing poker. What have you been up to?"

"That bitch attacked me," Little Len said, pointing at the wound in his neck. "And I've broken my ankle as well."

"What do you expect if you insist on wearing those ridiculous shoes?" Seb chided him. "They don't make you look taller, they just emphasise how short your legs are."

"Just get me out of here," Little Len snapped.

"Swing your legs towards me so I can have a look at your foot."

Little Len slowly dragged his body around so his legs were protruding under the bottom rung of the fence. Seb crouched down and cupped the swollen ankle in his hand. He squeezed it in several places before Little Len noticed that Seb's pockets were leaking money. Several crumpled five-pound notes lay on the ground and others dropped out as he shifted his position.

"You've been nicking from behind the bar," Little Len said.

"What?"

"Why else would you have all that cash on you?" Little Len gestured at the notes. "There's over thirty quid there."

"That's mine," Seb replied, gathering up the cash.

"Why was it all screwed up in your pockets?" Little Len demanded to know. "That's an obvious sign of a thief. Do you think you're the first to nick from us? I bet you've been doing it for years."

"That's a very serious accusation," Seb warned Little Len.

Undeterred, Little Len continued: "I know you overcharge the drunks, because there's been complaints, but I assumed that was going in the till. I never thought you would betray my dad, not after all he's done for you."

"How do you know I didn't have some luck on the horses?"

"There's no racing today," Little Len sneered. "And even if there was, you were working all afternoon so you wouldn't have had time to put your bets on and collect them."

"I didn't say it was today," Seb replied.

"That's how the bookies pay out winnings now, is it? In crumpled up five-pound notes? You must lose a fair bit if it falls out your pockets every time you bend down."

Seb dropped Little Len's wounded foot, causing him to howl in pain as it bounced on the hard ground. "You're a smart little bastard when you want to be, aren't you?"

"Get one of those shovels," Little Len ordered Seb. "I'll hold onto it, and you can pull me out and lift me over the fence."

Seb dutifully brought one of the shovels across to Little Len. But instead of dangling it over the fence for him to grab, he suddenly forced the sharp end through the gap in the fence which Little Len's chest was up against. The head of the shovel tore through the fabric of the denim shirt and buried itself in his flesh. Seb used his boot to drive the shovel in further. It oozed with gooey blood and made a squelching sound as Seb pulled it out. Little Len's face was a bizarre mix of terror and disbelief. His mouth opened several times, but no words came out. After a few seconds he slumped backwards, prostrate among the pigs' faeces. After kicking the body several times to check for life, Seb walked back towards reception, where he would inform Carol and Verity of Little Len's demise.

Eric continued filming. He emerged from behind the tree and zoomed in on the corpse, ensuring he got close-up footage of the face from every angle. So this is how Little Len's remains came to be in the woods. But something didn't add up. If Seb buried Little Len's body here, why would he have allowed the woods to be developed? It was inevitable that the remains would be discovered. But he'd seemed genuinely astonished when the body was identified as Little Len.

The sound of Woodland Manor discharging its drunken patrons out into the night came travelling up to Eric. A group of men were singing rugby songs with rude lyrics, others were arguing about politics, and several women were laughing hysterically.

Doors banged loudly as taxis turned up and the car park began to empty. Several of the people driving cars were inebriated, judging by the way they bellowed their farewells at each other. Where were the police? Oh yeah, playing poker in the bridal suite with Big Ben. And investigating the break-in at Meek's Mini Market. Silence eventually returned, but not for long. Eric could hear footsteps approaching and the muted voices of two men. He continued filming even though he knew there was very little chance of the resulting footage being viewable.

"This had better be important," Elvis complained. "I still had some chips left."

"It's pretty important," Seb said, illuminating the corpse with a handheld torch.

"What's this?" Elvis said.

Seb sighed. "Isn't it obvious?"

"You've killed Little Len?" Elvis cried. "Are you fucking mental?"

"Keep your voice down," Seb hissed at him.

"Do you know what Big Ben is going to do to you?"

"He's not going to do anything," Seb said, handing Elvis a key. "Because you are going to carry Little Len down to reception and put him in the passenger seat of Big Ben's MGB. Then you're going to drive up to Llandegveth reservoir, put him in the driving seat, and roll the car down into the water. The drought has exposed the banks, so you'll have no problem getting the car onto them, and they're sloped so it will go right down into the deepest part, where it will remain undisturbed for decades."

Elvis laughed and jabbed his index finger repeatedly into the side of his head. "You really are fucking mental!" he scoffed. "Why the fuck would I do that?"

"Does Big Ben know you've been shagging his wife?"

"What did you say?" Elvis snarled at Seb.

"You know exactly what I said," Seb said. "And don't bother acting the hard man with me. I've seen how you hide when trouble kicks off."

Elvis stared at Eric.

"You must have developed a nose for it," Seb continued. "Because when someone gets out of hand in the bar, who sorts it out? It's either me or Big Ben. It's funny how you're never around, isn't it?"

"You've killed his son," Elvis said.

"That's not his son," Seb said. "I mean, look at the size of them both – you'd think Big Ben would produce a strapping specimen like me, wouldn't you? Not some weedy little string of piss who can barely see over the bar. How long have you been hanging around the family? Maybe Little Len is yours?"

Elvis's whole body was trembling with rage.

Seb struck a thoughtful pose. "Or have Ma Butcher's legs been open for business to all and sundry for the last 20 years?"

"You are vile," Elvis said.

Seb said in a serious tone: "If anyone asks, Little Len drove off with one of the girls from behind the bar in the MGB. Is that clear?"

Elvis lowered his head, a beaten man. "Okay," he said.

"Right, I'm going to cash up the tills while you're taking Little Len for a moonlit drive up to the reservoir," Seb said. "Understood?"

Elvis nodded.

Seb began walking back towards the hotel. "Don't worry, I'll cover for you, I'll say you were with me all night. But not in that way – I've got standards."

"How am I supposed to get back from the reservoir?"

"You've got legs, haven't you?"

After Seb had left, Elvis spent several minutes staring at Little Len's body. He climbed into the pen and cradled his face in his hands. Was he sobbing? He grabbed the shovel from outside the pen and tried to dig the ground. It was too hard, even for such a sharp blade, so Elvis emptied the water trough into a section of the pen near the fence and used the empty trough to keep the pigs from getting in his way. He was still unable to dig into the ground, however.

Eric watched as Elvis sprinted back towards the hotel. After a few minutes he was back, holding the head of the extra-long industrial hose pipe that was attached to an outdoor tap at the rear of the building. Big Ben used this to water the plants and shrubs in the hotel's gardens, despite a nationwide hose pipe ban being in place. Water was gushing out of the head of the hose and Elvis used one of Little Len's shoes to hold it in place, so it continued watering the same patch of ground that he'd poured the pigs' water on.

Elvis walked back down to the hotel, and this time Eric followed him, still recording. The doors to reception around the front of the building were still open, and Elvis casually went behind the deserted desk and picked up the phone. The outside darkness kept Eric hidden from Elvis's view while the bright lights inside allowed him to record in pin-sharp detail.

"Clive, how would you like to buy a car?" Elvis said into the phone.

Eric couldn't hear the response.

"I know it's late, but this is a one-off opportunity too good to miss," Elvis said, looking at the spare key Seb had given him. "It's a 1971 green MGB. Low mileage, mint condition, leather seats, wooden dash, the works. Give me £400 and it's yours."

The other party responded and after a few seconds Elvis said: "Of course it's fucking nicked! What do you expect at that price? But put some new plates on it and no one will be any the wiser. The owner thinks his son took it, so he won't even report it stolen... Never mind what happens when his son comes back. He won't be coming back. Alright, nice one. I'll be down in about an hour or so. I've just got to take care of something here first. And I'll need a lift back, okay?"

After he finished the call, Elvis took a dark grey blanket from the linen cupboard and returned to the pig pen. The water from the hose had saturated the ground and he was finally able to dig into it. He kept the water running continuously as he dug, which allowed him to create a long thin hole in under an hour.

When he judged it was about the right size, he wrapped Little Len in the blanket, gently placed him in the hole, and covered him with the wet soil. He dragged the empty water trough from the other side of the pen across to the grave and used it to hide the wet ground. Finally, he started shovelling the slops into the food trough. When the bin was half-empty, he was able to lift it and empty what remained into the trough. Pausing briefly to catch his breath, he took the hose back to the hotel and turned off the tap before climbing into the MGB and roaring off into the night to make himself £400 richer.

## CHAPTER 29

### THURSDAY 19th DECEMBER 2019

Opening his front door, Eric was surprised to see a bundle of hair curled up on his doorstep. The Yorkshire Terrier's tiny face appeared disappointed to see him and he rushed inside looking for his mistress. He scampered from room to room, even doing several circuits of upstairs, before returning to the front door, panting with exhaustion.

"That's probably the most exercise you've had in years," Eric said to the dog as he scooped him up into his arms and gently placed him in the Lexus. The dog was evidently unused to such an environment as it immediately urinated on the leather seats. There was a time when this would have upset Eric, but he just laughed, returned to the house for a toilet roll, and set off for Brookvale, with the dog whining in the passenger footwell.

Mrs Freeman was delighted to welcome Andrew back into her arms. "Where did you find him?" she gushed as the dog yapped with excitement.

"On my doorstep this morning," Eric replied. "There must be a gap in your back garden fence, so I'll send someone around to sort that out for you."

"That would be so kind," she said to Eric.

"Still happy?" Eric asked her.

"Very much so," she replied. "It's a blessing not to have to deal with stairs."

"If there is anything you need – anything at all – please do call me," Eric said. "And how's Mr Freeman getting on?"

"He's watching Escape to the Country," she replied. "I told him, this is it for me. If he wants to escape anywhere else, he'll be on his own. Do you want to come in and see him? There's tea in the pot."

Mr Freeman was sat on the same faded orange and red check fabric sofa from his previous house, with a steaming cup of tea balanced on the sofa's thin wooden armrest.

"I've brought Andrew back," Eric explained.

Freeman rolled his eyes. "Thank you very much," he said unenthusiastically.

"Say it like you mean it," Eric teased. "And while I'm here, do you have the original digital files for your photographs?"

"They're on the PC," Freeman replied. "Do you need them?"

"Just the ones from the shops of the town centre album," Eric said. "The gallery wants to blow them up for mounting."

"You'll need a large capacity USB drive then," Freeman said. "Because they're too big to email."

\*\*\*

Eric looked up, shaking his head in defeat, and yelled across the showroom to Ryan: "How do I email a video to someone?"

"From your phone? Just choose the little box icon with the arrow sticking out of it, select the mail option, and then fill in the recipient's address."

Several minutes later, Eric said: "It's just crashed."

Ryan took the phone from him and prodded it back into life. "Yes, it would do," he finally said. "You can't email a file this size."

Eric sighed heavily. "Why don't things just work?"

Ryan said patiently: "You're making an unreasonable request."

"By asking why things don't just work?"

"By trying to email an 80GB attachment," Ryan explained. "Email servers have size limitations. They'd crawl to a halt if they didn't."

"I didn't ask it to be that size," Eric protested.

"You did, in your settings," Ryan corrected him. "Your iPhone is currently shooting in 4K at the highest frame rate, so just one minute of footage will take up about 2GB. This file is enormous and using up just about all your phone's capacity." His face suddenly grew serious. "It's not porn, is it? I don't want anything to do with that."

"No, it's something I took," Eric sighed.

"Have you backed it up?"

"I don't know how to," Eric sighed. "This is why I'm asking—"

"You really should," Ryan said. "What would happen if you lost your phone?"

Eric did not want to entertain that possibility. "Can you please just get it off there for me?"

Ryan considered his options. "Probably best to install a file transfer app and send it to a PC," he said. "Then you can move it to an external hard drive or a USB stick. Or you could upload it to the cloud if your plan gives you enough storage space. You could compress it of course—"

"Please just copy it to a USB drive," Eric said, his hands in a praying gesture. "I can understand how they work."

"We haven't got any big enough," Ryan replied. "You'll have to buy one. Get the largest capacity you can find."

"You'd better do it," Eric said. "Just in case I get the wrong thing. Actually, get a few of them."

With Ryan out of the showroom, Eric could make a few calls in peace. He could make them while Ryan was there, but – with the pish bowl incident in mind – he didn't want anything he said to provide Ryan with an anecdote for his next placement.

First up was PC Ripley.

"Believe it or not, I was just about to ring you," Ripley said. "The town centre CCTV has captured some cracking images of your erstwhile employee smashing his way into your showroom. He didn't even wear a mask, which suggests his actions might not have been premeditated. Probably more of an impulse, drunken or otherwise."

Eric asked: "Is it enough to charge him?"

"Criminal damage, when it's more than £5,000, is a serious offence, so he can expect to be prosecuted," Ripley confirmed. "If he's convicted, he might even go down for it."

"That's good to know but that's not why I'm calling," Eric said.

"Oh?"

"Some fresh evidence in the case against Carol has come into my possession."

"Has it indeed?" Ripley could not hide the suspicion in his voice. "What does this fresh evidence consist of, and how did it happen to come into your possession?"

"It will be easier if I show you, rather than explain over the phone," Eric said. "Are you at the station now?"

"Give me an hour to clear my desk," Ripley said.

Cwmbran Police Station was situated within walking distance of the town centre and Eric agreed to meet Ripley later. Next on his call list was Tom, from the phone shop. He was surprised to hear from Eric, but delighted when asked if he fancied making a career change – not least because his current contract ended in January.

"January will be fine," Eric said. "That's when the showroom is being refitted. Email me your CV and references and we'll take it from there."

"I'll do it this evening," Tom said eagerly. "Can I just ask why you chose me?"

"I was impressed with the care and attention you gave me as a customer," Eric said. "That's exactly how I'd like my customers to be treated." He paused for a few seconds and, remembering Mr Barrington's words to him, added: "The profession has been good to me and, if you work hard, it will be good to you too."

Eric's next call was to Zack at the Cwmbran Evening Star.

"Hey man, how's it going?" he greeted Eric. "Let me guess: you're looking forward to the feature and you want to book some ads around it?"

"The feature can't run," Eric said. "One of the members of staff in the pictures no longer works for us."

"That's no problem, I can take more pictures," Zack suggested.

"Not in the showroom you can't," Eric said. "Are you aware it was vandalised?"

"Yeah, that was not cool."

"You can therefore understand why I don't want the article appearing until the business is back up and running."

"Oh man," Zack sighed. "The article has been laid out, it's on the flatplan, and my boss is not going to be happy if we have to make alternative arrangements for the space."

"In that case I've got good news for you," Eric said with a flourish. "How would the Cwmbran Evening Star like a world exclusive scoop?"

Eric's final call was to Mrs Ducreux.

"Darling, I thought I'd scared you off," she laughed. "I thought 'that old bastard is ghosting me'."

Eric had other matters to discuss. "I've got the digital files of all the images of the town centre, and I'll put them on a USB drive for you," he said, sticking to business. "Also, the Cwmbran Evening Star is going to be covering your opening."

"I beg your pardon?" she trilled. "I'm not sure I want my opening in the press."

"The opening of your gallery," Eric clarified. "They were running a feature on me, but I've persuaded them that you're far more deserving of the space."

***

Eric and PC Ripley sat alongside each other at a metal table that was bolted to the floor of the grim windowless room. It was one of several used to interview witnesses and caution suspects at Cwmbran Police Station, so there were cameras in the corners of the ceiling and recording equipment, resembling a garish '90s Dixons own-brand hi-fi, stacked on a trolly. Eric had read somewhere that police interview rooms were kept deliberately cold in order to increase the anxiety levels of the person being interrogated, and he could believe it because he could almost see his breath when he exhaled.

Eric handed over the USB drive and Ripley plugged it into his laptop. After a few seconds, the screen displayed the footage of Little Len and Verity carrying the pig bin.

"What's this?" Ripley asked.

"That's the person whose remains were found in Woodland Manor," Eric said.

"But he's been in the ground for decades," Ripley said. "This looks like it could have been filmed yesterday."

Eric talked Ripley through the footage, identifying each person and explaining their role in the incident.

After the video had finished playing, Ripley said: "How long have you had this?"

Looking at the USB drive, Eric was able to say, quite truthfully: "It came into my possession this morning."

Ripley used the laptop's file explorer to look at the MP4 information. Ryan had converted the footage into that format, from the iPhone's native .mov, in order for it to be viewable on more devices. "The date stamp on this file says it was created less than two hours ago," Ripley said.

"Really?" Eric replied. "I rang you as soon as I received it, once I realised what it was."

"Received it from who?"

"I can't say," Eric said. "It was posted in a plain envelope through the letterbox of the showroom. Santa is in the town centre, so there were loads of people outside at the time."

Ripley narrowed his eyes and glared at Eric. "But you've still got the envelope?"

"It got thrown out," Eric said.

"Well, can you at least…"

"And the bins have been emptied."

"How have you managed to earn a living as an estate agent all these years?" Ripley sighed. "Because you are absolutely pants at lying."

Pointing to the laptop, Eric said: "This proves that Carol had nothing to do with the incident, doesn't it?"

"She admitted covering up a murder," Ripley shook his head. "That is a serious offence."

"That's not quite true though, is it?" Eric argued. "The murder Carol thought she had covered up didn't actually take place. Verity was defending herself, but she certainly didn't kill him. You just saw that."

"No, I suppose that's true," Ripley said.

"So, what can Carol possibly be charged with?"

"That's not for me to say," Ripley said. "I won't be making that decision."

"You've just seen who the murderer was," Eric said.

"I know, and this is going to take some explaining when I take it up the line. You're going to have to come up with better answers than the ones you gave me for how you obtained this footage."

"Can't you just say it was given to you anonymously?"

"Lie to my superiors?" Ripley was outraged. "Are you insane? Have you any idea what they'd do to me?"

"Recommend you for a commendation for solving the case single-handedly?"

As Ripley showed Eric out, he said: "I don't understand how someone could just film that and not intervene at any point."

Eric shrugged. "They must have had their reasons."

\*\*\*

As Eric approached the bar, Seb grinned and wagged his finger at him. "I wondered when you were going to show your face again," he said. "I was rough as a badger's arse yesterday. That's the last time I'm having a drink with you."

"It might well be," Eric said. "Can I order a coffee? A flat white would be nice."

"I'm glad I'm not the only one suffering," Seb said, pressing buttons on the steampunk-inspired brushed stainless-steel bean-to-cup device.

"I owe you an apology," Eric said.

"For getting me pissed and making me rue the day I was born?"

"No, for insulting your mother."

Placing the elegant black china cup and saucer containing his coffee in front of Eric, Seb asked: "What do you mean?"

"That is your mother, isn't it, looking all regal on the horse in the painting behind the reception desk?"

"No," Seb replied.

"I'm pretty sure it is," said Eric.

"Are you calling me a liar?"

"I wouldn't have chosen to put it in such stark terms but, being as you've asked, yes – I am calling you a liar," Eric said casually. "I can see why you'd want her there, replacing one of Big Ben in an almost identical pose."

"Was there a shot of it in that old photo album?" Seb asked.

"There must have been because I remember seeing it," Eric replied. "And I thought, why would Seb want a picture of such a – forgive me – plain woman in such a prominent place unless she meant a lot to him? But of course, she's there out of spite, isn't she? To rub Big Ben's nose in the fact that she is the queen of what was once his kingdom, even though neither of them got to see it."

"You be very careful what you say about my mother," Seb warned Eric.

"I have nothing but admiration for her," Eric said. "I mean that. It must have been so difficult raising a child in the '60s as an unmarried single mother, especially with no help or assistance from the father."

Seb poured himself a coffee, opting for a cappuccino in a tall transparent mug. "She never got a penny from him," he said. "She worked in his shop, and he sacked her when she told him she was pregnant by him."

"And when you grew up you got a job here to be close to him?"

Seb laughed at the suggestion. "In a way, yes," he said. "But only so I could get back at him."

"You certainly did that," Eric said.

"How do you know?"

Eric gestured with his arms. "Because you now own it."

Seb took a sip from his coffee. "Technically, the bank owns it," he corrected him.

"You got back at him in other ways too though, didn't you?" Eric said. "Like pocketing cash that should have gone in the till."

"Everybody was at it," Seb said defensively. "But they were too stupid to get away with it."

"I'm not criticising you," Eric clarified. "Lots of people had good reasons to get back at Big Ben. How did you get away with it?"

"By not being greedy," Seb said. "Or stupid. Some people would take a couple of tenners out of the till and think they wouldn't be missed."

"Amateurs!" Eric scoffed. "I'm sure your scam was more sophisticated than that."

"When arseholes who thought they were better than me asked for doubles, I would serve them singles and pocket the difference," Seb said.

"But that wasn't getting back at Big Ben though," Eric pointed out. "That was just overcharging the customers."

"True, but I had other wheezes on the go," Seb chuckled. "Because I was young, they used to make me deal with all the empties and take out the rubbish. And quite often I would 'inadvertently' include still-sealed bottles of spirits with the empties. A mate would collect them in the night, and we'd split the profits. There were no EPoS systems monitoring the sales and matching them to stock levels back then."

Eric raised his coffee cup in a 'cheers' gesture. "I don't blame you at all," he said. "Because it must have been bloody hard, watching your father dote on what he thought was his son. While you, his real son, was working alongside him every day. The irony is, he probably would have been very proud of you if you'd made yourself known to him."

"Where has all this come from?" Seb arched his back and glared at Eric.

"Whatever happened to Elvis?" Eric said. "Did he take off with Mrs Butcher?"

Seb continued to glare at Eric, his face reddening.

"You can thank him for the sale of the woods falling through," Eric said. "He didn't dump the body and the car in the reservoir. He buried Little Len with the pigs."

All colour left Seb's face and his breathing grew shallow.

Eric continued: "You know that now of course. What you might not know is he sold the MGB to a mate of his. He got £400 for it too. Not bad for a night's work, especially back in those days."

Seb's expression changed to defiance. "Where's this coming from? Are you trying to shake me down? Is that what this is? Your own business is so shit that you want to muscle in on mine?"

"You didn't need to kill Little Len," Eric said. "God knows, he wasn't the nicest of people, but he didn't deserve that."

"You didn't have to put up with him lording it over you," Seb spat. "The little runt was always threatening to tell his father if I didn't do what he wanted. Hang on – who said I killed Little Len?"

"I did," Eric replied. "But you let an innocent 15-year-old girl think that she did. And even though you've always been a good friend to me, I cannot forgive you for that."

Seb snatched Eric's coffee from him. "I guess I won't be seeing you in here anymore," he said. "Even though what you're accusing me of is just conjecture, I don't think I'll be comfortable having you on the premises."

"I can understand that," Eric replied, taking his iPhone out of his jacket pocket. "But you might want to watch this video. It's quite long but the narrative is gripping."

Eric selected the videos folder in his photos. He pressed play on the most recently recorded one and Seb watched transfixed as Little Len and Verity struggled with the pig bin.

"Who filmed this?" Seb asked.

"Just watch it," Eric said.

The footage continued, showing Little Len's clumsy attempts at courtship and Verity lashing out at him. His tumble into the pig pen might have elicited riotous laughter in other circumstances, but both Eric and Seb knew what was coming.

When young on-screen Seb crouched down to assess the damage to Little Len's ankle, Eric expected the current Seb to turn away or ask him to stop playing the footage, but he continued watching, right through to Elvis's grave digging and his driving off in the MGB. The only comment Seb made was about himself: "I really was hot back then – and I thought I was fat."

Seb snatched the phone from Eric and immediately started watching the footage from the beginning again. "Where did you get this?"

"You wouldn't believe me," Eric replied. "You couldn't believe me."

"There was no one there filming," Seb said. "And even if there was, for that person to stand by while a crime was being committed – and to say nothing for all these years – could be seen as conspiracy. Or at the very least perverting the course of justice. Isn't that what your receptionist has been banged up for?"

Eric took the phone from Seb and handed him a USB stick. "You can watch it as often as you like now," he said. "And Carol is not my receptionist."

Seb grabbed the USB stick. "Did she film this? What did she film it on? Portable video cameras didn't exist."

"No, she didn't film it, she was on reception with Verity, remember? She was consoling a 15-year-old girl who thought she had committed murder."

"Who filmed it?" Seb demanded.

"My guess would be some little person who decided not to look the other way."

## CHAPTER 30

### SATURDAY 3RD JULY 1976

"What is that, some new kind of television?" an elderly man in double beige asked in a disapproving tone.

Eric quickly slipped his iPhone into his jacket pocket. He had been alone at the bar reviewing the footage for his presentation, and the old man's soft soled sandals had allowed him to stealthily creep up behind him and peer over his shoulder. "I suppose it is," Eric said.

"What's the point of that?" the old man scoffed.

Turning to face his inquisitor, Eric took in Woodland Manor's garish red patterned carpet and dark wood panelled walls laden with unpolished horse brasses. He took a deep breath, inhaling the less than enchanting confection of last night's beer slops and this morning's spray polish, which now had a hint of citrus from the old man's Blue Stratos aftershave. "Oh, it's got a point," he replied.

"But it's microscopic," the old man scoffed. "Japanese, I suppose?"

"China actually," Eric said.

"China?" the man guffawed so hard he made himself cough. "That I very much doubt."

The commotion attracted the attention of a young barman with a wispy beard and shoulder-length brown hair. "Good afternoon Mr Reeves," the barman greeted Eric's companion while placing a short-stemmed glass on the bar. "Bristol Cream?"

"Croft Original," Reeves corrected him. "Dry sherry when light, sweet sherry at night."

"I'll try and remember that," the barman said, reaching behind him for the distinctive dark green bottle and bringing it towards the glass. "Though I could have sworn you had a Bristol Cream last Saturday lunchtime."

"Dry sherry should be served in a glass with a long stem," Reeves chided him. "Otherwise, your hands will heat the drink."

"I do apologise," the barman said, pouring the sherry into a long-stemmed glass.

Reeves handed the barman 30p in small denomination coins and tutted. "This place has gone downhill since—"

"Come on now, don't upset yourself on this beautiful day, Mr Reeves," the barman gently cut him off, aware of how the sentence would end. "It's been over ten years since you passed on the baton. Wasn't it Menander who said, 'time heals all wounds'?"

"Never heard of him," Mr Reeves retorted, holding his glass up to the light. "And he's wrong. It doesn't."

"Looks like another scorcher today," the barman said. "They say it's going to be hotter than the Costa del Sol…"

"Even this glass is grubby," Reeves grumbled. "How often are they cleaned?"

"…And it looks like we're going to have one of the warmest summers on record," the barman continued, while nodding a greeting to Eric.

"Famous last words," Reeves mocked, taking his sherry and choosing a stool further down the bar, close to the big television.

"For the record, my last words are going to be 'I wish I'd spent more time in the office'," Eric said.

The barman lowered his head, allowing his hair to fall forward and frame his face. "That's a slightly unusual thing to say, sir."

"Yes Seb, it is," Eric conceded. "But the next time you hear someone say, 'No dying man wishes they'd spent more time in the office', you can reply 'Actually, Eric Meek did'."

"Are you dying?"

"I hope not, but wouldn't it be satisfying to shut down the next bore who comes out with it?"

Seb frowned in confusion. "Actually, it was you who brought it up," he said. "Are you here for the tennis?"

"Not really," Eric replied.

"We're having Wimbledon on the big television today," Seb continued. "When the women have finished. It's the Men's Final later, and we'll be serving complimentary salmon and cucumber sandwiches."

"I'm more interested in a cold lager, Seb," Eric said, eying up his options. "What do you recommend?"

"We've got Harp, Carlsberg, Heineken, and the new Stella Artois," Seb said, extending his arm along the bar taps with a flourish. "But can I ask, why you—"

"I'd better stick to Skol," Eric said, pointing at the tap.

Seb dutifully filled a pint glass, etched with another brand of lager, and placed it in front of Eric, who offered him a ten-pound note. Seb glared at the large denomination note. "I'm afraid we haven't long opened, sir. Do you have anything smaller?"

Eric didn't. "Will it help if I have another?" he asked.

"Another Skol? Already?"

"It is pretty hot out there today," Eric said, gesturing towards the windows as he gulped down the cold yellow liquid. "Have one for yourself and get Mr Cheerful over there another Croft Original."

"Thank you very much, sir," Seb said, pouring another pint from the tap. "I'll have a tomato juice so that will be £1.26 altogether but—"

"You didn't even need the till to add that up," Eric observed. "That's quite a skill."

"It comes with practice," Seb said, slightly blushing. "But I'm afraid I still won't be able to change—"

"Don't worry about the change," Eric said, placing his now empty glass on the bar and immediately starting on the freshly poured one. "It's only money, right?"

"Very droll, sir," Seb said. "I'll see if reception can break a tenner."

"I'm not joking," Eric said. "Keep the change."

"But sir, you've given me a ten-pound note and—"

"Tell you what, throw me a packet of JPS and we'll call it quits," Eric said, pointing to the packs of cigarettes lined up along a glass shelf behind the bar. "Because there's no problem with me smoking in here, is there?"

"None whatsoever," Seb said, handing Eric a pack of John Player Special along with a box of matches. "Let me get you an ashtray. And thank you so much."

Eric unwrapped the cigarettes, savouring the aroma that escaped from the distinctive black and gold box. JPS had been his brand. He'd quit decades ago but recent events had seen him relapse on a few occasions. He lit the thin white tube, inhaled, and blew a plume of smoke into the air. It took on a blue hue from the harsh midday sun pouring in through the dusty windows.

"Can I just ask," Seb said, placing a chunky glass ashtray on the bar in front of Eric, "why you called me Seb?"

"You are Seb, aren't you?" Eric said, taking another gulp of Skol.

Seb whispered: "No one in Cwmbran calls me Seb, only my college friends. Everyone around here knows me as Simon."

Eric studied him. "You're not really a Simon though, are you?"

Seb stared suspiciously at Eric. "Are you trying to pick me up?"

Eric guffawed: "In your dreams!"

"What does that mean?"

"It means I am absolutely not trying to pick you up."

"You wouldn't be the first older man to come on to me," Seb said. "And you'd be surprised how many of them were supposedly happily married."

"You know, I'd completely forgotten how enjoyable it is to be able to smoke indoors," Eric said, ensuring that he blew smoke in the direction of the empty lounge rather than towards Seb.

After delivering the Croft Original to Reeves, Seb returned to Eric and said: "I don't think I've seen you in here before. Are you new to the area?"

"You could say that," Eric replied.

"Well, if I see you again you can count on me serving you first, no matter how crowded the bar is," Seb said conspiratorially.

"You'll definitely see me again," Eric said. "Though maybe not for a while."

Reeves interrupted their conversation by complaining about a cobweb he could see on one of the wall lights, and while Seb left the bar in search of a duster, Eric retrieved his iPhone from his jacket pocket in order to cue up the footage.

"How can you watch anything on that?" Reeves sneered, repeating his trick of silently creeping up behind Eric and catching him unawares.

Eric hastily placed the device on the bar, screen side down. "No need to thank me for the sherry."

"Why even bother with a television that small?" Reeves scoffed. "I've got a colour Sony Trinitron at home, and you can see every detail. It cost over two hundred pounds."

Eric took a large gulp of his lager. He briefly considered pointing out that the iPhone's 458 pixels per inch screen resolution was far superior to a 1976 Sony Trinitron television, but he thought better of it.

"Who would buy something like that?" Reeves continued. "What sort of person is so addicted to the telly that they need to carry one around in their pocket?"

With the wall light freshly free of cobwebs, Seb was back behind the bar. "What's that, Mr Reeves?" he said. "Were you talking to me?"

"I was just wondering how depressing someone's life must be for them to bring a television into a bar," Reeves said to Seb.

Seb looked around the bar. "Who has done that?"

Reeves jabbed a finger in Eric's direction. "Mr Big I Am here."

"This gentleman has just bought you a drink," Seb pointed out. "And the only television in here is ours."

Reeves pointed at Eric's iPhone on the bar. "That's it, there."

Seb stared at the device and frowned. "If the gentleman told you that was a television, I'm sure he was only joking."

"I saw it working," Reeves said. "He obviously wants attention, throwing his money around buying drinks for strangers and showing off his tiny little television."

"I can assure you that attention from you is the last thing I want," Eric said.

"Honestly, it's pitiful," Reeves persisted. "He's so desperate for everyone to see his pocket television."

"I haven't seen it," Seb said.

"He's probably waiting for me to go," Reeves said. "So he can impress you with it. He looks like a pervert to me."

"If I was waiting for you to go I wouldn't have bought you a drink," Eric pointed out. "Which you still haven't thanked me for, incidentally."

Reeves continued: "Can you imagine trying to watch the cricket on it? You wouldn't be able to see the players never mind the ball."

"Actually, it's not just a television," Eric blurted out. He held the iPhone in front of Reeves and pointed to his apps. "It's also a cinema, notepad, address book, organiser, newspaper, dictionary, thesaurus, encyclopaedia, banking portal, weather forecaster, street map of the world, calculator, music player, instant messenger, camera – for still and moving images..."

Reeves was staring incredulously at Eric, as was Seb.

Eric finished with a flourish: "Oh and it's also a phone."

After several seconds of astonished silence, Reeves said dismissively: "A telephone? Utter rubbish! Where do you plug it in, for a start?"

"It doesn't need to be plugged in," Eric said.

"Ring someone then," Reeves challenged Eric, removing a crumpled white handkerchief from his shirt pocket and wiping the perspiration from his balding pink head. "Let's see you use it."

"I can't do that," Eric said, starting to regret his outburst. "It's currently experiencing technical issues as a result of this being 1976."

"I thought as much," Reeves scoffed, shuffling back to his stool. "It's just a children's toy. Telephone indeed. It hasn't even got a dial!"

Eric downed the last of his lager and considered having another. Probably best not to. Getting half-sloshed would only undermine his upcoming presentation.

Reeves was now ranting at Seb from the other end of the bar. "You shouldn't let shysters and con men in here," he yelled. "There are plenty of other pubs in Cwmbran for people like that. I'll speak to Mr Butcher about this."

"I'm sure the gentleman wasn't being serious, Mr Reeves, let me get you another sherry, on the house," Seb tried to placate him, before rolling his eyes at Eric and asking: "Seriously sir, what is that thing?"

"It's an iPhone XS Max," Eric replied.

"But—"

"Remember the guide in 'The Hitchhiker's Guide to the Galaxy'?"

"The what?"

"Sorry, forget I said that," Eric grimaced. "It might not have been published yet."

"Can I see it?"

"Probably best if you don't."

The door to the lounge bar suddenly swung open, and filling its frame was the intimidating figure of Big Ben Butcher. Sweat was running down his enormous bald head and, with no eyebrows to halt its progress, cascading into his eyes.

"It's bastard hot out there," Big Ben announced. "Chuck me a towel, Simon, I'm sweating like a glassblower's ballbag."

Big Ben perched on a bar stool between Eric and Reeves with all the casual arrogance of someone who owned the place – which he did – and mopped his head and face with the bar towel. He pointed to the Stella tap and Seb immediately began pouring him a pint. He knew the drill.

"The weather people say today is going to be the hottest day of the year," Reeves said to Big Ben.

"I can believe it," Big Ben replied, then turning to Seb, he demanded: "Why haven't you got the tennis on? The tarts must have finished by now."

"The Men's Final is due to start at quarter past one," Eric said.

Big Ben turned towards Eric. "And it will probably be over by two," he said, slamming his empty glass on the bar and pointing at the Stella tap for another. "It's going to be a walkover."

"I don't know about a walkover," Eric said.

"Mark my words, it's going to be a straight-sets victory," said Big Ben. "Bang, bang, bang."

"You've got that right," Eric agreed.

Big Ben laughed: "Nastase is going to knock that Swede all over the court."

Eric shook his head. "No, it's going to be a straight-sets victory for Borg," he said.

Big Ben roared with laughter, and looking at Seb and Reeves in turn, asked: "Has this nutter escaped from the Grange?"

"He's been coming out with all sorts of nonsense," Reeves said, obsequiously laughing along with Big Ben.

"They should never have been allowed to build a loony bin so close to a residential area," Big Ben said. "They haven't got enough staff to keep tabs on them all."

"The man's a charlatan," Reeves declared. "He was just bragging to me that he had a telephone in his pocket."

Big Ben continued: "Borg hasn't got a cat in hell's chance. Not a cat in hell's chance."

"You're wrong," Eric said.

Big Ben glared at Eric. Very few people would have the audacity to tell him he was wrong. Especially not in his own bar. "What did you say?"

Eric replied confidently, though without making eye contact: "You're wrong. Borg is going to win in straight sets."

"What are you, an astronomer?" Big Ben sneered.

"In a way."

Big Ben moved his head closer to Eric's. "And I suppose you can predict the score too, can you?"

"Do you want to know the score?"

Big Ben leaned even closer to Eric. "Go on then, smart arse," he said, eyeballing him aggressively.

Resisting preceding his prediction with the term 'spoiler alert', as it would have been wasted on this audience, Eric said: "It finishes 6-4, 6-2, 9-7."

Still remaining seated, Big Ben stretched an enormous arm across the bar and pressed the 'no sale' button on the cash register. He removed Eric's ten-pound note from the drawer and slapped it down in front of him. "Put your money where your mouth is then," said Big Ben. "I'll give you odds of ten-to-one on that being the score."

Eric smiled to himself for a few seconds before slowly removing three ten-pound notes from his wallet. He ostentatiously waved them in the air before placing them down on the bar next to Big Ben's tenner. "Ten-to-one? I'm not really a betting man but I can't turn down those odds. Let's make the bet £30, shall we?"

While Reeves and Big Ben made themselves comfortable, Eric casually strolled from the bar out to the reception area as Seb stood on a chair to tune in the big television.

"Make sure he doesn't go anywhere," Big Ben shouted through to Carol. "He owes me money."

Carol smiled awkwardly at Eric.

"Not yet I don't," Eric assured her. "Can I ask you something, Carol?"

"Of course," she replied.

"What do you want to do?"

"I'm sorry?"

"Do you want to be stuck here for the rest of your life, putting up with arseholes like him?"

"He's not that bad," she said.

"He absolutely is," Eric corrected her.

"Are you offering to take me away from all this?" she asked. "Because I've heard that old flannel many times from drunken middle-aged men."

"I'm not drunk."

"That's what drunks always say," Carol said. "Besides, I don't even know you."

"Would it make a difference if you did?"

She considered the question. "It might."

Eric pulled his iPhone out of his jacket pocket. "You do know me," he said. "Would you like to see the proof?"

Carol stared in amazement at the high-resolution image of her that appeared on the screen. She was wearing the same clothes she had on today. Then Eric showed her the footage he'd shot of her outside the Old Oak. Of him asking her what her favourite song was, and what was number one in the charts. And following Eric's encouragement, she hummed 'You To Me Are Everything'.

Carol covered her mouth with her hand and shook her head. "This is impossible," she cried. "I haven't been out there in years. And that song is number one now."

Eric moved on to the next video, which showed both him and her on screen at the same time. "Where are we, Carol?" the on-screen Eric asked.

"The Old Oak," she replied, pointing towards the building behind them.

"And are you having fun?"

"I'm having a day I'll never forget," she laughed.

Eric turned the phone off and returned it to his pocket. "See? You do know me."

"I don't understand," she said.

"I know you don't," Eric said. "Do you want to?"

"I don't know," she said, before a look of concern crossed her face. "Am I dead or something?"

Eric reassured her: "No, you're not dead, but if I tell you, you must promise me you won't freak out."

"I can't promise that," she replied. "But try me."

"I'm from 2019."

Carol's face hardened. "Do you think I'm an idiot?"

"Of course not," Eric whispered. "Which is why I'm giving you the chance to come back with me."

He went on to describe how he'd shot the footage of the two of them on a previous visit, and how everything was reset once he returned through the portal. Which was why she had no recollection of her afternoon at the Old Oak.

Her confused expression suggested he had lost her early in the explanation. "Assuming what you say is true, and I don't necessarily believe it is, why me?" she asked suspiciously. "Out of all the people in the world you could come back for?"

"Because you begged me to take you with me last time I was here," Eric said. "I couldn't do it then, but I can now."

She looked at Eric. "Are we married in 2019?"

Eric shook his head. "We're not, but you are."

"Do I live in a big house and have lots of children?" she asked excitedly. "Have I got grandchildren?"

"No, you work in an estate agent's office with me," Eric said. "And you don't have any children."

Carol's face crumpled and tears formed in her eyes. "I've always wanted children."

Eric gently put his hand on her shoulder. "If you stay here, that will be your future. Your husband seems a decent chap, but he spends most of his spare time fishing."

Carol sobbed: "Why are you telling me this?"

"Because I'm fond of you," Eric said. "The future you. We're good friends."

"Do I have to sleep with you?"

"Absolutely not," Eric assured her.

"So why are you doing this?"

"Because you can be whatever you want if you come back with me," Eric gave her shoulder a tender squeeze. "I'll help you start your own business, doing whatever you want to do, and you can follow whatever dream takes your fancy. If you want to buy a VW Camper Van and travel around Europe, you can. If you want to move to New York, you can."

Carol eyed Eric suspiciously. "And what do I have to do for you?"

"In return? Absolutely nothing," Eric reassured her. "I only want to help you."

"I can't believe I'm saying this," she said. "But okay."

Eric smiled.

"But if all this is some sort of wind-up," she warned. "You'll be sorry."

Eric looked at his watch. "I'm going to cause a commotion in there when the tennis finishes," he said. "All you've got to do is come with me when I leave."

"I mean it, you'd better not be lying to me."

"I promise you I'm not," Eric said, holding up his iPhone. "You know I'm not."

"Is your time machine parked nearby?"

"It is," Eric said. "You won't have to walk far, so you can even keep your heels on."

"I can't believe all this," she said. "Tell me again why I can't remember being with you at the Old Oak…"

"Because that happened to a different you," Eric explained. "And if I come back tomorrow and try to do this again, I will be speaking with a different Carol again. I have to reintroduce myself to you every time. And the you that I'm talking to now will never have another chance to come with me. You will live out your life in Cwmbran and still be working when you're 70. There's nothing inherently wrong with that, lots of people will do the same, but I know you, Carol. If you'd been given an opportunity when you were young you could have done so much more with your life."

"It all sounds so unbelievable."

"I know," Eric agreed. "But this is your opportunity."

***

Big Ben retrieved the last of the cash from the safe in the office and furiously stuffed it in a plain white envelope. As he entered the bar area, his entire head, as well as his face, was deep purple in colour. "Can you bastard believe this?" he snapped at a uniformed policeman who was glaring suspiciously at Eric. "He got the score exactly right. What are the chances?"

"Sounds very fishy," the policeman replied, using his fingers to slowly caress his bushy horseshoe moustache. "Very bloody fishy."

Eric smiled at PC Roy 'Spanner' Tanner. He'd seen that look many times before on Spanner's chiselled face.

"He didn't even watch the match," Reeves piped up. "He spent most of it sniffing around the girl on reception. It's disgusting. He's old enough to be her father. I said when he walked in that he was a pervert. I could tell."

"There you go," Big Ben said, handing the envelope crammed with £300 in used notes to Eric. "A bet's a bet. Never let it be said I don't pay my debts."

The lounge bar was almost full now. Most had come to watch the tennis and take advantage of the free sandwiches, but word had also spread during the afternoon that Big Ben was in danger of losing a huge bet, and there were plenty of people eager to witness what would happen next. Some of their faces were familiar to Eric, especially the kitchen staff, but he was a stranger to them.

Eric opened the envelope and started counting the cash onto the bar. "I'd better check it, Mr Butcher," he said. "Just in case you've given me too much."

Several people laughed, until Big Ben silenced them with a glare.

"As you can see," Big Ben said in a loud voice that carried over the heads of the crowd. "I am a man of my word. And now PC Tanner has kindly agreed to escort this gentleman to his vehicle, to ensure that nothing untoward happens to him or his winnings."

The look on Spanner's face strongly suggested that something very untoward would definitely happen to Eric once the two of them had left the building.

"What a generous gesture," Eric said, as he divided the cash into two piles. "But that won't be necessary as I won't be taking the money off the premises."

"You what?" Big Ben said.

Eric handed one of the piles to Seb and said: "Would you mind dividing this up among the staff, including the kitchen porters?"

Seb accepted the cash and some of the younger members of staff descended on him, squealing with excitement.

"And I'd like all you lovely people to join me in celebrating Borg's victory," Eric barked at the gathering while offering the other pile of notes to Reeves.

"Why are you giving me this?" asked Reeves, unsure if he should accept it.

"Mr Reeves here is holding the money," Eric said. "So please ask him to get you whatever you would like to drink for as long as the cash lasts."

A loud cheer erupted in the room, and as Eric made his way through the pile of bodies rushing to the bar he was slapped on the back and even granted a brief chorus of 'For He's A Jolly Good Fellow'.

Big Ben's face suggested it was about to commit murder.

Carol had been standing in the doorway, watching the astonishing scene unfold. As Eric emerged from the throng, she rushed up to him. "I'm ready," she said.

They strode through reception and out into the hot afternoon sun. Their footsteps crunched on the gravel as they made their way down the drive towards the Freemans' garage where two suits and helmets, made from an incredibly reflective material, were waiting.

*If you enjoyed this book, and even if you didn't, it would be hugely appreciated if you could spare a few moments to post a review of it online, either on Amazon or wherever else you usually post book reviews. Thank you.*

**Other books by this author:**

**The Honey Peach Affair**

A social drink with Britain's hottest adult entertainment star is the starting point for the biggest adventure of film reviewer Bruce Baker's life.

When her sister asks for his help in investigating the star's disappearance, law-abiding Bruce chalks up a charge sheet worthy of a career criminal, during his encounters with the unscrupulous and the fearsome – while dealing with a disagreeable boss who is looking for an excuse to sack him.

Sharing his journey is a virtuous anti-porn campaigner, whose cause Bruce inadvertently elevates to national prominence, and it culminates in Bruce sitting on one of the biggest stories any journalist could ever hope to uncover.

But he doesn't want to write it.

**From Sex Shops To Supermarkets: How Adult Toys Became A Multi-Billion-Pound Industry**
With almost every major UK supermarket now devoting shelf space to adult toys, From Sex Shops To Supermarkets chronicles the phenomenal growth of the sector, and how mainstream television, cinema, and celebrities have rushed to embrace it.

The book features many of the industry's milestone moments, including the consumer electronics giant that launched its own sex toy, the private prosecution that could have threatened the Ann Summers business model, and the great jiggle ball shortage of 2012.

It also explains how Lovehoney used clever PR to build its business and reveals the strategies behind some of its most successful campaigns. The book concludes with venture capitalists investing in leading players and merging them into 'supergroups'

Printed in Dunstable, United Kingdom